Classic Book Reviews & Timely Stories

by

Charles J. Scott

The contents of this work, including, but not limited to, the accuracy of events, people, and places depicted; opinions expressed; permission to use previously published materials included; and any advice given or actions advocated are solely the responsibility of the author, who assumes all liability for said work and indemnifies the publisher against any claims stemming from publication of the work.

The book-review portions of this book represent the author's opinions, beliefs, impressions, interpretations, feelings about, and his reaction to the books being reviewed. As part of the work of fiction, these reviews should, therefore, not necessarily be considered as being completely factual, entirely truthful, or always accurate.

All Rights Reserved
Copyright © 2021 by Charles J. Scott

No part of this book may be reproduced or transmitted, downloaded, distributed, reverse engineered, or stored in or introduced into any information storage and retrieval system, in any form or by any means, including photocopying and recording, whether electronic or mechanical, now known or hereinafter invented without permission in writing from the publisher.

Dorrance Publishing Co
585 Alpha Drive
Suite 103
Pittsburgh, PA 15238
Visit our website at *www.dorrancebookstore.com*

ISBN: 978-1-6491-3399-1
eISBN: 978-1-6491-3536-0

TABLE OF CONTENTS

Part 1: Crime Spree a la Mode (Chapters 1-33) 3

Part 2: Double Dee Disco Insanity (Chapters 34-66) 141

Part 3: Fat Fee Guacamole (Chapters 67-end) 299

Classic Book Reviews
& Timely Stories

CHAPTER 1

Book review of the novel

The Glassblower

by Petra Durst-Benning, published in German in 2003, published in English in 2014.

What her big sister did.

This novel is a captivating story of three loving sisters. They are charming and crafty young women who rise above their trying circumstances at the turn of the 19th century in a remote rural village of central Europe, where medieval tendencies may still be prevalent, perhaps even today. The book is well-written, abounding in local traditions and folklore. Be warned, however, some wanton violence erupts in the natural course of events, and there does not appear to be much in the way of an active legal judicial system in the immediate vicinity to thwart it. The possibility exists that the villagers simply prefer to avoid encounters with the authorities at all costs—especially those within the jails and dungeons of feudal castles. The sequel should prove to be interesting reading material indeed, as the hopeful, good fortunes of the three girls catapult them into the limelight.

R. Royce remembers Colonel well. Colonel was no ordinary hound dog. He was white with black and brown spots all over. When they went fishing in the creek as kids, Colonel would jump into the creek and return with a fish in his mouth. When they went racoon hunting in the farmer's hay fields late at night to see if the new hunting dogs their dad and his best friend recently acquired in Arkansas would live up to their reputations, he was the only dog to tree a racoon on that wild moonlit night, while all the other hounds ran away chasing rabbits. They weren't any good at all as hunters.

CHAPTER 2

Book review of the novel

Ministry and Moonshine

by Fred L. Funk, published in 2012.

It's snowing in North Texas.

You've heard it said, "Down-home country folks would give you the shirt off their backs!" And "Times may be hard today, but not like the way it was back then."

"People made do with what they had and did the best they could."

"I walked for miles to school through deep snow in a blizzard."

And so it is, the author, Fred L. Funk, has written about a simpler place and time. You may be tempted to ask, "Who's going to argue with chicken-fried steak, green beans, mashed potatoes with gravy, a jumbo dinner roll lathered in butter that will melt in your mouth, and make you stand up and holler, particularly if you accidentally bit into a jalapeno pepper and tried to swallow a large glass of iced tea to quench your thirst afterwards—if you're seated at the dinner table next to the local minister?"

You may begin to wonder, "What is he going to do with all those varmints scurrying around in his own backyard at night, 'when you can't see too good' and aren't sure if they're squirrels, jackrabbits, coyotes, or skunks? Moreover, when he gets involved with real, live colorful characters who have strong personality traits and a certain way of doing things, sometimes you just aren't sure what might happen next in the course of human events, especially after a neighbor convinces him to buy a gun to protect his home and family, when he's never owned one before, or even learned the proper use of a firearm. Talk about a possible tragedy in the works!

On the other hand, people say, "The more things change, the more they stay the same," which might apply to this novel, as well. For example, while "bootleggers" of the 1950s and 1960s might have brought moonshine or "white-lightning" into your law-abiding, God-fearing, dry-county community way back then; in more recent times, out-of-town drug dealers would distribute methamphetamines or designer drugs into your neighborhood if you let them. But, then law enforcement got tougher today. Only, that's a different story, I suppose, speaking of the devil.

R. Royce thought about the chestnut horse that was kept in the barbed-wire fenced pasture around the curve and up the road from where his family lived when he was 13 years of age. They lived in a rent house situated precisely on the curve. His brother and sister were younger by three and five years, respectively. He wanted to go horseback riding, like they did when they rode the ponies, when they lived in Altura, Colorado, a few years earlier, but this particular horse hadn't ever been broken to ride. The animal wouldn't allow the kids to enter the pasture, without charging after them. So, Royce did the next best thing. He borrowed his mother's camera and snapped a photograph of the horse. That would have to do. It was too dangerous for them to go into the pen with the wild animal.

He remembered later that summer, when the kids woke up early, and their parents had gone to work, they ventured out into the open field next to their yard to look for box turtles. They noticed a huge circle of faded, decayed, or dead vegetation had been burnt into the field. Right away they knew that the cause of the circular markings had been from a UFO, which had landed next to their yard late on the preceding night.

When the kids went to see the chestnut horse, afterwards, they saw at once that the animal had been thoroughly spooked. It would never be the same. The horse now appeared as harmless as a baby with new diapers and a pacifier. It didn't make any attempt to stampede you or bite you, or try anything malicious ever again.

Around the Fourth of July, their father had purchased a slightly used console color television for the family to watch from the brother of his sister-in-law. He told the kids before he left for work not to turn on the television, "unless you want to see sparks fly." Apparently, there was some sort of short in the electrical circuit, so he'd planned to return the television for a refund when he found time. The unsupervised kids couldn't resist turning on the television set. Sure enough, they saw sparks, and turned it off again, before there was trouble.

He never did return the television, having abandoned it there, when the family moved away from 7th Street to 5th Street in the same town, but south of the railroad tracks. He wanted to live closer to the creek for coolness. He'd even bought a humidifier, which had an electric fan inside a big, square, vented metal box, to which he'd attach the garden hose and let it trickle water, sort of like air conditioning before portable air conditioners had been invented.

Once, he bought a 1950 big, round, and curvy Ford panel truck delivery van from the fresh fruits and vegetables store downtown on Vann Street for the family to get around in and travel in style, with the produce company advertising letters still painted on the side of the vehicle. Having gone fishing in Big Cabin Creek south of town about ten miles, and returning late one starry, starry night, all of a sudden the lights went out in the vehicle—both headlights, the tail-lights, and dashboard lights. None of them could see where they were driving. Luckily, their fast-thinking dad pulled the vehicle over to a complete stop and exclaimed, "There it is, the UFO, streaking across the sky." Years later, the family noticed that a new house had been built on the curved road property where they had formerly lived and made inquiries. Apparently, the old house had burned completely to the ground, and to this very day, no one knows whether it was because of the faulty television wiring, the flying saucer, or the horse.

CHAPTER 3

Review of a collection of short stories,

Octopussy and The Living Daylights

by Ian Fleming, published in 1966.

Lucky 7

This book, by author Ian Fleming, encompasses a collection of four short stories about the adventures of the character "James Bond," agent 007, of the British Secret Service. He appears to be a confident, sensible, down-to-earth, and highly trained fellow. He appreciates the finer things in life: good food in chic, expensive restaurants; beautiful and glamorous women in exotic locations around the world; and intimate moments by candlelight or moonlight over cocktails, with snazzy jazzy orchestra music playing low, softly in the background. Ah, but this may be the impression you get from Hollywood movies! True, he is well-dressed in a tailored business suit and striking tie. He wears buffed and polished patent leather shoes that have him shine in the eyes of his fans. His hair is neatly combed and fastidiously trimmed, not a hair out of place. He's frightfully clever, always knowing what to say and do at the appropriate moment. Essentially, James Bond is a Company man, who is given a difficult, specific assignment in each of the stories, which were published in the early to mid-1960s. Bond's missions include investigating a serious breach of conduct by a rogue British agent; identifying a top-level foreign agent who funds espionage; providing protection and security for an agent who attempts a border-crossing from a hostile nation into a neutral one; and attempting contact of a former British agent who becomes involved with an agent of a hostile foreign government. His success rate is three out of four. On the fourth mission, I believe, he adopts a "Don't go there" rationale, when he becomes reassured that agents of the FBI and CIA can better resolve the matter on their own turf, rather than taking matters into his own hands.

R. Royce thought about the Christmas gift he'd received his senior year in high school. He tore into the holiday wrapping paper with eagerness and enthusiasm. He knew exactly what he wanted.

"A portable color television set," he proudly exclaimed. "Just what I've always wanted!" Upon closer inspection, however, he discovered the shocking truth about the electronic device.

"Black and white," he almost declared out loud, feeling dismal. To say that he had been suddenly disappointed and mildly shocked would have been a profound understatement.

He got over it, though, fifty years later when the Ultra-4K 40-inch flatscreens came out. He bought one right away, added the high-tech Boss sound bar and a compatible digital DVD disc player to make the home entertainment system complete. Payback is not bitching about it.

After all, four of his favorite television programs had been filmed in black and white, *Route 66*, *Honey West*, *The Avengers*, plus the early episodes of *The Saint*. He includes *Kung Fu* as a favorite in the black-and-white category, since he and his dormitory-suite mates from college regularly watched the series on the black-and-white television set he received for Christmas.

When he asked a friend in the Army a few years later why he didn't go into electronics, he'd replied, "Why, I'm colorblind." Apparently, he was unable to differentiate a red wire from a green wire or a black wire. Sometimes, you have to empathize with people in order to gain a better understanding of the world around you. These days, the chief concern is no longer the sound and picture quality you receive, but the signals being transmitted out from your living room through the television Wi-Fi and internet connections. You wouldn't want your neighbors to complain about what's going on in the privacy of your living room.

CHAPTER 4

Book review of the novel

Centennial

by James Michener, published in 1974.

Two hundred years of progress

The novel **Centennial**, by James Michener, published in 1974, is purely historical fiction, yet strikes a familiar chord of truth. It is an epic, dramatic story of the Rocky Mountains and the highly diverse, itinerant peoples who have lived on the eastern slope plains areas roughly bounded by Cheyenne, Wyoming, and the Platte Rivers to the north; and Denver, Colorado, and the Arkansas River to the south. He writes mostly about the hunters, ranchers, and farmers, whose livelihood depended on the beaver, buffalo, cattle, and crops, such as sugar beets, potatoes, and wheat. These peoples often clashed and endured great hardships, trying to survive in the wilderness. Generations of them fought for a decent standard of living. Their world was changing rapidly, becoming ever more modern as time progressed. Living conditions gradually improved. Better forms of transportation and technology helped make work easier. Food became more plentiful. Civilization was on the rise and they began to enjoy their civil rights and stability. People slowly came to realize that they depend on each other, and that they must cooperate and act in harmony with nature. We can only hope that mankind has the wherewithal to survive on this planet longer than did the dinosaurs of forty to eighty million years ago grazing and roaming the plains. Centennial has brought us through the Jurassic Age, the Stone Age, the Iron Age; up to the brink of the Industrial Age, the Nuclear Age, the Space Age, and beyond—

the present Age of computers and the Internet. Where we go from here is the subject of years of deep research. Only time and our divinely human nature will tell where we end up.

R. Royce remembered an amusing anecdote a classmate told him during an on-the-job training seminar about a happily married couple. A man comes home from the doctor's office one day and tells his blushing new bride the prognosis is that he has a serious medical condition. He reports what the doctor advised him, that he can do most any form of exercise he normally enjoys—hiking, running, jumping, swimming, bicycling, basketball—except for one thing. He can't sleep in the same bed with his wife. They must maintain "social distancing." The mere act of consummating the marriage could cause him to become overly excited and have a fatal heart attack.

"We need to begin sleeping apart," he tells her, calmly, yet decisively. He suggests that he can sleep in the guest bedroom on the ground floor level, while she continues sleeping in the master bedroom on the second floor, effective immediately. Much later that night, they confront one another on the stairs.

"Where do you think you're going?" she inquires, hesitantly, but determined.

"I was going upstairs to commit suicide," he admits, hastily. "Where were you going?"

"Downstairs to kill you," she confesses, sadly. Their instinctual need to procreate was stronger than either one of them had anticipated.

CHAPTER 5

Book review of the novel

The White Queen

by Philippa Gregory, published in 2009.

*They did it all for love.
A match made in heaven.*

"What was she thinking?" The "White Queen" tells us all, revealing her secret, innermost thoughts and reflections in this first person narrative epic drama for more mature readers, a hard-hitting historical novel by author Philippa Gregory, and part of a series. This insightful book is the culmination of perhaps years of scholarly research for the time period covered. The events of the novel take place during the years 1464 to 1485, a mere span of twenty-one years, or a little over a single generation in the life of a royal family. For genealogy enthusiasts, the family tree chart has been included in the book. Royal family fans may be tempted and tantalized by a wealth of intimate details and juicy gossip from within the hallowed castle walls and secluded chambers seemingly derived from firsthand experience. History buffs can delve into the battle plans, strategies, and warfare tactics associated with medieval times—as well as developing an almost too real sense of relevant facts which have shaped and defined a great nation. The magical storyline, then, evolves around the two principal characters: the young, honorable, clever, faithful, and very beautiful Elizabeth Grey and the youthful, brash, tall, strong, and chivalrous Edward York.

They meet, fall in love, marry, and raise a family. Indeed, over the years, their family grows to include eight wonderful, independent-minded children.

Since he happens to be King of England from the moment of their initial romantic encounter, she later becomes Queen. Together, they rule England, generally through the terrible times of war and find little peace. Fortunately, they share the love they have for each other and their family throughout their entire lives. All in all, it is an incredible story if you pause long enough to think about it, and not just another Cinderella story. You might even get an eerie feeling of history repeating itself, or deja vu.

When R. Royce first met Meghan, aka Raquel, he'd felt confident in his chosen profession and abilities, but felt somewhat insecure in the ways of the world. She decided that he was lacking in certain social graces. He needed refinement. She taught him to relax a little and dance really slow. That seemed to remedy the situation for the moment. As time went on, she continually refined him and defined him. They wined and dined the night away. They became the life of the party. Ultimately, they achieved great success in all of their endeavors.

CHAPTER 6

Review of the nonfictional book

Haunted Joplin

by Lisa Livingston-Martin, published in 2012.

"Ain't Afraid of no Ghost."
Isn't she afraid of ghosts?

It's just the wind. Something is moving around out there in the shadows, obscured by the fog. We should have gone home before it got too dark outside to see. That's the sound of raindrops on sheet metal. Rusty door hinges began to squeak. The floorboards creaked. What was that noise? Somebody must have thrown a rock against the wall. It sounded like a door slamming. I'm starting to feel a distinct chill running up and down my spine. You're shivering? Maybe we should have lighted a campfire on the high ground by the sandy shoal of the creek. Do you hear voices in the distance? Growling? Howling? Shush! I believe I heard the rustling of leaves somewhere out there in the woods. Twigs snapping or tree branches crunching. The car ran out of gas and we're stuck out here tonight. The area is remote and desolate. Isolated. I can barely see. It's pitch dark. Do you get the sneaking suspicion that we are not alone? Sure, the party in Joplin died after midnight, but maybe it wasn't such a great idea to drive out here past the cemetery, across Cry-baby Creek to the old abandoned hunting shack near Lover's Leap, just so we could watch a full moon rise over the ridgetop and reflect in the pool of Hidden Lake, like some magical crystal ball. I'm beginning to get a really creepy feeling. Slime. The hair is standing up on the back of my neck. Maybe we should hike back to town instead. Nah, let's calm down and relax for a moment. Shall we? Did you bring a flashlight? I'll go back and look for the Ouija board. Have a sip of warm tea from the Thermos flask. I sense a charge of electricity in the surrounding atmosphere. The air smells pure and clean, sort of like ozone following lightning during a rain shower.

Be that as it may, such postulations do express some of the signs, misgivings, and apprehensions which might have motivated more than a few midnight marauders and late-night adventurers to bring along a Paranormal Science Laboratory (PSL) Team of spirit-world detection specialists with them on their next romantic rendezvous or seance. Their thoughts and experiences can only lead to rampant speculation and wild imaginings otherwise.

On the other hand, the book *Haunted Joplin*, by Lisa Livingston-Martin, provides a solid basis for confronting the fears and trepidation associated with supernatural phenomena. Seriously, in reality, this nonfictional, no-nonsense, thought-provoking book is supported by numerous, genuine photographs and well-documented facts culled from news reports of the day and describes in fine detail interesting local historical events which actually happened in and around Joplin, Missouri, and brings to mind the turbulent times of Jesse James, William Quantrill, and the Civil War through the Great Depression; Bonnie and Clyde; Viet Nam, the peace movement, and the misguided teenagers in Carl Junction who murdered an innocent classmate; Timothy McVeigh, the Alfred P. Murrah building; and up to, most recently, when the powerful F5 tornado devastated Joplin in 2011. Whether or not such traumatic events relate to or are the cause of ghostly manifestations is left up to the discretion and better judgment of the reader. One thing is for certain, however; specific individuals have been terribly wronged, or victimized, or suffered from tragic accidents over the years. As a result, the evidence of criminal trespass or transgression may still be present out there. We know the legal system can help prevent such horrible acts and violence. But, I believe, all in all, we are searching for a higher authority, attempting to fathom the universe, trying to explain what has been happening in the twilight of our lives.

Good thing R. Royce had his soft leather pouch of "mojo" with him. He wasn't sure that he would have survived the "visitation" without its contents. With the assortment of herbs, charms, stones, bones, and incantations, he harbored no doubts whatsoever that he would heal up eventually; get his strength and energy back, provided that he kept his wits about him and persevered. As it was, he watched the tornado clouds pass by to the south of his yard, traveling in a northeastern direction last year, in March of 2019, during which time his own physical body was the jolted recipient of a powerful bolt of ground electricity emanating from a nearby cloud to ground lightning strike. He was watching the severe weather report on television in the living room at the time, while reclining on his sofa. Half a dozen electrical outlets had been knocked out along the south wall in the living room. He had an electrician drop by a few days later to take a look at the problem. He had to reset the G.F.I.s.

In the aftermath of the storm, it was determined that over two hundred custom-built homes had been utterly destroyed or severely damaged in the adjacent golf course community to the south of him, by the tornado. There might have been another one that night which spun off and went in a northly direction. It stayed in Kansas, while the first tornado continued to wreak havoc in several Missouri communities to the east.

Not two weeks later, Royce was bitten by a snake in the lower right abdominal region of his body, while mowing and weed-eating the tall weeds and grasses beside the concrete drainage ditch at the back boundary and leading edge of his row of houses. He must have scared the creature as he went by.

Later that Spring, he thinks he might have been exposed to "agent orange-like" chemicals from crop dusters in the nearby farming community, or noxious weed and pest-control exterminators in the neighborhood. He thinks he could have gotten lime disease from a tick while walking in the woods. Or, it might have been because of the numerous mosquitoes that had bitten him during the rainy season, which could have been carrying the West Nile virus. A spider bite?

To make matters worse, he was overcome by the hot, summer weather while working outdoors in the hottest part of the day, mowing yards. He overdid it and felt the debilitating effects of fatigue, heat exhaustion or heat stroke, take your pick. His out-of-shape body was feeling the physical effects of years of wear and tear on his tired, aching muscles, his creaking joints, stretched-out tendons, and old bones, because of his war injuries, from various sporting mishaps, and other, sundry miscellaneous accidents, such as slips, trips, and falls. In short, he had become a nervous wreck, trying to rationalize the causes of his sickness. He was afraid of becoming a hypochondriac, merely thinking about listeria, e. coli, and salmonella.

He could barely move his muscles. It could be arthritis. Inflammation. He had serious difficulty getting in and out of bed, putting on or removing articles of his clothing, particularly his shirt, socks, and shoes. He didn't feel much like eating. He was sleepy all the time. Day and night. He was always thirsty. So, he drank quarts of water and electrolytic fluids, and lost a considerable amount of weight. It has taken him months, so far to heal naturally. He's had lingering doubts, because he was unable to pin-point the causes of his illness, and find a cure, but he is improving. He is mobile again and gets around okay. Up and at 'em. He was never an Olympic athlete, but he was always active. He may have felt the effects of old age, but he has acquired a newfound respect for life in general. He has spirit. He deserves that much consideration.

Most everyone else is much more concerned with "Tony Corona," these days than "Typhoid Mary"—so much, in fact, that Royce may be the only one in the community who's noticed the same clump of trees growing alongside the creek bank that was struck by the destructive tornado last year, just east of the newly built highway bridge over Center Creek, has been hit hard by high winds again this year. Fortunately, the newly rebuilt and remodeled houses on the ridge, as seen in the distance, appear to have been spared. The whirling cloud must have lifted in the nick of time, or the funnel cloud did not drop too soon. It must be a good sign. He's not complaining. He's only passing through. Some of us have to live here. I've been here five years myself, so far, and have seen enough to know better. We only have two alleys in the neighborhood: the bowling alley and tornado alley.

"Like they say, what doesn't kill you will make you stronger," said Cornelius Korn.

Royce was suddenly reminded of something his cute girlfriend, Gina Carina, asked him when they first met, many years ago, attending college, parking in the mobile home community, watching the stars, "You don't have any communicable diseases, do you?" Her friends called her "Karma." They were young, inexperienced, and innocent—so much in fact, that when they went out drinking together for the first time ever in a public tavern on her 18th birthday, the bartender checked their IDs and said, "Sorry, they just raised the drinking age from 18 to 21 in Kansas."

CHAPTER 7

Book review of the novel

Mission Compromised

by Oliver North, published in 2002.

Trouble spots around the globe

The novel *Mission Compromised*, by Oliver North, the famous retired U.S. Marine Corps officer from the time of the Reagan Administration, makes me think about the kind of employment such a distinguished highly decorated war veteran might seek as a civilian in peacetime. Naturally, I arrived at the foregone conclusion that he would go into either politics or some sort of corporate business—something on a grander scale. Just for argument's sake, one might suppose that he might decide to go into a major marketing business, and something international in scope. The reason for this conjecture is that the position as local sheriff in a hometown community, sort of like Andy Griffith in "Mayberry RFD," from the long-running television program, probably would not be commensurate with the level of his professional training and real-world experience while on active military duty. The author just doesn't strike me as the beloved, happy-go-lucky sheriff type. At the other end of the spectrum of government service, I think he might have a tough time running for President of the United States in the next election. Opposing either of the Clinton or Bush dynasty candidates, namely Hillary Clinton or Jeb Bush would be much too difficult of an assignment, especially since there is a current push on to place a female photograph on the new twenty-dollar bill, as decided by popular vote. Personally, I believe Hillary Clinton's photograph should appear on one of the Federal Reserve notes, should she be elected.

In any event, the burning question remains: "What kind of enterprising business should the promising author, or better yet, his alter-ego in the novel *Peter Newman*, delve into?" In my humble opinion, he should apply for a top-level executive position for a giant international conglomerate corporation such as the FedEx Company. One can almost visualize him working diligently as the director or CEO in such exotic places as Syria, Iraq, Yemen, Libya, Afghanistan, and Somalia—wherever there is no current, stable, or reliable government in place. His special delivery "care" packages should pass along gentle and specific guidance, and be sent forward to qualified, well-chosen government leaders who have demonstrated peaceful intentions for running their nations in accordance with proven democratic principles, having civil rights protection in place, and guaranteeing appropriate checks and balances. Furthermore, the leaders should honor and respect the separation of religion and state.

The United States, as a matter of course, in my opinion, should help "prop up" and "back up" these freely elected leaders with martial law as necessary. For example, in Iraq, both Sunni and Shia leaders should represent the country, and they should lead in a fair and just capacity, rather than that solely premised on selfish religious bias. Moreover, there should be an impartial and equitable judicial system put in place which has both the power and authority to punish criminals and terrorists alike. Of particular concern, all improvised explosive devices must be banned everywhere in the region. Finally, if the people of the region do not know the difference between right and wrong, then the government should educate them and teach them to respect all human life. The fact of the matter is, nobody gets rewarded as a martyr in heaven, or Jannah, by harming and killing other people here on earth, no matter what the printed word says in a pamphlet. It only makes sense.

Realistically speaking, these government agenda items will probably never happen in the real world, the one in which many well-meaning people of third-world nations live, and certainly not anytime soon. To make a long story short, no one is going to offer the esteemed author, or the main character of his novel any such most desirable employment opportunity the average executive seeks. What they might offer instead, however, is the subject of this book—a clandestine, top secret, search-and-destroy mission to take out some of the major players in the militant world of mass destruction and state-sponsored terrorism. Hollywood would jump at the opportunity to produce a bold new action adventure film, based on suggested material from the book, except they would probably not be able to film on-location due to the extremely dangerous and hazardous conditions prevalent there, since Iraq, Syria, Yemen, and others are presently struggling with civil war, or the potential for wartime activities. Indeed, a great many diverse peoples are presently fighting the huge group of organized religious fanatics who want to found a new state of Islam, which covers territory in two, if not several weak, desperate, and war-torn countries. As if we don't have enough problems with the already existing Moslem (aka Islam) sovereign nation of Iran. A couple of questions immediately come to mind from reading the book.

"If you can't trust the United Nations, who can you trust?"

"Why can't you travel freely and peaceably throughout the Middle East?"

Finally, one additional obtuse observation, oil prices certainly have dropped significantly since Muammar Gaddafi left office in Libya, in 2011, having been ousted by a newly formed government led by the National Transitional Council. That's the way it is in the short-term!

Having lost his sense of purpose and direction, and dropping out of college, R. Royce decided that he needed some form of self-discipline. When he went through the Army basic training program, he somehow qualified as an expert marksman with the M-16, a product made of dense plastic and metal material, supposedly manufactured by the "Mattel Toy Company," and was considered more serious-minded equipment than "Hot Wheels" cars or "G.I. Joe" dolls. As an incentive to excel, the Drill Sergeants allowed the experts to take turns firing an AK-47 they'd brought to the field for weapons-testing purposes. They were supposed to shoot at an empty metal ammunition box one of the sergeants tossed on the ground about thirty yards downrange. Royce had discovered then and there that he couldn't hit the broad side of a barn with the infernal contraption. Ditto, a few days later, when they let him fire a Colt .45 automatic for small-arms weapons familiarization. When scorers looked at the targets and counted the holes, they noticed he'd fired some of his rounds on the next shooter's target. He had a hell of a sense of humor. For some reason, his preferred weapons of choice were a 50-caliber turret-mounted machine gun, a TOW missile launcher, and the LAW.

CHAPTER 8

Book review of the novel

Maggie's Mistake

by Carolyn Brown, published in 2003.

"Born Free."

O.P., Bea, Fife, and I were just waiting around for an airplane to arrive at the Aviation Center when I began glancing through the Entertainment section of the newspaper one lazy Saturday evening—it must have been sometime back in 2000 or 2001, when I happened to notice the advertisement for an upcoming concert performance. Not one to keep current with the music scene, I saw the words "Lee Ann" in extra-large letters on the page, so naturally, I thought that "Lee Ann Rimes" was coming to town to give a concert performance. I'd seen her popular single music video on television at the Blockbuster video store and at the laundromat. The incredible range, timbre, and sheer volume of her singing voice left a lasting impression on me. I was thoroughly excited in anticipation of seeing her perform live on stage. Looking more carefully and closely at the ad, however, I noticed that it wasn't really her, but, in actuality, one "Lee Ann Womack" who was going to appear live in concert. I expressed my dismay and distinct disappointment to the others, when O.P. casually mentioned that Lee Ann Womack was a pretty darn good country musician herself. He knew quite a bit about country and western and we respected his opinion. Isn't it funny how you remember scenes from the past like that, as you grow older and become sentimental, sitting on the verandah on your rocker?

In any event, I finished reading Carolyn Brown's romance novel, *Maggie's Mistake*, yesterday and was trying to think what kind of background music would make an appropriate theme song for no apparent reason. right away I arrived at the conclusion, "Of course, Lee Ann Womack." I can almost visualize the gorgeous and alluring "Maggie," her fiery red hair cascading in the breeze, looking lovingly and longingly out over the ocean, while the song "I Hope You Dance" plays. Then, not a moment too soon, "Everett," her rugged, dashing and debonair beau, driving out to meet her in a shiny, sparkling metal-flake moss-green classic Cadillac convertible with a luxurious tan, soft Corinthian leather interior turns on the radio and listens to Glen Campbell singing "Gentle on My Mind" as he cruises toward the beach and parks.

High society may have to keep up appearances, but these two practical, down-to-earth, responsible, caring, and giving individuals have every right to enjoy their lives in privacy. You might think the book could be a little more sensationalized, as if Annie Oakley meeting Doc Holiday at Buffalo Bill's Wild West Show were apropos. You might even go so far as to believe that Maggie should not have left the barndoor open and let the horse get away, if you only judge the book by it fine-arts graphics cover. But one thing is for certain in the book, Maggie never forgot her vows.

R. Royce, too, had been madly in love, once upon a time, but it was never really meant to be. He hadn't yet become fully mature enough to understand the required implications, explanations, and subtleties of unrequited love. He was kind of flaky, and his demeanor was a little shaky. In other words, he lacked the total confidence and means to follow through on his good intentions and lofty promises.

CHAPTER 9

Book review of the collection of short stories

A Darker Shade of Sweden

by John-Henri Holmberg, published in 2014.

Exquisite candies in a gift-wrapped box

What types of high crimes and misdemeanors could possibly be found in a peaceful, free, modern, progressive-thinking, open society, such as that of Sweden, which boasts an excellent standard of living and universal healthcare for its citizens, as well? All kinds, as it turns out, if one judges by the diverse collection of crime-fiction stories included in the book *A Darker Shade of Sweden*, presented by John-Henri Holmberg.

In many of the stories, extremely well-written either by expert authorities in the field of criminology or by world-renowned, award-winning literary giants, things seem to "go to hell in a handbasket" in a hurry, so to speak. If the perpetrators were brought to justice in a courtroom setting, lawyers for the defense might well make the argument that government, religion, society, culture—even the weather was at fault. Mental illness, duress, or instability could have been a deciding or mitigating factor. And of course the prosecutors would have a field day gathering evidence. In any event, the stories are fairly representative in similarity to programming segments which you might have seen on any night of the week on any evening news channel in the United States; or on the late-night news, if the details were too excruciatingly gruesome, gory, or otherwise beyond the dramatically sensationalized media material suitable for prime time. Most are of local news caliber; some, national in scope. The subject matter of a few of the stories could easily have made the tabloids' front-page, with imagery magnified and exposed in all of its graphic splendor, conspicuously placed on the shelves of every supermarket checkout lane, had they been real, live events that actually happened. In their present form, however, they are simply stories with an amplified message for our own edification, growing awareness, and self-improvement to help make us better human beings on the road to self-fulfillment. Which isn't a bad thing, per se. We do need periodic reminders of what not to do and, most importantly, how not to become victims ourselves.

To enumerate them; nay, as in some form of renumeration, the stories encompass solved, unsolved, or otherwise resolved crimes which involve or evolve from the following facts, circumstances, or motivations:

1. Youth and innocence lost
2. A serial killer
3. An abused spouse
4. A labor dispute
5. The Last Will and Testament of a parishioner
6. An inappropriate teacher-pupil relationship
7. Mail fraud in a mining town
8. Medical malpractice with serious health consequences
9. Police detectives playing cards with fiction writers
10. The lack of a good alibi
11. A shunned daughter
12. A missing child at the carnival
13. A tight-wad millionaire on a cruise
14. An unassuming fashion-conscious girl under surveillance by British Intelligence and the Swedish Secret Service, reminiscing
15. Two fishermen who discover a human skull in a rowboat drifting near an island
16. Exported cultural property being sold at auction to finance military action in a third-world war-torn country
17. An expired statute of limitations

Any more details might spoil the surprise in store for the readers of such an outstanding collection, jam-packed with top-drawer crime-fiction stories. Thus, the ominous review is concluded.

R. Royce asked a rhetorical question, "What's the first thing Rolf does when he comes sloshing and running out of the lake?"

"That's an easy one," replied Cornelius Korn. "He shakes like a dog."

CHAPTER 10

Book review of the novel

The Charm School

by Nelson DeMille, published in 1989.

Show the love.

Sylvester walks nonchalantly into the apartment, a stack of today's mail in his hand. There is an advertising flyer from the florist. "Say it with flowers." He enters the dining room. There are roses on the table. Moving quickly and quietly now into the living room, he views a plain wicker basket of plants on top of the TV cabinet, overflowing with an abundance of intensely purple petals. Violets on television.

He reflects on the video game he witnessed being played out by a youth at the corner convenience store. Measurable levels of health, strength, weapons, and funds were prominently displayed to the side of the onscreen virtual-reality activity. You must maintain a high level of energy to continue the battle against a tough, well-armed, skilled, and resourceful opponent. Otherwise, game over.

He sits on an inviting sofa cushion, opens a long envelope, and begins to read the review of a recently cancelled television series, modernized and loosely adapted from the theme from Nelson DeMille's 1989 novel, *The Charm School*.

Reality check, you expect a middle-aged, overweight, out-of-shape, desk jockey technocrat, purported to be a mid-level Air Force manager and ex-fighter pilot, assigned to an embassy post in the USSR. Someone who sort of reminds you of another DeMille character, the joke-cracking, "legal eagle" wise guy—John "Rambo He's Not" Sutter, only all grown up and mature at present.

What you get instead is the very impressive character of Sam "Haul Ass" Hollis, a walking-talking Hardened-Man Dynamo of excess energy and instability, who appears to be on a daily regimen combination of steroids and "Viagra," yet his is a healthy diet of pure, natural foods, rich in body building proteins, vital nutrients, and source vitamins. It must be the fresh air and exercise that makes him this way.

He goes out to explore Moscow, only to discover to his dismay, that the food is terrible, the service is worse than intolerable, and he can't seem to get decent results in any of his search efforts. As a matter of taste, there's no Cordon Bleu cooking school inspired influence to be found anywhere; refinement, no Butler academy graduates in the vicinity to lend a helping hand in a pinch; or, for purposes of his ongoing professional development, ready access to a spare F-15 in reasonably close proximity is simply not there. To add insult to injury, he is badly mistreated by some of the local inhabitants. His rivals bully and intimidate him. Apparently, he does not fully comprehend the mentality and brutality of his KGB counterparts.

Be forewarned: the plot of the novel may seem incongruous; farfetched, preposterous, even bizarre at times, "nyet"—impossible. Hollis has the primary mission of locating missing U.S. Air Force pilots from the conflict in Viet Nam, who may have been relocated to Russia for some inexplicable reason. He asks around for possible leads and follows up on some of the information he receives.

His boss, the embassy station chief, Seth "All Systems Go" Alevy encourages Hollis in his duties, provides guidance, and tasks his ex-girlfriend with assisting him. The boss does reveal his conflicted "inner child" and war-mongering tendencies in the process. So, for example, he includes weapons of mass destruction in his contingency plans—a worst-case scenario, one might suppose. He seeks to make a profit on his business ventures in Moscow as a sideline, but this is not a high priority. In contrast, he is perceived to be generous to a fault, and a prolific giver of gifts.

Hollis's new girlfriend, then, Lisa "Tsarina" Rhodes, is allegedly young, beautiful, scholarly, and sexy. You wonder if she and Hollis didn't fall in love, she might have been a "sleeper," on her way to the pinnacle of the personnel charts within their diplomatic corps. The real trouble begins when Hollis invites Lisa along on one of his fact-finding missions into the vastly remote countryside and isolated villages some distance away from the center of Moscow. Here, you are cautiously reminded, that there are some places in the world where you just wouldn't want to be caught wandering around without at least two or three regular Army Divisions, plus some extra Marines, and dedicated air support.

I would not want to hazard a wild guess, or even contemplate any of the more serious implications of Hollis's and Alevy's decision-making process, and their ultimately chosen courses of action in a real-world scenario. One can only be thankful and feel genuinely humbled that the novel is merely an extension of some kindhearted, sentimental narrator's hyperactive imagination running rampant, but you can't help but wonder from where the megalomaniac personality and the persecution-complex induced tendencies for revenge and supreme domination springs forth. As if they had gone on an incredible road trip, or a mind-blowing ego trip, but really wanted to go on the world's scariest roller-coaster ride. You might also be curious about what they do to relax, chill out, and calm down afterwards. What would they try for an encore? Another covert military operation?

Oddly enough, Sam, Lisa, and Seth sort of remind me of the three principal characters in the original *Star Wars*, if you really want to stretch the point of an "evil empire" way out there into the farthest reaches of the galaxy. They do get to drive around town and drag Main Street in a cool transport vehicle.

All in all, a considerable amount of team research and "boots on the ground" detail went into planning and producing every single chapter of this extraordinary novel, and packing it with interesting facts and tidbits of information about the host nation. The reader should bear in mind, however, that the world has changed drastically since when the novel was first published.

Currently, there are a great many extremely dangerous, extraneous troublemakers stirring the pot of dissent, who originate in any of several other high-profile countries around the globe besides the U.S. and Russia. Nonetheless, the U.S. and Russia remain steadfast and ideologically opposed. Both strive to expand their spheres of influence throughout the rest of the world. It's a stalemate in as far as most are concerned.

R. Royce was reminded of a story he'd once heard about an elementary school girl in Oklahoma, who once wrote an impassioned letter during history class. Having discovered that a few of her former classmates, who had teased and tormented her mercilessly, without rhyme or reason, suddenly moved away with their families to live in Texas, she tactfully penned the following credible information:

"Dear President Gorbachev: Tulsa is no longer the oil capital of the world. Please aim your missiles somewhere of more immediate strategic concern. It makes better sense sending rockets to Mars for pre-positioning canned food provisions, vital supplies, and critical equipment for space missions in 2030 and beyond. The future of our civilization might very well depend on it."

Apparently, she did not bear a grudge or harbor ill-will. Neither did her big brother.

By Charles J. Scott,
submitted on 8/8/2015.

CHAPTER 11

Review of the collection of short stories

Guilt

by Ferdinand von Schirach, originally published
in 2010, and later translated by Carol Brown Janeway.

Dial up the heat.

Due to the recent phenomena of numerous crime scene investigations shows appearing on television, such as the *C.S.I.* programs set in New York, Miami, Los Angeles, Chicago, and New Orleans; the latest version of *Hawaii 50; Cold Case;* and the Courtroom Dramas, such as *20/20, 48 Hours, and Dateline,* it is no wonder that the stories by Ferdinand von Schirach in his book *Guilt* might be well-received in television format, except perhaps these stories may be considered too European, mundane, or twisted for prime time. They differ from these programs in other respects, as well. The police, detective, and investigator shows focus on finding, catching, and bringing the perpetrators to justice; and the courtroom shows zoom in on prosecutors proving the perpetrators actually committed the crime and then convincing the jury they did it. Most of them go to jail.

The stories in the book, on the other hand, have been filtered through the keenly perceptive and benevolent eyes of a tough-minded, Big-City attorney. You can tell instantly from the manner and style of his prose that the author himself has been a highly successful public defender, touting years of experience under his belt and expert knowledge of the finer points of German juris prudence. Undoubtedly, he has been called "a damn good lawyer," who doesn't mince his words or pull any punches. Obviously, he has won the respect and admiration of his peers and judges alike throughout his long, illustrious career.

International in scope, most of his stories are about foreigners living in and adapting to life in Germany. The book is gushing with the spirit of diverse cultures. A thoroughly modern city environment, as well as a smattering of small town locations form the backdrop of events as they unfold in a plain-spoken, straightforward way. Including three or four stories from the author's companion book, *Crime*, would have really spiced up the book, packed as it is—sort of like cranking up the heat a couple of notches by basting an incredibly hot jalapeño sauce onto the steaks already sizzling on a fiery grill. You can tell it's going to be a wingding of a barbeque, because you get the distinct impression that the author doesn't just resolve crimes with smoke and mirrors. Somehow, I don't anticipate a third book coming out any time soon with either of the titles "Remorse" or "Regret." A book called "Relief" is possible, since you get the sense of "That's what the victim must feel when the verdict is reached!" in many of von Schirach's stories. Poetic justice is served. "You can't be serious," a book of German short stories, called "Syrians"?

Nonetheless, there does not appear to be a great deal of pulse-pounding passion, or real sensitivity and emotion in the unique characterization of these stories. Some characters strike me as being awfully cold and devoid of feeling. I suppose they did what they did, in a harsh milieu and under the burden of a difficult situation. Complicated trial proceedings follow. Then, life continues all around them as before. In effect, they were bowled over by life—more like being run over by a train, something that happens sometimes. They are never the same ever again afterwards. The courts try to pick up the pieces and assemble them back together as best as they can, like "Humpty-Dumpty." But, it's not always easy or a pretty sight to see. Mistakes have been made before. Yet, compromised and broken as they may seem, they are lifted upwards toward the clear blue sky, a burnt offering to the gods.

The narrator sticks to the facts throughout the story, gives enough specific detail to make his point, and offers graphic descriptions of events as they unfold. As an artist, he paints a sharp, vivid, and contrasting picture of the subject, his surroundings, and significant circumstances. As any daring art critic worth his salt might boldly conclude, the author achieves a satisfying result each time, leaving the moralizing to the reader.

"He's as guilty as sin," said R. Royce.

"That's for a judge and jury to decide in a court of law," replied Cornelius Korn.

"He all but confessed. The eye witnesses to the crime were credible," said Royce.

"The prosecution still has to prove beyond a reasonable doubt that he is guilty," continued Korn.

"The defense doesn't have a leg to stand on," stated Royce, unequivocally.

"What would a reasonable man of average intelligence have done under similar circumstances?" inquired Korn, playing the devil's advocate.

"He wouldn't have killed a defenseless man in cold blood," Royce admitted, in all truth and fairness.

"I don't think he committed the crime, either," Korn concluded, candidly adding, "He'll stick around to face the music."

>Review by J. C. Scott,
>09-18-2015.

CHAPTER 12

Review of the book

Religion and the Decline of Magic
Studies in Popular Beliefs in Sixteenth- and Seventeenth-Century England

by Keith Thomas, published in 1971.

Whatever floats your boat.

"Your belly will bloat up like a party balloon, sitting there in your reclining chair all day long every Sunday, watching football, dipping fondue, and guzzling draft beer."

Making such an astute observation and having the audacity to tell someone living in the sixteenth-century Magic Kingdom—no, not Disneyland, but the mighty, chivalrous nation of England, you could have been accused of witchcraft by anyone who presented himself with an enlarged stomach, be bound and turned over to ecclesiastical authorities, and prosecuted to the full extent of the law. As you may have heard, or learned in school, the penalty for witchcraft was death by incineration, way back then. Most regrettably, witchcraft was a heinous crime against the Church, punishable by a tribunal of its prominent leaders. In case you weren't aware there were three main, recognized church groups in 16th-century England: Catholics, Puritans, and Anglicans. They each offered a different perspective to the faithful and blessed.

According to Keith Thomas in his hefty, historical nonfictional book, *Religion and the Decline of Magic Studies in Popular Beliefs in Sixteenth- and Seventeenth- Century England*, the Church was in the process of undergoing a drastic, cataclysmic upheaval. It may be inferred that this was because the people were changing, society was changing, the government was changing, and the times were changing. In a nutshell, the ideas of rational-thinking intellectuals were beginning to catch on and take hold, based on scientific methods and concrete proof. The author then goes into great, painstakingly elaborate detail, describing the people, their thoughts, their beliefs, society, day-to-day activities, government, the laws, the environment in which they lived, and—most importantly, considering the subject matter and theme of the book, the power and influence exerted over them by the Church, during five crucial time periods: medieval times, the Reformation, Civil War, Interregnum, and the Industrial Age.

In my humble opinion, Keith Thomas reveals the terrible truth that the various religions of England appeared to be in an almost Olympic-like competition for winning God's favor, being held in highest esteem by the Grace of God, and perpetuating good health, prosperity, and happiness exclusively for church members. In essence, each church strived to become the sole, direct intermediary between God and men. A result of this endeavor and the authority gained thereby was to put them at odds with the other rival churches. Yes, certainly, it caused them to excommunicate, ostracize, ban, and burn all persons who were not of their faith. This is probably why, in later years, the Pilgrims sailed for America on the *Mayflower* and many others caught the first available sailing vessel bound for Australia. Probably about this time, it transpired that some "planetary travelers" began thinking about eternity in earnest.

Of course, the individuals most likely to be burned were non-members who believed more in the power of natural magic, than that of the established Church, in all of its majesty, pageantry, ceremony, and rich history. Mostly, these castaway people were probably poor, destitute, mentally or physically ill, beggars, thieves, or laborers, and were considered a burden on society. In effect, all they had going for them was their indomitable spirit, the will to fight the battle of man versus nature, a few meagre lucky charms in their pockets, some knowledge of medicinal herbs, and the light of the moon and stars to help guide them on their way. You might even go so far as to say that they had become victims of religious persecution by the Church.

Eventually, the English government itself got involved, enacted and enforced strict statutes against the practice of witchcraft in cases where "maleficium," coupled with evil or harmful intent were found. Essentially, what this means is that a person caused physical injury to another person, or damaged his property or goods. Throughout history, such an action constitutes a criminal act, and the guilty party is subject to punishment as decreed in a court of law.

Some cases were easier to prove than others, however. For example, it is much more straightforward to prove that someone repeatedly stabbed a victim in the chest with the sharp point of a sword and consequently he died from his wounds than it is to prove someone merely looked at him, giving him the "evil eye," and he dropped dead in his tracks while everyone present watched on, horrified.

In any event, the book is definitely worth reading. It might even challenge your beliefs and restore your faith in the divine Providence, if not your trust in humanity. Henceforward—and I realize I skipped and glossed over a tremendous amount of encyclopedia-source and biographical information which is included in the book, magic was simply not taken seriously anymore—except possibly in the more recent or present time by the likes of Walt Disney and an army of animators. Strangely enough, I sometimes wonder whatever became of Jeanne Dixon?

>   Review by Charles J. Scott,
>   09-16-2015.

CHAPTER 13

Book review of a collection of short stories,

Nine Stories

by J. D. Salinger, published in 1948-1953.

Sink or swim.

The children of a large dual-denominational family react to and rebel against their strict, religious upbringing by lashing out in various ways throughout the precocious and impertinent phases of their luminous existences, however brief or prolonged. If he could only have torn himself away from his clinging family, the eldest son, Seymour, might have grown up, gone away to become a famous reclusive monk in a Far Eastern monastery, and lived happily ever after. Who knows, a generation later, the youngest daughter might have become a devout and faithful follower of Jesus Christ, completely at peace with herself and in perfect harmony with the world around her, a full generation before anyone ever heard of "Woodstock" or "cults." You can tell the children didn't have many friends for very long because hardly any of them would ever be able to meet the high standards set in the realm of their imaginations and through the arduous process of "home-schooling," which presumably would have included proof of sainthood, miracles and all. Their education may have been limited, but they appeared to be wise, knowledgeable and well-counselled. For instance, they appeared to see beyond the Great-Wall facade represented by education and the public school system as well as through the "Glass-Ceiling" of life in general, as administered by mere mortals, possessing human frailties and the more serious flaws of character, as if they were repeating the same amusing anecdotes over and over again. It just didn't seem very humorous the second time around, evolving as they were, seeking a higher plane of existence, or another dimension of reality. Similarly, they were probably cute once upon a time, themselves, like the kids on *The Art Linkletter Show* or *Captain Kangaroo*, but most of them eventually grew out of it.

Controlling and manipulative—spoiled brats, some would say, they had a very difficult time playing nicely with others in the sandbox. Vocal and strong-willed, they did things their way and took their sweet time about it too. You can begin to visualize the complicated psychiatry and psychotropic medication at work on the horizon in the not too distant future for their generation. In 1948, when the book was first published, no one accurately predicted the long-term health risks associated with smoking cigarettes. No Surgeon General's warning label appeared on the packages of tobacco products. Smoking was cool, chic, fashionable, and happening. Ditto for alcohol consumption. You wanted to make the scene, be sociable, and be seen. Again, no warning labels against drinking excessively and attempting to operate motor vehicles and other machinery. A bite of sandwich, a cigarette, and two mixed-drinks for lunch and you wonder why did you begin to feel ill all of a sudden? Must have been the excitement of Game Day.

All in all, there were some really good stories in *Nine Stories* by J. D. Salinger about a nostalgic New York family of vaudevillians trying to cope, adjust, and rebuild their lives in the wake and shadow of WWII. Seymour was a tough act to follow for his younger, more impressionable siblings. The youngest ones idolized him, I believe. He could have baptized the girl in the pool, or tossed her overboard into the deep blue sea—he was that profoundly unpredictable in a couple of stories. And the girl he met at the Derby could have gone on to become the next Queen of England, for all we know. In an unforgettable encounter, she undoubtedly inspired him and eventually saved his life. This is evident when, much later, showing symptoms of post-traumatic stress syndrome, he was healed by the power of pure, divine love. So, she obviously left a lasting impression on him. Ironically, the moral of the story is that you should never under any circumstances send kindergarten teachers off to fight a holy war in distant lands.

CHAPTER 14

Book review of the novel

The Swiss Spy

by Alex Gerlis, published in 2015.

You can put that in the bank!

The British Intelligence Service becomes intensely curious why some prominent Germans and a group of exiled Russians have been putting incredibly large amounts of money into secured bank accounts in Switzerland during 1939-'41. They seek credible inside information in order to determine who is making these tremendous deposits, and for whom they are being made. To help in this ambitious undertaking, they recruit a dual-national citizen of both Switzerland and Germany. He becomes an intermediary between two banking conglomerates, having offices in the two countries. A respected business executive, he travels freely and easily across the border, intercepts highly sensitive documents, and passes the information along to his British handlers. What could be simpler? There are complications and potential implications. Germany is at war with Great Britain, for instance. Shady dealings are revealed, involving money laundering, coupled with military war plans gone astray. Russian intelligence officers get wind of the clandestine activity. German State Security suspicions are aroused and they delve into the matter. The military police is placed on heightened alert. British operatives notify their contacts and marshal their resources. They make new travel arrangements with better connections. Meanwhile, throughout the turmoil, the unassuming Swiss businessman navigates through dangerous, uncharted waters in all kinds of inclement weather, as a manner of speaking. In the course of his extracurricular nighttime activities, under reduced visibility, and sometimes with clouded judgment he perseveres through trying ordeals, difficult situations and great adversity, but delivers the goods—for the most part.

The Swiss Spy, by Alex Gerlis, is a first-rate thriller. The book is a historical fictional account of events that gives keen insight into who and what really drove Germany into ruination as a world power during the early years of WWII. The list of suspects include the hopelessly insane, megalomaniac German leaders, their zealously overextended military-industrial complex, their faulty ideology, Russian forces, and British forces. It had to be a combination of these diverse, unmanageable factors. For the reluctant conservatives and other political hangers-on, the situation must have been like cruising in a leaky high-altitude hot-air balloon, ever so slowly deflating and gradually descending, ultimately bringing the basket case back to earth, the stunned occupants realizing the grave errors of a new, untested leadership and knowing they can't wait until the next fair election, which may never arrive. It must have been a truly humbling experience, that would place them back on solid, but terribly cold, muddy, and untenable ground decades later. I believe the war-mongers drove Germany into ruin, eventually destroying the country, much like a hostile corporate raider ransacks a company which stockholders and investors alike believe is "too big to fail," selling off its equipment, material, and assets, radically downsizing, then absconding with all of the savings, revenue, and profits, leaving behind a wrecked, defunct, useless shell of a company, bankrupt and out-of-business. It reminds me of a country and western song which suggests that individuals who own gold in California deposit it into their Los Angeles area bank accounts for safekeeping. It just goes to show you, average people do what they can making their way in life despite the odds. So much for "community development." Newsflash! History repeats itself in Syria today, a torn and troubled middle-eastern country which can boast the dubious distinction of being simultaneously at war with two super-powers, the vengeful Russia and the unabashed United States. Where have we heard that scenario play out before? Oh!

CHAPTER 15

Review of the novel

Look Homeward, Angel

by Thomas Wolfe, published in 1929.

Fate Drops a Plum into the Palm of his Hand!

The community of Altamont, North Carolina, which I found in my worn, dog-eared, but trusty 2004 edition Rand McNally Road Atlas, might not be the same one described in the novel *Look Homeward, Angel* by Thomas Wolfe, but then again…the town I located is in the vicinity of four nearby or connected counties: Avery, Burke, Caldwell, and Mitchell. It is situated in an area surrounded by the Blue Ridge Mountains which traverse toward the northeast into Virginia, and the Appalachian and Iron Mountains angled toward the northwest from the easternmost part of Tennessee, south of Johnson City. The unassuming town is located on the Blue Ridge Parkway between Asheville and Boone, North Carolina. The Pisgah National Forest lies to the southwest. There are numerous mountain peaks, lakes, state parks, and recreational areas throughout the wilderness region. At higher elevations, the area looks like an excellent choice for a scenic drive, a fine vacation destination, a good place to go to escape the sweltering summer heat in Georgia and South Carolina, and possibly find a retirement home in a peaceful, quiet, and natural setting. Out of the way, you might not have the social amenities such as shopping centers, marquee concert hall entertainment, the international cuisine often associated with fine dining, or major-league professional sporting venues found in the more developed population centers such as Winston-Salem-Greensboro, Raleigh-Durham, or Charlotte, but then you probably wouldn't have the hustle-bustle, traffic, and big-time crime either. Or jobs. Moving to a remote mountain town might not be the wisest upwardly mobile career decision you could make—if you are Harvard-educated corporate-business executive material. But you never know, someone might come up with a miracle cure for brain cancer, and a prominent community such as Altamont focused on the future might become the next world-renowned center for breakthrough medical research. A pharmaceutical company's dream come true.

If you had been living at the turn of the twentieth century, when the spiced-up, earthy novel took place you might have found yourself in or driving by the "Dixieland Boarding House," of which the author fondly reminisces and where his family of amazing tobacco-smoking, whiskey-sipping', God-fearing characters lived for the greater portion of their highly dramatic soap opera charged lives. Even more, you read the novel and you get a condensed course in the Classics and Antiquity. It is a primer of primitive cultures and a touchstone of ancient traditions. Oliver Gant, a stonecutter by trade, the patriarch of the family has a distinct flair for the dramatic. He is a well-practiced, accomplished oratory oracle of the sublime and infinite universe. In his own way, he seeks the affirmation and approval of the almighty God and Protector of his family and home. His blessed, frugal and sensible wife, Eliza, holds the family together, in my opinion. Her business savvy and smart real estate investments keeps them from starvation and out of the poor-house. His youngest son, Eugene, carries on the impromptu speech-making tradition and puts it all down in historical, at times poetic, written chronicle form. Eventually, he goes on to college and becomes a man of letters. Like the rest of the family, he likes to travel, but tends to wander, stray, and get lost along the way. When war looms on the horizon for the nation, the family philosophy of protecting individual freedom and the inalienable rights of all Americans actively involves them in the effort. Eugene goes to the shipyards in Virginia to help supply Navy vessels with arms and munitions. His brother Luke joins the Navy as a seaman. In general, they are a family of metaphysical voyagers, ever searching for something over the horizon, they know not what. Inevitably, Eugene has to "look away" from Dixieland. Correct me if I'm wrong, but I believe the novel is his story. In a sentimental way, it reminds me of the charming family film *Spencer's Mountain*. And a little of Carson McCuller's novel, *The Heart Is a Lonely Hunter*. So you get a little of the bitter with the sweet.

"Would you like a scoop of vanilla ice-cream on top of your lemon-berry pie?" asked Meghan.

"Just like Grandma used to make," said R. Royce.

CHAPTER 16

A book review of

The Teachings of Don Juan:
A Yaqui Way of Knowledge

by Carlos Castaneda

They let the genie out of the bottle!

You can almost visualize author Carlos Castaneda traveling to Mexico City and meeting a couple of tour guides who want to show him the sights around town, such as the museums, restaurants, shopping boutiques, and other featured popular attractions. Doing so would be a pleasant diversion. To pursue this line of speculation, then, a liberal arts student from South America with a background in anthropology, philosophy, religion, sociology, and psychology, he makes discreet inquiries about opportunities for medical research, especially those concerning the inner workings of the human brain. After all, several of the universities in the city do offer advanced professional degrees in the health sciences field. He learns, it just so happens, that a certain individual has been searching extensively for a qualified new apprentice, but his scholastic program is neither accredited nor recognized by any of the institutions of higher education in Mexico, nor by the American Medical Association, the truth be told. His curiosity aroused, the undaunted, intrepid author goes forth to seek further information about the alleged Don Juan, his particular whereabouts, his teaching methods and his credentials. On the other hand, you might just as well believe that the author simply went to Mexico to buy pharmaceuticals he couldn't get in Los Angeles, California, where he had been attending college. As you may know, the apothecaries south of the border do not always check for a prescription from your physician. And they may not be overly concerned about FDA approval. In any event, *The Teachings of Don Juan: A Yaqui Way of Knowledge,* published in 1969 by Carlos Castaneda, describes the author's experiences in diary format as he embarks on his apprenticeship to seek the warrior's true path of knowledge.

He travels a rugged, rocky road along the expansive corridor of the Great Southwest, that begins in central Arizona and leads him to Sonora, Mexico. The hot, dusty, winding road ends in the mountains and desert, which is where the humble, happy home of Don Juan Matus is located. He attempts to learn the ancient ways of the Yaqui Indian medicine man. In his diary, Castaneda relates his most extraordinary, spiritual, and supernatural encounters with the candid, humorous, lucid, enigmatic, practical, and knowledgeable Don Juan, who guides him in his quest to understand what it means to seek the path of a cosmic warrior. In brief, Don Juan introduces him to three types of psychotropic plants: peyote cactus, which relates to a spirit known as "Mescalito"; Datura stramonium, otherwise known as "Devil's Weed," which has the potential to conjure up an animal spirit "ally"; and finally a concoction referred to as "a little smoke," which is vaguely described as a precisely measured mixture of secret dried plant ingredients, including a sprinkling of ground-up small bright yellow flowers, with a powdery substance from a specific kind of psilocybin mushroom tossed into the preparation—according to my limited interpretation of the reading material. It actually sounds like a medieval alchemist's formula.

I can just imagine the two of them chewing on peyote buttons plucked from cacti found in their evening desert wanderings, spitting out the fibrous pulp, as if they were chewing gum that's lost its flavor, then chasing these unusual hors d'oeuvres with shots of tequila. After a while they begin watching great performances by the genie who escapes from the bottle. I can even see them scampering and scurrying around chasing gigantic lizards through the desert over rocks through the arroyo and into the canyon, after imbibing several bottles of Jimson Weed tea. But to see them soaring like eagles beyond the Siquero cactus and high above the mesa, while a flock of lazy, unsuspecting crows circles aimlessly below would be a most impressive sight.

Seriously, I begin to wonder, what were Don Juan's ancient ancestors and their neighborly fellow inhabitants really doing roaming around in the great Southwest for the past several millennia? Besides escaping war, poverty, slavery, and the various and sundry miscellaneous crimes of other advanced civilizations. Of course, they must have enjoyed their lives and freedom, exploring the new world, doing a little prospecting, and otherwise communing with nature. Besides frolicking on hallowed ground amidst the flora and fauna of a faraway frontier, there is a great deal to be said for survival, self-sufficiency, and gathering empirical evidence. Once upon a time in recent memory....

Maybe we can't explain all of the mysteries of the universe, past or present. Strange events have taken place in our own lives. For instance, last Wednesday at 8:37 A.M. on October 27, I awoke and, looking up, was startled to see a distinctive pair of large oval shapes, like eyes, directly above my head, reflecting off the bedroom wall, apparently from diffracted morning sunlight passing through the glass window pane and between the slightly opened blinds. One eye was red and yellow. The other eye was green and yellow. The phenomenon might just as well have been attributed to eyes from the spirit world. Who can say for sure? It only happened once. May their eyes shine upon your better nature!

CHAPTER 17

Book review of the novel

The Martian Chronicles

by Ray Bradbury, originally published 1946 - 1958.

Mars Scores Wars Cars & Candy Bars.

Life on Mars is conceivable from your imagination, including the extraneous conditions of life on the planet and the Martian environment. All you have to do is reflect upon and encapsulate humanity, our lives in the microcosm we call Earth, our history, the major achievements of mankind, our impressive array of capabilities, and the vast natural resources with which we have had to work. You can project the facts, factors, statistics, and general data out there into the farthest reaches of the universe, or onto any other planet out there in the solar system, such as Mars, the next closest planet to us, going away from the sun. You can think of the planets as if they were arranged in a complex pattern like a long curvy line of dominos. If they were part of an amazing infinitely complicated domino effect, Mars would certainly be one of the earliest ones to topple. Astronaut travel to our moon proved to be a challenging achievement, but the government today does not offer enough incentive or motivation to return anytime soon. It would be a different story if there were beneficial resources on the moon which could promote and sustain life. Happiness and comfort living on or visiting any celestial body is important. But oxygen and water are the critical resources we must have in order to live anywhere. There is a good chance oxygen and water exists on Mars. So, boom or bust, Mars appears to be the next logical choice for future exploration. Obviously, you can't send expeditions toward our Sun. They would incinerate, melt and burn to ashes. Traveling toward the farthest reaches of our galaxy makes perfect sense, traveling toward the next galaxy, as if we were sailing along with the debris from the "Big Bang." For the immediate future, Mars would be the ideal stepping stone, if not the ultimate projected destination of mankind on Earth. NASA should make a feasibility study on the subject right away.

Destination Mars depends on the terra firma of the planet. Specifically, exactly how hard is the ground when you land on it? How deep and how solid does the rocky surface extend when you dig into it? Are there pitfalls, sinkholes, quicksand, and quagmires? You don't want to land your rocket on a sinkhole! Or, do you? The perfect location might well be an underground missile silo, offering the best protection from the elements and the climate. Farther away from your Red Crystal Trailer Park and deeper underground, do you drill into molten lava, gaseous material, or liquid chemicals? Potential sources of fuel and heat. How about a water source? Arriving flight crews will have to become explorers of the "New World" for this commodity, which is probably more precious than gold on Mars, and they must be resupplied periodically with pure drinking water. Electricity should be simple: bringing solar generators and wind turbines should do the trick. You need shelter. Caves and cliff dwellings are possible. Or they could convert the rocket fuselages into shiny new "Airstream" travel trailers. Oxygen would be thin on Mars, if breathable at all. Crews would no doubt need a life-support system for oxygen. The gravity on Mars is significantly less than that on Earth, but should be about twice that on the moon, so getting around should be easier. Walking on Mars should be a breeze. Explorers can make great strides by leaps and bounds, and cover greater distances. Until a viable water source is located and the flight crew can grow their own food, their food must all be provided from the pre-packaged food stocks brought with them aboard their flight, until they can be resupplied. Can they find proof of life on Mars? Doubtful there are any Martian rabbits hippety hopping around the bunny trail; tasty vitamin-rich vegetables, or even edible insects. Basically, the life they find on Mars will be the life they bring with them. Nonetheless, flight crews should be trained to look for ephemeron specimens on Mars. How are wind conditions? Hurricanes and tornadoes, nonexistent. But, is dust a problem? Like the Dust Bowl in Oklahoma in the 1930s or recurring, raging sandstorms in the Sahara desert? Definitely undesirable!

It may be inferred from a recent news report I heard on television that the main reason Mars looks so barren through a telescope or from Voyager probe satellite images is because there is no magnetic field on Mars to protect it from cosmic winds and solar radiation. Life on Mars might have just been "blown away." This suggests two things: First, the planet probably does not have a solid iron or metallic core at its center, or a magnetic polar axis. Secondly, it is difficult to sustain life forms on such a planet due to the inherent physical, chemical, and thermodynamic properties of matter. Not that I'm an expert on the matter. Specifically, I believe that it is difficult to sustain life forms when conditions favor entropy increasing more dramatically than enthalpy. In other words, thermodynamically and atomically speaking, substances have a greater tendency to disassociate, separate, or fall apart rather than to attract, combine, and fuse together. A molecule would more readily have a tendency to break apart into atoms, rather than atoms naturally forming into molecules. As you probably have already guessed, complex molecules are the building blocks of life, which have formed from combining atoms into simple molecules, which fuse together from simple inorganic molecules into the more complicated organic molecules, with DNA present. Somehow, life forms in the process transforming from reactive chemical substances into biological creatures. Again, this favors an enthalpy thermodynamic reaction and organic chemistry. A breath of the Holy Spirit might somehow enter into the equation. Or the atmosphere on Mars might have to change with global warming. An artificial magnetic field and greenhouse gases might have to be generated. Then again, a sudden impact from a random collision with a water comet might instantly improve conditions for life on Mars.

Be that as it may, you can never know for certain what living conditions are really like, until you actually set foot on Mars and try to survive there. Ordinarily, under more favorable conditions, travel to Mars would be like going on a camping trip to a remote wilderness region, only you couldn't drive back to the convenience store for flashlight batteries, sodas, hotdogs, and marshmallows; gasoline, a warmer sleeping bag, matches, or a fishing lure. Besides, there might have been life on Mars in some way, shape, or form eons ago, before the time of dinosaurs on Earth. Plus, what do we know about the Martian moons? It might be worth a side-trip to go sightseeing there en route, approaching near enough to shoot some close-up photographs for *National Geographic.*

Newtonian physics applies to rocketry just as it does for cars driving down the interstate highway, except rockets have to overcome the force of gravity in order to escape from the atmosphere surrounding Earth. Funneled gases from onboard fuel storage containers must propel them through millions of miles of outer space, just to reach the orbit of Mars. That's a requirement for a great amount of fuel. If it takes a rocket a little under two days (under 1 and 7/8 days) to reach the moon, then it would take roughly a year to reach Mars, according to my fuzzy arithmetic, allowing for rest stops, refueling, and any scenic side-trips—not to mention, time for dodging asteroids, meteors, and comets. Consequently, launching a rocket from Earth's moon to Mars might be more sensible and economical. A newly arrived flight crew on the moon could board and "blast-off" in a freshly fueled and fully stocked rocket from a permanent base on the moon. Eventually, quantum physics will send rockets to Mars faster.

The first mission to Mars itinerary: Earth to our moon, moon to Martian moon, Martian moon to destination Mars. One-way ticket. No return trip. Travel timetable: 1 year, approximately 50 million miles. Flight crew volunteers plan to spend the rest of their lives on Mars. Follow-on missions to Mars are programmed and scheduled at semi-annual intervals for the next five years. So, after five and a half years, the personnel from ten flight crews should be included in the census of current population on Mars, assuming a 100-percent success rate, no fatalities, and no cancelled flights due to budget cuts, war, inclement weather, natural disasters, or accidents.

Given all of the above information in the rapidly changing, scientifically challenged world in which we live today, if Mars is even remotely similar to the fictional fantasy world depicted by author Ray Bradbury in his 1950 novel, *The Martian Chronicles,* the newly arrived settlers on Mars can expect a tremendous amount of heartache, trouble, suffering, sorrow, and soul-searching. In a more realistic, pragmatic, and Darwinian universe, though, I believe the early inhabitants of Mars will be more like our pilgrims, soldiers, explorers, fortune-seekers, and western expansionists in the United States. If there ever were any Martians in existence, I believe they are long gone by now.

Forty years ago and decades before the "Martian Land Rovers" landed on Mars and began sending images back to Earth, there was a natural history, geology, and astronomy exhibit in a large glass enclosure, tucked away in a dark, dreary, and dusty corner of an obscure science and engineering building on campus. Maybe it was a student's idea for a science fair project. Inside the display case was a robotic gadget, some reddish orange soil samples, various rocks, and a few Polaroid photographs. The contents might have been red rocks from the Rockies and sienna soil from the Red River Valley. Who knows? They could have been the same rocks and dirt you'd find on Mars. There might even have been a top-secret mission to Mars and the proof arrived from the Smithsonian Institute in Washington, D.C., having been sent to the lab for further scientific analysis, placed on display, and promptly forgotten. We know rocks came back from the moon.

The war years were difficult and uncertain times. Hysteria, paranoia, and riots ran rampant. Today, we can feel much more self-assured, confident, and secure in the knowledge we have gained. We have good intelligence, a fine free press, and uncensored news journalism, without hidden agendas favoring special interest groups or embraced by hostile foreign nations to thank. As we all now know, you can put tremendous amounts of information on the internet, but you can't store really impressive secrets for very long.

CHAPTER 18

Review of the novel

The Hangman's Daughter

by Oliver Potzsch, published in German in 2008;
the English translation, published in 2010.

Crosses to Bear and Axes to Grind.

The trouble began in earnest after R. Royce purchased a 1983 Ford Crown Victoria from a fruit and vegetable vendor at the Farmer's Market in Miami, Florida. The vender must have acquired the vehicle at a Dade County surplus auction. It was a plain-looking basic-stock automobile with only a few added options; namely, a high-performance eight-cylinder motor and a speedometer that reads 160 mph on the high end. The box-shaped Crown Vick used to be seen all over the city, because it was a sedan of choice by taxi drivers in Dade. There was plenty of leg room for passengers and a large trunk for luggage. He was in Miami in 1989 because he had landed a job at the airport that paid the bills. He lived in an efficiency apartment near the Hialeah horserace track. The vehicle had three major faults: first, the engine would shut down completely for no apparent reason and you couldn't start it up again. He would have the car towed to the neighborhood mechanic's shop, time and time again. Raphael would get it going again. Second, the transmission went out on a trip to Fort Polk, Louisiana. He had to get the transmission rebuilt in Tallahassee, which is as far as he got. Third, the vehicle failed the Florida exhaust-emissions test. Luckily, a good Samaritan with a mechanic's business card was there waiting for him as he exited the "Clean Air Act" facility. The mechanic from the shop just around the corner adjusted the carburetor, and the vehicle passed inspection.

He drove the car in that condition for about two years when someone took it upon himself to steal it during the night, while it was parked adjacent to the apartment building next to the road. He filed the customary theft report with the police department, and thought, *Well, I can kiss Vicky goodbye.* In Dade County, Florida, car thieves stole about 300 vehicles per month on average during those years. As they say, "That's part of the cost of doing business in South Florida." He commuted around town on busses. Or he relied on his "leather personnel carriers" for transportation. In other words, he walked to and fro.

A couple of months later, the police dispatcher left a message on his answering machine, saying, "Your vehicle has been recovered and is presently located at the Impound Lot. It had been abandoned on a side street west of town." He paid the storage fee and had the vehicle towed to Raphael's garage. The damages: two broken windows, a dented trunk lid that had been prized open, and miscellaneous papers and personal effects strewn about the car's interior and floorboard. Someone had painted a graffiti design with pink hearts on the left rear fender. But he had his car back. He had a feeling the vehicle would shut down and the thief would not be able to start it. Raphael replaced the windows and trunk lock. The mechanic got the vehicle going again. Royce drove it home and around town normally for a few months. Ultimately, he decided to have a newly rebuilt engine installed. An overhaul shop in Medley did the work. The car ran like a dream, and the motor purred like a kitten. He could hardly wait until he could drive the Crown Vick across the country on his next vacation.

He had planned to drive up I-95, go around the NASCAR track in Daytona Beach, travel further north to Macon County, in Georgia; west past the peach and pecan orchards; north again over the rocky and hilly terrain in Arkansas to intersect the famous Route 66; then turn westward. What a wonderful trip that would be! His vacation would begin on Wednesday.

The vehicle was stolen for the second time on the prior Monday. *No point in going on vacation now*, he thought. He took the bus to work at the airport and postponed his vacation. When he had to go on Army Reserve duty, he flew on a commercial airline. Once he arrived there, he rented a car for local transportation. Afterwards, he flew back to Miami and returned to his regular day job.

Months later, watching the 10 o'clock news one evening, he noticed a news segment that featured a retail business establishment on the causeway to Miami Beach, which had been robbed late on Saturday night by a brazen group of loud and dangerous-looking thugs. The manager reported that the robbers had stolen a large amount of cash from the safe and fled. Tape from video cameras in the parking lot showed the getaway car, a light-blue four-door Ford sedan in rough condition. That might have been the last time he ever saw his 1983 Crown Victoria.

He bought himself a 1982 Cadillac Cimarron to get around town, the smallest Cadillac ever built, boasting independent rack and pinion suspension on all four wheels, modelled after European sports cars, with a reputation as fine driving machines, which allow you to accelerate faster and feel every curve in the road. He was not pleased with the car's performance. It was too underpowered. You want luxury and comfort. You expect a smoother, quiet ride. You don't want to feel every bump and pothole in the road. He traded it in on a sleek Mercury Cougar in Fort Lauderdale, freshly painted in color-shifting shades of shiny metal-flake cobalt.

A couple of years later, he was informed that a certain item having a unique serial number, which had once been placed and locked in the trunk of his Crown Vick had just been recovered by the police. The stolen item, hidden behind the back seat of a vehicle, had been found during a routine traffic stop downtown. A passenger in the vehicle had been promptly arrested as a result. The next day, however, he posted bail and was released from jail pending trial. Unfortunately, he skipped out on his court appearance. Royce never learned if the authorities had ever recaptured the fugitive from justice. The missing item? He was not exactly sure about that, but he believed it must have been a "Lo-Jack" device with an electronic kill-switch in silent alarm mode for added security.

I began thinking about the book I'd just read. *The Hangman's Daughter*, by Oliver Potsch, published in 2008, proved to be a devilishly good yarn about a conscientious executioner and sanitation engineer who plied his trade in the mid-1600s in Bavaria, Germany. You might say, "He had an axe to grind," if not a long, heavy sword to sharpen and wield. *The Dark Monk*, *The Beggar King*, and *The Warlock* are his other books in the series. The novel *The Monk and the Hangman's Daughter*, by Ambrose Bierce and Adolphe Danziger de

Castro, transitions nicely into the same medieval genre. For contemporary music fans, who want to enhance their reading experience even more, Elle King's album "Love Stuff" will really pump up the adrenaline and get you going, as you listen to her down-to-earth, raw, resonating modern rendition of folk rock. Her music is quite unlike the primordial, animalistic screaming and screeching; the pulsating, pounding, and hammering sounds you often hear from heavy metal. Maybe I'm exaggerating, or stretching the truth a bit. She purrs like a kitten.

CHAPTER 19

Book review of the novel

State of Siege

by Eric Ambler, published in 1956.

*Beach Blanket Bingo.
Forts, ports, and saints.*

Royce enjoyed hiking around in the jungle looking for unusual butterflies, interesting tropical foliage, exotic birds, and such. He saw the big iridescent blues that live high up in the canopy of the humid rainforest and the migratory monarchs. He saw banana trees, the mangoes, the coconuts, limes, and mahogany. He saw the magnificent bird of paradise, every variety of parrots and finches, and the toucans. Kuda mundis, sloths, howler monkeys, and giant iguanas live in harmony. He saw a large bird of prey rolling down the side of a ravine, clutching a coiling snake in its sharp, jagged claws, in a classic struggle of nature, the survival of the fittest. He spied the lean, sleek black-coated jaguar out for a stroll in the airy sunshine of an open field, unperturbed, nonchalant, unafraid.

Sometimes he went swimming at Devil's Beach, relaxing, floating lazily on an inflated innertube from a deuce-and-half cargo truck, wearing a straw Panama hat and dark glasses to keep away direct sunlight—until a large ocean wave bowled him over, capsizing him, submerging him, driving him under, into the murky depths, into a swirling sticky sandy cloud of saltwater. He returned reluctantly to the sandy beach, like a washed-up chunk of driftwood. He laughed as he lay down on the soft bright cotton fabric of his striped beach towel, resting and napping as his skin dried in the warm sunshine and gentle breeze. *You have to have the right equipment when you go to the beach*, he thought. *A big, floppy hat, cool-ray sunglasses, surfer trunks, tank-top, T-shirt, and sandals.* He remembered the glowing moon rings, the stars of the southern cross, and the bonfire his friends and acquaintances had built on Christmas Eve, as cresting ocean waves rolled in, pounding the beach. A Christmas party. He heard it said, "Every wave is new, until it breaks." He reflected on the jobsites, further up the winding dirt trail through the jungle. Battery Pratt, Battery Mackenzie, then the fort. Helicopters were buzzing and zipping around everywhere like horseflies. They repeatedly warned the pilots over the CB radio to stay out of their airspace, but they never would listen. A balloon goes up anyway. Afterwards, a bottle-rocket like on the Fourth of July. Go-fast speedboats putter about Gatun Lake. The fishermen reeled in peacock bass. He thought about the prehistoric-looking rock fish he'd reeled in once beneath the bridge along the Treasure Coast. He was curious to know if the species had sharp teeth that bite, and he discovered that it did. Later, they went to the Tarpon Club for dinner. Those traversing the Isthmus met the train at the station in Margarita. The pace of life was slower, simpler. He was completely at ease. He thought about Florida's naming their towns after forts, ports, and saints.

Fort San Lorenzo overlooked the mouth of the Chagres River, where it converges with the Caribbean Sea and the Atlantic Ocean. Henry Morgan, the pirate, attacked the fort hundreds of years ago. Rusty cannons pointed ominously toward the ocean. The fort is in ruinous condition. Vines, sawgrasses, and lush, tropical plants have invaded and taken over. The Chagres River is where the French had hoped to build their canal in the early 1900s. They soon gave up on the formidable project. Mosquitos and malaria added to the confusion. A few decades later, the United States went on to construct the Panama Canal, which connects the Atlantic and Pacific Oceans. It begins a few miles away in Lymon Bay.

One fine Saturday afternoon, Frank Magnifico, a coworker, asked him if he wanted to go snorkeling in the nearby lagoon. He'd never gone before and wanted to try it. He quickly learned the proper use of the borrowed equipment—a clear-glass mask, swim-fins, and breathing tube, with a highly visible orange floatation ball. They swam out to the coral reef and floated on the calm, glassy surface above the clear body of warm ocean saltwater, peering underneath for signs of life. A miraculous, colorful world of gracefully beautiful creatures and other delights in the depths near and far below awaited them, opening up among the cliff-faced outcroppings, the bizarre wavy overgrowths, the splendid coral rocks, and mysterious caverns, ultimately leading to the presumably sandy bottom of the ocean floor. They held their breaths and dived deeply into the depths to obtain a closer inspection of the many tropical fish species swimming all around them. The dazzling creatures were present in all different sizes, shapes, and colors. The two snorkelers surfaced, cleared their masks and breathing apparatuses. They dived again and again to see what they could see under the deep blue sea. After a while, out of the corner of his eye, Royce noticed something most peculiar.

In the exact spot where only an instant before where a small, slender, insignificant-looking, ordinary, typically silver ocean fish, had been suspended, resting momentarily, a tremendous, gigantically round, spherical fish appeared magically in its place. This happened in the blinking of an eye. The unexpected surprise event frightened Royce to such an extent that he immediately responded by propelling himself upwards to the ocean surface by rapidly flutter-kicking the long rubber swim fins he was wearing on his feet. He undoubtedly wanted to put as much distance between himself and the perceived danger as fast as he possibly could—namely, the Unknown Sea Monster from the Deep.

Once he reached the surface, he searched all around the watery area for Frank. There was no sign of him floating anywhere in the immediate vicinity. He naturally became agitated and was concerned for the safety of his fellow snorkeler. Then, looking far into the distance, he spied a body waving his arms up and down in a frantic gesture. A person was standing on the old wooden wharf, located about a hundred yards away. Relieved when he recognized that it was his buddy Frank standing there all safe and sound, he removed his face mask and calmly dogpaddled over to the dock. He called up to Frank, saying that he just saw the biggest, roundest fish he had ever seen in his entire life. A little fish was there one second, and a gigantic fish instantly appeared out of nowhere.

Frank replied that the fish he saw was nothing more than a common blowfish! They frighten easily and expand like a balloon. He continued, "Did you see the hammerhead sharks? I've been out of the water for over an hour already. It's shark feeding time in the lagoon, every day around four P.M. You didn't know that?"

The next time I go snorkeling, I'm wearing a waterproof watch on my wrist and carrying a sharp, rust-proof diver's knife in a rubber sheath around my ankle, he thought to himself. *You can't be too careful these days.*

Having read Eric Ambler's international thrillers, *State of Siege* (1956) and *The Mask of Dimitrios* (1939), I can honestly say there must be considerable incentive in making a lot of money by working overseas, if you have the proper knowledge, training, and skills. In the first book, a British consulting engineer gets caught up in a military coup in a rapidly developing Indonesian country, whereby one military regime tries to wrestle control of the government away from the military regime presently in power. In the second book, an English writer of detective short stories decides to look into the background of a man with a long criminal history who has come to the attention of the Chief of Turkish Police. The Police Chief shows him a thick dossier on the subject. The Englishman becomes curious about the man and wants to learn more by visiting key cities in Turkey, Yugoslavia, and Bulgaria.

In the first book, you get the general idea that the situation would be greatly improved if fair elections were regularly held in a peaceful manner, and if there were some semblance of civil law and order in place. In the second book, you have border disputes among nations that do not trust one another. A violent state of nature occurs within each country. They fight with each other like animals. They'd barely survived WWII, and the threat of war is always looming on the horizon.

In both books, you wonder why the countries do not separate state and religious institutions. The problem is that groups in control of government have a terrible tendency to punish their adversaries, and other groups who think differently than they do, in an excessively harsh manner. They would drive them back into the stone age if you let them. They become exorbitantly cruel, and they rule by fear. You have to ask yourself the following basic questions: "In most legal cases, in their system of government, does the punishment fit the crime?" and "What is the country's human rights record?" On the flipside of the coin, you have to solve the problem of terrorism by bomb-throwing extremists. Essentially, the same problems which existed in the 1930s through the 1950s still occur today in the more dangerous and troubled countries.

CHAPTER 20

Book review of James Jones' 1951 novel,

From Here to Eternity

You're in the Army now.
Three squares, a pickle suit, and a crib.

How R. Royce found himself in the Army is a story in and of itself. At the conclusion of the Viet Nam Conflict, the Nixon administration terminated the draft. As an alternative, they began to establish an all-volunteer, peacetime military. Royce had been attending classes at a fine liberal arts college in Missouri, up until one overcast, gray autumn day, when he flipped his ten-speed racing bicycle, riding down a steep hill on campus. He made the drastic mistake of applying his front-wheel caliper brake during a rapidly accelerating descent halfway down the hill. In doing so, he catapulted the bike and rider headfirst onto the hard, unforgiving pavement. This incident happened years before manufacturers began mass producing and distributing Styrofoam bicycle helmets, with the sporty-looking plastic shell and chin-strap seen in every neighborhood today. He was quite fortunate that he didn't crack his skull open like a ripe watermelon someone accidentally dropped on the tarmac. He felt stunned and a little dizzy. He appeared momentarily dazed and unwary. A bump on his head began to swell up. He sensed that he had some purpose in life. There was something important he not had yet accomplished. He needed to go to class, he remembered, but he had lost his drive and motivation. He didn't give the accident another thought, however, and went on his way. His instinct for survival must have kicked in at some point in time. He stopped everything he was doing. He loaded his disassembled bicycle, his clothes, a few books, and miscellaneous possessions into the trunk and onto the backseat of his 1965 Chevy Impala. Next, he drove home to his parents' house in Oklahoma. In this way, he dropped out of college and closed that chapter in his life forever.

Once he was safe and sound in the bosom of his family at his childhood home, he fell into a coma. It was like a deep, mind-numbing sleep, without dreams. His parents didn't know what to do with him. They didn't know what was wrong. So, they transported him to the emergency room. Doctors admitted him into the hospital for further evaluation. He was in a coma for two weeks, then just snapped out of it one day. He came back to his senses and didn't remember anything ever happening. He was given some anti-anxiety pills and went home to recuperate and, presumably, live a long, normal life.

After a few weeks, he traded his beat-up tan Chevrolet in on a white 1968 VW Beetle. Then he proceeded to drive south for the winter, toward the Gulf of Mexico, chasing sunshine and ocean surf. He made it as far as the outskirts of Beaumont, Texas, renting a ramshackle motel efficiency unit, with a wooden screen door, a Kelvinator refrigerator, and a gas-heat cooking stove. He chatted with an automobile accident victim staying next door. His lawyer and wife visited him daily. They advised Royce that he could get a job at the nuclear power plant under construction. He found employment at a Mexican restaurant for a while instead, but didn't see the future in it. Eventually, he quit and drove back north. Running short on money, he sold the VW for cash to a mechanic at a tire repair shop in Waco. Then, he caught a Greyhound bus to his hometown in northeast Oklahoma. He stayed a few days at his parents' house, then enlisted in the Army.

In 1976, earlier that year, he'd attended the Mississippi River Festival under the gateway arch in downtown St. Louis, on the Fourth of July, with his girlfriend, who grew less infatuated with him day by day. What impressed him most were two staged events: First, the soldiers in the Air National Guard, who stepped out of a helicopter which landed nearby, didn't exactly look or act like they were the toughest, bravest, smartest, or the most experienced candidates for the job. He was inspired that a mild-mannered fellow like himself might stand a good chance of fitting in with such an energetic, enthusiastic, exuberant, and highly motivated group. Only, he wanted to join the infantry, where the soldiers keep their feet firmly planted on solid ground. He had gained a keen sense of belonging. Secondly, he was very impressed by the demonstration of F-15 fighter jet capabilities. The jet had appeared over the crowd, motionless and suspended in thin air, like a hovering flying insect, then propelled itself across the sky like a raging rocket, darting into the wild blue yonder of the distant horizon until it stealthily disappeared completely from view. Technologically advanced machinery fascinated him. He had serious doubts about the Air Force, as you might well imagine. "Aim low, avoid disappointment" was his motto. "No guts, no glory" seemed an appropriate catchphrase.

The Army he joined had changed considerably from the brown boot, heavy M1 rifle-toting military organization which James Jones described in his 1951 bestselling novel, *From Here to Eternity*. But, in general, the quality of military life was about the same. A generation later, you were still guaranteed three square meals a day; a clean, starched, and pressed green cotton field uniform; and a warm bunk in the barracks in which to sleep. You were expected to learn self-discipline while you received specialized training in a battery of basic military skills. You stayed physically fit by performing regular group exercises. You were prepared to travel on short notice to other military posts around the country, or for overseas tours of duty. You understood there would be insubordination in the ranks, and outright treachery, due to the nature of the duty assignment. "You knew the job was dangerous when you took it." You've heard of cases of sabotage, espionage, even treason. "It goes with the territory." You remain steadfast, poised, ready, and vigilant. You remember the general orders for an infantry soldier: "I will guard everything within the limits of my post. . . I will quit my post when properly relieved. . . I will report all violations to the relief. . .," and so on.

Sure, the publishing house probably convinced the author to exaggerate a few key passages and salient features in the story. Later, Hollywood-hype would sensationalize the plot and scandalize the leading characters in order to make an award-winning movie. But, they couldn't downplay the heroic actions of brave soldiers stationed in faraway overseas posts around the world in time of war.

Today's modern military, in comparison, with all of its camouflage uniforms and electronic equipment, lethal weaponry, and highly mobile responsiveness can support, defend, and protect U.S. interests almost anywhere in the world if and when necessary. The problem with Congress, which wields the majority of this power and mass-destruction capability, is they don't know if and when it's necessary to send in the troops. The fact that many of the troops are women or gay; sometimes inebriated or under the influence; and don't really care one way or the other what happens to them in combat is immaterial. No one said it's a perfect world; we're perfectly human to think otherwise.

"What do we do about the duds and candy wrappers, Sarge?" asked the new Private, indicating pallets of surplus "American Standards" and other materials recently admitted into the warehouse.

"The commodes are for the Black Operations latrine. I can file the documents here. We recycle the remainder. Meanwhile, you need to attend Diversity Awareness and Sensitivity Training classes," replied the Supply Sergeant.

"I'll see if I can learn to tolerate what I can't accept," quipped the Private, candidly.

"I can take the edited, G-rated version any day of the week myself, expletives deleted," said the Sergeant cordially, smiling slightly. He was a good role model for new recruits, who strenuously objected to the designation of field artillary reconaissance scout platoon forward field observation units as "cannon fodder."

CHAPTER 21

Review of the novel

Treasure Island

by Robert Louis Stevenson, published in 1882.

Beastly and Ugly in Orlando.

R. Royce exited the train from Miami in Orlando. He took the first available taxi to the International Airport and picked up an airline ticket to Tulsa. He rented a peppy sub-compact at the Avis counter. He drove the low-mileage, fiery-red vehicle to the mall off the Silver Lake expressway. The year 2000, too early for summer, he thought. The weather was too warm, humid, breezy, and sunny. He bought a dress shirt for business meetings, then strolled over to the food court. He ate a slice of plain cheese pizza, seasoned with garlic powder. He drove to a nearby motel and stayed in one of the all ground-level rooms in the back building, away from traffic noise. He parked the car in one of the row spaces just outside his door. He went inside his room and watched cable television for a while, then walked over to the Steakhouse on the corner for dinner. He returned to the room, performed a series of calisthenics, and went to bed. He planned to fly to Oklahoma to visit family and friends and get back in shape for military reserve duty in Maryland immediately afterwards. He had orders. His flight was scheduled to depart at one thirty P.M. the next day.

He awoke early the next day and completed a regimen of three S's: shave, shower, and shampoo. He felt squeaky clean and fully refreshed, from the tip of his nose to the tips of his toes. He was ready to greet the dawn of a new day. He opened the motel room door to let the sunshine in, so he would feel the full effect of the southern exposure. He was calm and relaxed.

Within a few moments, two tall, dark males in their late 20s, one heavyset and flabby, with loose-fitting black polo shirt and charcoal Docker pants; the other of lighter complexion, comparatively, and average build, but muscular and high-strung, wearing a green plaid button-down shirt and non-descript jeans, sauntered and shuffled into the room. One of them closed the door. Royce stood up and faced them. He asked simply, "What are you doing?"

In lieu of a courteous reply or a reasonable explanation, the mean-looking perpetrator lifted a Saturday night special out of his pants pocket, canted the hand grip sideways ninety degrees, and raised the pistol above his head angled forward and slightly downward, the barrel pointing directly at Royce, giving the appearance of an L.A. gang member greeting, or a Las Vegas gangster-style assault. He didn't know which.

Several fleeting thoughts ran through Royce's mind at the time. First and foremost, *Was this a hit?* Didn't make sense, they didn't act quickly and decisively enough. The milli-seconds ticked by. They weren't professionals. *Thank God!*

Robbers. His heavy hard-sided suitcase. The porter at the train station had lifted it and felt its bulkiness. The Avis parking valet eyed it. He was after all coming from Miami. Must be money, narcotics, or valuable merchandise.

He was too far from the telephone, couldn't dial fast enough. Average people don't do well in pressure situations, he'd learned. If he had to react, he would have to equalize the odds. Gun. Martial Arts. Stiletto. Not while traveling commercial carrier. He could throw the lamp to distract them. Under different circumstances, he could be a dangerous adversary. In the present circumstances, his repertoire of defense mechanisms included wit, charm, personality, and grace. Plus, he didn't want to pay for damages to the motel room and furniture. He was under orders. He didn't want to have to explain his delay or absence to the duty officer. He focused on, carefully scrutinized the revolver. He saw no lead or copper tips protruding from inside the five-shot cylinder. Probably empty. He would play along and see if it helped matters to cooperate. They were muggers. Purse snatchers. Crude, petty thieves. Tough guys who end up in jail, the hospital, and the morgue. Common small-time criminals. They are always eventually apprehended.

Beastly told Royce to empty his pockets. He stepped toward Royce in order to collect his wallet and the gold Yachtmaster watch he was wearing on his wrist. Intensely Ugly continued to cover him with the raised revolver. He never said a single word throughout the grim proceedings. Fat City Beast instructed him to go into the bathroom and stay there for thirty minutes, until they were gone. They must have practiced their strong-arm technique before.

Not hearing any more noises, Royce peeked out of the bathroom after two or three minutes. He saw his suitcase had been left opened and upright on the floor. The contents had been thoroughly rifled through, but his belongings were intact. He opened the motel room door and looked cautiously outside. He saw nothing moving and nothing out of the ordinary. The two of them had fled the scene. His car was in the same parking spot.

He went over to the telephone on the nightstand and called the front desk to report the robbery to the police. Next he retrieved the car key from the side pocket in his leisure slacks. He went outside to the vehicle and opened the trunk. The trunk contained his carry-on bag, from which he extracted a checkbook and a second, backup credit card. Inside the checkbook was the toll-free phone number to his stolen credit card company. He reported the theft over the phone and asked the company representative politely to cancel the card.

The local police arrived within ten or fifteen minutes and he reported the details of the crime. Royce was invited to the police station to look at current suspect photographs, but none of them matched. The Orlando Chamber of Commerce offered to reimburse him for the hundred dollar loss, but he would not accept the money. They were concerned about their image. How it might affect tourism. He felt that he was justified with his actions.

The police returned the victim to his motel in a timely, professional manner. He found that he had plenty of time to return the vehicle to the airport and catch his flight to Tulsa. He'd dodged another bullet, and he'd kept his promise never again to fly out of Miami.

I've wanted to read the book *Treasure Island* by Robert Louis Stevenson ever since I was a kid, and finished reading the novel only yesterday, generations after my childhood years have long ago elapsed. You must have cherished the memory of Disney pirate adventures from childhood just as much as you did the idea of Robin Hood's adventures in Sherwood Forest, and those of King Arthur, Merlin the Magician, and the bold, chivalrous Knights of the Round Table. Then, suddenly one day you grew up, had to earn a living, and care for your family. You woke up and arrived at the stark realization, "You aren't playing basketball in Kansas anymore." Similarly, I'd read the story book *The Wonderful Wizard of Oz* by Frank Baum in its entirety as a child and was fascinated by the imaginary, fantasy world. While in college, I'd asked fellow students during our fireside chats on favorite books and interesting reading material naively, "Do you know why they call 'Emerald City' by that particular name?" Even today, I like surrounding myself with intelligent people. It turns out no one I met had admitted to ever having read the book. Certainly, they'd seen the movie on television, but they'd never really read and understood the book. So, I guess, it just goes to show you, many people will go through life and never really know for sure the reason why.

CHAPTER 22

Book review of

Stories from Iran:
A Chicago Anthology (1921-1991)

edited by Heshmat Moayyad

"What are you running from, a bear?" he asked the jogger, facetiously.

R. Royce glanced at some citrus fruits that had fallen out of a suitcase and rolled across the polished linoleum floor at DFW International Airport, belonging to a family arriving via Heathrow. He suggested that they eat the fruits before arrival or put the prohibited items in the Agriculture bin for disposal. One of the family members gave him a tasty pastry containing pistachio nuts, fresh from a bakery in Tehran. It made for a delicious complement to his morning coffee. He thought about the neighbor's Calico cat, with its "coat of many colors."

His neighbor Natalie brought the cat home as a kitten, but it didn't have any outside playmates. Her dogs stayed at her mom's house across the road and one house over, inside the house, or in the backyard. Rascal liked to wander, roam around, and explore her jungle, as would any lion cub. She became friends with the squirrels that lived in the trees in the yards of several houses, including his. Royce lived directly across the street from Natalie. Rascal would climb up the tree trunk and out on a limb after a squirrel. But the squirrel would leap over to a dangling branch of the next closest tree. She scampered around the yard, playing with them. She enjoyed chasing them. She learned to swish her tail back and forth as would a squirrel. She visited Royce every day, racing to the storm door so he would let her inside. He would comb her hair with a brush and give her tidbits to eat. She guarded his house and would fight off prowling cats, the intruders from the south end of the block. She was very protective of him and they watched television together. She accompanied him as he watered the four dozen or so rose bushes he grew around the perimeter of his back yard. Growing roses was a relaxing hobby. The birds, bees, and butterflies seemed to like them. He was especially fond of the little redheaded woodpecker that woke him up in the morning and the hoot owls that he heard before going to sleep at night. He enjoyed the cooing sounds of the doves that came to town during hunting season. They escaped a shotgun reward.

Royce was the kind of fellow who would rush down to the creek in eager anticipation of a flash flood. He felt perfectly safe from tornadoes. Once while driving toward the Red River in a U-Haul moving truck on I-35, he shot the mile-long gap between slow-moving twin tornadoes travelling in a perpendicular path from west to east directly in front of his north bound vehicle. He drove on through the wind and the rain to northeast Oklahoma.

He missed living in west Texas—except for in July and August, when the temperature often soared above 100 degrees and the searing sun beat down on you mercilessly. The heat was overpowering and sweltering at times. Neither did he miss the biting insects. Standing in a bathtub of cold bleach-water, he found a viable solution for the stinging welts on his feet and ankles. Wearing leather boots instead of sandals would have helped. Too, he was still trying to wrap his head around the idea that "fracking" gas wells and horizontal drilling may have caused earthquakes in the vicinity and cracking in the walls of his nice brick home.

I wanted to read the book *Catherine the Great* first, thinking *Stories from Iran: A Chicago Anthology (1921-1991)*, edited by Heshmat Moayyad and published in 1991, would prove dull and tedious reading. Silly and pointless, by way of comparison. Fairytales. "Arabian Nights." "Sinbad the Sailor," "Ali Baba" and all that. The culture and people must be completely alien to the western civilization subjects about which I have been used to reading. On the contrary, I found the stories appeared more interesting and with greater depth of character than I had originally thought. Perhaps, this is because the authors were generally well-educated and well-traveled. Many were educated in European countries. Some might have visited the United States. Many were professionals—doctors, lawyers, engineers, and prominent civil servants. They were affluent people who knew what it takes to build a nation. Some were dissidents and exiles, who knew you cannot impose your will on the people, dictating extreme laws and harsh rule, forcing your strict religion on those whose beliefs differ, and inflicting cruel and excessive punishment on offenders. In doing so, no national leader could ever expect to achieve peaceful, prosperous, and positive results. Indeed, these authors could have provided the inspiration for social reform in the Iran of today and tomorrow. They might have made the Middle East a better place to live and visit. Highly esteemed and influential, some of the more recent authors are probably still living today. If so, they undoubtedly would be pillars of society. Most interesting to me, at any rate, is the fact that one of the authors was the son of a Moslem cleric. He lived to the ripe old age of 104 or 105 years. He seemed clever and witty enough, judging from the caliber and quality of his writing. He also appeared to be a very wise man, due to the simple fact that, having been stationed at the Iranian embassy in Berlin for a number of years, he had the good sense to leave the country just before the rise of the third Reich and World War II began. A truly wise man anticipates and gets out of harm's way.

A good variety of stories have been included in the book. If I counted correctly, there are thirty-five of them. The substance of the stories—the nuclear core, if you will, as I have grasped their meaning, significance, and concept is as follows:

1. "What's Sauce for the Goose Is Sauce for the Gander" is about the general conditions of life in Iran, according the a prominent leader's secret masseur. Fact or fiction, you get the idea that you want show up wearing the right kind of hat. They're sort of like the Quakers, in this respect.

2. "Abj Khanom" is about the sibling rivalry between two sisters, one of whom is more worldly and the other, more religious. One of them becomes radical and fanatical. She is so inclined as to drop a bombshell on the party at any given moment.

3. "Mirza" is about a wealthy conservative Iranian who fled the country without his wife and daughter. While living in Paris, he meets his grown daughter. They have a heart-to-heart chat.

4. "The Snake Store" is about the temptations faced by a beautiful, young Iranian wife in a rural village. Her jealous neighbor baits and sets a trap for her.

5. "The Wooden Horse." The good, persevering wife lights a Trojan horse on fire. It symbolizes everything she loves, honors, and cherishes in life. It represents her hopes, aspirations, and dreams. Afterwards, there is nothing to look forward to but pain, suffering, and death.

6. "The Grave Digger" is about a poor, destitute, pregnant teenager who needs love. All she wanted out of life was a pony or a puppy. A teddy bear!

7. "The Half-Closed Eye" is about a family who strives and connives to get ahead in life. They smuggle and sell drugs for a living. Some get hurt along the way.

8. "Emat's Journey." A young girl runs away from home. She goes on a pilgrimage to Mecca. She learns to serve God and man. A deeply religious man teaches her and offers her shelter.

9. "The American Husband." A spoiled, rich Iranian woman marries an American day laborer. He makes an honest living, but she expects more out of life.

10. "The Little Native Boy." A village boy falls in love with an English girl in an oil industry boom town. Union members, local officials, company representatives, police, and agitators interact to create a volatile situation. Violence erupts.

11. "Through the Veil of Fog." A female college student gets an education in England. She socializes with others who share common interests.

12. "Glorious Day" is about an official who goes on holiday and meets the girl of his dreams. She pleases him immensely and recites poetry to him. She becomes the most unforgettable person he ever met.

13. "Moths in the Night" is a story about an epiphany. It's a reality check of sorts. You're not really sure what happened, what went wrong, but you sense that something terrible did go wrong. The first step of course is to recognize you have a problem.

14. "The Cast" is an incomplete story about a dentist who takes care of business. It is as if the story should be the first chapter of a novel that should have been written instead of a short story. You think, *Can you expound, expand, or explain what's going on?* You sense that a crime has been committed, but you don't see the big picture. You don't know the situation or circumstances. There is no edification. No feeling of justice or heroic action. You don't get closure. Nobody wins.

15. "Adolescence and the Hill." This is a story about a child who never grew up. Peter Pan with serious weapons and no purpose or direction in life. He lacks guidance and opportunity.

16. "Mr. Hemayat." A man battles with his alter ego, his true self. The man interacts with himself throughout the day. Together, they have quite an extraordinary day, short of a real adventure. A field day for a schizophrenic. "Walter Mitty," he's not. Mental instability is a concern.

17. "Shadowy." A story about a man who takes refuge in the world of his imagination. Cleverly thought-provoking and philosophical ideas permeate his universe. He is not terribly practical. You don't visualize him working as a craftsman on "This Old House."

18. "Love." A sad, tragic story about a girl who marries too young. The arranged marriage has fatal consequences. There should be laws.

19. "The Two Brothers." The younger one works for a living and meets a nice girl in his apartment building. The older one lives with him and loafs around all day. They have their differences. One meets his reward. The other meets his destiny.

20. "Mourners of Bayal." Because a boy's mother is dying and the family carts her off to the hospital, and they visit the cemetery, he is delayed from picking up his bride, per an arranged marriage. The bride's family smokes while waiting for him to arrive.

21. "Sacred Keep Sakes." The story is about a reclusive wounded soldier during a new year's celebration. He behaves badly.

22. "The Trench and Empty Canteens." After struggling his entire life, a man wants to live out his life in peace and quiet in a nice house on the outskirts of the city. He longs for the good life in suburbia.

23. "The Wolf." A doctor's wife is lured by the "call of the wild." She could have drawn the curtains. He could have built a privacy fence. They could have called the animal control office, or the dog-catcher.

24. "Portrait of an Innocent." A sculptor dies trying to complete his life's work. Posterity loses out.

25. "The Discrete and Obvious Charm of the Bourgeoise" is a story about the progress made by western civilization as we know it, from the perspective of someone who never lived it and wanted it all to just go away. The narrator is like the puppet master at a "Punch and Judy" show. The people at the party are like stereotypical puppet-toys. Is that any way to treat your party guests?

26. "Aziz Aga's Gold Fillings" is about the daughter of a dysfunctional family of misfits and other educated free-thinkers. She befriends the school bus driver.

27. "Brother's Future Family." A typical family and relatives get together for the holidays. You may not always like them, but you're stuck with them.

28. "Smell of Lemon Peel and Fresh Milk." A sick Russian girl endures her medical treatment in Iran. The strong will survive.

29. "Hard Luck." A weak boy is raised by the owner of an opium den. He has wild dreams.

30. "Night Journey." A hitch-hiker catches a ride on the oil-company bus. He appears to be a bandit on the run.

31. "The Sad Brothers." Two brothers encounter and raise a big "E.T."-like bird in their basement. The creature escapes and everyone in the vicinity finds out about it. In this way, Thanksgiving might have once been celebrated in Iran.

32. "Trial Offers." An intelligent, precocious young woman becomes engaged to a respectable civil servant. The have a promising future together, but she discovers that he is a chauvinistic pig, who would go to great lengths to make her life miserable. She resents this, and would return the favor double, given half a chance. They agree to a separation, then sever ties. She becomes involved with a liberal-minded professor. They experience happiness and joy. Their future together is not assured, however. They exhibit self-destructive tendencies.

33. "The Long Night" is a rite of passage story about a prepubescent girl in Iran who watches her best friend grow up before her very eyes and marry.

34. "Narcissus" is about a young man who sells bouquets of flowers beside a busy roadway. It's a living!

35. "The Mirror" is about an old lady about to be taken away by the grim reaper. She mocks him repeatedly. She laughs at death.

CHAPTER 23

Review of the historical book

Catherine the Great: Portrait of a Woman

by Robert K. Massie, published 2011.

Drones Fly Off Store Shelves in Christmas Shopping Season!

R. Royce lost his crown on Christmas Day. He felt something give way when he bit into a ham sandwich. Shortly thereafter, it dropped into a bowl of cornflakes and milk. Fortunately, the bone structure underneath was solid and intact. Had nerve endings been exposed, he might have experienced excruciating pain. He planned to drop by the dentist's office for an appointment on Monday. Saturday, he ran out to the convenience store to pick up a couple of items. He asked the clerk, "Did you get everything you wanted for Christmas?"

Amy Mae replied, "Yes, I got to work on Christmas. Nobody else would come in." Royce gave her a big toothless grin and walked outside into the cold and rain. He remembered the weather man saying we can expect five to eight inches over the weekend. Something about warm water in the South Pacific.

Sunday, a volunteer fire fighter knocked loudly on the front door. He said, "The creek is 25 feet above flood stage, and is expected to rise 10 more feet. Be ready to leave if you have to." Royce begins to closely monitor the situation. He reflects on some of the interesting times of his life.

Basic survival training in the Army many years ago, the same kind of cold, gray rainy day. The Deltas ran through a live fire exercise, using the buddy system. Crawling, standing, then moving rapidly, weaving and dodging as they went. The squad negotiated a wooded, hilly obstacle course. The idea was to shoot, move, and communicate wordlessly in reaching a hypothetical objective, known only in whispers. That was when perhaps the only time in his entire life he had done so, he leaped before he looked. It was sort of like falling out of bed onto the floor and rolling underneath the mattress, at the same time a tornado rips the roof off of your house, implodes the walls, shatters window glass, and destroys everything all around. Only, in this scenario, you jumped into the nearest deep hole, a crater, ravine, or ditch. It gets more interesting than eating stockpiled C-rations in tin cans dated 1945.

The group moves noiselessly, in single file along a narrow, winding cowpath of packed clay through a field of tall grasses and into a dugout, like for a baseball team, only it's a longer trench dug deep into the ground. One of them walks cautiously around the berm, and steps out to the summit overlooking a steep hillside. A SME, or "subject matter expert," hands him a spherically shaped metal object, with a handle and ring attachment. Standing beside him, he calmly pulls out the ring and tells the individual, "Throw it over the cliff, downhill." Soon, they hear a popping sound, like a pop-gun or a firecracker in the distance. The sound is muted because they wear ear plugs. The next Delta moves toward the front of the line in the dugout. He steps up and moves out to the summit. The process repeats. All goes smoothly and according to schedule, until one particularly inept individual steps up to the plate. The SME hands him the metal ball and pulls the ring-pin. The trainee immediately drops the ball on the ground at his feet. The SME reacts instantly. He grabs the individual in a bear-hug around the midsection of his field jacket, lifting him vertically up into the air. In a single solitary motion, they both dive over the painted heavy-gauge iron barricade behind them and lay flat on the ground against the opposite side of the wall. Within seconds, the group witnesses the percussion effects of a live, exploding grenade firsthand. The iron wall clangs like a church bell.

Having recovered and shaken out the dust, the SME signals a nest of machine gunners to fire a stream of 50-caliber bullets above the dugout, followed by bursts of intermittent rifle fire. The Deltas didn't need to be told twice to duck. That was how Royce learned to tell when someone is shooting at him or in his general direction. A few days later, they experienced the nighttime disorientation associated with walking from a state of total darkness and silence into a fiery inferno of very loud and bright explosions. Temporarily deaf and blind, they discover it's difficult to keep their wits about them. Nonetheless, they survived training under simulated battlefield conditions. The question is, "Can they survive in a real world war, when the rules of engagement keep changing?" The results can be disastrous when the hunters become the hunted. No surprise there.

Royce decided to see a couple of college basketball games in town. Along with the costume-lion mascot, he saw other supernatural creatures milling about, reminding him of warm and fuzzy cartoon characters on parade, only these were meant to promote a fantastic new movie in area theaters for the holidays. He watched the second half of the women's game, then decided to go out to his vehicle in order to retrieve a foam-rubber cushion before the beginning of the next game, since the stadium seats were made of an uncomfortably hard plastic. On the way back inside the field-house, one of the attendants asked to see his admissions ticket. Royce fumbled around in his pockets looking for the ticket and beseechingly remarked, "Please don't turn me into one of those *Star Wars* characters!"

Having read the history of Sophia Augusta Fredericka (1729-1796), according to the book by Robert K. Massie, published in 2011, entitled *Catherine the Great: Portrait of a Woman,* I gradually came to understand what an incredibly impressive world leader she really was and how she created and shaped the Russia we recognize today. First of all and foremost, she was a daring survivor. She survived wars, revolutions, political rivalries, public opinion, tragedy, and disease, namely the bubonic plague and smallpox. The powerful empress went on to rule Russia for 35 years, an amazing feat for someone who devoted practically her whole life to public service. How very incredible, too, considering the harsh toll war, poverty, rebellion, and pestilence took on the population and the nation. By comparison, the rulers of most European nations had bland, mediocre careers of limited duration, and they made far less impact on the rest of the world. At the time of Catherine II's rule, the United States was in its infancy.

All the American colonies had going for them was a vague set of principles, called a Constitution, borrowed from the revolution in France; the desire for independence, freedom, and opportunity; and a vastly unexplored wilderness. Times certainly have changed over the centuries. You can turn on the television and see for yourself.

Today, the United States and Russia are on about equal footing. Russia is a closed society, with the same expansionist tendencies and sphere of influence that it had 250 years ago, more or less. The United States has since matured and grown up. It is an open society, has a free economy, and boasts cutting edge technology in all sectors. Both have military might and excellent resources. Both have problems at home and in the Middle East—namely, in Syria and the vacuum left by a severely weakened Iraq, each struggling with civil war. In order to resolve such concerns, we know who is in charge in Russia and who can make a difference from that podium. Without a doubt, there are subtle differences between the two great nations. We aren't so certain in the United States. The President is on his way out. The Senate and House have been gridlocked and indecisive for years. Penny-pinching, nitpicking, and bean counting preoccupies the country. Where is the magnanimity?

So, the burning question remains, "Which U.S. political candidate for President is best qualified to further U.S. interests at home and abroad, given present-day circumstances?" The U.S. needs good guidance and great leadership. We are always looking for a bright and promising future. This is the beauty of our election process. The voters will decide next November. Until then, all we have are popular opinion polls and plenty of sensational media coverage. Backers and detractors. Big business and the Pope. The Earth spins and revolves through a continuum of space and time.

CHAPTER 24

Book review of the novel

Myst

by Rand and Robyn Miller with David Wingrove,
published in 1995.

"Standing in a maze of tall cotton, but not forgotten," said the master of disaster. "You're lost in a lost world."
Lost on a deserted island.

R. Royce didn't own a computer until September of 1994. He used one routinely at work, accessing filed information from "DOS" databases and for communicating letters or memos, using "WordPerfect." But that was it. A colleague asked him innocently one day if he owned a computer. He replied bluntly, "I wouldn't have one in my home." Apparently they were catching on, though. People were buying them for their own personal use and enjoyment, to enrich their daily lives. They stored photographs on them, played musical favorites, challenged themselves intellectually with amusing games, and had encyclopedia information stored at their fingertips. The more enterprising, ambitious, and upwardly mobile professionals sorted letters, organized other forms of trade correspondence, scored certificates of achievement, even updated their resumes on their own computers. All of their personally identifiable information was readily accessible yet private. Naturally, this was before the worldwide web and the internet became the rage, and years before chic, smart cellphone proliferation.

Royce received orders for a temporary position, working in support of the Army staff for a military unit assembled a few hundred miles north of Miami in a place affectionately known as "the shack in the swamp." His reporting date was October 1994. The Colonel in charge sent him a letter of introduction as well. At the end of the letter was an unassuming and innocuous post script, "P.S. Bring your computer."

Royce bought his first personal computer (PC) through an advertisement in the classified section of a local newspaper anyone can pick up at the local convenience store. The PC came with "Microsoft Windows" version 3.1 installed, some reference books on DOS and the Windows operating system, a laser printer, a bulky CRT monitor, a compact disc (CD) drive, a mouse, and some cables. He thought he was in business. He learned how to make extra use of the computer immediately by buying, installing, and playing all kinds of video and arcade games. Just for good measure, he added an atlas and a word processor. He filled the PC hard-drive program storage unit completely with miscellaneous games and such. Then, he had a computer technician piggyback a second hard-drive on the PC for additional storage space, which he also filled up rapidly with even more game software. *Definitely not job-related, but an excellent practical exercise*, Royce thought. After all was said and done, and he had finished performing his official duties, he had the Post Office ship the awkwardly cumbersome, heavyweight computer to his parents' house. The computer arrived dropped, dented, and seriously damaged. No matter, the machine had become obsolete after only a few years. Ever since then, he had stored the unused PC in their attic, where it collected dust, and was long overdue for disassembly and recycling.

The "Myst" interactive CD game must have come out sometime in the mid-1990s and probably used the earliest Windows 3.1 operating system. The video card requirement was modest, since the game used a low-resolution screen and fewer colors. The RAM memory requirement was most likely also in the low range, possibly half a megabyte. To play the game, you simply pointed the mouse and clicked on the mouse buttons, moving the mouse around on the pad to indicate the areas on the computer monitor you wanted to explore. The game probably can't "plug and play" anymore on the later, much more efficient Windows version PCs, since the later generation PCs ran much faster computer chips (CPUs), had ram and hard-drive memories of far greater capacity, and had much more complex main circuit boards, known as motherboards. In short, the CD game became as obsolete as vinyl records for a turntable or clumsy tape cartridges for an 8-track tape player. The good news was, for those of us who didn't have the time, patience, or intelligence to figure out complicated puzzles and secret passages, you were able to buy a revealing booklet of Myst hyperlinks, clues, keys, and codes in order to gain rapid access to the different Ages entered from Myst Island.

The game did sport undeniably beautiful artwork, accompanied by cool, natural sounds. You were never really sure what was happening, however. It was like being immersed in a mystery that you didn't have time to solve. There were no virtual detectives around to offer wise solutions or illuminate the way. Since the game was on an interactive CD, you basically inserted the disc into your CD player and manipulated your mouse to explore the sights and sounds of the island. You eventually encountered someone trying to communicate with you through an old television set of some sort, but it had poor reception, a fading signal, a snowy picture, and audio masked by static. He must have been stuck in a time warp. Perhaps, the garbled message was meant to heighten the effect of suspense in anticipation of unknown danger. Perhaps, he wasn't sure how to get the contraptions in the Age of Electronics and Mechanics started and wanted you to rescue him.

Twenty-two years later, you saw the book *Myst: The Book of Atrus*, published in 1995, by Rand and Robyn Miller, and David Wingrove, on a shelf somewhere and you decided you really might enjoy reading it. You began feeling nostalgic and became curious to know if the book would help you understand all you missed out on two decades ago, when you tried to play the Myst interactive CD on a PC that regularly froze up, having had faulty electronic components and an early prototype Windows operating system, which frequently crashed the program and automatically shut down the PC for no apparent reason. In other words, you wanted to leave the world of virtual reality behind and enter the sublime universe of your sometimes perversely misdirected, tangentially traveling imagination. You hoped to reopen the doors to your expansive, reawakened imagination, because you were inspired by the novel ideas and clever insights gleaned from the minds of true video gamers.

You quickly discovered the book was certainly thought provoking the more and farther you read. The story and drawings easily captured your interest. You found out that the evolving concepts which the authors shared with you were definitely intriguing and quite utterly fascinating. The magnificent Ages you read about added a certain charm, awe, and flair to what might otherwise have been a dull, lazy afternoon in your typically ordinary life. You clung to the spirit of adventure. You wanted to go out and explore stimulating, desirable, and fantastic new worlds. Then, your thoughts were invaded by a keen sense of foreboding and conflict. Something was seriously wrong there. Good and evil forces were at work behind the scenes. You became fearful. Hesitation and trepidation became your new watchwords. *Beware!* you thought. Things were no longer what they seemed. People were not behaving normally or rationally. You didn't know whom you could trust. Who could you turn to for help, sustenance, and guidance? Your parents, your grandparents, the inhabitants, your newly found friends? "For heaven sakes!" you exclaimed. You suddenly realized that you'd better get out of there somehow! A cataclysmic upheaval could occur at any minute. "Get a grip on yourself. Think. React. Do something, even if it looks all wrong." Maybe you became too emotionally involved. "What can you do?" you ask, ponder and reflect. You have to judge for yourself when you read the book.

CHAPTER 25

Book review of the Chris Holm novel

The Killing Kind

published in 2015

Rocking adrenaline pumping action.

For R. Royce meeting girls was as awkward as speed dating. He had the worst luck ever meeting the right girl. Once, he sat next to an attractive brunette and said, "I don't believe I've ever seen you in here before."

"I just got out of prison," was her curt reply.

"What did you do?" he inquired, nonchalantly, undaunted.

"Killed a guy who tried to pick me up in a bar," she said, matter-of-factly.

On another occasion, a cute redhead sat down beside Royce. "Anything interesting going on?" he asked her.

"I helped my boyfriend rip off my uncle," she bragged, proudly.

At a burger grill on the beach, a striking blonde motioned toward him from the center of the room, and loudly proclaimed, "The last time I saw him was when I was pregnant with my third child."

It gets better. "Can I buy the lady a sandwich and drink?" he asked the man behind the counter.

"You should ask my husband. He's my bartender," she interrupted.

Calamity Jane was his all-time favorite, though. They hit it off right away. Both were students at the university. She was studying sociology and freelanced for a newspaper in her spare time. Royce finished his tour of service in the Army and was attending college on the G.I. Bill. He majored in general studies, not wanting to commit to anything more specific. He'd walk through an arctic blizzard in combat boots to see Jane. She invited him home for the holidays to meet her parents and see where she grew up. Reaching into the back seat area of her Monza for a snack package of cookies, as she drove south on the highway, he noticed a pair of cowboy boots on the floorboard.

"There's a revolver in your boot, Jane," he said, downplaying the significance of his discovery.

"Home protection," she replied.

"You've only got five bullets," he said, calmly, holding them out in his palm for her to examine. "There's one missing."

"That one's for you, if you ruin my Christmas," she said.

Royce was the shy, slightly insecure type. Humble and introspective, he had to travel far and wide in order to overcome his sense of inadequacy and low self-esteem, so Jane proved more than he could handle in the long run. She was smart, talented, and beautiful; a career woman, who was outgoing and cheerfully optimistic. She came from a Fortune 500 family, one of the oldest and most respected families in Philadelphia, twice removed. They probably complained about the oats and put the crack in the liberty bell. She resettled in Kansas. She obviously had a bright future before her. He arrived from the wrong side of the tracks and had to earn his way in life, every step of the way. So, it didn't last. They drifted apart and casually went their separate ways. "I'm not going to chase you," she said the last time they communicated. He felt a deep, resounding sense of relief. Years later, having endured and ended two excessively arduous careers, he thought about going into paralegal work or private investigations. He wasn't smart and savvy enough to get into law school, or tough and dedicated enough to work as a police detective. He fondly remembered Jane's passion for "The Fall Guy" on television, about a bounty hunter in California who chased bail jumpers. Either career opportunity seemed plausible and a worthwhile pursuit. Years later, he saw a girl in Laramie, Wyoming, while grub-staking a prospecting claim in the Rocky Mountains, who closely resembled her in manner and demeanor. She was the most beautiful girl he'd ever seen his entire life. "Forget the bears, you'd better watch out for the mountain lions!" she told him. "The cougar, by its very nature will stalk you, slowly sneak up on you, and pounce when you least expect it."

Royce was working with his cousin, a carpenter, rebuilding and remodeling his mother's house in northeast Oklahoma, in the spring of 2013, a job that required over five months of steady, strenuous labor and attention to detail. He couldn't find a contractor who had time to rebuild the older two-story house with the steep roof, and install a metal roof on top. So, he and his cousin did the job themselves. Afterwards, he decided to take a leisurely road trip to Missouri for a couple of days' R&R.

Royce checked into a quiet, comfortable motel room for the night, kicked off his shoes, showered and settled back on the bed feeling refreshed and totally relaxed. He felt a keen sense of accomplishment from the completion of his construction project. He sipped a soda, which boosted the sugar and caffeine in his system. He flipped on the television set with the remote control provided. The local evening news was on and featured a double homicide in the city. The heinous crime must have occurred only a few days prior to his arrival, he deduced. The news spoiled the evening for him and the trip. His internal radar system went on, and he reflected on universal matters of the heart. He checked out of the motel early the next morning and drove back to Oklahoma. Triple whammy! He left feeling hexed, vexed, and perplexed.

Homicides occur with greater frequency in larger cities, along with the more violent crimes, he believed. A double homicide would be a rare species. A husband and wife double homicide would most likely involve a serious domestic problem, or an irreconcilable marital dispute. The case should have been open and shut. Not so in the Ozarks double murder. The police were baffled for months. First of all, they determined that neither spouse killed the other. He didn't kill her and she didn't kill him. This meant a third party must have killed them both. Someone murdered the married couple in their affluent, suburban home, where crime rates are very low, and serious crime, probably nil. Even worse, the police had no suspects and few clues. Pertinent news reports came few and far between. Circumstantial evidence suggested that the murderer could have been a close personal friend and longtime business associate of the husband. Someone who had known the couple for many years. But the police lacked concrete proof to pin the crime on him—namely, they didn't have the murder weapon and there were no eye-witnesses. Eventually, the police did obtain enough evidence to name the friend as the chief suspect, and they were ultimately able to connect him to the crime scene and arrest him. However, as the months passed, with the accused suspect locked up in the county jail, it appeared that no prosecutor was going to assemble a solid case against him, and no judge would try him.

Interested in how the case would be resolved, Royce was able to verify the status of the case by searching current newspaper articles on the internet at the public library. In December 2015, having checked the most recent news reports on the case, he learned that the man accused of the crime had finally confessed. A judge had convicted and sentenced him the previous July. Thus, the cold case was closed, over two years later.

According to the story, the defendant had gone to his friend's house one fateful night in the spring of 2013 to borrow a large sum of money. The friend did not want to give him the money. Perhaps angry and desperate, the defendant killed his friend for the money that was secured in the safe in his home. Next, he was forced to kill his friend's wife, because she was there and probably fought back, in defense of her husband and herself.

If true, that would mean an easy open and shut court case. Verdict, guilty. Due to lack of sufficient supporting evidence for a jury trial, the prosecutor probably accepted the confession and forwarded the case in order to obtain the "second-degree murder" conviction, as agreed upon by the defendant and his lawyer.

Questions remained: "Why did the defendant need the large sum of money?" and "To whom did he owe it?" Apparently, the defendant had a serious gambling problem and felt compelled to pay a tremendously large gambling debt he had accrued. That answered the first question. The second question was more complicated and required a fair amount of slick and tricky detective work, which may or may not have been performed to the satisfaction of all parties concerned.

If he owed money to his best friend and couldn't or wouldn't pay, and he was indeed physically capable of committing the atrocious act of murder, then the defendant did have the most likely motive for murder. If, on the other hand, he (or they, meaning he and the victims, possibly his partners) owed the large amount of money to "someone else," this someone else could have had a better motive for murdering the couple in their home than the best friend did, particularly if this someone else knew about the money in the couple's safe. Applying this simple logic concerning the essential facts in the case tends to make one speculate on who else might have committed the crime. That's why the experts say, "Follow the money and find the criminal."

Royce ultimately decided that reading detective stories is a far safer hobby than actively engaging in real-world P.I. work, where you invariably ruffle feathers shaking the nest, and "gun control" means how straight you can shoot in self-defense. The line of work is entirely too unhealthy and downright dangerous for amateurs who snoop around for answers to hard, personal questions best left to trained and authorized professionals.

I found the crime novel *The Killing Kind*, by Chris Holm, published in 2015, surprisingly well-written and insightful. The author goes to great lengths revealing the thinking processes and psychology of his characters. His plot runs wild and rampant like a flooded river, coursing through certain life-altering events, bulldozing over everything and everybody in its destructive path. Role models for the two leading characters could have been "The Incredible Hulk" and "Supergirl." But the characters themselves appear to be real people, trained and skilled in their fields of endeavor, who have chosen to place themselves in extraordinarily dangerous situations. Tongue in cheek notwithstanding, the novel fits in perfectly with Lee Child's "Jack Reacher," lone wolf, and soldier-of-fortune novels; and those of Robert Crais' private investigators, "Elvis and Pike." You begin to think, now there's someone who can even up the odds when Lawrence Block's "Keller" calls. The book is definitely action-packed. Hollywood seems to thrive on hard-hitting adventures that can deliver a punchline when necessary. So, a movie may not be completely out of the question. You do sort of wonder how these rogue heroes manage to live long enough to tell their story, after so many harrowing, narrow escapes, time and time again. Reading the book will keep you on the edge of your seat. A word of caution. You may get the adrenaline pumping feeling that reading about crime fighting heroes has become a national pastime.

CHAPTER 26

Book review of the Jo Nesbo novel

The Leopard

published in 2009, and translated in 2011 by Don Bartlett.

Leopard changes hot spots in spine-tingling, frigid-air thriller.

He longed for the bygone era when summers seemed endless and the worst crime imaginable was leaving your best girl home on a Saturday night. So it was, the "Beach Boys" sang about the best times of their lives. Obviously. They were on a perpetual "Surfin' Safari" for about half a century.

R. Royce contemplated about the secluded swampland he'd bought years ago in central Florida. Actually the densely overgrown lots were situated on fairly high ground. Half forest, half jungle, he remembered vividly. He visited there every opportunity he had to get away from it all, spending his leisure time camping out in his camper-topped Dodge Laramie pickup truck, tending the roses he'd planted and cultivated, clearing the land like he was the reincarnation of Daniel Boone, or living the life of Tarzan the Ape-Man, often darting over to the pristine beaches, by driving roads less frequently travelled a short distance north and a few miles east over the Causeway to cool down and chill out. The Atlantic Ocean was only a couple of miles away, as the crow flies. He delighted in sifting through seashells by the seashore at sunrise, just as much as one might enjoy watching waves and gazing at free-spirited girls in bikinis playing "Beach Blanket Bingo" later in the day.

He reminisced about Raquel, fondly remembering what she had once said, "I would make you so, so very...very...miserable."

"Maybe so, but would you make me sleep out in the rain?" he replied, nuzzling her affectionately, as if he were an adorable puppy. As you can probably tell, he made friends easily. And he was a nature-lover. Time seemed to stand still for him.

He discovered two Artesian wells, one on the adjacent property to the east first, later, one hidden practically under his very nose in the underbrush beneath the intertwined clump of ornamental thorny, grafted sour-orange trees in his own backyard. Consequently, he enjoyed a viable supply of free fresh water in close proximity. His near-term goal was to reclaim the yard space created by the former owner, Mrs. Swinsen, who abruptly returned home to her family in New York, having abandoned the property after one of the hundred-foot-tall Australian Pine trees toppled and fell on her house. The City had no choice but to demolish the building eventually, out of health and safety concerns. The year was 1991.

It's always one thing or another, Royce thought. *If it's not the invisible biting bugs and mosquitoes, it's the snakes and sharks. If not the sweltering, oppressive heat and humidity, it's the hurricanes and tornadoes.* In fact, a snake was the reason the nice family living in the quaint cottage to the west unexpectedly and suddenly decided to pack up and move to Tallahassee. It seems an indigenous reptile had bitten one of their pet Boston terriers, a small black-and-while rascal with a cute pug nose, wagging tail, and wet, dangling red tongue. It had such a friendly demeanor and pleasant disposition.

"Generally, they're harmless," people say, "if left alone." They are seldom seen and live their lives underground mostly, amongst the rich reddish brown mulch and earth formed by century-old layers of fallen and decomposing tree trunks, limbs, leaves, and pine needles. The neighbors offered words of caution to snakebite victims and rose gardeners in the form of a simple nursery rhyme: "Red yellow black, and you're coming back. Black yellow red, and you're not." So, as it turns out, the coral snake with its distinctive alternating brightly colored stripes is the deadliest creature in the forest, not to be confused with the scarlet king snake. Others, including the Bushmaster, rat snake, and Pygmy rattler, all swamp dwellers, would not win any consolation prizes from Darwin. They are all plentiful and exceptionally scary. In the swampy area miles to the north, Royce heard tell from a local road grader, "The bite from a Pygmy rattler might not kill you, but you'll wish you were dead."

When Royce first began clearing the land, he couldn't even drive off the paved road into what was once a manicured lawn. Several Florida Palm trees had grown up and were scattered about, the biggest one smack dab in the middle of the single gravel driveway access. They're short and big around, with overlapping tough, fibrous husks surrounding their trunks, and long, waxy leaves that draw in copious amounts of rainfall. He overcame the formidable obstacle with a newly purchased chainsaw, brute force, and persistence. The nice 87-year-old neighbor living in the modest wood-framed house across the road, a retired botanist, with tangerine trees in her front yard, asked Royce if he'd ever tried "swamp cabbage." She went on to say the succulent delicacy is actually the heart of the palm tree, boiled and seasoned, until it's soft and tender. The downside is every time you prepare a delicious meal of swamp cabbage, a tree must die.

Months later, as he cleared the yard toward the back of the lot, chopping down shoulder-high sawgrass, various pasture grasses, and obnoxious weeds in his path, he came upon a tall stone cross, undoubtedly a monument to someone's ingenuity. He initially thought it must have been a grave marker from the days of Ponce de Leon and the search for the fountain of youth. He became somewhat agitated, concerned that he might have been treading on holy ground. Trudging onward, like a good Christian soldier, he was mystified to discover a second stone cross. That's when he realized their true purpose: they served as clothesline poles, to his profound relief. He would soon string up galvanized metal lines between them to support the weight of his sweaty t-shirts, grubby work-pants, dirty socks, and damp towels.

The most pleasing discovery of all was when Royce ventured through the thickets and into the dense forest to the west. He was astonished to find a large and solitary fruit-bearing ruby-red grapefruit tree in their midst. The granddaddy of them all! He gathered the grapefruits in five-gallon buckets, and lined them up on top of a curvy concrete block wall structure he'd constructed in the clearing to dry and ripen in the sun. He figured if a wild animal ever attacked him, he would be able to run around the wall faster to escape imminent danger. They were the sweetest grapefruits he'd ever tasted. He took them home and made gallons and gallons of juice. Drinking the stuff is good for weight loss, and chocked full of vitamins and nutrients. The tree was protected by a large hoot-owl, which roosted silently in the top-most branches, but was ever vigilant.

Tending the roses was Royce's favorite hobby. He'd planted a row of velvet red and golden yellow tea roses along the edge of the woods, parallel to the grassy ravine, alongside the paved road. The neighbors complimented him on how beautiful they looked, and how often they bloomed. His pride and joy, however, was the heat-tolerant, neon-pink California hybrid rose. These large, hardy roses grew about five feet tall, in the crater of a fallen tree he'd filled with topsoil, and looked like something outside of this world. They were absolutely magnificent specimens!

Two hurricanes, Frances from the east, and a few months later Jeanne from the west, swept across the land during the same season. Multiple tornadoes had spun off, traversing Royce's yard-space, according to the steadfast neighbor who lived north on the other side of the clothesline. Several neighbors' homes had been seriously damaged, their roofs blown off, or utterly destroyed, but not his. He calmly sat on his second-story screened-in back porch late throughout the evening cordially sipping coffee, while watching trees snap like toothpicks, the tree branches sent flying, monitoring and surveying the carnage and extent of damage. He'd build the solid concrete block stucco house using the money Lowe's paid him for his original property, which had been located where the corporate owners wanted to build their new superstore in town, in the shopping center on the main drag to the north and west, just off the interstate. Royce had planned to take his sweet time clearing his land in maybe ten or twelve years, but the recent activity of high winds had drastically accelerated his timetable for converting the area into a scenic park, a modern-day Garden of Eden. In reality, the area looked more like a disaster area or a war zone that summer. He was able to clear the land much faster afterwards. There was room enough for three fine, spacious mansions to be built there someday, when he sold out and moved to Texas.

Underneath the sandy topsoil and tightly compacted coral rock from millions of years of sedimentary settling, there exists a naturally flowing underground river. They call it the "Florida Aquafier," which is actually a good source of pure drinking water. That's undoubtedly why the trees grow so tremendously big and tall in the region. Their roots must have penetrated through the layers of sand, dirt, and coral earth and dipped into the bubbling, dripping, and gurgling springs deep below.

One can easily understand why a Norwegian police detective would want to go on a leisurely vacation getaway or take a long business trip to a warmer climate. It would be a welcome change of pace for Harry Hole, the main character in Jo Nesbo's novel *The Leopard*, written in 2009 and translated into English by Don Bartlett in 2011, especially after having repeatedly braved the trenches under arctic conditions in the frozen tundra and persevered through many a harsh Russian winter in another of his novels, *The Redbreast*. These are two of several novels about the exploits and dangers faced by this persistent detective, who usually ultimately gets the job done one way or the other, while confronting his demons and dealing with other issues, impediments, snares, and entanglements. The reader finds that he possesses a certain charisma throughout his ordeals. You can't help but like the guy. He has pizzazz, and a real knack for investigative research. You get the feeling that he is competent in his job and has excelled in his endeavors. He's arrived at the pinnacle of success in his field. He's risen to the peak of his profession. Indeed, he's found himself on the cutting edge of technology! Despite receiving severe criticism regarding his job performance, you can't really knock him for his efforts, considering that the vile villains he must bring to justice are some of the most sinister, diabolical, demented, deranged, and abominable criminals to ever walk the face of the earth. Like the "Dirty Harry" Hollywood movie character, starring actor Clint Eastwood from the 1970s, he packs plenty of "heat" and unleashes some serious firepower when necessary. At the same time, you won't find a gentler, more compassionate man, who manages to look after and care for his family with pure, loving kindness and humility.

Beyond the definitive characterization in his books, you've got to give the author credit for alluding to but not dwelling on the nightmares associated with having to interact with others who may embrace far different, diverse or alternative lifestyles and see things much differently than he does. He doesn't go out of his way to appear overly judgmental. He doesn't extoll virtue, as opposed to excessive deviation from normalcy. Case in point, he doesn't get wrapped around the axle about controversial personal preferences, such as tattoo artistry, body piercings, spiked hair, trendy gothic, militaristic fashion, techno-rock, raves, substance abuse; or a predilection for rude, crude, unorthodox and antisocial behavior. I believe he views these as being basic facts of life. He plays the role of a criminologist, not a sociologist or a psychologist. As a result, Harry is a perfect, prime example of an archetype character who has the good sense and common decency to watch his step and tread lightly in settings involving office politics, bureaucratic organization, and functioning law enforcement. He also appears to be on relatively good terms with journalists from the media and the press, which is really nothing more than a big ball of wax involving rapport, the timely presentation of key facts, possessing insight into what matters to the community, and having the keen ability to close cold cases quickly, using the sources of intelligence that are available to him. After all, everyone loves a good human-interest story.

CHAPTER 27

Book review of the novel
by Joseph Finder, published 2015, titled

The Fixer

How to get the most out of your dilapidated old house and a 60-minute job interview.

R. Royce was sleeping peacefully in the hammock he'd strung up between two scraggly live-oak trees in the scorching hot and dry California desert a few hundred miles northeast of Sacramento. Everyone else was dug in and hunkered down on the ground, camouflaged and hidden, oblivious of reptiles and rodents. The year was 1987. He was in the Army Reserve fulfilling a military duty requirement. He should have been in the lush, beautiful state of Washington during the sunniest, driest, and most pleasant time of the year there. He reflected on apple-blossom season and picking ripe, delicious, crunchy apples from the tree. His infantry unit was at Fort Lewis learning a new set of survival skills and testing out some prototype equipment for functionality, durability, and reliability. His company commander had shown some initiative when he simply relieved Royce and several other augmentees of their unit responsibilities for the duration of the summer. In other words he detached them from Company A, which was at full-strength, and deftly reassigned them to Company B, which was short of key personnel in certain skill-level positions. Since Company B suddenly went active, and was quickly mobilized for a training mission prior to being deployed overseas, "mission top secret, destination unknown," Royce went with them. He didn't mind. He was flexible and adaptable. He liked adventure. He was eager to get a visual on some of the northern California terrain and scenery.

Years ago, he'd been flown from his duty post in the D.C. area to Phoenix during the coldest part of the winter. It was much warmer in Arizona by comparison. A good place to host a Super-Bowl, he thought. He and his two civilian counterparts were sent to emplace stationary targets for the Air Assault Brigades operating in the desert southwest just across the border from Mexico. The three of them rented a full-size sedan at the airport for local transportation. The sights were impressive, even spectacular. Cowboy movies had been filmed in the idyllic, rugged, sandy region of cacti, mesas, burros, and canyons. The Lost Dutchman's mine was out there somewhere. John Wayne made several movies in the vicinity. Billy the Kid had spent a considerable amount of time in Yuma. Royce dug a hole in the dusty ground for a wooden sign post and miraculously found water. Of all things, an underground water source.

The duty in the summer California desert would be similar, only much hotter, but now he was tasked with finding the well-hidden targets instead of placing them, then coordinating for their elimination and annihilation. It was a seek and destroy mission, essentially. Much more interesting, but commensurably more dangerous, by several orders of magnitude. It would be like going from tons to megatons of firepower. Or, from standing out in the open, wearing a Kevlar helmet and bulletproof vest to going underground, protected by several inches of armor-plated steel and a concrete bunker.

The Colonel asked Royce and Sergeant Armeni if they'd ever been in a Huey, a UH-1, and wanted to go for a ride in a helicopter. Armeni said he hadn't and volunteered to go. They went on a routine aerial reconnaissance flight of the area northwest of their present location. In the meantime, Royce busied himself with setting up the communications links from their forward LP-OP operations base to the 34th Attack Squadron. Next, he coordinated for repairs assistance from the 8th Aircraft Maintenance Company and with the 19th Air Ambulance Company for medical evacuations. Done, he prepared and ate a satisfying meal from an MRE pouch mixed with lukewarm water from a canteen. Then, he rested. He fell soundly asleep, until about 0400 hours the next day, when he was rousted out of bed by loud, thumping sounds of turning rotors, the rotor blades chopping and churning as they displaced great volumes of air; and the high-pitched, whining noises generated by the engines of half a dozen Apache Helicopters and Cobra gunships landing nearby. He was rousted out of bed, by the storm of whirling dust and flying, sandy debris. In other words, he fell out of his hammock onto the hardened earth waking up startled, stunned, and slightly disorientated.

Apparently, the Colonel and Armeni had located viable targets concealed somewhere in the vast desert wilderness, and called in the 27th Cavalry Regiment for imminent, active engagement. Because he hadn't volunteered to recon the region on the previous day, Royce tagged along at the Colonel's insistence for the D-Day activities commencing at first light, or daybreak. They immediately climbed aboard the spotter aircraft and departed under cover of darkness. Within minutes, they departed with the so-called advance party. A-10 Warthog fixed-wing aircraft and some Harrier Jets from an allied unit had been dispatched for added security and the subsequent cleanup. Troops from the 4th Air Assault Battalion stood in readiness by their Chinooks. They would seize the installations and take complete control over the fortifications on the ground moving in from planned rendezvous and staging points. It would be like the Vikings storming the castle and ransacking the city during medieval times, only in a much more subdued and professional manner, without the "ravish, pillage, plunder and burn" aspect. Their modern warfare tactics would seem almost civilized in comparison, but the results, far from tame. The weapons they were about to unleash were far more lethal and long-reaching. They fire automatic weapons having a high-capacity firing rate. They fire a multitude of different kinds of rounds: concrete-wall penetrating, phosphorous, tracing, percussion, and NATO. A combination of these rounds would cause massive damage to engineered infrastructures and weapons systems alike. Plus, they would cause mass casualties to enemy combatants who offered armed resistance. Moreover, this type of military operation could play out anywhere in the world, under virtually any conditions, natural or manmade. They're particularly suited for fighting in urban terrain, from an idealistic standpoint. Royce thought about it for a moment. There are places in the world today where he wouldn't want to go at all, without being accompanied by at least one well-armed and fully-equipped Army at total-strength. Plus, he would want solid military units positioned in active reserve for backup and contingencies, just in case the operation went sideways. Sad, but true. It's gotta be. They don't call him the most interesting guy in the world, because he doesn't have much to say about himself. No, they call him the million-dollar minute man, because the soldiers know every time he orchestrates a full-scale military attack, it costs a million dollars a minute.

In his well-crafted novel, *The Fixer*, published in 2015, Joseph Finder came up with a humdinger of a whopping "tale of two cities:" the Ivy-league bedroom and boardroom community of wealthy, prosperous, and white-collar professionals on one hand; and the suburban landscape developments of rising middle-class citizens, blue-collar workers, and organized labor. Really, you'd think they should all learn to work in harmony toward a common goal, for the betterment of their utopian ideals, and for improving their living standards. But this does not always happen in the real world. The scenarios change because of poverty, crime, lack of opportunities, everyday misfortunes, and just plain bad, or dumb luck.

Ethics and morality aside, the novel reminds me of the telling movie *A Simple Plan*, starring Billy Bob Thornton and Bridget Fonda, in which greed evolves as an integral part of human nature, figuring prominently as one of the "seven deadly sins." The historian Gibbons documented these characteristically human traits long ago from the distant past, in *The Decline of the Roman Empire*. The movie and the book remind me of the horror stories about lottery winners from the past. They lost it all after only a few short years. And, they ruined their lives in the process of having to deal with all of the implications of their sudden wealth. As the sayings go, "Money is the root of all evil" and "Power corrupts and absolute power corrupts absolutely."

Perhaps it is only human nature that makes you want what your neighbor has, but that's often the way it is. "The grass is always greener" on the other side of the fence. There are those who struggle to make ends meet; those who strive to get ahead; and those who want it all and want it now. That's the rub, the rubber, the robber, and where the greatest friction occurs.

On the obverse side of the coin, we've all heard they're "too big to fail" and "You can't have too much money." Au contraire, "You can't have enough." That's why rich, multi-national corporations retain the highest-powered teams of the sharpest lawyers, accountants, business managers, and stockbrokers they can find. And, that's why the rich have influential friends in high places. For instance, in the very seat of government itself. By and large, however, they have made a gallant attempt to insulate themselves from all of the pain and suffering in the world. Have they succeeded? Probably not. They must pray for help.

Was the novel historically accurate? Politically correct? Doubtful. Supercharged emotionally? Not really. But, not too cold and calculating either. The leading character wanted to get at the truth. That's all. He must have believed the truth would ultimately set him free. As an idealistic, investigative journalist, he wanted to give his readers exactly what "enquiring minds want to know." And, winning a Pulitzer prize along the way wouldn't hurt the average journalist's chances for having a successful career.

CHAPTER 28

Book review of the historical novel,
by Iain Pears, published in 1998,

An Instance of the Fingerpost

A risqué novel about a hack, quack, snitch, witch, and the once rich.

R. Royce was trying to cure the common cold. He remembered the stages in the process a person goes through from an obscure and all but obsolete book on biology, printed in 1950, that had been shelved in a corner bookcase in the living room. First contact: the microorganism enters the human body. Incubation phase: the microbes find a warm, moist, dark place in the body and begin to multiply, exponentially. They begin to overwhelm the host. Sickness: the host becomes desperately ill. His body weakens considerably. He feels fatigued, lacks energy, and wants rest. He loses his appetite. He alternately sweats and has chills. His head pounds and his muscles ache. Recovery phase: his immune system begins to fight against the invading microbes. White blood cell production increases dramatically in his bloodstream. The blood cells produce phlegm, which gradually covers, overwhelms, and encapsulates the microbes, which have been steadily growing in numbers, rapidly expanding their territory, reproducing in his mouth, nose, and throat. Return to health: he can begin to breathe easier, his appetite returns, and he feels like getting out of bed again to greet the day and participate in normal daily activities.

At first, he thought he had at home all the ingredients necessary which would bring about a quick, easy cure: steaming chamomile and lemon teas, chicken broth, rest, and faith. After three days with a runny nose, however, his swollen sinuses began to clog and his breathing became labored. He periodically blew out the slimy mucus from each of his nostrils into the bathroom sink, but one nostril or the other would invariably re-clog, and he would have to exhale warm air from his mouth to complete the respiration process in the most efficient manner possible. His eyelids grew heavy; his vision, dim and blurry.

He reminisced about friends from long ago. Whatever happened to Pete Bates, from middle-school days? Tall, skinny, shy kid who milled about the schoolyard with the rest before the bell sounded, and didn't have much to say that was very untypical, except that he thought he could fly. He always carried a bottle of "Formula 44" to prevent the flu in the pocket of his winter parka. So, it would seem that he sometimes got carried away with visions of grandeur. One early morning, a crowd of kids pointed to the top of the school building and there he stood on the rooftop. Many in the crowd pointed fingers, and everyone looked skyward, amazed. A roar went up. Some of the schoolkids shouted, "Show us you can fly, Master Bates!" Then, they began to chant, "Jump, Pete, jump." Fortunately, the unruly disturbance caught the attention of the school principal, who went topside and coaxed the delinquent back inside the building. The principal must have convinced his parents that the undisciplined boy would be an excellent candidate for the junior military academy located in the next town, because that was his last day in school, and that was how Pete finally cured his cold.

The next morning, when Royce thought he might be getting a sore throat as a result of his illness, he drove to the local convenience store and picked up some lemon-lime soda and nighttime cold medicine. According to the textbook, some persons had resorted to the use of stimulants and depressants. The medicine would help him sleep better throughout the night, he believed. The downside was he'd wake up in the middle of the night soaked in a cold sweat, his sheets and pillowcases cold and damp. He'd climb out of bed to change the sheets and pillowcases for dry linens, tossing the wet items in the washing machine. The next morning, he'd wake up in a cold sweat again, having slept on cold, damp sheets and pillowcases. So, he had to change the sheets and pillowcases a second time. He tossed the damp ones into the washer, and those from the washer to the dryer. He reflected on the fact that you sort of wanted to generate a little body heat, especially in the middle of winter. All he felt was cold and damp.

A few days later, he developed a harsh cough and began to get a sore throat, partially from the cold-causing microbes and partially from the cold medicine, which tended to dry out the mucus membranes of his esophagus. He began to cough repeatedly, trying with all his might, attempting to expel the perceived irritant on the inside wall of his throat.

Because of the persistent cough he'd developed, Royce returned to the store for another 12-pack of lemon-lime sodas and a large package of wintergreen-flavored mint candies, something that might soothe his irritated throat condition. Candy-coating his esophagus with mint and lemon-lime flavored syrups seemed to work fairly well and his throat began to feel much better. Particularly so, after numerous rigorous bouts of gargling with warm saltwater, during the night.

Gradually, over time, he began to breathe easier and he was able to rest much more completely. His muscles were still sore and his joints ached, but he was becoming more alert. And he had finally felt the fever that had flamed up within him, warm, burning, inviting—like the woodfire in a cozy, rustic cabin fireplace made of rocks, stacked and cemented together all the way to the chimney top. The next morning, he cooked an omelet for breakfast and had a cup of coffee. He was slowly but surely returning to normal. "What doesn't kill you will make you stronger," he recollected someone having recently said in the office, as he began to gather his wits about him. Thus, the "physician" healed himself after all. "Feed a cold; starve a fever," he proclaimed loudly in defiance!

Only it wasn't just the common cold he was trying to cure. A week prior, he'd been afflicted by the deadly tsetse fly toxin on his way to the exiting airport. It caught him unaware, as if a poisoned dart had just sailed by him while he was strolling along the sidewalk, window-shopping in the fashion merchandise district. As he paused to turn the corner, the sharp needlepoint barely nicked him, scratching the exposed skin on back of his neck. He swatted too late. The fly zipped through the air, ultimately striking a wooden-framed bulletin board made of cork dead center among the routinely posted government notices and the list of active, precautionary safety measures found on the advertising kiosk. It felt like a mosquito bite. Harmless enough. Maybe. He didn't stop to read the writing on the wall.

One might wonder if the pocketful of raw, rare gemstones he had concealed on his person were so precious as to risk his very life in the process of couriering them across remote international borders, not his own, for an undisclosed employer, funded by a temporary employment agency. Lucrative, but not much said about job security. But then again, it beat flipping veggie burgers for a living at the delicatessen back home by a long shot.

The historical novel *An Instance of the Fingerpost*, written by Iain Pears, published in 1998, proved to be just the kind of realistic reading material—food for thought, you could sink your teeth into. The story seems plausible enough. An Italian medical student goes to London, England, in the middle 17th century and tries to learn enough and earn the necessary credentials to become a doctor. He feels the calling to heal the sick and improve the lives and health of everyone he meets. A noble ambition. He has a crude idea of man's mortality and his short lifespan, but does the best he can under the circumstances. Not everyone he tries to heal gets the cure. Not every physician is perfectly gifted, suitable, or perfectly qualified for the job. Basically, he meets a number of other "quacks," quite unlike himself, and a variety of other quirky characters. The profession becomes frustrating to him, but he perseveres. He learns useful home remedies from practitioners of local folk medicine. He gains accolades from the renowned colleges of medicine. And he gets an inside look at the politics of medical healthcare.

In fact, the politics of healthcare applies just as much today as it did 350 years ago in sunny old England, even though today's doctors are better trained and we've all enjoyed the benefits and miracles of modern-day medicine. Nonetheless, you might want to think twice about having your appendix, tonsils, gall bladder, et cetera, removed, simply because you have experienced slight discomfort and moderate inflammation, and because you have the necessary health insurance to cover the expense. Likewise you might want to consider a second opinion or multiple opinions before you consent to and give preference to one form of medical treatment over another. For all you know the anomaly revealed might be completely harmless and you have 40 more years to live, before you die of natural causes. We know that we all have to go some time, but we'd prefer to prolong the inevitable. Likewise, you might not want to overdo it with the tremendous volume and kinds of available medication. You don't want to abuse pharmaceuticals, and you certainly don't want to become addicted to them. At some point in time, you might want to ask yourself if you really need the pain pills, sedatives, anti-anxiety medication, et cetera. Rehab, detox, "cold turkey," "drying-out," and "going on the wagon" are alternatives.

Is the stress and pressure from your job killing you? Does your type-A personality dramatically increase your chances for a heart-attack? My philosophy is "Run like hell!" Save up and try something different. Change your lifestyle. Quit. Sell out. Move. Get a hobby. Relax. Go where people live longer, sensible lives, without the hustle and bustle. Retire, even if you have to live more modestly in moderation. What sense does it make rampaging through life like a raging bull right up until the very moment he meets the point of the sword? Unless, of course, you really love your work. In the immortal words of a former coworker, "Law enforcement is my life!" But then again, she resigned after a few short years and married a doctor. Sensible girl. The gentle people love her so.

CHAPTER 29

Book review of the novel

The Treasure of the Sierra Madre

by Bruno Traven, published in 1935.

*All that glitters is not gold.
The light at the end of the tunnel.*

The man returned the photo ID R. Royce gave him, and said, "You are who you say you are." Royce was at a real estate office in north Texas selling a house. The year was 2015. August. He was oddly reminded of the first time he ever visited the Alfred P. Murrah federal building in Oklahoma City years ago, in 1986. The OIC flippantly asked Royce, "What kind of badge do you want?" He handed the security officer a letter of authorization for Revenue Agent credentials. It would be Royce's first professional job. Turns out, he lasted throughout most of his probationary period. He had been terminated in just under a year. Deemed unsuitable, sort of a dud. Regrets, he had none. He essentially lacked the requisite basic accounting skills and a qualifying business background. Hired "off the street," he was thankful for the opportunity presented, and he had learned a great deal about getting along with people in the corporate world.

Afterwards, between jobs, he tinkered with television sets, repaired automobiles, and performed part-time military duty as an Army Reservist in the IRR. During this period of uncertainty in his life, he put in various applications for gainful employment, including one for an interesting Soil Conservationist position, and one for Medical Examiner. He liked the idea of saving the world and the people in it. When he did not receive a reply for either job, he called each of the respective employment offices on the telephone to inquire why. One of the secretaries said that he could not be considered at all, since another office had held onto his application and would not let go. It seems someone at the "South Florida desk" wanted him to work in the capacity of an information specialist with their I.T. Section. In other words, their organization wanted to train him in information technology. Then, they would grant him "peace officer" status. When they did finally hire him, the equipment they issued him included a tin star, electronic access to the intranet, and a "heater." For the most part, he behaved in a professional and responsible manner, and did not create too many waves. "Don't rock the boat," he was told. To make a long story short, he latched onto the job and held onto it, like a hungry pit-bull biting into a chunk of raw meat. Unlike the dog, however, he divined a major long-term goal of living a normal, healthy, and happy life; the thought safely hidden away within the mysterious recesses of the more highly developed cerebral portion of his brain. Toward the end of his fruitful career, he transferred to Texas, where he was ultimately to retire in a small, quiet, out-of-the-way duty station. There, he continued to maintain a low profile. He began to see daylight at the end of the tunnel.

Looking back over the years, Royce realized the job entailed inherent risks. Unlike in the Army in which, "You knew the job was dangerous when you took it," the risks associated with his civilian job were such that, for example, the pool of employees in Miami averaged one suicide every six years; in Dallas, one heart attack victim every three years. He didn't want to become another labor statistic. When he gave the supervisor his "two weeks' notice," Royce told him that the most stressful thing he planned on doing in the future was to watch the grass and trees grow, and the flowers bloom.

What he neglected to mention was that he was going to the mountains for a breath of fresh air, looking for kimberlite. One fine day, he packed a GPS instrument and a geology book among the personal effects and camping gear already loaded in the vehicle. That very afternoon, he drove away in the direction of the setting sun.

The book *The Treasure of the Sierra Madre*, written by Bruno Traven and published in 1935, is a prime example of an author's literary work who was perfectly at peace with himself and in perfect harmony with the universe, even though he lived through tumultuous times of great chaos and discord, caused by war. He was fully knowledgeable of mankind's evil, selfish, and injurious nature. He was wise to man's wicked ways. Yet, one gets the clear and distinctive impression that he kept himself aloof nonetheless. Without a doubt, he had set himself to a higher standard. Furthermore, he prophesized the prevalent tendency for dominant feudal rule, and the rising tendency of dictatorship in government. He also predicted the resulting anarchy which inevitably follows the weakening, downfall, and ultimate collapse of any and all antagonistic and oppressive totalitarian regimes, for example, the ones you see on the evening news every so often with regularity, in which the dire consequences, and pathetically uninspired results of wholesale chaos and terror are apparent. It makes you wonder. There must be a higher power at work somewhere in the supremely metaphysical universe.

In any event, if one adheres to a strictly grassroots approach to life in general, B. Traven's short stories are just as telling and just as revealing as any of the graphic details portrayed in the novel. Among the cleverest stories with a true-to-life, down-to-earth message are "The Story of the Nun" and "The Silk Scarf," in my opinion. These are must reads for Traven fans.

CHAPTER 30

Book review of Robert Penn Warren's book,
published in 1931, entitled

The Circus in the Attic and Other Stories

The cream of the crop.

R. Royce reflected on living on five acres in the woods above a hidden hollow in 1970. The white, wooden-framed house was situated alongside a rocky, red-clay dirt road on a flat stretch of the rolling hillside above a muddy Cabin Creek. The house is long gone now. The last time he drove by, there was a double-wide mobile home in its place. That must have been thirty years ago. The garage and well-house were still there. So was the pear tree, in the pasture east of the house. His mother preserved the fruits in dozens of Mason jars during the autumn harvesting season. In the summertime, the children picked wild blackberries, collecting them in large tin cans from the bushes in the thorny thickets, brought them home, and scooped them into cereal bowls, pouring milk on the berries and sprinkling granulated sugar on top. The farmer and his wife, who lived across the road were long gone, too. Their son and his family lived there in a new house they'd built much farther back from the road, out of sight. Royce used to help haul hay for the family in the summertime and put it in their barn. Generally, they used a flatbed five-ton truck and bale-loader. They lifted and stacked the square bales manually with curved hay hooks made of shiny stainless steel metal. Sometimes they used the Beaners' pickup to haul hay. It was a rugged 1965 two-tone blue and white Ford half-ton. The hay meadows were across the creek, uphill from the weathered, screened-in fishing shack, that had a wood-burning, cast-iron cook stove inside. Fisherman liked to spend weekends there catching sand bass when they were running the riffles. They drank beer and slept on cots.

He remembered the chestnut racehorse they owned—Gypsy was her name, and how she ran away with his brother, barely a teenager then, trying to outrace the neighbor girl, on her motor-scooter. He couldn't control the horse. The bit and leather reins he held didn't slow the horse down at all, and he rode without a saddle. The experience proved bumpy and terrifying for him. But she stopped without fanfare at the crossroad, her finish line. Royce remembered, too, the gray pack-mule his father bought for his prospecting trip to Arizona. "Brighty!" Now there was a sensible, easygoing creature if there ever was one. Never in a hurry. Never a concern. Unlike his granddad's matched pair of prize mules, of which he was so proud, and to which he routinely harnessed up a heavy plow-shear and tilled the fertile topsoil for the garden at their house alongside the highway north of the truck stop, about four miles west from the white framed house. They were all business. Big, plump, ripe red tomatoes and tiny green hot chili peppers were the garden specialty, the fruits of their labor. The coffee in the pot he kept going on the campfire all day long was so thick a spoon could stand upright in it, they said. "Strongest, syrupy, worst-tasting coffee in the world. Like drinking mud," someone complained. At least the cooled milk from the dairy farm a mile up the road, and a section over to the west was fresh. The family bought their milk in large glass jugs directly from the farmer back then. Recently, Royce began buying refrigerated farm-fresh milk in half-gallon glass bottles from his local grocery store. It takes him back to days gone by.

Only last week, he visited James, whom he's known since junior high school. His family was in the dairy business until the mid-1980s. Royce told him that he started buying milk in glass jugs again. He got a kick out of the concept. James and Louise live on the family farm, where they raise beef cattle. The grandkids visit them, and they help with the chores. The couple enjoys watching their grandson wrestle competitively in his school's athletic program. James retired from the Monumental Rock Quarry yesterday, the last day of March, 2016. "Now, he can take it easy," as his mother would say.

The Circus in the Attic and Other Stories, written by Robert Penn Warren and published in 1931, is a fine collection of southern fiction which takes place roughly from the time of the Civil War to the end of WWI. The stories are about the unsung heroes of the Old South and their struggles, misfortunes, suffering, and tragedies. They're about ignorance and poverty, the depression years, the influence of family values and religion on justice, bondage and servitude, pride and vanity, love, honor, and loyalty. They're about people's hopes and dreams. They're about courage and resignation in the face of adversity. It's no wonder that the author would go on to write a novel about politics and a potential savior, someone who would go out of his way to work miracles in the valiant attempt to improve the deplorable living conditions in the South. That best-selling novel was *All the King's Men*, written in 1946.

I don't know if an ordinary reviewer of books should "dare to compare" the preeminent Robert Penn Warren's short stories to those of the later writer John Grisham in his *Ford County: Stories*, published in 2009-'10, but why not? There are an abundance of similarities in their subject matter, incorporating the good folks of the Sunbelt, their system of beliefs, and their wholly unique way of life. The authors' talent, style, and flair are self-evident. Their stories, revealing. Not that style and flair should play any significant role in storytelling, from a purely historical point of view. It's just that conditions have changed so very drastically and dramatically (even if traditions may not have changed so greatly, "Thank G.!"), and there have been such surprising new developments, sprung on the unsuspecting populace over the years, for better or worse.

Namely, after the time of R. P. Warren's Stories, there was the advent and proliferation of modernized institutions: hospitals, prisons, nursing homes, casinos, the military services, manufacturers, distributors, and established law firms. To spice up matters, a number of the lawyers representing these concerns appeared to be slightly shady or tricky, if not exceptionally meticulous. And that's where J. Grisham went on a hellbent tangent, in his novels.

In summary, to make a long story short, these excellent, tangled and twisted tales of the surly, sultry, saucy, sassy South, past and present, make for quite interesting and intriguing reading. Indeed, they are just as relevant today as they were a hundred years ago. As a former college sweetheart once smugly retorted, "We do have a past." And I predict the stories will be just as relevant a hundred years from now. Contrary to whatever the Delta "drama queen" coach might have meant when she shouted up to the open window on the second floor from the street, broadcasting her message loud and clear, "It will never happen again!"

"The cream of the crop," mused Royce. "For crying out loud."

CHAPTER 31

Review of the book by Conrad Aiken,
written 1922-1950, entitled

The Short Stories of Conrad Aiken

As the man read, his hands trembled and the book shook. As the curtains fluttered, he shuddered. The resonating host had inspired ghosts and fired desires.

Their bruised and deflated, tremendously fragile egos left them devastated.

R. Royce drove the Mercury south on I-95, the cruise-control engaged, leaving Maryland far behind, after completing Army Reserve duty in the summer of 1988. His destination was Miami, Florida, where he had finally located what could prove to be a real, steady job. He hoped to find a place to live and be gainfully employed by mid-September. Along the way, he decided to stop for fuel in Savannah, Georgia. For some inexplicable reason, quite by accident, really, he pulled the car over near downtown, along Abercrombie Street, parked the vehicle, and went for a leisurely stroll, for a proverbial walk in the park. The day was gray and dreary, and humid. It could rain any moment. The sky was overcast with low-lying stratocumulus clouds. Not in the least weary, but feeling perky and energized, he stretched his legs as he moved quickly and quietly along the beaten path. He spotted a historical sign which caught his attention beside the tree-lined sidewalk, in front of a row of two-story buildings and houses, which must have been majestic in their time. They reminded him of Baltimore, their houses having long ago been built too close together for comfort, in his opinion.

The sign indicated that this particular abode was where the highly esteemed and well respected author Conrad Aiken once dwelled. Perhaps where his descendants still lived. Who knows? Royce recollected having read one of his short stories from a textbook in English class at school, years ago—required reading, the one about an adolescent's obsession with "global climate change."

The really unusual thing about appearing suddenly and unexpectedly, practically on the famous author's front porch step, on such a dark and mysterious day, in such a strangely peculiar setting, was that when he happened to glance up, then look intently, searchingly upstairs at the second-floor window, Royce was startled to discover that while no lights were on to illuminate the shadowy interior, the half-open curtain seemed to move, ever so slightly, as if someone were hiding behind it, peering out. He suddenly felt self-conscious and embarrassed. He felt like an intruder, or a night stalker, even though it was the middle of the afternoon, eavesdropping on somebody's privacy, or at least at a guarded intimacy. But mostly, he felt like he'd just conjured up a ghost from somebody's past or past life. He was spontaneously spooked. He was overcome with such an eerie, creepy feeling that he felt compelled to vacate the premises immediately, abruptly leaving the hallowed shrine of the landmark. He hurried back to his vehicle and drove away from the scene as fast as he could safely do so. He didn't stop until he arrived in sunny Florida, the 'Gator State.

Driving along, he thought about his best girlfriend from Denver and his buddy from White Oak, both sixteen in 1970, years ago. His family had moved from Colorado to Oklahoma a couple of years prior. He reflected on the "rites of passage." She had collided her automobile into the concrete pillar beneath the overpass of the new interstate highway, on her way to Hinkley High School one chilly morning, according to a letter sent from her mother to Royce's mother that spring, and was killed instantly. She must have lost control, skidding and sliding on the icy crossroad.

At the end of the school year, that same spring, going on a high school picnic, the students were loaded up on a bus, and they traveled to Grand Lake. His best friend and another classmate decided to swim across a large pool of water below the dam. "He must have cramped up," some said. "He fought wildly and must have panicked." The other boy said he tried to reach him and save him, but was pushed away. The fact of the matter is, he sank like a rock and drowned. The body was recovered from the murky depths by a scuba diver later that afternoon.

It was a rough year for a boy and his youthful friendships.

The Short Stories of Conrad Aiken is a fabulously impressive collection of stories written by Conrad Aiken between the years 1922 and 1950, and assembled together into a hefty book of some 416 pages, without a wasted word or frivolous phrase anywhere to be found. After reading the stories over the course of about a week's duration, looking over my copious scribbled notes, reviewing the table of contents, and tabbing to a couple of the stories for brief skimming, in order to refresh my memory about the "gist of the story," I searched for stories which for one reason or another did not quite "measure up" to the high-caliber quality and sublime, lofty standards of the average Aiken story, I quickly determined that there were none. No such animal. They were all excellent stories by any standard or rule of measure. Next, I decided to pick out the ones which impressed me the most. My favorites.

There was a long list of these. They include five flights of imagination or pure fantasy; five conflicted interpersonal relationships; five reality checks; five deeply philosophical meanings; five existential crises; and five appeals for divine intervention. Oh, wait! I must have miscounted. Six categories times five stories in each category totals thirty stories. But there are only 29 stories in the entire book. There must be a simple explanation for this. And there is: many of the stories fit into multiple categories. Like action-adventure, romantic-comedy, or courtroom-drama for types of cinema films.

At any rate, I was most impressed by "Strange Moonlight," "A Pair of Vikings," "The Last Visit," "Silent Snow, Secret Snow," "Hello Tib," "By My Troth, Nerissa," and "Your Obituary, Well Written." The stories just go to show you what great character development is possible, nay, certainly achievable, when extraordinary people who have tremendous egos interact and become emotionally involved, especially when they possess the means and the ability to get whatever they want out of life. It sometimes follows that their bruised and deflated, tremendously fragile egos leave them completely devastated and terribly damaged. Unknowing, the rest of us live out our relatively insignificant, miserable, little lives and try to eke out a meager existence—all the while dreaming about and drooling over their privileged circumstances on "Snob Hill," which ends up becoming their fiercest battleground, their "Boot Hill"—until we come to realize that our own lives are not so bad after all.

"Those who are about to go into battle, we salute you," exclaimed Royce, probably misquoting a character who must have been inspired by Atilla the Hun, from a long-forgotten motion picture about Vikings he had seen at the Fox Theater in Aurora, Colorado, on Colfax at a Saturday afternoon matinee when he was an impressionable teenager. Then, he thought, *I'm free, glad to be alive, and making money.* He's humbler and friendlier now, since he's become older and wiser.

CHAPTER 32

Book review of

Graham Green Collected Stories

by Graham Green
the book published in 1973, the stories published 1935-1975.

What did you do during the War, Dad?

R. Royce looked oddly in the general direction of the couple seated at a nearby table in the restaurant when she suddenly exclaimed to her companion, "You're the man!" He couldn't help but wonder, *Did she mean "the man in charge!" or "the man the police are looking for!"* He felt certain she meant it as a compliment, in either case, dismissed the thought entirely from his mind, and continued eating his burger with relish and all the fixings, along with a side order of home-fries, gooey ketchup, and mild salsa while he reflected on the events of the day from the headlines of the local newspaper.

"You gotta watch out for him," she cautioned. "He'll turn on you when you least suspect it. Like a dangerous, cornered animal," she advised.

What the hay? thought Royce. *Where are the authorities when you need them?* Her boyfriend must be some kind of martial-arts, ultimate prize-fighter, or some such bonified character from the World Wrestling Federation she's promoting. Royce slumped down in his chair and tried not to look too intimidating. He raised the sports page of the newspaper and hid behind it.

When they left, he followed them out of the building, trying to be as inconspicuous as is humanly possible. In the parking lot, he climbed into his late-model gray Ferrari and tailed the Hollywood starstruck couple, following at a reasonably discrete distance. Who knows where this little adventure would lead?

He located them in a roadside park with picnic tables beside a lake where some ducks were swimming. He sauntered over to their vehicle and did a tap-dance on the driver's side window with his index finger. Abigail rolled down the window. It was steamed and so was she. The Bruiser didn't react to the intrusion whatsoever. Little did he know, the interruption would probably cost him his career, but save his life in the end.

"Could I trouble you for a light?" Royce asked her. Reclining in his seat, the Bruiser was oblivious to the world. He was out cold. She was supposed to deliver him in time for the "Main Event" that evening.

"Do I know you from somewhere?" Abigail inquired, as she handed him a flashlight from the dashboard, smiling like a Cheshire cat. She climbed out of the automobile, walked over to Royce's and got in.

"He sleeps like a baby," Royce said, as they drove away, wealthier and wiser.

At some point in time in his early childhood, one might think, if he didn't know any better, his parents must have taken away all of his toys, confined him to a room with a minimum of bare necessities, and sent him to bed without his supper. Not exactly bright and cheerful, Graham Greene's stories can be that depressing and gloomy in places. The privations the author must have endured seem to have been reflected in his writing. To make matters worse, he projected an image of someone who has experienced more than his fair share of misery, terror, and phobias. His greatest fears concerned God and mortality. Apparently, he was gravely skeptical of religion in its many shapes and forms and might have appeared to be faithless and agnostic in crucial moments throughout most of his life, one might be led to believe. His view of the world and the future of mankind was largely pessimistic, clouded by doubt, frustration, and the utter futility of it all. True, he lived in highly uncertain times, having written about life in wartime England in the early twentieth century. He wrote realistically and convincingly, however. He didn't mince his words, and he didn't sugarcoat his perceptions. Life was harsh enough and the characters he described were not the toughest or the strongest people in the world. They were hardened by circumstances and their environment. But not many would be deemed to be heroic; or, survivors, either, for that matter. Actually, his characters tended to be weak, ordinary, and sort of flaky or quirky. They generally displayed multiple faults, flaws, and weaknesses to an excessive degree, which led them down the path toward self-destruction and their senseless demise. No exaggeration.

Yet, there is great substance to his stories, which has superlative redeeming qualities, which transcends the humdrum mediocrity and lack of promise of the shadowy existence many must have experienced during the foggy gray, dreary era. He had a tendency to mock and poke fun at himself and the glaring limitations of others, I believe. For example, he certainly "let the cat out of the bag" in the story "The Over-night Bag." And he elaborated and expounded on the theme "What happens when the flame just won't go out?" in the story "Mortmain." He told exactly what happens "when pigs fly" in the story "A Shocking Accident." He explained the necessity for "sunshine laws" as a requirement for "transparency in government" in the story "The Root of All Evil."

Then, just when you would want to write him off as a crackpot and the world's greatest cynic, he came up with a heart-wrenching, sentimental story about a "match made in heaven" in "Two Gentle People." He questioned his faith in the Almighty in "A Visit to Morin"; then, the power of prayer in "The Blessing"' and finally, the traditions associated with Christmas celebrations in "Dear Dr. Falkenheim."

Reverting back to the years of childhood, he described what happens when children are left unsupervised, unattended, and on their own recognizance for prolonged periods in "A Discovery in the Woods" and "The Destructors."

He reveled in the prospect of professionalism and careerism in "When Greek Meets Greek," "Men at Work," and "A Chance for Mr. Lever." He reminisced about unrequited love and lost youth in "The Blue Film" and "The Innocent."

But mostly, he scoffed at the various types of failures, losers, incompetents, and other persons with problematic personalities in several stories, most notably, "I Spy," "Cheap in August," "Dr. Crombie," "A Church Militant," "Dream of a Strange Land," "Special Duties," "Alas Poor Maling," "The Case for the Defense," "A Drive in the Country," "Jubilee," and "The End of the Party."

Lastly, he revealed how "crime just doesn't pay" in "Across the Bridge" and "The Basement Room." All in all, Graham Greene's collection of stories are as diverse a mixture as the grab-bag assortment of discounted merchandise one might have found at any nickel-and-dime store in America in the 1960s, maybe not the most glamorous products on the market, but they did include the basic sundry items you needed to keep around the household for those little emergencies which tend to occur almost on a daily basis now and again—like extra buttons, needles and thread, plenty of bandages, and penny candy comfort food; all to make you feel better again despite yourself.

CHAPTER 33

Book review of the
Collected Stories of Wallace Stegner
by Wallace Stegner, published in 1990,
written 1938-1990.

*Spoken like a true Samurai Warrior.
Truer words were never spoken.*

As he was driving his newly acquired Caprice in Tulsa one fine summer day, R. Royce was thinking about a lecture series of information briefings he had attended in the latter part of 1994, during a Combined Arms Seminar. Since discussion was encouraged, in order to provide constructive criticism and instantaneous feedback on the various topics being presented, he decided to contribute something positive after listening to a particularly moving and uplifting speech about the daily activities in an Army Mechanized Infantry Brigade which had once been located somewhere in central Louisiana. The post boasted a slower, more relaxed pace of life. It was a place where older soldiers eased into retirement gradually, quietly and gracefully, without much fanfare. Processing was sort of like putting old racehorses out to pasture in a field of morning glories and daisies. At the end of the speech, Royce had made the comment, "Spoken like a true Samurai Warrior."

In the summer of 2006, Royce had found a late-model Buick for a neighbor and swapped it for her buffed shiny silver 1995 Caprice Classic. He needed a reliable commuter car for transportation back and forth to work in and around Dallas at the time. He was living on the edge of the city, in the suburbs near the Speedway. Largely obsolete now, compared with the latest models coming out of Detroit, this particular vehicle had the unique distinction of being shaped like a big lemon, and was rapidly becoming a very popular car to customize, in certain inner-city circles. The body, paint, and leather interior was already in showroom condition. The sticker on the frame indicated the presence of an economical 4.6-liter motor, but someone had removed it altogether and dropped in a new 5.9-liter V-8 instead, which transformed the vehicle into an excellent highway car. Most importantly, it was a clean car with a clear title. All Royce had to do was tune up the motor, change the oil, install an aluminum radiator from California and a heater coil, replace the hi-fi stereo and speakers, add a lift-kit, and put a sharp set of 16-inch alloy wheels and new high-performance tires all the way around. Once completed, the modified vehicle was an eye-catching sight to behold, a one-of-a-kind original.

As Royce steered the Caprice into the "Seven-eleven" parking lot he noticed a pale green four-door Monte Carlo parked off to the side of the building, but didn't think too much about it at the time. He stopped his car and walked cheerfully into the convenience store for refreshments. He located the soda fountain and snack aisles. While waiting patiently in line, he heard a deep resonant voice behind him mutter into his ear, "I want your car."

What an odd, uncouth thing to say to somebody you don't even know in a busy, crowded convenience store, Royce thought. Sometimes acting normal and doing nothing is the best course of action to deescalate a potential incident. You never know when someone might come unglued, become unhinged, or fly completely off the handle. So, Royce ignored him.

The tactic did not work. The short man of bulky stature—perfect for any eight-man football running back position, he thought, repeated himself, only louder and with a more insistent tone of voice this time. The youth had a dark complexion and a round smiley-face which gave him the appearance of a "Pillsbury Doughboy." Was he merely pretending he was a tough-guy, and wise to the ways of the world, instead of being a junior college dropout or some delinquent reject from technical training school?

"Not for sale," Royce stated matter-of-factly, plainly and calmly, turning slightly to get a better angle on his antagonist, looking directly into his steady gaze and dull eyes. There is safety in numbers, Royce considered. Too many people around for trouble, he rationalized. He stepped up smartly to the cashier, paid for his soda and chips, and walked calmly outside, creating greater distance between himself and the other.

Moving quickly to his vehicle then, Royce got in, started the motor, and put the transmission in reverse to leave the scene immediately. That was when he noticed there were actually four young men in the green Monte Carlo, including the one who tried to strike up a conversation a moment ago, who had just returned and taken a back seat. Punks, he thought. A Sunday driver and his joyriding friends. Nothing to be taken seriously.

Across the busy boulevard at the next intersection was a branch office of Royce's bank. He had planned to withdrawal cash for his trip back to Texas there, having visited family and friends in Oklahoma for a few days. Now he had to go back to work. As he exited the empty teller-machine lobby and strolled to his car, he couldn't help but notice, of all things, the green Monte Carlo with the four occupants moving slowly forward, leering, almost prowling. They pulled up and stopped their car beside his vehicle. Their windows were all rolled down. They must have followed him over to the bank, it appeared. Royce climbed into his Chevrolet and rolled down his window, too. He smiled as if he were meeting old friends at "Walmart" by chance.

"What do you have under the hood?" one of them asked, the taller, slender, bucktooth passenger in the front seat, with a gold-plated incisor. His inquiry did not appear to be made in a menacing or threatening manner, but you never know how someone might react, if you say something rude, insulting, or terribly offensive. So, Royce wanted to be careful how he responded.

"A big V-8 engine," Royce replied pleasantly, not too smugly, hoping they wouldn't want to street-race for money. "And there are several notable safety and security features built right into the vehicle," he continued. "Standard issue." He let this information gradually sink in. There was no overt reaction by the other party. As long as they stayed in their vehicle the situation was cool. Nobody could accuse Royce of being modest and humble. Or shying away from trouble for that matter. He actually considered himself more of a Cowboy, than a top-rated NASCAR racing driver, which really meant that he could be counted on to drive fast if the need had arisen to get from point A to point B in an awful hurry, but he would rather roam around on the range.

Becoming much bolder and braver now, he suppressed the urge to grimace, groan, and growl. He stifled his trademark snarl, sneer, and howl. He thought of himself more as being among the rugged, trail-riding, cattle-driving cowboys who galloped horses across the silver screen and into the history books. So, no, he didn't want a drag race.

"See you around," said Bucktooth, postponing the inevitable.

"Not if I see you first," replied Royce.

They had obviously reached an impasse, a watershed moment in their daily lives. They might have reevaluated the situation or made a rapid risk-assessment, but nobody said another word when Royce grinned and calmly drove away at a leisurely pace through lively city streets, and onto the Broken Arrow expressway leading up to the turnpike gateway. He didn't expect them to follow. And they didn't.

Cruising in a westerly direction on the Interstate toward OKC, Royce pushed the speakerphone button on his beeping phone. "Good evening, Mr. Royce. Did you meet the backup unit?" he was asked.

"Greetings and salutations, Mr. Wright! Yes, I certainly did, but it was more of a confrontation. I wasn't made to feel overly enthusiastic by the enigmatic encounter with Destiny's children."

"They have been trained in undercover work, and they know the city."

"Bunko Squad definitely knows how to ruffle a fellow's feathers. But, at least they don't act like game rangers or look like rent-a-cops."

"Can you keep me informed when the deal goes through?"

"Sure, Chief. I always try to keep you in the loop. But, when you're up against organized crime and a crooked Ponzi scheme in a high-stakes poker game, you can't always predict end results.

When I read the *Collected Stories of Wallace Stegner*, published in 1990 and written between 1938 and 1990, I gasped almost in disbelief and concluded, "Truer words have never been written." I reflected on the group of them. Imaginative stories generally require a "suspension of belief," or so I'd heard, in order to get anything really meaningful out of them. But Wallace Stegner's tales ring true any way you shake them. They smack you like a fist-punch in the face. You feel as if you'd just been blindsided while talking on your portable telephone. You weren't watching where you were going and you blundered, walking directly into a corner-post column made of impervious six-by-six treated pine lumber. Knock on wood. Of the thirty-one stories in the book, I would estimate that over a dozen fall into the categories of most interesting, quite extraordinary, and unparalleled fiction-writing which is capable of captivating a wide range of audiences from coast to coast. The three that impressed me the most were "The Maiden in the Tower," because I like visiting my old haunts; "Women on the Wall," because I can relate to corresponding with loved ones over great distances; and "Blue-winged Teal," because I'm a sentimental and an incurable romantic. Of course, there's "Berry Patch," which is all you need to know about true love, in my opinion. The author included a longer story, "Genesis," which turned out to be a common-theme storyline for many an epic Western novel or Hollywood film about courageous cowboys.

Many of his stories are about growing up in the wilderness and have frontier settings. They are all about survival.

The stories I could least relate to, being from a mostly rural county, a proverbial hayseed of infinite possibility, depicted a sensible, moralistic photographer and his liberal-minded, idealistic, social-worker wife trying to convert their sprawling city into some form of perfect utopia and revitalized cosmopolitan metropolis, if not actually improving the living conditions there. My immediate reaction was, "Why are you wasting your time bringing losers home with you, trying to educate them? They're animals." On the other hand, eradicating them would be completely wrong, I suppose.

At the other end of the spectrum, the stories which involve living among high-society misfits and malcontents did not make much of a suitable impression on me or do anything to significantly improve my edification, either. These kinds of stories are not meant to inflate your ego or soothe your psyche. I merely believe that they are stories meant to be about living among wolves in sheep's clothing.

CHAPTER 34

Book review of

The Complete Stories of Truman Capote

by Truman Capote, published in 2004,
written between 1943-1983.

The big bird flew into a rage.

The big bird went berserk, absolutely bonkers. While great flapping crow wings beat furiously, mercilessly, ruthlessly and repeatedly against the tinted glass side window of the neighbors' new white Japanese import parked in their drive-way one hot, humid sunny summer day, a second crow which had been perched precariously on the edge of the garage roof peak observing every detail, swooped lazily, gracefully, effortlessly down, landed on the automobile roof to investigate the matter, and hopped around, wide-eyed and frantic in anticipation. R. Royce, who had just then walked outside his house to check his mail noticed, and immediately ran across the street and over to the vehicle to frighten them both away, thinking that they might scratch and damage it in their efforts to gain access to food or shelter. Within minutes after they had both flown away, he realized that the larger, overprotective male crow must have become inexplicably insanely jealous of his mate and had actually believed he spied another crow much like himself, a most formidable, territorial adversary, in the mirror of the car window. He flew into a rage. Essentially, he had been cock-fighting his own glass reflection.

Later that very afternoon, while tending the roses in his own backyard, Royce saw the female crow perched quietly on the electric wire suspended between two telephone poles, high above, pondering him in awe, watching him in wonder: how quickly and completely the man had resolved their conflict, making their terrible problem vanish into thin air. *When fools rush in*, she must have thought. Undoubtedly, they are highly intelligent, observant creatures and have very keen vision. On this particular day he would not have to "eat crow" for his sometimes callous actions and indiscrete, unprofessional behavior. After all, he was no birdbrain or idiot.

Which curiously and fondly reminded him of his childhood at Grandma Lea's:

You're a little kid at Grandma's house and you want to play in the muddy ditch filled with fresh rainwater and look for crayfish. She lets you explore these majestic surroundings to your heart's content. After a while, you want to go indoors for cornbread, chili beans, and fried potatoes she's prepared especially for you—and a buttered dinner roll with strawberry jam and milk for dessert. She lets you enter the house through the screen-door porch and glide across the linoleum-tiled kitchen, but only after spraying you down with water from a garden hose until you are squeaky clean. The tiny water-spray droplets sparkle and glisten, in contrast to the glorious blue sky. You are bathed in sunshine. You are barefoot, shirtless, wearing cutoff jeans. You feel overjoyed and comforted. You've seen the baby fawn, the pet racoon, and incredible swimming crustaceans.

A few days later, July 6, the story was different. He had made a serious error in judgment: he should have worn gardening gloves. Royce had been stung five times simultaneously, reaching into the dense foliage of an ornamental bush planted in his backyard, as he attempted to grasp a clump of tall marsh grass and pull the blades of grass up, roots and all. The waxy-leaf bush had grown and thrived near the verandah, but so had the tall grass. Instead, he stirred up a nest of angry red wasps. Several of them flew out from the bush unexpectedly, and he ran toward the house to avoid further retaliation, agitation, and complications. His hand stung with sharp pain and it swelled up tremendously for a few days. He put ice on the hand, and was very fortunate that he did not exhibit dangerous symptoms of allergic reaction. A week later he was basically back to normal, with some slight visible scarring.

The selections in *The Complete Stories of Truman Capote*, published in 2004 and written from 1943 to 1983, all exceptionally well-written, may be placed in four main categories: the family at home for the holidays; art and dreams; midlife crises; and appeals to healers. In the first category, I would put my all-time favorite, "A Christmas Memory," then the other fine gems, "Jug of Silver," "Children on Their Birthdays," "Thanksgiving Visitor," "One Christmas," and "My Side of the Matter."

In the second category, I would place "Headless Hawk," "Master Misery," and "House of Flowers."

In the third category, goes "Among the Paths to Eden," "A Mink of One's Own," "Shut a Final Door," "Preacher's Legend," and "The Bargain."

In the final category you might discover "A Tree of Night," "Diamond Guitar," "Mojave," "Miriam," "The Walls Are Cold," and "The Shape of Things."

You should be forewarned, however, substance abuse and alcoholism; pervasive, extreme poverty; and pockets of ignorance are common threads that run throughout the stories as a whole. On a positive note, you have been gifted with the southern sunbelt version of a loving, caring, god-fearing family not too unlike the ones depicted in "the Waltons" of mountainous West Virginia and the "Little House on the Prairie" of cornfed Iowa, seen in television reruns.

CHAPTER 35

Book review of the historical account of

Washington's Spies

by Alexander Rose, published in 2006.

A Capital Recipe for Horse and Buggy Intrigue.

R. Royce enjoyed a leisurely lunch late one morning at Fort Belvoir's dining facility in the spring of 1980. Two incidents happened on that particular Sunday that made it most memorable. First, a newly arrived uniformed MP took it upon himself to step forward to the front of the chow line, since he had been told by his peers that he could cut in front when on duty. Much to his chagrin and dismay, the other soldiers in line took exception to this policy. They did not exactly agree with his tactics and gave him considerable verbal abuse as a result. Several made insulting and derogatory comments in protest, while others waited patiently in line, as steamy food was being heaped onto his tray. Comments such as "Where do you think you're going, 'Lone Ranger'?" and "Heavy-Duty Harold has to hurry back to his super-hero comic book." and "In reality, he's picking up the Colonel's daughter at Falls Church in about an hour." could be heard.

The second incident occurred incidental to the All-Army Cooks Championship Baking Competition, about to be judged on that very day—in fact, that very afternoon. Supposedly, the esteemed panel of guests included high-ranking officials from the Pentagon. Photographers and journalists would cover the story, and several dignitaries would preside over the awards ceremony to follow. The event was a big deal for promoting community service. A sizeable area of the dining hall had been cordoned off and a few dozen lovely decorated cakes were lined up for display and inspection on tables covered with white linen tablecloths, ornately folded napkins, newly polished silverware, and gleaming stacks of fine china plates.

It so happened that the platoon of soldiers waiting in line in fatigue uniforms had only just returned from bivouac, where they had been camping out in the cold in pup-tents and running through several days of field training exercises. Really, they had been performing typically ordinary maneuvers, only in muddy terrain, under wet-weather conditions.

Wet-weather training reminded Royce of the time the Mechanized Infantry unit had driven their M60 Tank into a pond and promptly got it stuck in the muck. The recovery team had arrived onsite to pull it out using a complex block and tackle apparatus, composed of thick steel cables and multiple heavy pulleys. Royce had just returned to the field after CQ duty and noticed a single, solitary soldier standing alone near the crest of a hill at a considerable distance away from the others. Everyone else was standing up close and personal, surrounding the tank sunk in turret-depth muddy water, chatting and observing the process of extracting the tank from the pond.

"Who are you?" asked Royce. "And why are you standing way over here?"

"I'm the safety officer," the man explained, calmly. "I once saw somebody cut completely in two, by a broken steel cable that had whipped around and swashbuckled wildly in the air. Too much tension had been applied to the cable pulling 60 tons of machinery up a steep slippery slope."

Consequently, the platoon of soldiers trooped back to the military post weary and hungry for a hot meal, where they could sit-down in more comfortable surroundings, relax, and unwind. Only, somebody forgot to tell them about the Baking Contest. They didn't notice any off-limits signs, so naturally they went for the desserts after the main course. Several soldiers sliced themselves large, generous portions from over a dozen of the most beautifully decorated prize-winning cakes that Royce had ever seen in his entire life. If the cooks didn't want the cakes to be eaten, they should have posted a guard, he figured.

After lunch, Royce thought about going for a hike around the golf course to help digest the food he had eaten. Along the way, he thought about some of the tactics employed on maneuvers: parachuting out of an fixed-wing aircraft; rappelling down the side of a sheer cliff wall to the beach far below; traversing a rope bridge across the river valley; ziplining through the forest at treetop heights; feeling their way through mysterious caverns and underground tunnels; and wading through the swamp in chest-deep pools of water. Why couldn't they just for once canoe across a shallow, gently flowing pool of cool, sparkling clear water one lazy sunny afternoon with a cooler full of beer on ice. The effect on morale would be sheer poetry in motion.

After reading some of Alexander Rose's historical narrative in his book, *Washington's Spies*, published in 2006, I just couldn't resist writing a poem to commemorate the Declaration of Independence and the birth of our great nation. The title of the poem is "Washington's Pies."

It goes as follows:

> Simply put, Herman was a pie man
> And Washington's biggest fan.
> Quite an inquisitive fellow was he
> Sociable and pleasant as he could be.
> Toasting good company with tankards of ale
> The mission he accepted could not fail.
> The bakery goods he would carry
> Hid Revolutionary Wartime secrets moved by ferry.
> Apple pastry, rhubarb, berry
> Lemon meringue, pumpkin, cherry.
> While appearances can be deceiving
> What they say, seeing is believing.
> Ship-loads of soldiers were promised on the shore
> Fireworks celebrations, guaranteed galore.
> Ask him no questions, he'll tell you no lies;
> Boston's the place to look, if you're seeking spies.
> The next installment may seem deliciously free,
> But if you savor sweet peaches, shake not the tree.
> "Paul Revere is not here, as you can plainly see,"
> He would exclaim with vituperations and formally decree.

Alexander Rose's exceptionally well-documented book presents a factual and historical account of some of the events which helped shape the course of our early history in parts of the United States, specifically, during the time when Americans were colonial subjects ruled by King George and England, up to September 3, 1783, when the Treaty of Paris was signed. In other words, the book roughly covers the time period from the 1770s to the end of the Revolutionary War. Upon reading the book, you quickly get the distinct impression that certain individuals living in New York then had sensed the urgent need to get vital information to Washington, as soon as possible. And by Washington, the author was referring to the General of the Continental Army—the top military leader, not a specific place on a map. General Washington, himself, as well as his Army, was constantly on the move during those years, or on the run from the British Army.

There are other choice tidbits of information which the author presents or to which he alludes, including the fact that the community of Long Island, New York, must have been quite a "hotbed of political activity." Indeed, the good friends, neighbors, and pillars of the community living there were completely surrounded, thoroughly infiltrated, and totally inundated by " 'taters and traitors."

"'Taters?" you ask. Sure: dictators, agitators, and facilitators. The dictators were King George and the military leaders of the oppressive British Army and Navy representing him in the Colonies. Martial law had been imposed and was in full effect. The British military was the predominant occupying force there. Not everybody was happy with the unpopular laws that were enacted, and many of the king's "brave new world" subjects became unruly and rebellious.

The agitators were a terrible grab-bag assortment of pirates, privateers, profiteers, robbers, thieves, arsonists, looters, smugglers, and counterfeiters. Many acted as common criminals, but some were sanctioned by the military. Most actions could be attributed to a long series of war-related complications, consequences, repercussions, and reprisals. To make matters worse, there was an incredible amount of retribution and retaliation.

Facilitators were legitimate tradesmen and businessmen. They were buyers and sellers of commercial goods and those who provided services. They were the ones most likely to follow the rules and obey the laws. But factions of them were also members of the Continental Army and the Continental Congress, Whigs, pacifist Quakers, and other normally peaceful religious groups. Individuals from these groups wanted to create a free and independent nation. They wanted representative government. Hence, the friction that ensued during those difficult years of social strife and civil unrest.

Traitors? Benedict Arnold was mentioned, and the party that exposed him and tried to turn him in, was identified in the book. Then, there were several members of a large political contingent of Tories, known as Loyalists—those loyal to England and King George. These Loyalists were perhaps less well known to history, if known at all, but they gave many of the local inhabitants quite a scare on occasion.

Finally, there were what I would refer to as the "perpetrators." These were government officials, diplomats, and military leaders from two extraneous countries: France and Spain. They were not exactly disinterested parties to the proceedings. Evidently, the Continental Congress had obtained many of their farfetched and revolutionary ideas from France. They were also assured of much needed military support from this country. Spain, on the other hand, being much more conservative, kept its distance and had its own ideas about involvement in the "New World."

People from Spain began settling in and developing what would eventually become valuable winter-vacation real estate and resort property in such diverse places as Florida, Mexico, and the Caribbean Islands. I believe, the people from this country had the most insightful and far-reaching influence in the Western Hemisphere up to that time. Not that their conquistadors were among the most beloved arrivals. Of course, because all of this is not explicitly or expressly spelled out in the book, I may be going off on a tangent in expressing my own opinion. There remains this certainty: within a couple of centuries later, North America would be carved up and parceled out like a full-grown Thanksgiving Day turkey at dinnertime.

CHAPTER 36

Book review of

The Romanovs 1613-1918

by Simon Sebag Montefiore, published in 2016.

How many Feberge eggs were commissioned during the reign of Tsars Alexander III and Nicholas II? The book tells you. Imagining a "Hillary the Great" or "Donald the Terrible" invasion is as inevitable as insidious, irresponsible journalism.

R. Royce asked his good friend and retired former boss why he enjoyed shopping at Harp's, having located him there, placing paper bags of groceries in the trunk of his British racing green fastback Shelby Mustang. "I like the neighborhood, it rhymes with Earps, and I am after all is said and done basically a law-and-order man."

"You certainly know how to stay under the radar after an operation. Reclusive and as elusive as a submariner. There's no telling where or when you might surface. By the way, how did you come up with your new identity?" asked Royce.

"Simple. I was minding my own business, driving a long and winding stretch of highway somewhere in Kansas, passing acres and acres of wheat fields, when I happened to spy the galvanized gray metal spout of a tall grain-elevator filling a semi-truck trailer, shooting out a steady jet-stream of dried golden corn kernels, reflecting and scintillating magnificently in the warm afterglow of afternoon sunshine. Hence, the name, 'Colonel Korn.' "

"A decent and respectable name if I ever heard one, the difference between ordinary glass and fine crystal. You flick the rim of the beer glass with your finger-nail and all you get is a dull thud. You flick the rim of the crystal vase, and you hear a chorus of musical notes, a heavenly ringing vibration, the humming sound of a tuning fork, clanging wind chimes, a strumming guitar chord."

"I'm thinking about dropping the 'Colonel.' How does 'Korn Pone' grab you? Or 'Korn Cobb'?"

"Not too flaky, now that you've gone and re-invented yourself," quipped Royce. Do you remember the time you wanted to meet up at 'Cowboys,' the truck-stop in Atlanta, at midnight?" Royce asked Korn.

"Sure do, but the name had been changed."

"I went into a highway cafe on the route for directions, only none of the patrons ever heard of the place. Fortunately, a lovely, young waitress overheard me and exclaimed, 'I know where you can find Cowboys in Atlanta.' It was the new '76' Station at the next exit." Royce had come a long way from selling silk-screen muscle car T-shirts out of the trunk of his classic Dodge at the beach somewhere along the Atlantic coast of Florida.

Back at Korn's house, Royce prepared a steaming plate of tasty fried potatoes from an old family recipe. He expertly peeled, sliced, and diced a large baking potato and put the bits and pieces into a hot Teflon-coated skillet over a melted pat of margarine. Next, he added a generous, finely chopped mixture of fresh, firm orange bell pepper, mushroom, and sweet onion. He sprinkled on a pinch of sea salt and some ground pepper, then fried the food over medium heat for several minutes, turning the potatoes every so often with a spatula to keep them from burning, until they were golden brown and ready to serve.

Having relaxed over a cigar and a snifter of cognac each, Royce asked Korn plainly and matter-of-factly, without mincing his words too much, "Now that the small-talk is out of the way, where is my half of the proceeds from the last business transaction?"

Colonel Korn stood up from his overstuffed cushion on the colorful flowery divan. He calmly walked into the study and returned momentarily with a leather briefcase. He handed it to Royce, without any reservation or hesitation on his part whatsoever. "The client was pleased that we recovered his funds," he said.

"At 110% return on investment, he should be," replied Royce, hoisting the case as he abruptly stood up from the comfortable plaid Scotch-guard fabric armchair in which he sat. The broker was not one to renege on what he personally considered to be the deal of the century.

"Now would be an excellent time for a long vacation," said Korn, jovial, knowingly, his eyes gleaming benevolently.

Simon Sebag Montefiore's historical account of *The Romanovs 1613-1918*, published in 2016, was a long, difficult book to read and digest. You have to be patient and persevering if you want to get through all of the material. There's a lot of information inside, fine-print and footnotes. How many Faberge eggs were commissioned during the reign of Alexander III and Nicholas II? The book tells all. It's not too dry, and the reading is worthwhile, in my opinion. Including a wealth of information, you learn a great deal about early Russia, about which most people in America have no idea and probably never will. As a pleasant diversion, and to keep myself alert during the full two weeks I spent reading the book in installments, I stopped periodically to watch the full seven seasons of *Mad Men* on television, one DVD disc at a time, one sequential episode after another. Doing so really brought the book material to life and kept me interested and motivated.

It just so happens that the executives from the television series behaved just like the Romanov family might have, had they been part of a corporate advertising family in NYC, rather than a family of tsars from the annals of Russian history. Like I say, it would have been a lively comparison from which you may draw your own conclusions.

In either instance, the story they told would make an incredible bill-board advertisement for a better way of life. You almost want to shout out, "Skip the drama, mamma, and get to the point." The characters were driven by a surfeit of success and excess. They have acquired power, wealth, and influence—and not too strangely, they wanted more. Yet, they discover that they can't deal with the responsibility of stepping on other people's toes. Their lives become a vicious circle, a dog chasing his tail. They become frustrated and angry. They seek peace of mind, and life somehow gets better. For a time.

The parallels between the premier advertising agency of the 1960s - 1970s and the Romanov dynasty lasting three centuries are indeed striking to say the least. But what is the bottom line? Advertising executives and the Romanov Tsars alike were selling products they believed the people wanted to buy. All any of them really wanted was someone who appreciates the finer things in life. In charge, they were convincing. In uncertain, or perilous times, convinced. Beans or bullets. Feast or famine.

A more contemporary parallel example of the Romanovs' story? Imagining "Hillary the Great" or "Donald the Terrible" in their place, or in similar present circumstances, invasion is just as inevitable as insidious, inept, and irresponsible journalism. They conquer the same territory. We survive, and the world turns.

CHAPTER 37

Book review of

The Lamplighter

a novel by Anthony O'Neill, published in 2003.

A fundamentally flawed philosophical argument of Biblical proportions in an epic battle of good versus evil, implicating a conspiracy of religion, psychology, and medicine.

Genuinely supernaturally terrifying and spooky stuff, that may well scare the hell right out of you.

"Better to light one candle than to curse the darkness."

"You aren't really Steven King, are you?"

"What must I do to convince you of my true identity? Write my name in blood?"

What has R. Royce gotten himself into this time?

The Lamplighter, a novel by Anthony O'Neill, published in 2003, is a gothic, tall tale about a vibrant, bustling, progressive-minded community in 19th-century industrial-age Edinburgh, Scotland. The devil of a "bad influence" moves into the neighborhood, and local residents try everything within their power and everything they can think of in order to evict the responsible tenants. Eventually, they do, but at what steep tariff? The very foundation of their deeply held beliefs, their towering faith and firm resolve has been shaken and put to the test in the process.

A scant generation later, during this "age of enlightenment," several seriously vicious and deadly crimes begin to haunt the humble and normally peaceful, law-abiding inhabitants, disrupting their otherwise tranquil lives. Chaos reigns in the city, as more of the crimes occur, and the murders continue to baffle the police and terrify the citizens. Not superheroes in any way, shape or form, three unlikely detectives match wits against a most formidable adversary. They band together in a tacitly accepted alliance and take up the challenge to unmask the mysterious presence lurking in the fog and in the shadows. They embark on a search and destroy mission one cold, dark night in a gallant attempt to save the city from its plight, in what must appear to be an epic battle of good versus evil. But in the end, the results they have achieved all seem to point to a big, long philosophical argument that they have perpetuated among themselves while attempting to solve a "cold case" and bring the instigators to justice.

Exactly, what has R. Royce gotten himself into this time? At present, he has become the sole owner and exclusive, authorized dealer for a treasure trove of valuable ornaments and unusual artifacts in the form of a baker's dozen of "knock-off" hand-painted porcelain eggs. At first glance, from the outside, you see the bright, shiny, colorful shell of an ordinary hard-boiled Easter egg. But, if you were to key and crack one open, then look inside, you would be dazzled, tantalized, and mesmerized by the marvelous diorama display of truly magnificent and unique, highly crafted, artistic design features. The contents of each unassuming egg reveal an antiquity in miniature made of precious gold, platinum, and fine, rare jewels not seen anywhere else in the world. Each one, priceless and fit for the ruler of an empire—if, indeed, authentic; that is, the genuine article.

So, how has this incredible turn of events come to pass? One day, a certain Mr. K. Cobb having a sterling international reputation, but considered somewhat of a rogue and eclectic, placed a Styrofoam insulated carton of these eggs in the back of a locked, secured, and well-lighted glass display case, away from prying eyes, which was situated in a booth-space which he stocked with the cluttered odd assortment of various dusty antique glassware, wooden furniture, and vintage collectibles, and rented from a local flea market vendor.

Unbeknownst to the vendor, however, while he could have sold any number of the eggs to a "valued" customer for $199 each; generally, a cost-prohibitive amount to pay to the "average" buyer, for such a so-called generic enamel-painted ceramic egg placed on a dull lead-weight pedestal, Cobb on the other hand would sell the corresponding catalog-egg key to the "knowledgeable" buyer for close to a hundred thousand dollars, made payable in advance in cash directly to he, himself. In theory, it was a win-win business deal all the way around for such quality merchandise.

Except, unbeknownst to Mr. Cobb, one of the eggs also contained a tiny nested blue porcelain Robin's egg, into which was secreted an even tinier memory chip, which held the digital file of a treasure map, readily downloadable to pc. The map would lead adventurers to a lost, buried national treasure of real, genuinely priceless Faberge eggs, as once commissioned by Tsar Alexander, and spirited away by some of his more conservative and enterprising descendants, who shall forever remain anonymous. So, how did R. Royce become involved in a caper of such great magnitude?

An avid junk collector, who thinks that he "knows a good bargain when he sees one," walked into the shop unannounced that very same afternoon, and purchased the egg that contained the egg that contained the map. Later, in the privacy of his own home, he cracked them both open without the benefit of a key. You might say he took a wild chance on the item, then, and had it evaluated by a qualified "Antiques Road Show" appraiser for a confirmed estimate of its true worth. Afterwards, he found a trustworthy buyer through a broker, who turned out—lo and behold—to be the very same, inimitable Mr. Korn Cobb. Like they say in the business world, "What goes around, comes around."

Royce modestly stated afterwards, "I don't necessarily get paid for what I do, but I do get paid for what I know."

CHAPTER 38

Book review of the historical fiction novel

Airshipmen

by David Dennington, published in 2015.

Full of hot air.
What happens when the balloon goes up?

Cornelius Cobb has stumbled onto something unbelievable: "Secure Net." Typical for him, he makes the most of it. "Do you know where the farthest most advanced CPUs are now manufactured?" he asked R. Royce. Cornelius was an educated man. He once attended college at Cornell.

"Tough question, Korn," said Royce, in reply to his longtime good friend, addressing him by his nickname. "Could be in any number of cities around the globe. Tokyo, Hong Kong, Singapore, Chicago, San Francisco, even San Jose, Costa Rica."

"Try Dresden."

"What difference does it make? They're all fast computer chips now. They all power, drive, and operate the PC when it's connected to the internet. None of them are that much faster or more powerful these days. Playing fantasy video games is their main purpose in life.

"Maybe so, but the Dresden computer with their latest version CPU, aptly named 'Recluse Spider,' simply can't be hacked. Operating with stealth pico-nano layered technology and broadband digital fiber optics, it is too technologically advanced for any of the other chip makers to reverse engineer," explained Cornelius. "Connect a Spider PC to the worldwide web and it's virtually invisible and indestructible. Signal encryption and filtering is achieved at the subatomic particle level, and masking or redirecting signals hide the optically filtered signal altogether. You won't need antivirus software to monitor and check for machine errors either. The Spider chip is completely error-free and totally reliable, with built-in 'fail safe' technology embedded into its micro-circuitry."

"Sounds impressive, doesn't it. In other words, a 'Mickey Mouse' signal conceals the real-deal information. An ordinary PC displays a 'Goofy' cartoon and you get a 'puzzle palace' of covert operations," stated Royce. He'd seen the brochure. "Can you order a dozen units right away?" asked Royce. "We'll call our new startup venture 'Security Net Live.' "

"You might as well tell your clients that they can kiss 'freedom of information' goodbye forever," replied Cobb.

"What happens if one of the Spiders falls into the wrong hands?" asked Royce.

"The Spider Network is 'fail-safe,' but not 'fool-proof,'" stated Cobb. "What more can I tell you?"

"Can I put a Spider PC in undisguised mode, unmasked and uncloaked, as it were, when I want to connect with musician, novelist, and movie-star celebrity-chat sites? You've heard of surf and turf? I surf and text."

"As I said before, the system is not completely foolproof. You should use a Spider only for its intended purpose. Strictly business. You wouldn't normally cruise main street in a formula-one car for a burger and milkshake at the local 'Sonic' drive-in the night before racing the Indianapolis 500, would you?"

"Is that what you think the IBM engineer from rural Missouri did with his programmable proto-type circuit board? Word on the street is mobsters would have caught up with him eventually over a supposedly bogus exorbitant gambling debt, had he not gone to prison on murder charges."

"Unfortunately so. Innocent people were swindled in the scam. To make matters worse, close friends of his were robbed and killed, when the couple's home was ransacked during a home invasion. Valuable items were recovered from a pawn shop in town. But, there may be another unrelated explanation for these events," suggested Cobb.

"Let me take a wild guess," said Royce. "An undisclosed foreign field intelligence service was after his computer equipment. They wanted the design and blueprints, for some nefarious reason, such as wanting to wreak havoc on our well-functioning and perfectly fine-tuned capitalistic free-enterprise system. The murder was incidental collateral damage, nothing more than a red herring."

"It could be that they are still seeking this kind of technology. Shortly afterwards, a dance-club manager died suddenly under similar suspicious circumstances in the same area. While the two clubs he managed have ties to racketeering, the FIS could actually have been covering their tracks. A new group from Chicago has already moved into the vicinity and took over the business. The real culprits are most likely back in their condominiums in sunny Miami, cooling their heels, hoping and praying somebody doesn't spill the beans on them; or frijoles, as the case may be."

The very next day, R. Royce flew to Florida aboard a charter aircraft to snoop out additional information. He rented a compact automobile at the executive airport, then booked a motel room in Fort Lauderdale, just across A1A from the Atlantic Ocean. Following a good night's sleep, he awoke early fresh and alert. He inserted a Bond-movie music CD into the rental car's disc player and drove to South Beach in Miami, where he parked on a side street. Then he went for a leisurely stroll toward the sound of cascading ocean waves an hour before sunrise, keeping a sharp lookout for sea-turtle-egg poachers among the mangroves, Brazilian pepper trees, and dense clumps of tall grasses.

"Who goes there?" inquired Royce, suddenly.

"The Mayor of Miami Beach and I live here," said a man wearing baggy cargo shorts, T-shirt, and boat shoes, who'd just stepped out of the shadows and into the clearing, onto a barren sandy dune. "You're the one who is trespassing and transgressing."

"Is that a fact? This is a public beachfront," replied Royce. He tensed his muscles in preparation of lunging at him, and would have wrestled him to the ground, had he had a legitimate reason to carry out such an act of aggression. The fleet-footed, slender stranger appeared to be friendly, at ease, and cooperative, however. He did not brandish any weapons. Nor did he attempt to intimidate Royce with flagrant, open hostility and harsh words, which might have escalated the situation. Instead, he became docile and subdued. But he wasn't exactly a happy puppy.

"The cafe across from Penrod's is open. We can grab a cup of coffee and have a quiet, uninterrupted breakfast there," the man said amicably.

"Lead on," said Royce.

At a corner table in the cafe, they ordered omelets and stacks of pancakes. They drank coffee while they waited for their breakfasts. They surveyed the dining room. There was not much business going on that early on Sunday morning. The beach clubs had all closed down, and their patrons had gone home to sleep it off. Somewhere somebody blissfully satisfied was dreaming about a beautiful woman bedded down for the night, if not for the duration.

"You've heard what happened to John in Springfield?" Royce asked, after a slug of coffee.

"They say he had a heart attack," the man said.

"John was as healthy as a horse. In the prime of life," replied Royce.

"Wasn't he trying to sell computer software in his spare time, as a sideline? It's a competitive market, you know. Maybe the pressure got to him."

"What kind of software?" asked Royce. "Video games?"

"Nothing quite so imaginative or inventive," said the man. "I believe it was a quick and effective program that searches through corporate financial data. Something to do with business profits and earnings."

"No wonder his days were numbered. 'The Kiss of Doom,' mixing high finance business and pleasure the way he did," said Royce. "Do you know who bought the program from him?"

"Sorry. I think we've reached the end of the line with him," said the beachcomber. Every one of his known associates have been apprehended and arrested by the FBI. Something to do with megabucks credit card fraud."

"Guess I'll have a heart-to-heart chat with Rene, next," said Royce. In the winter of her discontent, when he needed her most, the rose froze, but he believed in her looming potential still. The flame was not to blame. Deer-hunting season was fast approaching, and the dame was game. "There is some life in the old girl yet," he muttered.

"So, you're thinking about moving your business to Chicago?"

"To get through the tough times and lean years, as we both know from years of experience and hardship, it certainly pays well to expand and diversify."

The Airshipmen, a historical novel by David Dennington, published in 2015, was as incredible and interesting as the science and technology that went into the production and flight of the massive high-flying, lighter-than-air dirigibles during the late 1920s and early 1930s in Great Britain. While not nearly as aerodynamic, supersonic fast, or highly maneuverable as other flying machines, to be built in the later eras of aviation history, they did offer elements of beauty, grace, and poetry in motion. Back then, the rare and unique "Zeppelin" appeared singularly in the sky as a spectacularly gigantic carnival-circus creation which is rivalled today only by the floating 'Disney' characters sailing above and meandering through the heavily populated streets of New York City, suspended by long ropes in their traverse, during Macy's Thanksgiving Day and Christmas parades, and, of course, by the distant "Goodyear Blimp" floating as quietly and unobtrusively as a peaceful, pastoral, and puffy cumulus cloud suspended far above the much too pre-occupied crowd of spectators at a Super Bowl stadium. Oddly enough, the whale-size blimp has the same basically ellipsoidal shape as an ordinary handheld football. But the blimp isn't supposed to spin, or spiral through the air like a football does as it flies through the skies. Which is not to say that it couldn't spin. For example, should NASA someday become inspired and decide that the best means of travel through the vast empty void of outer-space from Earth to Mars would be in a Zeppelin. Then, our astronauts and future colonists would be able to carry their own atmosphere and air supply with them to the new planet. Who knows? They could even fill Zeppelins with fresh water. We know how much fun "water balloons" can be.

CHAPTER 39

Review of the book

The Billion Dollar Spy

by David E. Hoffman, published in 2015.

The man definitely knew his squat thrusters, gyro-casters, and gravitons.
   One disgruntled federal employee in the military-industrial complex can ruin your whole day.

R.oyce lived in Aurora, Colorado, as a boy in the summer of 1965. Oftentimes he wandered and meandered aimlessly through the paved side-streets and cobblestone alleyways off Colfax Avenue, searching for "castaways"—namely, empty glass soda-pop bottles worth 2 cents each for the deposit refund at "Gorman's Supermarket," which was situated on the corner of Fulton. Sometimes he used the money he earned to buy a small waxy-white paper sack of broken cookies from "Pratzel's Bakery." Or maybe an ice cream cone, three scoops for a dime at "Jimmy's Frozen Desserts." Or maybe go to "Woolworth's" with April for penny candy. No wonder the Shamrocks' little leaguer called him "snaggle-tooth," forever eating sweet snacks and treats; undoubtedly, the leading cause of tooth-decay. He didn't say it in a derogatory or demeaning manner. "The tooth was going to fall out anyway," Royce rationalized, as he sped away on a stingray bicycle with the ape-hanger handlebars and banana seat. To add insult to injury, he wouldn't discover that he was nearsighted and couldn't see very far away, until four years later, when he couldn't read the scoreboard from the bleachers at a baseball game in Oklahoma. It was a wonder how he ever caught Schofield's practice pitches on the front lawn.

Once, the Altura trailer-court manager saw him walking downtown, crossing his path. Old Man Sealy called out and immediately attracted Royce's attention, saying, "Look what I found!" as he reached into the cavernous depths of one of his deep, baggy pants pockets and extracted a round, smooth disk-shaped nugget. R. had been impressed by the shining glint in his eye and the gleaming golden metal object he held out. His dad and Mr. Sealy sometimes went panning for unusual stones in the mountain streams.

Early mornings, Royce and Schofield would catch the uptown bus to Denver to pick up a supply of several half-dozen-size packages of freshly baked glazed donuts from "Mr. Doughnut," then sell them to people they encountered along the return route as they played and walked back home. Typically, they sold out every day, and made a tidy profit that summer.

Sometimes on Saturday afternoons, they would go to the movies at the Fox Theater with the other kids in the neighborhood. They would all be seated together in the same center row, their wide eyes big and fixed on the enormous silver screen in anticipation of something wonderful or incredible. They saw flashy beach movies and wild western shoot-outs. They became Annette Funicello and Wyatt Earp fans. Surprisingly, Frankie Avalon appeared "live" in person on the theater stage during intermission one day. He talked about the best time of his life. At the time, most of the kids did not realize that he was actually the film star they had just seen in the movie they had just watched. *They were just too young and innocent to make the connection,* he thought, years later. It was then and there in that mostly empty void of an afternoon matinee movie theater, the sudden realization that "all is fair in love and politics" began to dawn on him.

Royce's mother would make batches of popping-corn for them, filling up half of the large brown-paper grocery bag for the kids to carry into the show as a healthy snack. Decades later, when Royce visited "the old neighborhood" to see if any of the neighbors were still living there, he saw Schofield, all grown up now, who'd asked if Royce's mom still makes the same tasty bacon-grease-flavored popcorn that she did when they were kids. Royce said, "Probably so." Anticipating a cautionary tale, he went on to say that he doesn't go to the theater and pay the price of admission in silver dollars anymore.

When I first began reading the Hoffman book, I immediately thought that the story could just as well have been about Edward Snowden, the former

NSA federal employee who fled the U.S. not too terribly long ago, wandered around the world, and wound up in Russia. He was the person in the news who had exported a boatload of top-secret, classified, and otherwise confidential information when he left. It just goes to show you how one disgruntled employee can ruin your whole day. Instead of snapping photographs of official documents with some sort of miniature "Kodak" spy camera and passing along rolls of unexposed film to dubious, shadowy characters, he must have quite simply uploaded umpteen tera-bytes of sensitive computer files at a time to the worldwide web, also known as "the internet," in a matter of seconds all in his spare or leisure time, posting them to anonymous "clouds" of data, the files fully accessible by anyone, anywhere in the world almost instantaneously by email. Then it dawned on me, "His book will never be published in Russia." The reason is because Russian leaders greatly value their secrets of state, their own privacy and confidentiality much, much more highly than the right of the people to know. In fact, sadly enough, I seriously doubt if anyone in the West will hear from him ever again.

The Billion Dollar Spy, by author David E. Hoffman, published in 2015, is a well-documented, nonfictional account of CIA and KGB intelligence-gathering activities and collaboration in Moscow and Washington, D.C., during the 1980s, which culminated in the U.S. invasion of the Persian Gulf in 1991, all of which has had tremendous repercussions and consequences felt even today—like the aftershocks of a major earthquake. As we all know, when diplomacy fails, military action often takes its place, as the military-industrial complex "marshals their forces."

From what the average person may conclude from reading this book, standard U.S. military equipment, such as fighter aircraft has vastly increased its range and capability, since U.S. experts have been looking over the shoulders, as it were, of Soviet engineers, scientists, and technicians to see what they have on their drawing boards and have built into prototypes, newly created designs, mockups, and working models. Then, they have reverse-engineered these "virtual reality" creations into their own uniquely superior fabrications, overcoming newly found deficiencies, and exploiting now-known weaknesses and flaws.

As proof of this "American ingenuity," the author cites the overwhelming success of the U.S. military when they invaded Kuwait and Iraq in the Persian

Gulf War. True, the F-15 fighters might have destroyed Russian-built MIGs dog-fighting in the open skies above Iraq, but the statistics fail to consider a few key facts: First, the Iraqi pilots were undoubtedly inadequately trained and the MIGs they were flying were most likely improperly maintained, underpowered, and without the latest technology available and critical equipment aboard, including missiles, guidance systems, and adequate radar defense mechanisms. You'd think, if they fly military aircraft, they must know their squat thrusters, gyro-casters, and gravitons! Apparently, what they flew were military aircraft suitable only for air-shows and parades, and then to be flown only with an abundance of caution out of concern for the safety and welfare of pilots and spectators alike.

So, if the premise is true, that the U.S. military establishment stole their advanced equipment designs from the Russians, then it obviously follows that the Russian spy who sold the CIA this type of information, must have given it away with the blessing of the KGB, since they would have known well in advance that the F-15s would eventually be opposed by the MIGs of Iraq and a bold, brash, and brazen Saddam Hussain. The Russian intelligence community merely wanted to sit back and watch the ensuing fireworks and observe the most advanced fighter planes the world has ever seen in wartime action against their obsolete MIGs out of pure curiosity. After all, high-stakes poker players don't usually go around showing their hands to everyone they meet.

CHAPTER 40

Book review of the autobiography

Good Vibrations:
The Story of a Beach Boy

by Mike Love with James S. Hirsch, published in 2016.

Oh, look what washed up on the beach!
 A most curious, gigantic, brilliantly colored deep-ocean sunfish washed up on the beach one day.
 BB's Greatest Hits Volume 1 favorites list: 3, 5, 6, 9, 12, 13, 14, 15, 17, 19

R. Royce was tooling down the highway in his red 1976 Chevy Malibu, with the quintessential, unassuming white vinyl top without a care in the world, when he stuck a "Delaney and Bonnie" cartridge in the 8-track tape player factory-built into the dash. He was contemplating about how he could have made something of himself in life.

Take music, for instance. He could have taught a course in music appreciation at the community college. He was very knowledgeable about a variety of trendy sounds from pop and country to classical. But, alas, he was also a classically under-rated underachiever. For sure, he might have lacked the necessary qualities of ambition, self-discipline, motivation, focus, and several other positive traits normally exhibited by highly successful professionals, entrepreneurs, and businessmen in their field. So what?

Instead, on a whim, he decided to go and see the ocean firsthand for himself. He'd find a decent job that pays at least minimum wage when he arrived.

He planned on spending the winter in a warmer climate than North Dakota for a change.

A week later, he pulled the car into a vacant parking spot at "Wendy's" off A1A, directly opposite the Atlantic Ocean. He calmly strolled over to the rectangular metal box vending machine, chained to a light-pole, put two quarters into the slot, and extracted a recent edition of the local daily newspaper. He walked into the fast-food restaurant, bought a combo meal, then sat down to read, eat, and watch the waves roll in. He felt an undeniable sense of exhilaration and exoneration sweep over him. Having rapidly skimmed the wanted ads, he turned back to the front page. He was astounded by what he saw. No, dumbfounded would be a more accurate description. A mysterious, gigantic, brilliantly colored sheeny iridescent blue and intensely yellow deep-ocean sunfish had washed up on a sunny, sandy dry grassy dune at Melbourne Beach, sporting an enigmatic smiley-face. Most curious, the rarely seen creature was about thirty feet tall and only four feet long. A bizarre sight indeed! He wondered what the big fish would weigh. How would you reel one in? Then, spontaneously, "What was he thinking?" said Royce aloud to no one in particular. He looked more closely at his sandwich. "Probably about 'the other white meat,' shark."

Good Vibrations: My Life as a Beach Boy, by Mike Love with James S. Hirsch, was published in 2016. It's an eye-opener! The autobiography tells an interesting story about the life of a rock-and-roll musician and member of the famous California group known all over the world, since the 1960s as "The Beach Boys." The group has sold millions of record albums and appeared in thousands of concerts in practically every major venue over the past fifty years. They are just as popular today as they were in the beginning. Their songs about fast cars, cute girls in bikinis, and surfing have spanned the generations and become timeless in their appeal. Their music is about feeling good. What more can be said about it? Informative and insightful, the book is better than any ordinary "kiss and tell" expose or the average, run-of-the-mill "kick donkey and take names" action-thriller novel currently out there. You quickly learn that these guys never had anything to prove, other than they always had the right equipment available for a trip to the beach: shorts, t-shirt, floppy hat, sunglasses, flip-flops, a towel. When they became rich and famous, everyone wanted in on the act and a piece of the pie. They dealt with it and went on living their lives. They continued to crank out the tunes. They sought enlightenment. They had families to support.

You know the songs you like best and you can play them over and over again, in high-fidelity, digitally remastered, theater-quality surround-sound. Having a holographic "IMAX" experience is even in the realm of possibility. And one of these days, when you most feel like "catching a wave," you might just run out on the spur of the moment and see the band "live" in concert somewhere not too far away.

CHAPTER 41

Review of

Night Games
and Other Stories and Novella

by Arthur Schnitzler, published in English in 2002.

Freudian analysis over a friendly game of poker and other harmless pursuits.
Virtue and vice in a decadent society.

R. Royce stood before the Royal Gorge and saw two protruding peaks; looming in the distance, the Garden of the Gods, as he opened his eyes and remembered fragments of a powerful, poignant dream. Sometimes, he had a difficult time distinguishing myth from legend. Apostle from disciple. "Then came Bronson," Christian biker. He tried to iron out the wrinkles. A boy who fell out of a tree. A friend who lived to tell the story. Something right out of *A Separate Peace*.

He turned on the television with the remote. "This is how I rip wood stock with a rip saw," explained the carpenter to his rapt, obviously enthralled studio audience. Momentarily shocked into silence, Royce muted the sound. He might just as easily have been a magician sawing a wooden box with his beautiful lady assistant inside in half.

He thought about "triple-A." Not the roadside assistance people. Not the military's anti-aircraft artillery unit. Something a colleague once told him long ago: "What every individual needs in order to grow and develop into a fully functional professional human being is 'achievement, affiliation, and an award.'"

He reflected on the Sunday morning cartoons of yesteryear. "Rocky and Bullwinkle." "Mr. Magoo." "Dudley Do-right." "Tudor Turtle," who would inevitably, desperately, and frantically call out for "Mr. Wizard" to rescue him from all harm, before it is too late.

The Wizard, then, would begin to chant an alliterative incantation, which concludes with reassuring words to the effect that the matter has been ultimately, immediately, and completely resolved. The turtle is able to live another day due to some form of divine intervention. And so, he saves the troubled tortoise from certain disaster."

The candlelit figure of a man appeared, suddenly materializing from out of the shadows. He held out a large, shiny steel, rectangular-shaped meat cleaver. Royce immediately felt threatened and intimidated; then, oddly, he interpreted the finely handcrafted, wooden-handled object as an offering, a present, if you will; a choice of weapon for dueling. He began to shudder. A duel with the "Grim Reaper."

"No thanks," he said. "I have my own." He brandished two flourishing, but obscure instruments, each having enchanting pearl handles. They radiated, shimmered, and gleamed with fluorescent white light—a stiletto-cross in his right hand, a switchblade in the left.

The next night, Royce was transported to Wrigley Field in Chicago for the seventh and final, deciding game of the World Series. The stadium was filled to capacity with bright, incandescent lights and cheering spectators. "Out!" heard Royce, loudly from some distance away. Then, again, only bellowing in baritone, much closer, and more distinctly this time—"Out! In that instant, he awoke. He considered the ordeal as an omen of banishment. Haunted, perhaps, but he would live to fight another day.

Night Games and other Stories and Novella, written by Arthur Schnitzler, who lived from 1862-1931, was translated from the German and published in English in 2002. The collection of stories includes nine selections. Any prominent psychologist of the era must have loved this contemporary author's stories, since he delved so deeply into the mind of his characters. To summarize most succinctly, the stories are about love and death.

Upon reading the stories, in which one of the characters abruptly "passes away," you begin to realize that the tragedy may not be so much the death itself, per se, but the life he's led, which may seem kind of ironic. You get the impression that the life he's led was a total lie. All he ever believed in was a total falsehood. He's been shaken to the very core of his being in the instant of revelation. The stories are bizarre, to say the least. To make matters even worse, the character attempts to answer the burning question, "Was it really love, or was I only dreaming?"

On the other hand, one could present a valid argument that these stories were actually meant to be more about the suspect values and beliefs harbored by rising middle-class professionals in Austrian society in the early 1900s, than about 'love and death.' To drive the point home, one could continue to argue that the stories take on the complete persona, the personality and psyche of an accomplished, well-known, well-respected physician, who encounters and views with surgical precision the complete spectrum of modern society in the course of his busy existence. Throughout his daily activities, he encompasses the lives of the unfortunate masses (the impoverished, untrained, slothful, non-productive, and those exhibiting symptoms of as yet undiagnosed illnesses or infirmities); the laboring worker bees; the self-improving, self-perpetuating middle-class; and the wealthiest upper crust, the seat of power.

The story plots are simple and straightforward. For example, a medical doctor goes out late one night to make a house call at the home of a sick and dying acquaintance. Afterwards, by chance, he sees an old friend. He accompanies him to observe a festive pagan ritual nearby. When he returns home very late and awakens his wife, he learns that she's been dreaming about the very same thing. He decides suddenly and momentously, that he wants to investigate the matter further. In the meanwhile, he dwells on mankind's baser instincts, his most ignoble tendencies, and scandalous behavior in general. The protagonistic detective begins to scrutinize the exploitation of human weaknesses. Furiously frustrated, he might more easily have changed careers and become an high-profile media-lawyer or a hostile corporate businessman, than discovering the identity of the mysterious woman he'd met earlier that night. In any case, inspired by Darwinism, he would have profited greatly from the often drastic and catastrophic mistakes of others.

CHAPTER 42

Book review of the collection of 32 short stories, written between 1859-1973, entitled

Finnish Short Stories

as translated by Inkeri Vaananen-Jensen with K. Borje Vahamaki, published in 1982

MN Braces for Warmest Superbowl Party Ever with Rock Bands Heated Bleachers and Bunsen Burner BBQ.

R. Royce decided to take the day off. He felt a resounding and exhilarating sense of accomplishment sweep over him, even though two hurricanes had spun off tornadoes which careened and cut crooked paths through his yard recently, Frances from the east and now Jeannie from the west, all in the same season, pruning and toppling trees right and left as they went. He'd meant to spend the next ten or fifteen years leisurely clearing the land he'd purchased and accumulated, which presently amounted to about a sixth of the secluded residential area. An overgrown jungle, half had been concealed by briars, thickets, and invasive potato vines; the other half was densely forested by towering Australian pines, live oaks, and palms. Now, he'd have the land cleared in a year.

The new neighbor to the east, a retired building contractor from Orlando bought the four vacant wooded lots on both corners, so he could be near his daughter and grand-kids. They lived only a few blocks away. He bulldozed down the trees, brought in semi-truck driven trailer loads of sod-grass and before long had an instantly lush and green-growing lawn on the south half. On the north side, he had forty or fifty dump-truck loads of fill-dirt dropped, mostly ground coral and pulverized mineral rock, which he compacted and allowed to settle over several months' time, creating an artificial plateau, so that the new CBS, brick, and mortar maintenance-free house he built soon afterwards would be high and dry with a solid foundation in the rainy season, overlooking the new swimming pool he'd also designed and built. To top off all the construction, he created a secure privacy wall, which separated his "estate" from Royce's as yet undeveloped parcel.

These drastic environmental changes prompted Royce to spring into action mode. He planted rose bushes everywhere that pleased him, in every nook and cranny. But the real reason that Royce was so tickled was because he'd filled the "moon crater," caused by the removal of a knocked over pine tree, giant root-ball and all, which had grown big and tall on the boundary and been in the neighbor's path of demolition and destruction, with fresh, rich, deep top-soil, and into which he had planted a hardy variety of disease-resistant hybrid rose bushes. Among them grew the tallest, fullest, most exotic leafy-green foliage that produced the largest, most exquisitely beautiful neon pink roses he'd ever seen anywhere up to that turning point in his life.

It also didn't hurt that his property value soared and skyrocketed by the practically overnight improvements to the neighborhood. The 82 acre fields to the south had sold to a developer and a gated community of expensive upscale homes was under new construction.

Just as much as he loves rose gardening, Royce enjoys ocean fishing. Once, he tried his luck fishing for the ever-elusive snook off the docks in Fort Pierce, near where he'd seen other fishermen catch pan-size fish for dinner, using a simple low-tech rod and reel in the shallow areas. He cast his fishing line was out into the deep water that evening. Lo and behold a mighty big fish struck the bait and made off in a flash, swimming away at what must have been ninety mile an hour plus speeds. He took great pleasure playing that sporting gamefish, probably the biggest one he'd ever attempted to reel in. He must have wrestled with that fish for a good twenty or thirty minutes. He had the monster of the deep nearly landed, when the line suddenly went slack. He knew in a second what must have happened: either the high-test line had snapped in two or razor-sharp teeth bit through the metal leader line. He reeled the line in anyway and discovered what had actually transpired. Tremendous tension in the line had completely un-bent the normally gracefully curved heavy-duty hook, until it was perfectly straight, shearing off the barb in the process. It looked exactly like an ordinary carpenter's finishing nail on the end of a fishing line. As a result, the powerful fish had simply slipped off the end of the hook and nonchalantly swam away.

Royce reported to work bright and early on Monday morning. He was helping a group of heavy-equipment operators with a new bridge under construction. On the previous Friday, the site supervisor had left specific instructions for the crew to lift up one last long section of pre-stressed concrete to top off two completed concrete columns.

"I told you guys to lift that bridge span, before you knocked off early for the weekend," he said, pointing to the concrete span on the ground at his feet.

"I thought we did," said the crew's straw boss, perplexed, shaking his head and smiling weakly. "The hurricane that went through here over the weekend and devastated the area, must have blown it back down to the ground."

Finnish Short Stories, translated by Inkeri Vaananen-Jensen with K. Borje Vahamaki, published in 1982, are some of the best early contemporary Scandinavian, uniquely fictional stories I have ever read in the English language, not that I have read that many. However, I did find them quite interesting, even inspirational in places, totally original, and delightfully provocative—if not the most current and up-to-date regarding subject matter, having been written in the years between 1859 and 1973. In any event, stories about global warming, Russian aggression, commercialized media such as popular music, the internet, and space travel have been omitted. The 32 stories included in this collection are about warm, loving, caring people who have lived in a cold, harsh climate, under adverse, sometimes severe conditions. Included are the following stories and topics:

1. "Eriika." Highly spiritual in nature. She becomes one with the universe.

2. "The Nurse Maid," "drops the ball" on the job and is quickly, unceremoniously terminated from employment. She seeks gainful employment elsewhere.

3. "The Watch" is about a fellow who saves up for a new time-piece, which quickly becomes his pride and joy toy. It just goes to show you that if you throw enough money at a problem, it goes away.

4. "A Summer Dream" is about "puppy love." The fellow grows up, moves away, and returns. He reminisces about his first true love in life.

5. "Liars?" is about two teenage fashion models. Art mirrors reality.

6. "The Bishop's Pointer" tells of elementary school-age pupils who learn early in life to read the writing on the wall. You expect a schoolyard brawl to break out any minute.

7. "The Gentleman and the Boor" is a fable about social justice and the state of nature in an inherently unjust society. It could just as well have been about a wise and benevolent oligarch and a strong, hardworking serf, who lifts himself up "by his bootstraps." They plant a garden.

8. "First Love." He falls in love with a circus performer in town for the weekend. A practical, practicing contortionist and lion-tamer might have had him temporarily jumping through fiery hoops, but would never take him on seriously as an apprentice trapeze artist.

9. "The Hired Girl" has no misgivings about true love. Do you ever get the distinct impression that time is running out and life is passing you by? She doesn't feel very good about it.

10. "Love" is an iron-clad prenuptial agreement which forms the basis of a more perfect union. What happens when a lawyer is the best man.

11. "When You Have Feelings" is about a well-rounded, pragmatic girl who does not defy convention or public opinion. She readily finds her place in society and then becomes an integral part of the community.

12. "Death" tells of a faithful wife who's lived a hard life, but accepts her lot in the end. You get the impression that "parting is such sweet sorrow."

13. "The Girl in the Rose Arbor or the Dying Sister." She is not the fortunate one. Unloved and unwanted. Maybe not. Life goes on without her, or does it? You become more sympathetic to the plight of others.

14. "Food for the Winter." A loving, hardworking couple ensure their survival through the winter. They feel warm and secure in their home with the knowledge that they might not starve or freeze to death anytime soon.

15. "Building a Bridge." A group of skilled employees have a job to do. One fellow anticipates going their separate ways when the job is done. At the railway station, he looks around and wonders, "Where did everyone go?"

16. "Military Splendor." It is a tough, dangerous job being a leader of men, especially in the military, in war or in peace.

17. "The Last Tree" depicts the rugged life of a lumberjack. He is sure to win a consolation prize in our hearts, to go along with the one for his valiant reforestation effort.

18. "The Unneeded Paradise." An ambitious young man seeks fame and fortune in the New World. He doesn't cut the mustard.

19. "The Apple Trees." A young novice away from home, on the job for the first time out in the world, seeks real-life experience and learns a valuable lesson about life from an old worn-out railroad worker.

20. "The Fur." We all have something to fear. True, we may be eternally hopeful, but what happens when "something really is out there"? Scary-fiction writers would have a field day penning the likes of this Halloween story onto paper.

21. "The Monkey." An idle, but curious newspaper and magazine street-corner vender observes "monkey-business." Apparently, it doesn't get him anywhere in life. He should know better than to "monkey around with another monkey's monkey." Notwithstanding, the meaning and gist of this story might have just sailed right on past me.

22. "Long Ago." A girl tracks down a "missing person." She wants answers, but gets more than she bargains for. If you're going to survive in this world you have to stand on your own two feet.

23. "A Finnish Landscape." Two buddies discuss the artwork of an esteemed, famous mutual acquaintance at a health resort. There's no sign of him in the picture.

24. "The Proposal." A girl tries repeatedly to tell her father that she plans to marry. He tells her wild, imaginative stories from his past. She cannot get a word in edgewise. Perhaps, she is too immature and inexperienced for matrimony and wedded bliss.

25. "Selecting a Play" is a clever story about a group of like- and civic-minded community members who want to perform in a new town play. Doing so has become an annual tradition, looking for a role you can sink your teeth into.

26. "The Frogman's Day" appears to be a funny story about a practical-joking amphibian. There may be more to "the creature" than meets the eye.

27. "Is My Hair Beautiful?" Is it about a vain man who is surely destined to become a Russian syndicate boss, once he discovers that his hidden talents are not fully or sufficiently appreciated elsewhere.

28. "The Pig Bitten." A pretty girl hikes a long distance to the lake with friends who are going fishing there, but abruptly leaves when she senses that the sun is about to set on her. She has set her moral

compass for home and does not look back. You have to admire her determination and resolute steadfastness. On the other hand, you might think that she has skipped out on quite a clam-bake.

29. "The Rock in the Sunshine" is a story of spiritual awakening and the rebirth of a man with responsibilities. He has a poetic moment of triumph.

30. "The Drunkards" portrays the sobering fact that alcoholism is one of the "real and present dangers" associated with living in a frozen wasteland. You don't want to drink to that.

31. "Aila" is one of my personal favorite stories in the entire collection, about a remarkable woman who raises her sister's daughter. She senses and protects her from life's little problems, pitfalls, everyday hazards, and all harm. She should have become a saint by now. In fact, I might have met someone who had an uncanny resemblance to her, matching the description of her niece, once years ago myself and could sense the suspense immediately, but recognized that she had been completely surrounded by an impenetrable "forcefield." She had been truly blessed and would continue to be for all the days of her life.

32. "Death of a Dog" is a story just as the title suggests, but with very graphic, disgusting, and gory details. You don't want to grow up on a farm like that.

CHAPTER 43

Book review of

The Alchemist

by Paulo Coelho, published in 1988,
English translation by Clifford E. Landers.

Fortune cookie says: Remove woolen outer garments in warm weather for a pleasant journey.

"Have you ever thought about going to Egypt?" R. Royce asked his good friend Cornelius Korn.

"I thought about ordering some crocodile shoes from a Cairo sporting goods catalog, once," replied Korn. "But I was concerned that the Nile crocs may be an endangered species. They might be prohibited from importation into the United States."

"Could be. Cowhide leather for me. Much more supple and comfortable on your feet, with a shorter break-in time," said Royce.

"Do you remember Richard Woodward?"

"The roofing contractor?"

"One and the same. When he and his roofing crew were putting new shingles on hail-damaged houses in Dallas, Texas, years ago, he told the others that he wanted to drive over to Bayou Country and find himself a new pair of alligator shoes," said Royce. "When he returned a few days later, one of the roofers inquired about his trip to Louisiana."

"We rented a flat-bottomed air-boat and searched everywhere through murky back-waters among the curtains of Spanish moss, hanging vines and Cyprus trees for the biggest, meanest alligator. When we finally spotted one, lurking around a swimming hole, we pulled the boat alongside. I reached out, grabbed the giant lizard by the tail, and wrestled it into the boat with us," he said.

"And you know what?" Richard continued. "That alligator wasn't even wearing any shoes."

"Sounds like a typical Dickie shoe story to me," said Korn.

I was uncertain what to expect when I read Paul Coelho's novel, *The Alchemist*, published in 1988, and translated from the Portuguese into English by Clifford E. Landers. Turns out, the book proved to be as inspirational and interesting as one might believe would be the case, if he were listening to the Pope speak on Easter Sunday. The book was that good.

It reminded me of a story about a goat shepherd on a farm near Adaleide, Arkansas—although it could just as well have been in the vicinity of Telluride, Colorado, or Weed, California, for that matter. One fine spring day, a shepherd boy decided to lead his flock of yearling goats over hill and dale to greener pastures some miles away through the national forest, alongside a mountain stream. Clearly, over paths less travelled. Hours later, while resting and grazing the goats on a pastoral grassy hillside, he fell fast asleep, on that warm, sunny afternoon.

When he awoke, he quickly realized that the goats must have wandered away. They were all gone. Vanished. He immediately began to look everywhere for them. Eventually, he followed a winding trail over the next hill.

It just so happened that not too far in the distance was a large, solitary wooden-frame house with a verandah, owned by a lovely, charming, and beautiful maiden, who'd inherited the house from her rich spinster aunt. She had been living all alone in the house for a couple of years now. A socialite, she often invited guests for garden parties, bingo, cards, luncheons, and ballroom dancing. She was very popular in the community and a promising civic leader. At present, trained and certified as a physical therapist, she was guiding a group of thirty-five college coeds in yoga relaxation techniques.

During the yoga session, some forty missing goats appeared and wandered into the yard. They began to mingle and cuddle with the students practicing yoga stress-relief. Such soft, gentle, innocent creatures they were, too! Yoga class became a petting zoo, to the delight of all participants and the instructor.

The goat shepherd arrived a short time later, prepared to make apologies. But no apology was necessary. This must have been how "goat-yoga" was invented. Only in America!

CHAPTER 44

Book review of
Norse Mythology
by Neil Gaiman, published in 2017.

Gods whose antics make you wonder who's really in charge of Valhalla.

Most everyone was duly present and accounted for inside the second-floor classroom. All alert, they listened intently to the operations coordinator, DI Quentin Thomas, who provided them with critical information vital to the success of their upcoming mission. Now, a high-pitched whirring, screaming, and whining noise could be heard outside the row of windows which faced the building entrance and the expansive front lawn, which served as a parade grounds, assembly point, and exercise area.

A VTOL aircraft descended slowly, surely, and expertly to the ground from just beneath Cumulus-cloud level. The precision landing was as smoothly and gracefully performed as a silvery spinning UFO in a Hollywood science-fiction movie. The aircraft touched down as softly as a grasshopper leaping on grass. Jet engine roar, avionic whine, over-pressurized gases escaping from nozzles could be heard by anyone in the vicinity, if there were anyone outside. There wasn't. The facility had been long deserted, and all but abandoned. The loudest noises diminished considerably by dozens of decibels, as the aircraft engines were being shut down and the air pressure valves closed. Soon all was as calm and quiet again as a whispering wind.

Class coordinator and operatives alike saw the hatch open on the aircraft underbelly, a ladder lower to the ground, and someone wearing an OD-green

Kevlar helmet with shaded face-shield, a shiny green flight-suit, and polished black jump-boots climb out. The aviator extracted a sword-like object from a hidden sheath, stabbed the point solidly and deeply into the grassy soil and earth. She removed her helmet and placed it gingerly on the jeweled hilt of the sword. A moment before, she appeared to have just claimed the hallowed ground beneath her feet for Queen and country, or King, as conditions warranted. She shook out the golden fleece that was her hairdo and walked confidently toward the brick building. She was obviously late for the briefing.

"Group, I have the distinct pleasure and privilege of introducing you to Major Norad. She will fill you in on the finer details of tonight's operation," said Mr. Thomas. "You will not be disappointed, I'm sure."

"Good afternoon, Deltas. We have a considerable amount of information to cover and not much time. So let's get to it," said Meghan Norad. "Where did everyone park their vehicles?" she inquired, for purposes of rapid orientation.

"Most of us walked over from the barracks. But, there is a faculty and staff parking lot behind the building off Perimeter Road for POVs," said one of the Delta pilots, seated in the front row. Miscellaneous and sundry aircraft, such as the Harrier jet you flew in on, have all been towed over to the remote hangars about a mile down the road. They're completely out of sight and away from prying eyes," said the pilot.

"I don't see our field agent," said Meghan.

"He's probably camouflaged and camped out on some isolated beach with his marine binoculars, spotting subs," said another.

"How does he know where to look?" she asked.

"We're compartmentalized. That's his bailiwick. It's what he does," interjected Quentin. When he locates a sub, he relays the sighting information to us. Then, the stealth pilots scramble and paint the vessel, so we can track it. The Coast Guard and Marines intercept any rendezvous vessels and contact parties they discover, including insurgents or subversives. What could be easier?" he asked. It was a rhetorical question.

"You claim that the man expects to make contact late tonight northeast of Sebastion Inlet," stated Meghan. "He must have a pretty darn good source of information, for someone who must routinely cover a thousand miles of ocean-front beach property."

R. Royce was telling his good friend Colonel Korn how a marine biologist colleague had recently trained "Rocket Man" and "Major Tom," two ordinary dolphins to explore the underwater coastline in search of foreign submarines. "They have had tiny sonar, camera, and transmitting devices surgically attached to their sleek, wet, and slippery backs," he said, matter-of-factly. "They're friendly and highly intelligent creatures. When they encounter an unidentified foreign submarine, for instance, they rub their bodies up against the hull—much like a bear scratching its hairy backside, to loosen an annoying cocklebur, by rubbing against a tree trunk. In the process, a transponder, or tracking device becomes detached from the dolphin and reattaches itself magnetically to the hull of the sub. Then, the Air Force or the Coast Guard can locate and track the sub to their heart's content wherever it goes."

"That still doesn't explain how you know for certain a specific sub is going to be at such and such location after midnight tonight," said Korn.

"They call it tradecraft for a reason," replied Royce, innocently shrugging off the question, indifferently.

"You don't think the UAW crew might try to torpedo your plan, do you?" inquired Korn. "They have a new underwater cruise missile they want to launch at the first opportunity. The electronics section says it has the motor from a 'Dixie Chopper' coupled with the six-speed transmission from a Mustang GT," he said. "It boasts peak acceleration and packs quite a punch on target."

"Not my decision to make," said Royce. "They should go play in the Pacific Ocean instead."

The book *Norse Mythology*, published in 2017 by author, Neil Gaiman is sure to surprise many readers, who have heard of the wise and omnipotent Odin; the powerful, hammer-wielding Thor; and the deceptive, demonic Loki, but may never have delved into the subject of the many myths and legends surrounding these larger-than-life characters. The included stories comprise a very diverse and impressive array of their exploits. The gods are boisterous, full of life and joy. They are adventurous, and they love a good, lavish feast. Indeed, they love to eat, drink, and be merry to excess. They are often rowdy and violent at a party. They make trouble wherever they go. All of their deeds are pure hyperbole, it seems; their actions are all so exaggerated you begin to wonder about their plausibility. They are strong enough to smash mountains, they can drink a river dry, they can soar through the sky like an eagle. At least one of them appears loud, obnoxious, crude, belligerent, arrogant, and vain on more than one occasion. The others behave more like high-strung, egotistical gameshow contestants than the tribal leaders of the free-world they represent. Theirs is a world inhabited by a great many unsavory creatures, trolls, giants, and ogres. A world of dangerous wild animals, including vicious wolves, venomous snakes, and other bizarre and deadly monsters. Indeed, even magicians appear, who create worlds of illusion which spin totally out of control. Only the dwarves and elves, who have designed and fabricated the necessary weapons and defensive artifacts for the gods, have helped preserve the lives of the gods under such adverse conditions and in such an arduous climate. After all is said and done, you cannot help but believe that there must have existed a higher form of intelligent life somewhere in the universe than that emanating from these seriously flawed mythical beings in the time before Genesis. That, or somebody must have gotten the story completely wrong and inexplicably, perpetuated the most outrageous lies and exaggerated falsehoods.

CHAPTER 45

Book review of the novel

The Secret Garden

by Frances Hodgson Burnett, published in 1911.

Young and Invincible.

"According to the early morning farm report, cotton-pickers are already in big demand this spring throughout the Sun-belt, especially in the Mississippi Delta region," said Colonel Korn.

"Of course, you're referring to the large, complex agricultural harvesting machinery made of iron and steel that plucks cotton balls from the tall, dried-out-looking, stick-like plants, undoubtedly devoid of chlorophyll, which have been grown in vast field acreages; extracts and separates out the seeds; then bales the cotton, weighs it, determines moisture content, and transports it to nearby climate-controlled sheds, for temporary storage until further transportation onto commercial railroad cars is made, I presume," replied R. Royce.

"Yes, exactly!" said Korn. "Furthermore, I predict a futures bonanza for that particular commodity in the coming months."

Dancing around the room, Royce spontaneously burst into song and merriment, singing parts of a lively tune he must have heard on the radio a long time ago that had been stuck in the farthest recesses of his brain, escaping only now:

"When I was a tiny little toddler, my mama used to rock me on my front porch swing, near those scorching hot hay fields we called Fling.

"We used to live in a shotgun shack just up the hill from Cabin Creek, by those plump ripe tomato fields we called Sleek.

"When those green, leafy plants began to burn, we couldn't pick very many berries, in those overheated briar patches we called Fairies, to protect us from our fear of bears."

"A folk legend is born. I wish I had a banjo…," Korn chimed in, smirking and carrying on a little despite himself and his normally reserved demeanor."

"I may not be able to sing like Johnny Cash, but three months on special assignment to an undisclosed, isolated, uninhabited, and remote tropical island, reportedly located somewhere in the South China Sea tends to make you appreciate home," Royce said.

"We should count our blessings that our next stop isn't a quaint and tidy little garden spot located within the Arctic Circle somewhere north of Korea," said Korn.

"All the blessed children tire easily when they travel. They just want to return to the simple life of nature trails, sand, and gravel. How far the Lord wanders, yet you only want to go to Flanders," recited Royce. "But, now you're talking Politics!" he said, as a matter of fact.

They continued to maintain camouflaged and blackout conditions, with strict radio silence. Royce monitored some satellite imagery instruments. Korn checked the cameras strategically placed on the surrounding perimeter. They were prepared to react quickly and move at a moment's notice.

"Quiet! Don't look now, but we may have a visitor," said Korn, observing a live-camera feed. As the intruder approached, he recognized a friendly, familiar reconnaissance scout. Evidently, Special Forces had sent them a message from "the Pueblo" to be hand-delivered in person. Their immediate future would hang in the balance.

"Code-name 'Amelia Erhardt' at your service," stated Major Thomas frankly, an Army Ranger and pilot, her flashing eyes beaming like a lighthouse beacon, her golden-blonde hair neatly cut into the style of a French Poodle, as she calmly and softly stepped into the grass hut, which had long served as their hidden lair, through an open doorway.

"Greetings, Meghan! What's a nice girl like you doing in a desolate place like this? Good news first," specified Royce.

"Looking for Livingston, naturally. What are you guys doing here? The good news: you were voted least likely to go out in a blaze of glory back at HQ," she said. "Just kidding. I really came to see you."

At this juncture of the dialogue, Korn cheerfully contributed a few heartfelt chorus lines from 'Ring of Fire' to the conversation. "Hallelujah, amen!" he concluded, with a meek smile. He innocently offered up a sigh of relief.

"You two really know how to defuse a situation and reduce the tension in the room," said Royce. "What's the bad news?"

"You've been scheduled to observe an air-assault and demolitions exercise up close and personal. But, if you'd rather do Karaoke, we can talk about 'Time Love and Tenderness,' said Meghan. Or, you can tell me all about 'When a Man Loves a Woman.'"

"Mission top-secret, destination unknown," replied Royce.

The Secret Garden, a novel by Frances Hodgson Burnett, was first published in 1911. The delightfully charming story about three young children, Colin, Dickon, and Mary possesses all of the endearing qualities to become a timeless classic of English literature.

The children have banded together and become friends in an idyllic, pastoral setting. Due to the severe limitations imposed upon them by a sometimes rather harsh human existence, they attempt to rise above their circumstances in life. Despite having sustained grievous injuries, they soon learn that they must persevere if they are to overcome adversity. They must make a gallant effort to negotiate the obstacles and pit-falls which they encounter along the path toward achieving their goals. Often, they succeed only through sheer determination and pure willpower. Because of the process of evolution, which obviously must be at work somehow in their universe—or perhaps because of other, even more powerful forces, there is an almost sublime interaction among the characters in their rite of passage. The trio reminds me of the plight of the Tin Man, the Scarecrow, and Dorothy in *The Wizard of Oz*. Indeed, their growth and personal development seems to involve a great many ordeals of mind over matter. Hence, the story actually appears to portray the triumph of the indomitable human spirit. Moreover, the theme of a "Garden of Eden" or "Paradise," running throughout the story as a "common thread" reveals the magic and majesty that is commonly known as "Mother Nature." So, above all, the story is a celebration of Life, which simultaneously expresses deep reverence for the Divine Creator, who is the Author of all Beings. Ultimately, you can't help but exclaim what you must have heard repeated over the years, time and time again: "They grow up so fast, don't they?"

CHAPTER 46

Book review of

The Collected Short Stories of Bertold Brecht

published in 1983, edited by John Willett and Ralph Manheim, and translated by Yvonne Kapp, Hugh Rorrison, and Antony Tatlow,

written 1920-1924 (11 Bavarian stories),

1924-1933 (14 Berlin stories),

and 1937-1940 (13 Scandinavian stories, in exile).

For the Love of Humanity and the Spoils of War.

The Collected Short Stories of Bertold Brecht were written between 1920 and 1940. The book was published in 1983, edited by John Willett and Ralph Manheim, and translated from German into English by Yvonne Kapp, Hugh Rorrison, and Antony Tatlow. The stories were grouped into three categories: Bavarian Stories, Berlin Stories, and Exile Stories, which was when Bertold Brecht had lived in Scandinavia. The author became more well-recognized as a playwright, than a writer of short stories, but he was an excellent writer of short stories. My personal favorites are numerous. They include "Before the Flood," "Muller's Natural Attitude," "Barbara," "The Monster," "Socrates Wounded," "The Experiment," "The Heretics Coat," "Lucullus's Trophies," "A Question of Taste," and "The Augsburg Chalk Circle." A brief idea, a concise summary, or my interpretation of the gist of each story follows:

1. "Bargan Gives Up" is a strangely bizarre pirate story in which undying loyalty causes him to walk the plank.

2. "Story on a Ship" ...a realistic, unpretentious tale about "the last straw" or "the straw that broke the camel's back," and depicts a final act of desperation.

3. "The Revelation." The author reveals his flair for the dramatic and the power of poetry.

4. "The Foolish Wife" was glad to see her husband return home after a prolonged absence and proves the law of diminishing returns. In other words, you rarely get out of a relationship more than you put into it.

5. "The Blind Man" depicts no end in sight to his long suffering.

6. "A Helping Hand" is a treatise on the futility of the feudal system. It provides insight for why 'the dog bites the hand that feeds him.'

7. "Java Meier." A fish merchant follows the newspaper articles pertaining to the untimely death of a neighbor, who literally becomes a victim of identity theft.

8. "The Lance Sergeant" concerns alcohol abuse in the artillery regiment, low morale, and loose cannons.

9. "Message in a Bottle" is not too dissimilar in concept from the printed label on the fire-alarm mechanism seen in many office buildings that reads, "Break in case of fire."

10. "A Mean Bastard" makes his bed and then has to sleep in it. It's a graphic portrayal of public relations and grassroots politics.

11. "The Death of Cesare Malatesta" proves the point that you shouldn't gossip about the people you meet in small towns, because they all know each other and are often related. Some thought that they were above the law.

12. "The Answer" boasts the best, most appropriate punch line in the volume, a decent reply to the burning question, "Do you still love

me after all these years?" Some persons suffer greatly their entire lives, but find out in the end, it was all worth the effort.

13. "Before the Flood" is a different version of the Biblical Flood story. One is a vignette about a prehistoric creature, extinct long before the time of the Ark. One is about an animal God must have created after the Flood. A tongue-in-cheek tale.

14. "Conversation about the South Seas." Living on an island paradise is obviously not his cup of tea. The climate does not agree with him. He is without a doubt unable to get along with the other vacationers, the local inhabitants, or the natives.

15. "Letter about a Mastiff." The narrator appears insulting and downright snobbish. He babbles on pointlessly and aimlessly. He takes himself much too serious throughout his ordeal, which appears more imaginary than real.

16. "Hook to the Chin" is about self-improvement in any endeavor. Basically, it's about managing your priorities in life, the outcome of which represents either success or failure. In the case of this story, someone repeatedly reminding his opponents to watch out for his left jab spells certain disaster. As we all know, there is a measure of risk involved in trying to dominate the world of boxing.

17. "Muller's Natural Attitude." He's very perceptive on the subject of mechanics, which must have formed the basis for much advanced German engineering and research, as the aircraft takes a tumble in midair. He is well-versed in the instinct for survival.

18. "North Sea Shrimp" is about a "happy Kamper'" and self-satisfied interior designer into which his so-called friends introduce chaos, calamity, and strife. As they say, "With friends like his, who needs enemies?" They would not represent ideal candidates for a house swapping vacation.

19. "Bad Water" relates to the legal proceedings in a tropical island community. When it is perceived that a crime has been committed by one of its members, the perpetrator is allowed to present his side of the story before the administration of justice.

20. "A Little Tale of Insurance" is about a nearly bankrupt financier who concocts a get-rich-quick scheme that is perfectly legal and highly profitable to himself. One might call it "a human interest story."

21. "Four Men and a Poker Game" pertains to the natural tendencies of sore losers who attempt to even the score.

22. "Barbara" is the reason he's "driving his life away." Even if he won't admit it, he is the jealous type. He puts the pedal to the metal as an exhilarating way to release stress.

23. "The Good Lord's Package" revels in good cheer during the holidays. In the immortal words of Bill Shakespeare, "All's well that ends well."

24. "The Monster" is the stuff of Hollywood legends, where reality TV is born, and art imitates life. It just goes to show you, you can't mistake greatness. The plot is much more subtle than having "Godzilla" or "King Kong" make an unexpected appearance at an exclusive skyscraper restaurant downtown, where you want to enjoy a quiet evening meal without any surprise interruptions.

25. "The Job" describes the process of exploiting the working class. You have to eat in order to live. You need a job to put groceries on the table. If he were alive then, and asked for his opinion, I believe the author would give a biting commentary on the state of the union address in the 22nd century.

26. "Safety First." The story on which the original idea for the classic film "Lord Jim" might very well have been based. A carefully planned retribution.

Class Book Reviews & Timely Stories

27. "The Soldier of La Ciotat" represents the iconic, heroic military man in practically any and every war and armed conflict throughout history. "Do or die" is his motto!

28. "A Mistake" reveals the similarities of opposing nations which yet possess diverse cultural tendencies. One is time-conscious and trusts the police. The other, not so much.

29. "Gaumer and Irk" lends credence to the notion that no crime goes unpunished in one or more of three realms: in this world, the next, or in the subconscious.

30. "Socrates Wounded" expounds upon the discourses of natural philosophy as told from the distinct point of view of a 'man of action.'

31. "The Experiment" shows that a practitioner of the scientific method is much more respected than a judge seated on the highest court in the land, no matter how benevolent he may be.

32. "The Heretics Coat" describes the systematic miscarriage of justice during the interrogation and inquisition on the person of an honorable, noble, trustworthy, kind, and fair individual.

33. "Lucullus's Trophies" tells about the might and power that was Rome before the time of Christ, as evidenced by the values displayed by a prominent military general, a fearless conqueror, and a preeminent statesman.

34. "An Unseemly Old Lady" casts off the bonds of servitude and begins to enjoy life to the maximum.

35. "A Question of Taste" is an intriguing detective story about a wartime atrocity and an unsolved crime.

36. "The Augsburg Chalk Circle" depicts a famous court case in Bavaria during the middle ages mishandled by an eccentric Spaniard judge.

37. "Two Sons" tells about a confused mother whose son is a soldier away at war. She encounters an enemy soldier who has become an enlightened POW and feels sorry for him. Meanwhile, marching home, over hill and dale, and through streams, it doesn't take "Wet Willie," otherwise known as her true son, very long to arrive one fateful day and reconcile in his own mind how and why the country he's defended with such bravery for so many long years is in imminent danger of losing two world wars in a row.

38. "Life Story of the Boxer" is an incomplete, fragmented narrative, which some might refer to as an unedited work in progress. The narrator rambles on about running away from home to join the merchant marines. He hires on as a deckhand, a crewmember on various international cargo vessels, travels the seven seas, and visits an untold number of foreign ports. He leads an adventurous life of pure escapism. Eventually, he should have discovered that you can't run away from yourself, and you have to go home sometime.

R. Royce was waiting in line at the convenience store early Monday morning when he overheard the customer tell the clerk, "Last night I sent my old lady out for beer and cigarettes. I woke up this morning and looked around. No beer. No cigarettes." Most of the other customers were just trying to wake up gradually with a minimal amount of shock to their systems and get to work on time. They were purchasing coffee, maybe a donut, gasoline for the car, a newspaper. The construction worker was undoubtedly on a different time schedule, and in a different frame of mind. His agenda was not the same. Royce went back home. Later that morning, feeling energized, he decided to mow the lawn.

"This lawnmower rides like a bucking bronco in a rodeo," he exclaimed. He had recently bought it new. The machine boasted plenty of high-octane horsepower. Royce enjoyed himself immensely as he bounced and shook in the saddle. The mower zipped around the yard like a hovercraft, cutting even thirty-inch swaths each time. When he finished, the yard looked like a magnificent green carpet, or so he thought, the green at a prestigious golf course on the PGA tour. He stopped to smell the roses growing and blooming in a neat row at the back of the expansive yard. He walked along at a steady pace in front of them, "inspecting the troops." A short, straight-line terrace wall behind, made of shaped rock blocks protected the flowers somewhat from the capricious nature of the wind. He looked intently at the intermingled array of orange Mexican poppies he'd planted from packets of seeds he'd obtained from the local garden nursery.

Next, he strolled over to the nearby creek-side park to see if the Canadian geese had arrived at their usual stopover on the trip back north. They had. He'd like to think the ones he observed were the same pair from last year. It was like their regular vacation spot. They honked at him as they waddled and piddled around in close proximity. Last year, they'd followed him as he rode his beach-cruiser bicycle, flying low above him as he rode along the jogging path adjacent to the golf course. Royce was elated and contented by all that had transpired as well as could be imagined.

That afternoon, he would drop off the long, tall, and narrow, naturally curved walnut accent table he'd built the previous week, routered, sanded, stained, and finished to a high-gloss luster at the flea market, which was his idea for introducing the bizarre into the bazaar. *It doesn't get any better than this*, he thought.

CHAPTER 47

Book review of

A Gentleman in Moscow

by Amor Towles, published in 2016.

He put his heart and soul into his work, then breathed life into it.

A *Gentleman in Moscow*, by Amor Towles, published in 2016, is an unassuming, but fast-paced novel about an ordinary fellow who happens to live and work at a centrally located hotel in Moscow. The story takes place from the early 1900s to the mid-1950s. The young man appears intelligent and well-educated enough. He demonstrates cleverness in most instances, and is well-versed, knowledgeable, and astute in his dealings with others. Sometimes, however, he has a tendency to offend persons in positions of authority without really meaning to do so. By nature, he is gregarious, friendly, pleasant, and personable. Even charming, up to a point. Having been assigned to a position of responsibility in the Metropole Hotel restaurant, he accepts the responsibility as a challenge and performs his duties in a punctual, proficient, and professional manner. But the Russia he has known practically all of his life and grown to love is rapidly changing before his very eyes—due to wartime strife, political and social upheaval, and the industrial revolution. He quickly learns to adapt, however, by assuming the roles of a father-figure, mentor, and teacher. In the process, he falls deeply in love with a vivacious young lady who goes on to become a glamorous movie star.

All in all, the storyline keeps the reader interested and motivated throughout the book. As the "plot thickens," you get a real sense of Russian history, poetry, and a pastoral life in general. You absorb page after page of interesting, life-changing events as the leading character reminisces, reflects, and observes the world turning around him. You begin to savor every sentence as you would sip fine wine and bite into a morsel of an exquisitely prepared entre during the bountiful evening meal.

During the course of his career, the conflicted leading character is ultimately forced to take action. Although, he has developed a heightened sense of self-preservation, he behaves heroically on behalf of others. His faith becomes great. He senses what makes the world "tick." You can't help but empathize with his plight and condition. Afterall, he is a decent sort of fellow. Always the consummate gentleman, he could have taught a princess and "Miss Manners" lessons on etiquette and refinement at the same time. You get the picture.

Undoubtedly, indubitably, inevitably you begin to wonder about the ominous, omniscient, omnipresent narrator who crops up now and again in some passages of the story, especially when he tells you in no uncertain terms how it will end for the leading character. He is quite a character himself, in my opinion. "Who is he supposed to represent?" you may naively inquire.

R. Royce was thinking that sensory deprivation is when you return to your hotel room, put out the "do not disturb" sign, lock the door, turn out the lights, climb into bed, and sleep soundly throughout the entire night and well into the next morning. "Sometimes it just doesn't pay to get out of bed in the morning." If only he had kept his mouth shut and his personal opinions to himself, his life might have turned out much differently, he thought. But these fleeting thoughts did not faze him.

"You have a lot of nerve marching in here unarmed and unannounced," said the barrel-chested businessman.

"Let's just say I wanted you to know how skeptical I am that a Hollywood movie based solely on a violent video game will sell," said Royce. He wasn't exactly a wiry kind of fellow himself.

"I could shoot you here and now, and nobody would be the wiser," said the man. He picked up a heavy loaded revolver and placed it on the table, holding onto the grip tightly for a moment of suspense.

"The bartender would know what happened," replied Royce simply in a calm and even voice that betrayed no lack of confidence. He placed a small, inconspicuous removeable storage device made of a durable anodized metal in front of himself on the table.

"How old were you when you first realized that you wouldn't be able to change the world?" the other man asked, redirecting by choosing a different topic.

"Old enough to know better. Where's the money for the information?" inquired Royce.

"I didn't bring the monetary instruments," said the man, turning the firearm ever so slightly.

"Before you do anything rash, which you might later live to regret, you should take a long, hard look at yourself in the mirror. There's a shiny red dot on your forehead," said Royce. He calmly retrieved the thumb-drive micro-device and slipped it gingerly into the smoothly lined side-pocket of his corduroy jacket. Then, he stood up and shuffled to the exit.

"Back to square one," exclaimed the businessman, straightening the lapel of his newly tailored sharkskin suit. He stretched out the starched, creamy yellow shirt, pulled on the teal-green silky tie, and inspected his highly polished coal-black leather loafers. "You don't know who you are dealing with!" he said in dramatic fashion to nobody in particular.

Neither did he. Their next fruitful meeting—or round of negotiations, would be scheduled for the day of the Kentucky Derby.

CHAPTER 48

Book review of

Victoria: The Queen

by Julia Baird, published in 2016.

"You come highly recommended by my young Aunt," she said, her rosy cheeks blushing.

If you are even remotely interested in genealogy, facts about the royal family, or the subtle intricacies of world history, you might want to peruse the contents of the in-depth biography of *Victoria: The Queen*, by Julia Baird, published in 2016. The book encapsulates the events of her long life; her loves and passion; and the stimulating and arduous times of one of Great Britain's most endearing and enduring monarchs. Within her milieu, you get a keen sense of rising civilizations overcoming the turbulence of war; the advancements made in the human rights arena; the triumphs over terrible suffering, injustice, and abject poverty; and the rampant effects of modernization and industrialization impacting our daily lives even today.

Practically every nation on earth has been affected by England's actions or influence in one way of another, for better or worse. When you think about it, we can only learn from her mistakes and be thankful for the independent-mindedness, wellbeing, and prosperity which she has demonstrated. How can you fail to be inspired by her tremendous energy and success, occurring most recently within the past two centuries?

To put things broadly into proper perspective, I am humbled by the thought of going out and celebrating the bicentennial of Queen Victoria's birthday in 2019! Remarkably, a photograph of the Queen in her later years reminds me of my own illustrious, esteemed grandmother.

R. Royce finally figured out why his thumb felt so numb and tingly. On the road trip, he'd noticed that he had acquired a habit of steering the Cadillac with the wheel pinched between his thumb and index finger for the last few hundred miles, or so. The "Land-Yacht" held the road quite admirably, as he had become well-aware. The powerful motor, independent suspension and taller new radial tires mounted on alloy rims allowed the vehicle to glide along easily, almost effortlessly, practically steering itself down the Interstate.

Perhaps, he was too tense. Perhaps, he had discovered a new way of releasing stress by pressing his thumb too tightly against the padded leather steering wheel. Who knows for certain? He began steering the car with the wheel gently squeezed between his index finger and the middle finger instead, alleviating the excessive pressure he'd previously applied to his thumb. He continued to enjoy the sights and scenery as he drove onward to his ultimate destination.

Cornelius Korn greeted him at the latched screen door when Royce arrived at the secluded mountain cabin and cordially invited him inside. He was most convivial and pleased beyond measure to see his old friend of many years again. He'd obviously remembered the simple directions to the cabin he'd been given:

"You just drive out of the main road in town until the road comes to a 'T.' From there you turn left and follow this road along the ridge-line and around a sharp curve. When the paved road ends, you travel a few miles further until the dirt road ends. Then, you follow a trail through the woods, until it ends. Eventually, you'll have to park the vehicle and hike a few more miles after that. Go in a northerly direction up the hillside until you see a steep ravine and a winding creek deep below. Look for a rowboat to cross the creek. Once you're on the other side, follow the foot-path through the forest until you reach the tree-line. From the clearing, you'll want to look for a snowmobile parked nearby. The key should be in the ignition switch. Then, all you have to do is ride up through the pass over the next mountaintop you see, descend partway down the other side and look for a cabin in the middle of the forest. It's the only one up there for miles around."

"Any difficulty finding the place?" asked Colonel Korn, mildly surprised at the presence of an unanticipated guest.

"Nah, but I have to admit I wasn't able to locate the rowboat or snowmobile," replied Royce.

"…reminds me of my younger days, when I went prospecting in Afghanistan," said Korn. "Did you bring the briefcase and funds?"

"Just a certified check," said Royce.

"Twenty million?"

"Just like you won the Powerball. All you need now is a helicopter and a satellite link."

"Yes, and I'll be as safe, sound, and secure as the Bank of England," replied Korn. "Have you seen Meghan yet?"

"Not since she opened a new investment portfolio. I'm sure to hear about her investment strategy in the next several days." said Royce, in complete confidence.

"What did she tell you the last time you spoke with her on Bond Street?" discretely inquired Korn.

"She said that your reputation preceded you," said Royce.

CHAPTER 49

Book review of

Hillbilly Elegy

by J. D. Vance, published in 2016.

We haven't seen that much drama since Dr. Phil toppled Jerry Springer from the prime-time television ratings chart.
 Sociology 101 on steroids for the sensitive, but motivated, mobile, and maneuverable opportunist.

Hillbilly Elegy, by J. D. Vance, published in 2016, is an autobiographical American success story about an astute young man who really was not meant to achieve lofty goals in life, largely due to his limited socioeconomic background. All of the statistical indicators pointed to a life of severe hardship, deplorable misery, and complete, abject failure for such a fellow. His family was problem-plagued, destitute, and on familiar terms with the local Police and Health and Human Services Departments. In his hometown, people were more inclined to abuse drugs rather than going to work and earning a decent living. Probably, the best opportunity available to him for purposes of "upward mobility" would have been to simply run away and enlist in the military. Hypothetically speaking, he could have just given up all together and stayed home instead, in the community where he grew up, "the new kid on the block."

"Get a job! You're talking to the Kid!"

Sure, he could have gotten by with living at home and blaming all of his personal problems on his parents—which works up until about age 37 or 38. Afterwards, at some major turning point in an otherwise hollow "affirmative action" existence, it becomes extremely difficult to convince even his closest friends, neighbors, and associates that all of his problems in life have been caused by his parents; it is his parents fault that he has failed. You would think at some critical juncture in his life he would discover, that he should grow up and take responsibility for his own actions. Blaming the government for all of his problems sounds even more foolish.

So, he ran away and joined the Marines. He experienced marketplace reality. He enrolled in some college courses. Trained and educated, he found himself on a satisfying career path. He married and had a family. He eventually became "management material." Hence, he lived the dream and had a fully successful life. This seems to be the gist of the story, at least on the surface. But, when you delve deeper into the social, psychological, and political forces at work in his life, you begin to understand more of his concerns.

Nevertheless, in my humble opinion, the book reads like Sociology 101 on steroids in places about a sensitive, but motivated, mobile, and highly maneuverable enfranchised and empowered opportunist. I'm not certain of the timelines involved, historically speaking, relating to the chronological events of the author's life in comparison with those of the great number of individuals in his peer group, but I'd venture a wild guess and speculate "the duly appointed Judicial Clerk hasn't seen that much drama since Dr. Phil replaced Jerry Springer on iconic daytime television."

R. Royce demonstrated his skills in salesmanship, and he was a good cash customer. When he brought bundles of money in large denominations into the bank in a neat, portable zippered leather bag, the clerk automatically deposited the funds into his savings account with no questions asked. Royce had been the proprietor of an upscale art gallery in town for almost three years. He specialized in exceptional quality paintings, signed lithograph prints, unique art-glass conversation pieces, and fine hardwood furniture. Because of his profitable hobbies, he avidly enjoyed his retirement years even more. It didn't hurt that his life was mostly hassle- and stress-free. He'd even made several new friends recently in the course of his business dealings. He had no competition to speak of. So, he appeared generally happy and contented. His patrons either appreciated the fine art and craftsmanship he exhibited in his shop and let it go at that, or they purchased some of it for whatever reasons. A win-win situation. Once in a while old acquaintances would drop in for a chat and they'd usually go out to a nearby cafe for an appetizing "home-cooked" meal.

Meghan stopped by Monday morning on her way to the city. She asked him if he wanted to ride along. He did, and they shared the sandwiches, slices of date-nut bread, and a thermos of coffee she'd brought.

"What has Cornelius got up his sleeve this time?" asked Royce.

"Very funny," said Meghan. "You know perfectly well that he deals in arms."

"Any long-range aspirations for the foreseeable future?" he inquired, slyly probing for details.

"Well, in as far as I can tell, his prospects are limitless," she admitted. "You can ask him yourself in person. We're meeting with him in about an hour." She accelerated the Porsche, before he was able to comment.

"I love NATO, don't you?" he said, after a time.

"Having strong allies is good for business," she said, calmly.

"We are after all in the business of security," said Royce, succinctly and to the point. Meghan continued to drive the speed limit as she passed the bar on the corner of Twelfth Street and Vine. "So, I assume we're not meeting Korn in the local pub or rathskeller, then," he said, observantly.

"Nope. Better a think tank, than a drunk tank," said Meghan. She turned onto the expressway, then after a few miles, onto an exit ramp, onto a twisty side-street, and into the underground parking lot of the most expensive and exclusive luxury hotel in the city. "We have the bridal suite all to ourselves," she said simply. She smiled pleasantly and provocatively.

"Champagne?"

CHAPTER 50

Book review of

The Inferno:
The World at War 1939-1945

by Max Hastings, published in 2011.

Belligerent power would not trade now clear ambition for all the tea in Ceylon.

Select and place token armies on the countries of the world map. Roll the dice. Remove or replenish the armies as required. You have a fairly accurate concept for a simulation of WWII.

A subjective, unvarnished account of what really happened in WWII from the point of view of those who were there.

Inferno, by Max Hastings, published in 2011, is about the war to end all wars. I simply could not put the book down. Powerful stuff! You would think the story has to get much worse before it can possibly get any better. You realize that all your life you've been insulated from actual past events by the bold newspaper headlines you've seen, by the news reels of a dreary, distant era, and by the brave actions of Hollywood actors shown on the large silver screen in "Panorama" and "Technicolor." You become shocked and horrified as you read further. The book takes a no-nonsense approach to what really happened from every conceivable aspect and perspective. It is a subjective, but unvarnished account of WWII from the point of view of those who were there.

Do you ever get the distinct feeling that you are going to war in the immediate foreseeable future? By inference and deduction you could verify in your own mind the proffered historical data, facts, and figures, and probably roughly assess your own chances of survival and success. You find that men at war are not always guided by the same abstract principles as Clausewitz and Sun Tsu. They're guided more by necessity, gut-instinct, raw emotion, and a driving rainstorm of ambition. In any armed conflict, you want posterity to honor and respect the man, his rank and uniform, and the weapon he carries, but this is not always the case. Which is a humbling learning experience to be sure for some.

Braced with long overdue diligence and steel-reinforced determination, then, the author takes aim from the moral high ground. He analyzes the facts and figures of each significant battlefield scenario as it unfolds. He looks from all directions for the big picture as he focusses his powerful binoculars on every minute detail in his narrative. Reading through the muck, the muddy and murky material will challenge your every belief and everything you ever thought you knew or didn't know about the war. You begin to approach war with stone-cold stoicism, if not outright caution and fearful trepidation. Yet, you believe in your heart of hearts that Roosevelt, Churchill, Stalin and the other Allied military leaders did what they thought they had to do in their day, right, wrong, or indifferent.

Certainly, as the author clearly points out on numerous occasions, the military operation could have been handled differently, if only the General modified his tactics, used all of his resources, or showed some initiative. But the truth be told, the outcome and strategy would most likely have been the same. Like the popular boardgame "Risk" you played as children in the 1960s, you look at the map, place your armies on the battlefield, roll the dice, and you get an outcome. You remove, replace, and replenish your forces and continue to march.

One side-effect of reading the book is how ravenously hungry you become for hot food, a meat sandwich basket with fresh bread, curly fries, and a pickle; or, anything else readily available in the refrigerator. You seek to quench your thirst as well as to satisfy your increased appetite. A plastic jug of fruit-flavored sports drink, mineral water, or lemonade would make a perfect combination for the "Rambo" combo. Unless you happen to have C-rations or MREs in the cupboard.

I read the second half of **Inferno** like a soldier on a mission, waking up early in the morning with renewed energy; exceptionally motivated, having a sense of heightened morale, having already put on a steaming pot of coffee. Prepared for a furious firestorm, I dug in for the duration. By the time I had read 3/4 of the book, I began to feel an almost uncontrollable urgency to just relax and return to my normal, peacetime activities and ordinary routine. I knew then that war is a dirty, ugly business. So, I took a break to finish the book later.

R. Royce was dressed in a newly starched uniform complete with an "Orkin" cap. He carried the usual typical brass metal canister with sprayer-hose by the handle, when he paused momentarily, and walked into the empty hotel room, having entered with a borrowed pass-key. He checked the suite for electronic surveillance devices with a sophisticated gadget he extracted from one of the pouch-pockets of his shirt. There were none. He quickly and efficiently bugged the room and left the premises quietly by the staircase exit and side-door unnoticed.

"The loving couple should arrive from the airport in about two hours," said Cornelius Korn, when he returned to the apartment in an adjacent dwelling. He turned on the receiver and attached a flash-drive recorder and L.E.D. monitor.

"We're all set to go, then," said Royce. He'd changed clothes along the way. He now wore a casual loose-fitting button-down shirt and comfortable stretch-waist slacks. They sat and waited for the business couple to arrive.

At approximately 6 P.M., they saw them enter their hotel room and begin to settle in for the evening. "What time is your business meeting in the morning?" asked the man's wife.

"10 A.M. sharp," said the husband.

"I'll set the alarm clock," she said, accommodating his requirements.

"We'll know by tomorrow afternoon if our firm has won the bid," he said. "Then we can celebrate."

"Our bid?" she asked, batting her eyelashes.

"A cool twenty-one million," he answered, confidently.

Back in Korn's apartment, then, he and Royce heard every word. "We had better relay the information to Meghan at once. We can relax now, but she has work to do," said Korn.

The very next morning Meghan dropped off their firm's bid at the CIA office building in Langely, Virginia, for the upcoming freelance project. Winning the contract would be worth millions.

"You don't think what we're doing is in any way unethical or illegal, do you?" Meghan asked Korn.

"Most certainly not!" he replied, appalled by the very thought. "What kind of unscrupulous businessmen do you think we are?" he replied.

"Good work, Meghan!" said Royce, most pleased by the results, searching her face and getting an instant reaction. She smiled unabashedly and most candidly. "The fact of the matter is, our competition employs unregistered agents from a hostile foreign government. They couldn't possibly win the bid for such an important clandestine operation."

CHAPTER 51

Book review for

The Great Quake

by Henry Fountain, published in 2017.

The Power of a Thousand A-Bombs, minus the Big Bang.

Mix in a scattering of meaningful, pertinent historical facts. Flavor with tales of local indigenous inhabitants set in their natural environment. Salt with the sentimentality of lifelong friendships; loving, caring, intimate relationships; a sense of harmony and community; and peace, wellbeing, and tranquility. Introduce a team of esoteric detectives with a prize-winning attitude and a scientific bent in their backgrounds. Toss in "the pink elephant," a giant upheaval in the form of a catastrophic natural disaster. You have all the necessary cookbook ingredients for a bestselling novel. A "Who Done It" narrative, inspired by true events that actually happened in our lifetime. The resulting book is *The Great Quake*, by Henry Fountain, published timely and recently in 2017.

You will be drawn into the story hook, line, and sinker; captivated, fascinated, and ultimately surprised by how scientific breakthroughs are made in a painstakingly slow, arduous process and by Herculean effort, sustained over long years of solid research. Suddenly, you realize "Life goes on," and you have to get back to it. Only now, you feel better prepared for the imbroglio of inevitable future crises.

"Send her in," said the Admiral, on the bridge of the aircraft carrier flagship.

"Who, Major Thomas?" asked the Air Force liaison officer.

"Yes, Meghan. Who else?" She had just returned from a seminar in Tokyo on using flow-chart logic applicable to wartime scenarios and contingencies planning.

"Did you enjoy your ride on the Japanese bullet train?" inquired the Admiral.

She almost said that the experience was "more fun than a roller-coaster," but held her tongue instead. She knew she was going on a mission of utmost importance. She grinned slyly, felt the keen desire to bounce around, practically going into convulsions, caterwauling, gyrating, strangely contorting her body, and rocking her midsection to and fro.

"Why did you quit your day job?" asked R. Royce.

"The money I was making wasn't worth the time I spent away from home," replied Colonel Korn.

"Take a good look around. We're lost and adrift in the vast South China Sea," said Royce.

"Maybe so, but we're making a lot more money now than we ever have before. Plus, there's the added benefit of job satisfaction."

"How long do you think before a Coast Guard aircraft or an ocean freighter spots our dinghy?" asked Royce.

"Within a few days, I suppose. We're pretty far out," said Korn. "We stand a better chance of being located by one of the Navy's Pacific submarines. I've been pinging our position to their satellite for almost a solid hour now."

"At least, we've completed our assignments and made a clean getaway," added Royce. "The hydrofoil jet skis lived up to all the hype and advance billing, with their high-performance engines and oversized fuel tanks."

"Maybe so, but we still ran out of gas, before we could make it to the island rendezvous point," said Korn. Forty-five minutes later, a periscope raised up out of the ocean's depths and they were positively identified. The submarine might have surfaced then and there to bring the two heroes aboard the submersible vessel, much to their dismay and relief.

"Did you see that?" asked Royce. "A periscope just broke the surface over there. They've spotted us." They were going home sooner than they had anticipated after all, they thought. Within minutes, however, the Captain must have given the order "Down periscope" and their hopes were immediately dashed, as a rush of tiny air bubbles distanced themselves, trailing away from them, disappearing over the wave crest, vanishing over the horizon.

"They just wanted to see if we made it out alive," said Korn.

"They're probably going to send out a Navy destroyer to rescue us, like astronauts returning from the moon," surmised Royce, blatantly disappointed.

"After what we did, they'll probably send a drone," said Korn. "If they don't get us soon, the sharks will begin to circle." He was not overly optimistic.

"Meghan knows where we are, approximately," said Royce, hopefully. Not long afterwards a recognizable jet aircraft painted battleship gray zoomed above, zipped by them, and dipped a wing.

"Oh, there she is now," exclaimed Korn. "Right on time, as scheduled."

"A Seal Team in three Apache helicopters is sure to follow. Fifteen minutes maximum," said Royce.

"No doubt they want the equipment back we borrowed, including the communications device with the portable e-library," said Korn. He was more excited than he might have been, had he just witnessed the "Shockwave Flame-Jet Semi-Truck" beat an airplane to the finish line at the "Alpha Aviation Airfest" extravaganza.

CHAPTER 52

Book review of the novel

Hausfrau

by Jill Alexander Essbaum, published in 2015.

You grab for the reins, hold on tight, and yell "Whoa Nellie!"
But there's no stopping her. You're just along for the thrill ride.

Extolling the virtues of the novel, *Hausfrau*, by Jill Alexander Essbaum, published in 2015, you might want to begin with the fact that the author takes the reader on a personally guided tour of a serene and scenic wonderland, a place where most of us have never been, but have always have wanted to visit; namely the Switzerland of "Heidi," maybe not exactly a classic fairytale kingdom, but as interesting and intriguing a dream destination as could well be imagined. The novel's leading character initially gives you the impression that she is a worldly woman who knows the city of Zurich and the surrounding cantons, practically as well as any native.

Fact two, you quickly learn that she is well-versed in the finer points of the English language and its antecedent grammar. Specifically, she dissects and conjugates sentences faster and easier than I could catch a fish in the creek, clean it, and have it on the table in time for supper. Moreover, she becomes so well acquainted with the Swiss version of the German language as to its structure and meaning in such detail, that she would suitably impress both linguists and ethnologists alike. She also translates Swiss concepts into the English vernacular rather well in the process.

Fact three, you are just as surprised by her in-depth knowledge of philosophical inquiry and deeply religious discourse. She presents valid, metaphysical lines of reasoning and complicated ontological arguments. For example, she openly questions free will, the nature and existence of a Supreme Being, and the After Life.

Fact four, you become fascinated by the progress she makes in revealing and explaining certain subtleties in the sciences of psychiatry and psychoanalysis regarding mental health, in general. You may feel awkward and uncomfortable about it at first, eavesdropping on weeks and weeks of regularly scheduled therapy sessions, like some sneaky, hedonistic voyeur, but at the same time, you become intensely curious about what actually happens in the condensed, underlying, transpiring thought processes. You think, there's one hard and fast rule: "You can't fool your shrink!"

"Or, can you?"

Then it slowly begins to dawn on you, "Nobody gets very far on booze, tranquilizers, pretentiousness, and modulating self-esteem on the road to recovery."

"Or, do they?" Moderation and modernization seems to be the key. Personally, at this point, I began reading between the lines, splicing plots into the story that simply weren't there, and interjecting subterfuges. "Is there a hidden agenda I'm missing?" I must have been reading too many pulp detective stories or watching too many episodes of "Greed" on television in recent months. Not to mention, the hot topics of war and spying that cropped up and creeped into my meandering thoughts. Even today, four decades later, there are people walking around out there who never got over the war in Viet Nam. It just goes to show you, "Not everybody can be as neutral and unaffected as the Swiss."

Fact five, the author sets the reader up with her character's complete lack of knowledge about high finance and the Swiss banking system. So, my mind is working overtime and operating in overdrive trying to figure out the best angles for how such tremendous quantities of bank funds are efficiently and effectively translated into private hands and individual pockets. But this tangential inquiry would be revealing too much and stepping on too many toes, I suppose. The author's leading character might have been so much more, but surely she was never meant to be an ordinary, conniving gold-digger, or a conspiratorial, overachieving socialite. Not that I wouldn't accuse her of emulating either one or the other. Besides she might have been pushed too far, too fast, and too much.

R. Royce checked his precision Swiss watch. "Let me see if I have this correct," he said, looking up. "You know someone who lives in a townhouse complex adjacent to a party who plays his stereo home theater system much too loudly on week-ends, and often late into the night. You told him that you would help convince this party that it would be in his best interest to keep the sound level to a minimum."

"That's about right," said Cornelius Korn, his friend of many years and a close business associate.

"Exactly how do you propose that we achieve this lofty goal?" inquired Royce. "I assume Sparky and the motorcycle gang, including 'Spuds Mackenzie,' the original pit-bull party animal might not want to cooperate and go along, peacefully and quietly."

"Right again," said Korn. "You're on a roll. But I've considered that possibility."

"So, what are we going to do about it?" asked Royce, in a noncommittal tone.

"Interestingly enough, and fortunately for us, Sparky, Spud, Spike, and their three vivacious girlfriends have solved their own problem for us," said Korn, obviously pleased with his recent discovery.

"How so, if you don't mind my asking?" said Royce, not yet entirely convinced.

"The gang has stolen two delivery vans to use as getaway vehicles, and they are in the process of holding up a large bank, as we speak," said Korn, resisting the urge to smile and suppressing the tendency to gloat at having learned inside information.

"Let me guess, damage control. You know where they're going!" said Royce.

Korn continued. "The guys will drop off the cash they've obtained, at the rendezvous with the girls, who will then transport it to the townhouse and put it in a hidden safe. The guys will drive to an isolated and abandoned warehouse, where they will leave the empty vans. From there, they will climb in their own vehicles and travel south for relaxation on a fishing trip that is long overdue. Their plan is pure and simple, but not foolproof."

The terrific trio made the ten o'clock news that very same evening. They had been surrounded, apprehended, and swiftly taken into custody by the sage Delaware County Sheriff and his deputies without further incident, in the vicinity of the second spillway at the Grand Lake recreational area.

The next day, Royce rapped gently on the townhouse door of the friend's noisy neighbors. Dolores opened the door and was confronted by someone she'd never met before, but would have liked to get to know better. He took his time looking inside the living room and saw Pebble and Fawn seated wide-eyed and innocently on the living room sofa.

"Good afternoon," he said, amicably. "I'm your 'Good Neighbor Sam,' with the Homeowner's Association. I hope I'm not disturbing you with this intrusion, but would like to take this opportunity to remind you of our 'quiet hours' policy. As you may be aware, we do not permit excessively loud music in the picture-postcard cottage setting of our lovely gated community. The first time you're given a verbal warning. The second time we issue you a nominal penalty, a token fine, if you will. We call it 'hush money.' Can we count on your full support in this matter of great import?"

"You've convinced me. We're certainly going to be much quieter in the future. We'll be on our best behavior. We've obviously been warned," spouted out Dolores, defiantly.

"I'm turning over a new leaf, beginning today," pouted Fawn, slightly modifying her original position.

"We'll be as silent as tiny little church mice on Sunday," said Pebble, reluctantly, but outspoken nonetheless.

"Thanks a million," said Royce. "We truly appreciate your understanding and cooperation. Have a nice day."

"They had to see what they could get away with, didn't they?" said Meghan. "Do you think we can find them jobs with the CIA? They seem like such nice girls."

"Enterprising, too. Perhaps something part-time during the party season," said Royce. "They'll require passports. Our former station chief would have been proud of us after this little escapade. He's always held such healthy, proactive, and openminded views concerning our extracurricular activities."

"Who? Hugh?" asked Korn, in disbelief.

CHAPTER 53

Book review of the novel

The Monkey's Raincoat

by Robert Crais, published in 1987.

The raving megalomaniac was furious. Mad at her? She hires a detective to find the answer.

Looking for some light reading material for purposes of amusement, while spending some quiet time at the local library one day; lo and behold, I found **The Monkey's Raincoat**, by Robert Crais, published in 1987. The client depicted in the novel isn't as weak, defenseless, and pathetic as you might imagine at first glance. She does have a well-meaning friend upon whom she confides for support and guidance. She leans on her for comfort in her hour of need. Neither of them exactly fits the bill for the stereotypical "Wonder Woman" criteria.

The private eyes they meet from the detective agency to help resolve her problem are interesting to say the least. You might be tempted to call them "Frank" and "Reliable." You discover that Lady Luck smiles upon them repeatedly. You get the idea. They are the kind of fellows who would make good friends and neighbors. They would bail you out and be there for you in a pinch, "when push comes to shove," as some might say. Yet, they are believable characters, as caring and lovable as teddy bears. You get the picture.

The setting is Hollywood Hills, with all of the glitz and glamour. Not unlike the bumper sticker visible on a customized farm truck in sparkling showroom condition dragging Main Street which offers a quick assessment of the situation, "too cool for New York, but savvy enough for L.A."

The plot—no job too tough for our illustrious, esteemed gumshoe investigators; involves a case of mistaken identity coupled with misplaced trust, amidst a raging monsoon of megalomania on the part of the antagonist. Before long, you start thinking, *Somebody ought to go over there and spank that monkey.* No doubt, you will want to read more about these detectives and their daring deeds in a future novel. Putting them together with the damsels in distress, the score from an arrangement of assorted "Looney Tunes" cartoon theme and poignant classical music, you'd have another "LaLa Land" movie hit.

"You want to remove the toxins from your body," said Meghan in a calm and soothing tone of voice, as she saturated a tub of warm, clear, cleansing bathwater with two handfuls of finely granulated salt crystals, infused with eucalyptus oil.

"It's good for the skin and the soul, isn't it?" replied R. Royce.

"I don't know about yours," she said, tactlessly, callously.

"Shall we change the subject, then?" said Royce, on guard. He was beginning to feel somewhat uncomfortable. He winced and looked away. Feeling mortally wounded, the fleeting thought occurred to him that a door to the next universe had suddenly closed before his very eyes.

"Who died and left Alexis Sue Shell in charge?" she burst out, bluntly, spitefully, and somewhat angrily.

"What brought that on, Meghan? It's too late for a soap opera."

"Someone knocks on Cornelius' door late one night and asks if he can help retrieve a cold and frightened kitten out from under the hood of a parked automobile. He calls Susan and brings her aboard to resolve the situation."

"So, she coaxes the cute and cuddlesome creature, forlorn and beyond reach, out with a warm saucer of milk. It's no big deal!" explained Royce.

"But then he put her in charge of communications!" said Meghan, frantic.

"Somebody has to contact us when there's an alert. We can't all be in the office all of the time, 24-7. He needed to free you up for more pressing matters. We have plans for you."

"Oh. What do you have in mind? You're telling me she doesn't have a mean streak or a vindictive bone in her body?"

"No, of course not. Neither do you," Royce began to reassure Meghan, and felt the universe expanding, as it should. "Which is why we're all meeting for a friendly breakfast early tomorrow morning."

She changed her tune and began to ham it up with a song and dance routine. "Don't tease me, please me. Hug me, kiss me, squeeze me."

At Denny's, Cornelius Korn told the others present about the novel he was reading and the solid wooden chair he was building in the shop out of hard-rock maple.

"I bet it's sturdy," Meghan commented. Susan laughed inaudibly, contentedly, catching on quickly.

About that time Korn showed them the tickets for their next vacation. "Pack your bags," he said, beaming. "We're going on a Caribbean cruise." Never once did he mention the next get-rich-quick scheme.

"To Atlantis," said Royce, looking over the itinerary. "A resort hotel named after the fabled lost city at the bottom of the ocean. Are we searching for sunken pirate treasure?"

CHAPTER 54

Book review for

In the Shadows of the American Century
The Rise and Decline of US Global Power

by Alfred W. McCoy, published in 2017.

> *Gulliver wishes to free the geopolitical constraints which bind him.*

In the Shadows of the American Century, by Alfred W. McCoy, published in 2017 is serious-minded, no-nonsense nonfiction. The book is about how the United States has evolved into the premier "superpower" that it is today and why it may lose this exclusive status within the next two or three decades—a deep subject definitely worth pondering. The material presented caters mostly, I believe, to politicians and other top-level government officials; senior military officers; executives of large corporations; historians, and other highly educated intellectuals securely ensconced in their ivory towers.

The rest of us would be better off reading or rereading *Future Shock*, by Alvin Toffler, which was written in 1970; or *1984*, by George Orwell, written decades before that. We can better relate to "sticker shock," wondering what "big brother" and "Uncle Sam" are really up to, and trying to remember a computer password or debit card pin number. This being said and all things considered, I went ahead and read the book anyway, being a naturally curious and basically inquisitive intermediate beginner in the realm of professional development. My conclusion is that the book represents technically brilliant photo-journalism at its finest. But it is totally unconvincing to me that a superpower would go rogue in such an unprecedented, irrational manner, even if the setting sun of imperialism were to cast the mere shadow of a doubt upon our bright future.

According to Toffler, you need "imagination" and "insight" in order to prepare for the future, and defend yourself against its effects. McCoy, on the other hand, may have you believing that all you need is a little "inspiration." I, however skeptical, representing people with common horse-sense, believe what any average American will tell you, that you also need original ideas, sound innovation, ingenuity, and good, timely information, if you're going to get anywhere in life and want to succeed in your endeavors.

If a certain superpower were endowed with good intentions, was a wholly human being, and you identified him by the Jonathan Swift character name "Gulliver," he would obviously be a "giant of a man." You might even go so far as to say that Gulliver has a great many responsibilities. He has obligations and duties to fulfill, as well. Like all of humanity, he has doubts and fears, along with his hopes and dreams. But above all, you can't help but think, "Gulliver only wishes to free himself from the geopolitical constraints that tie him down."

R. Royce had some time to spare, and so he went to the recreation center with the intention of bowling a few games. He warmed, stretched, and limbered up his muscles the first ten frames. His score improved significantly the second game. Along about that time, Cornelius Korn arrived. He was not so much inclined to concentrate on the physical aspects and dynamics of the sport of bowling itself. He was more the type who enjoyed rolling out the flashiest and most impressive-looking bowling ball anyone has ever seen before or since, on occasion.

"Did you enjoy the cruise?" asked Korn, mildly amused.

"Immensely! The islands were absolutely fabulous," replied Royce.

"Especially the part about the deep blue sea, pristine beaches, coconut palms, warm sunshine, and not a care in the world," commented Korn. "Listen, I was thinking about the old '56 two-tone Buick your folks drove back in the day when we were kids. The one that would never go in reverse gear."

"I'd completely forgotten about that," said Royce. "What do you have in mind?"

"You've seen the big, boxy, four-door, all-terrain Jeep I acquired a couple of months ago. A neighbor is trying to sell it for me. He owns the car lot in town."

"Let me guess. You want to add a splash of color to the bulletproof, glossy-black body as an added incentive to prospective buyers, because you're asking too much for the vehicle."

"That's right. What do you think about painting the doors lime green?" asked Korn.

"Might make too much of an impact statement. How about painting the rocker panels underneath the doors instead? Chartreuse should do the trick."

"Splendid idea! Into the paint shop it goes."

"Incidentally, did you sell the treasure map we acquired on the cruise ship?" Royce asked.

"Yes, the funds have transferred. They were deposited into your offshore bank account this morning," beamed Korn, pleased to relay the message.

"One last item on the agenda," said Royce. "You mentioned something about packing a parachute for our next vacation?"

CHAPTER 55

Book review of

The Black List

by Brad Thor, published in 2012.

Telecom giant and media movie mogul buy into televised terrorism; take the internet by storm.

You're at work or on the job one day, and you hear the unmistakable sound of gunshots, the projectiles striking objects in close proximity. A pane of window-glass shatters. Wood from a door-frame splinters. Holes mysteriously appear in the concrete block structure. You might at first think it's job-related. Later, on the way home, while you're in your own neighborhood, you hear more shots fired. You think, now it's getting personal. You become concerned, agitated, and a little unnerved at the sheer audacity of these random acts of violence. But you're neither at home nor on the job.

What's going on here? You're on a fine European vacation far, far away from home and the office. You're totally incognito. Nobody is supposed to know that you're even in Paris, France. Yet, you've just been ambushed. You remember something an old acquaintance once said to you, "Just because you're paranoid doesn't mean somebody isn't out to get you."

You've been brutally attacked and you don't know why or by whom. The situation worsens when you become suspicious that your every movement is somehow being tracked, and you're being followed everywhere you go. "What have I gotten myself into this time?" They are the words of another close acquaintance, back in the day.

You have to "make like a tree and leave." Perform the magician's disappearing act. Fly under the radar. Get off the grid, fast.

Silly, but you try to remember if you've paid last month's cable television bill. You have the completely bundled package deal: satellite television, fiber optics internet, and international phone coverage. You can almost visualize the newspaper headlines now: Telecom Giant and Media Movie Mogul Buy into Televised Terrorism; Take the Internet by Storm.

You begin to consider the entire gamut of conspiracy theory possibilities involving regular criminals, insurgents, mercenaries, terrorists, the Mob, and hostile foreign agents, any of whom could conceivably be targeting you. Particularly you, since you have the indubitably undesirable distinction of working as a deep undercover agent yourself. It's complicated, you know. Preposterous. Illogical. Unbelievable. Deniable. Ethically and morally reprehensible, but so begins the plot of Brad Thor's fast-paced novel, *The Black List*, published in 2012.

Boasting such a potentially diverse and ever-thickening plot, it's no wonder that the book has inspired the enormously popular Hollywood television series with the same title name, which has been running continuously for several seasons now. A different star-studded cast of characters may appear in the show than in the book; nonetheless, the program perpetuates a similar action-packed theme as does the novel. Be that as it may, the show goes off extensively on a multitude of tangents. What you might well imagine if someone converted a regular PC workstation into his own private PlayStation, with virtual-reality goggles and 7.1 surround sound, and he plugs in a different violent, interactive video game every week or so. I'd say the threat to national security seems real enough to me as it is.

R. Royce sat quietly in the driver's seat of his automobile. He was waiting for his cell-phone to ring. Within minutes, it did.

"Hello, Ironman," said Cornelius Korn, his business associate of many years.

"How's the surveillance going?" asked Royce. He wasn't about to be goaded by Korn. Too early in the morning. When you say "Iron-man," some people think about weightlifting, somebody who wants to build up the muscles in his body. Some think about a comic-book superhero made of—what else, iron. As in, his alibi is iron-clad. When winter rolls around, Royce simply likes to get out his "Black & Decker" appliance, plug it into the nearest wall socket, and press his freshly laundered, long-sleeved shirt on a towel he temporarily places on a walnut table in the living room while he watches the morning news program on TV. Putting on the garment gives him a warm, fuzzy feeling. Plus, he enjoys wearing the neatly pressed shirt. What's the big deal all of a sudden?

"Nothing shaking yet," Korn replied. "The hangar is empty. Pilot is nowhere to be seen."

"I should give Meghan a ring," suggested Royce. "She should know what's happening." He ended the call.

"Hello, Ironman," said Meghan, his other business associate. "Glad to hear your voice again! Your contact is right on schedule. He should arrive momentarily at the airport."

"I should drive on over, then," said Royce. "See you later, alligator." He ended the call. He started the Buick and drove to the aviation center. When he got there a Cessna Citation taxied over to the building and the sole passenger exited the aircraft. He wore a green plaid shirt, jacket, and khaki slacks. He was carrying a smart aluminum briefcase.

"Henry Kline?" asked Royce.

"Pleased to meet you, Mr. Ironman," said Mr. Kline. "The funds you requested are in the briefcase."

"Excellent," said Royce. "Would you be so kind as to follow me?" They went over to the Buick he had just parked in the lot minutes before. They got in and drove away. They only had to drive a short distance to the Scenic Charters' hangar, where they waited on another aircraft, this one a Learjet. The timing was perfect. It arrived within a few minutes of their arrival. Korn had them spotted in his binoculars.

"There she is," said Kline. An attractive young lady had disembarked from the Learjet and was walking toward them. He grinned and approached her. She appeared to be happy and healthy. She returned the smile, walked up to the man and gave him a big hug.

"How was your trip to Bogota?" he asked.

"Let's just say I'm very glad to be back in Texas and fortunate to be alive," said the lovely Virginia, his daughter.

"We have one more stop to make," said Royce. "We'd better get going." They piled into the big Buick, and Royce sped away. He drove to another airport not more than twenty miles to the northwest.

"Hello, Ironman," said Meghan. "How are your two passengers doing?"

"They're both exhausted. Virginia, from the trip, and Mr. Kline from the intense negotiations that got her here," said Royce. "But they're both doing well. We'd better get going."

"One more flight and you're both home-free," said Meghan. She led them to her King Air Turbo-prop aircraft. The three of them escaped into the wild blue yonder.

"Hello, Korn," said Royce. "The passengers are on their way home now. We're out of the woods."

"You still have a flight to catch," said Korn, over the phone. "There are three big bodyguards driving your way at a high rate of speed. I don't believe it's a social call."

"Thanks for the warning. I'm on my way," said Royce. He ran over and hopped into the nearest skydiving plane he could find on the airport grounds. The tail number matched the one he was given. The pilot was already aboard. He was also a certified skydiving instructor.

"Mr. Ironman, I presume," said the pilot. "I see you're wearing your parachute. That's a good sign."

"Ready to roll! Today is the most exciting day of my life," said Royce. "I've been completely cured of my intense fear of falling from great heights." The three thugs drove up and saw the plane ascend skyward from the end of the runway. They were obviously too late to question Mr. Ironman. Luckily for them. From a distance, Korn had them spotted in his sights.

"A day late and a dollar short," he said out loud. He turned the ignition switch on and began following their vehicle at a safe distance. He nonchalantly whistled a tune as he played follow the leader. The theme song from "The Bridge Over the River Kwai." At their destination, Korn drove up beside their vehicle. He exited his vehicle and walked over to the water-fountain, where they stood.

"You're all washed up," he said politely, wanting to make a good first impression. "When I spoke with your boss, he casually mentioned that you've been terminated. I have him on the phone in case you want to verify this information."

"You'll never work in Hollywood ever again," said their Boss and disconnected the phone.

"If you're looking for another job, maybe I can be of some assistance," said Korn. He was professional in every sense of the word, a real deal-closer. He handed the men a business card for a new construction and remodeling firm.

CHAPTER 56

Book review of the novel

The Secret History of Twin Peaks

by Mark Frost, published in 2016.

Very much alive in '65, he gave a hoot and a holler into the wind tunnel from whence they came.

How is ***The Secret History of Twin Peaks***, by Mark Frost, published in 2016? Forget everything you've ever heard, read, or seen. The officially accepted version in the form of a factual cold-case FBI file that's been inactive for 29 years, with supporting documentation going back 213 years, has just landed on your desk. You've been newly assigned as the most recent "control" officer for the unsolved mystery. Included are an estimated 3,000 pages of official classified government and secret military documents for "your eyes only" to peruse before you go into the field and conduct the full-on investigation into the matter.

Three thousand pages, with hieroglyphics, marginal notes, et cetera. Some of which may be strictly conjecture or purely subjective. You conclude, this certainly represents a conspiracy and a possible coverup! Shuffling through and skimming over the assorted pages, and copies of pages, you quickly realize the gravity of the situation. You proceed to leaf through the files with a fine-tooth comb and a magnifying glass. You carefully assess and cautiously evaluate each bullet item as you go.

First and foremost, there are the murders to consider; the missing persons; then the madness, mayhem, hysteria, and chaos to follow in their wake. You reflect: there has always been a perpetrator. Or perpetrators, plural.

You think solving the mystery should be as easy as helping yourself to a delicious slice from a large, frosted and appropriately decorated birthday cake at the office party. Or, even more apropos, like floating a sailboat downstream on a lazy river in the summertime. You simply have to "go with the flow." If your yacht were in the Atlantic Ocean, you'd naturally follow the Gulf stream to get where you're going; no doubt, a tropical paradise. Similarly, if you were airborne in the upper atmosphere of Earth in a high-flying experimental aircraft, you'd want to follow the jet-stream for the added boost of a tailwind. Taking the concept further, to the next level, if you dare, what if you were going to Mars and points beyond?

Why you'd just have to wait for the most opportune, historical moment when the planets and all the heavenly bodies in the universe and the next several galaxies line up properly, then follow the gravitational pull. Conceivably, under the right conditions, and circumstances, at the right place and time, you could attain a velocity greater than the speed of light to accelerate you on your way to your ultimate destination, past the stars of your own constellation, gliding and sailing along effortlessly through the remote regions of the frictionless vacuum known as outer space. The stuff of science fiction and crackpots, to be sure. I don't necessarily think so.

The only problem then would be slowing down and eventually stopping. You see yourself sitting on your garden-variety lawn chair, peering out over the horizon, relatively motionless in the gravitational field of your new home planet, in the distant universe of a faraway galaxy. But you're willing to cross that bridge when you come to it. And you begin to think that you are the best qualified candidate for the mission. After all, you've been recruited out of college and trained by the highly motivated instructors at Quantico; not to mention, the world-renowned scientists at NASA.

Three more inquiries you must make: What has happened to your predecessors, the two special agents you have replaced? Who will be your current partner and backup operative, your fellow field-officer? And where is your point of contact for the quaint little gingerbread-baking, storybook community, affectionately known as Twin Peaks?

You can hardly wait. You're eager to travel, get settled into your new living quarters, and begin meeting the local inhabitants. As they say, you are "loaded for bear," primed and pumped and ready for your new wildlife adventure. You plan on totally immersing yourself into the culture and nightlife. The experience you gain should prove exhilarating, exciting, and challenging, if not actually rewarding. You fully expect to work overtime, putting it into overdrive when necessary. You'll do the required due-diligence, and do it on the double as the situation dictates. If it doesn't work out, you can always take copious notes and "run like hell." You'll just have to see how it pans out.

You hope your new partner isn't too nutty, fruity, or quirky—as was the previous one. Mr. Spontaneous. You'd settle for normal, ordinary, and average. Competent and alert are plus-factors. But you'll take whatever help you can muster up. Otherwise, you are on your own out there in the wilderness. After all is said and done at the end of the day, to whom can you complain?

The answer: to anyone who'd give a hoot! You would go to great lengths obtaining useful information that yielded positive-proof results.

There has been a pernicious rumor lately circulating in the office about "little green men" captured by the USAF in the 1940s, who were said to communicate using telepathic messages, through the use of brainwaves and diffuse, cloudlike, softly reflective lights which gradually change their hues. At least one of them was still alive in the 1960s, reportedly conveying messages about locating a powerful source of potential energy.

Supposedly, this particular alien gave military and other government officials the distinct impression that he wanted to reverse-engineer the hulk of an alleged UFO spacecraft, long-since crashed and recovered in New Mexico, remanufacture a brand-new one, and return with it to a far distant galaxy via the "slip-stream," which incidentally bypasses the planet Mars altogether, but is in close enough proximity to make the trip most interesting and worthwhile. Scientists wonder, particularly the astrophysicists and astronomers. Interested parties want to know from whence he arrived, and would gladly finance the venture and several other projects.

What am I missing here? DNA evidence for an extraterrestrial? A genie in a bottle? See for yourself!

R. Royce awoke early on Christmas Day. He brewed a pot of coffee, poured a cup, and prepared a bowl of microwave oatmeal. A healthy meal choice for your constitution on any occasion, he thought. Lowers your cholesterol. The gooey concoction has all the grit, natural fiber, and roughage you need in order to cleanse the inside walls of your stomach and intestines, to make you regular again during the everyday process of food digestion. Along with fresh air and exercise. Afterwards, you feel as clean as a whistle inside and out. At least that's what he believes. He watched an episode of the early morning "Farm Report" on television. He especially enjoyed the featured story segments about harvesting evergreen trees in Virginia and raising reindeer in North Dakota.

He reviewed the messages on his telephone answering machine. There was a holiday greeting from his sister. She was at Ashleigh's Boutique, trying on evening dresses for a formal dinner party. So, he called his mother to wish her a Merry Christmas. She said that his brother was over at their cousin Donald Vann's house, welding a flatbed trailer. She was about to watch the parade at Disneyland on television.

There were no specifically pressing issues that he had to address on this day. He would rest, relax, and spend some quality time near the fireside hearth. It so happened that he was snowed in by a blizzard and couldn't go anywhere anyway. He thought about the "little green elf" he'd read about years ago, having been discovered wandering onto the highway from the desert one starry, starry wintry night. What if he had actually been the spiritual emissary of "intelligent life" elsewhere, visiting for the express purpose of wishing us "Peace on Earth, Good Will toward Men" only nobody was able to recognize him as such or even understand the message he conveyed? Of course, the disputed fact that he had arrived in a UFO, may have caused the government in its infinite wisdom enough consternation to cover up the story and make it go away.

He decided it was time to wake up Meghan Thomas, his business associate, the most merry and amorous significant other. He suddenly had the urge to go sledding down the hill in the snow on a toboggan designed for two, the way they did when they were children in the Colorado Rockies.

Down the slope, between the trees, around the big bend they went. At the base of the hill Cornelius Korn and Alexis Sue Shell were calmly seated on a snowmobile, overlooking a naturally occurring granite and quartz rock formation, the cleft of which surrounded an oval pool of steamy, clear bluish green water.

"Welcome to our Himalayan hot-tub hideaway," said Cornelius, cheeringly.

"We're having more fun than a barrel of monkeys," said Alexis Sue, enthusiastically.

"How long has this pool of spring-water been here?" inquired Meghan, cautiously dipping her hand into the water, obviously the last to know, but warming up fast to the idea.

"About thirty-five million years, " said R. Royce. "Champagne, anyone?" He held out a magnum and four glasses. "Caviar?" He indicated a tray of hors d'oeuvres which was strategically placed on a rock-shelf serving as a table. They were in for a treat. Swimsuits optional.

CHAPTER 57

Book review for the novel

Pompeii

by Robert Harris, published in 2003.

He observed the smoke rising from a campfire in the moonlight from some distance away.

One man's soul searching trial and tribulation, as he attempts to conquer a mountain of adversity.

Nothing on earth can quite match the therapeutic effects of a Roman health spa resort purification by fire.

The novel **Pompeii**, by Robert Harris, published in 2003, is an absolutely fascinating snapshot and account of life in southern Italy in the bustling coastal communities which had sprung up along the foothills of Mount Vesuvius by the year 79 A.D. A real sense of purpose and opportunity motivates the Roman citizens, subjects, and inhabitants residing or frequenting there. Senators, magistrates, scientists, admirals, engineers, naturalists, journalists, philosophers, prophets, builders, shepherds, farmers, craftsmen, and their entourage all make their homes in the vicinity. They have transformed the landscape by their creations and the fruits of their labor with no small measure of assistance from a great number of soldiers, sailors, other conscripts, and indentured servants. You begin to feel the repercussions and the sudden impact of civilization at the stupendous height of imperialism on all of mankind. After all, building a thriving metropolis with all its amenities has indeed been a daunting task over the centuries.

To insure their future, civic-minded leaders ask the "sibyl" for a favorable sign. "Where has the raven perched on the rock gone?" she wonders. The bird has gone missing. This is a worse omen.

Reading further, you get the distinct impression of longing and a sense of foreboding. Something is dreadfully wrong with this pastoral scene, something that you cannot easily put a finger on, something that you cannot simply repair with baling wire, duct tape, or a patch of Portland cement. The reader of the novel becomes intrigued by the developing mystery, the majesty, and the mounting suspense which has been left unvented. There are other indicators, but you need solid scientific proof and hard evidence of unusual natural phenomena. "What is happening here?" many ask, but no one seems to know for certain.

True, the people have literally built their homes on shaky ground. The ground trembles. Fish are found floating in the hatchery ponds. A river runs dry. The air is fouled and becomes putrid. Hence, the emperor of Rome, one "Titus Caesar," dispatches a knowledgeable expert in such matters, an hydraulics engineer, of all things—"Attilius," by name, to discover the real reason for all the troubling activity in the region. In my humble opinion, what the leading character encounters and the actions he takes, gives the novel substance. It lends credence to what makes life bearable and tolerable.

In the final analysis, while Pompeii has forged its place in history, the purely fictional story of Attilius provides incredible insight into the human condition. He walks through the gates of the Pan-Hellenic Council and enters into their abode. The room in which he stands was over-heated. It becomes a blast furnace. His trial and tribulation is more the story of human evolution, and the purification of his soul, rather than any form of revolution.

R. Royce sat and watched an extraordinarily delightful cooking show on television. "Marsey dotes an' dosey dotes, an' liddle lamsey divy," sang the charming and beautiful blonde chef as she removed the main course, an iron skillet of well-seasoned, steaming, and bubbling baked tomato, zucchini, and squash basking in their natural juices and infinite glory from the oven. "Woo who, whoa ho ho!" she exclaimed, carefully tilting the accompanying round pan of freshly baked apple pie dessert toward the viewing audience, revealing its heaping, golden brown, flaky crust. The smell of cinnamon and the other spices permeating the air must have been totally intoxicating. He had become mystified watching the scene unfold. He felt utterly astounded and dumbfounded. He was hungry for more! He'd never seen a finer, more eloquent meal prepared with any two of his favorite dishes. Perhaps this is a slight exaggeration, but no matter. He was given over to hyperbole.

"The preparation of such a wonderful meal deserves a toast!" he said aloud, and meandered into the kitchen without a care in the world. He extracted a chilled bottle of a most excellent sparkling wine from the refrigerator, poured half a glass-full, then sat down at the table to relish the moment. He helped himself to the zucchini casserole left for him in a covered ceramic dish placed on a trivet, the dish still very warm to the touch. Quite satisfied with the main course, he sliced into a freshly baked golden-delicious apple pie, also warm from the oven. Thus, his midday meal proved most tasty.

After eating his fill, he reached over and read the note on the table: "Hope you enjoyed lunch. It was especially prepared just for you. Gotta run, Meghan."

"Will wonders never cease?" he inquired out loud. It was uncanny how similar the meal had been to the one featured on television.

Royce discovered that it had snowed overnight. He retrieved a broom from the closet and swept the white powdery snow off of the exposed body surfaces of his automobile and started up the motor. He switched on the heater, raised the temperature level, and put the fan on high in order to expedite melting the frosted ice from the windows. The very next day, another cold one, he had to repeat the process, since it had snowed again. He called Meghan on the cellphone to find out when she might return.

"Thanks for the lunch," he said. "You didn't have to go to all the trouble. I could have gone out and grabbed a sandwich."

"Oh, I didn't make you lunch," said Meghan. "Your neighbor dropped by to introduce herself and left food on the table before we left. Did you know that she has a cooking show on television?"

"I do now," said Royce. "By the way, how are the road conditions out there?"

"Very unfavorable," said Meghan. "You should stay home if you don't have to go anywhere."

"How were you able to drive, then?" asked Royce.

"My car drives perfectly well on a solid sheet of ice in freezing sub-zero temperatures," she volunteered, without hesitation.

"Well, be careful out there. Otherwise, I might have to send out a rescue party to search for you," he said.

"If I'm not back by five P.M., you can tow me home yourself," she said. "I'll be at the office finishing up some paperwork and finalizing last-minute details."

"We're going to make a fortune from this deal," said Cornelius Korn, when Royce relayed the news to him. "So long as the plans we made don't go off half-baked."

"According to Meghan, our firm has submitted a successful bid for a major industrial contract to provide the water-lines necessary for an upcoming mission to Mars," said Royce. The flexible double-walled tubes are made from a very cleverly designed, lightweight, aeronautical material, which is actually an insulated titanium-reinforced carbon-fiber composite. They are very durable, puncture resistant, and unaffected by severe temperature extremes. The space between the two tube walls can contain super-heated steam. This allows a steady stream of liquefied water to flow through the central-core interior tube from the heated water reservoir, which is really only a large tank of melted water at the source, all the way to the underground base station a couple of miles away, without freezing somewhere along the way. As you may be aware, the base station has been located deep inside a cavern to protect astronauts from the harsh conditions of life on Mars.

"As I have often heard it said before," said Korn. "Good luck with that." A fine kettle of fish.

CHAPTER 58

Book review for

The Last Picture Show

by Larry McMurtry, published in 1966.

They let their puppies breathe free as they played in "the green grass of home."
Raw material for a sure-fire trip to Huntsville.

I vaguely remember reading the novel *The Last Picture Show* by Larry McMurtry, published in 1966, during my formative high school years. Sometime during my college years, I saw the infamous B&W film version, shortly after its release. The film pretty much followed the plot and characterization of the book fairly faithfully, but for a few slight alterations, probably for cinematic effect. Possibly because one of the actresses objected to performing a scene like that in public. There are numerous scenes with adult situations in them. Strictly R-rated raw material in my opinion. The story is about a group of rebellious high school students who live in a small town in Texas in the 1950s. One thing that impressed me then and now are the strong values instilled in the community involving family, friendship, and kinship. You could say that they really know how to circle the wagons. Their lives are permeated by the influence of the wild west in general, cattle ranching in particular, and, of course, the oil industry. They also have a strong sense of patriotism and independence. Many migrate to Dallas and Fort Worth after graduation. Some to Midland and Odessa. There's a thriving Air Force base in the vicinity. Some go to California; some to Mexico. It is all a matter of business and opportunity. You have to start out somewhere in life, whether you work as a ranch-hand on the prairie or roughneck in the oil fields or enlist in the army. There are two basic facts of life: you have to eat and you have to earn a living somehow.

In the novel, "Lois" is a concerned mother who tries in vain to explain the facts of life and the benefits of a good, solid liberal arts education to her precocious, wide-eyed, and innocent daughter, a high school senior, who doesn't seem to want to listen. Lois tries to lead by example to help her gain an understanding of the ways of the world by involving her in organized social events, such as extracurricular football game activities and the Christmas dance at the American Legion. Her immediate short-term goal is to enroll her in college in Dallas as soon as she can and get her out of "Dodge" fast.

Meanwhile, some of the local high school boys begin to "sow their oats," so to speak, and begin to explore the more nefarious aspects of the world around them. They want to broaden their horizons. Normally, they are responsible, rugged individuals who work hard in the oil fields and play hard on the football field. A few of the teachers in school try to teach them something relevant, but mostly they learn from the school of "hard knocks." Teaching them anything is like trying to educate a litter of feral hogs: all they want to do is root around in the mud, rut, and run wild through the briars and brambles, among the mesquite and cactus. Yet, deep down in your heart, you get the distinct feeling that there is a spark of humanity somewhere inside of them after all. They must shape their own destinies, make their own difficult choices, and take calculated risks. You can only hope and pray that they make the right decisions along the way. It is all part of the growing up process.

Still, there are pros and cons as to how exactly these rites of passage are to be accomplished. By brute strength alone. By survival of the fittest. Where only the strong survive. Maybe under certain conditions. By bullying and coercion. Doubtful. This is totally unacceptable behavior. It will simply no longer be tolerated. This is the reason why we have laws and the constitution. It is a matter of righteousness and fairness. It is only by the grace of God, among other things, that we live together in peace and harmony.

Moreover, by taking advantage of the weak, powerless, and susceptible, some invite legal battles and political action. They are shunned by the church. The moral indignation and retribution becomes overwhelming. They cannot win. They lose face, prestige, and possibly a big law-suit. The prospect of financial ruination looms over the horizon.

R. Royce was out watering his roses in the backyard from a garden hose. The neighbor's calico cat kept him company. The roses had been growing and blooming for about seven years. He lived in a big yellow-brick house on the corner in a small Texas town. Over the years, he had planted the rose bushes in a straight row between an ancient ash and an old hackberry tree. They bloomed periodically throughout April and on into November. The line of roses ran parallel to Bishop drive, a side street on the North side of the property. The residential area where he lived used to be mostly cotton fields in the 1960s. He was the second owner of the house. He planted a second row of roses along the back boundary, perpendicular to the first, between the tall trees which grew there in a long line. The boundary looked like a small inverted v-shaped ridge, and ran for miles in either direction, north and south. Royce planted two sturdy Lacy oaks to replace the ones which had been chopped down before he moved into the neighborhood. He thought the ridge was some sort of geological marvel, even though one of the neighbors said that it was just the edge of the cotton field that had risen up because the ground had never been plowed under. Royce had his doubts, and secretly believed that it conceals an underground spring.

The cat jumped from the lawn-chair on which she rested and began playing with a grasshopper that had begun leaping around the yard under the hackberry tree in the corner of the yard. All at once a dark gray bird of unknown origins flew out of the tree and assaulted the cat in a dive-bombing raid, flying just above the cat's arched back. The cat tried to defend herself and pawed at the air, but was too late. Next the bird flew in front of the cat, tempting the cat further, but she again swatted too late with her paw. The bird repeated its assault on the cat. Again and again the cat swatted too late. The bird was too fast for the cat. The bird vanished for a time. The cat resumed watching Royce water the flower bushes.

Moments later, the bird magically reappeared in the air. The cat alerted and went to pounce on the bird as it flew by. The bird flew a few feet away and landed in the yard nearby. It hopped about, limped along, and held its wing as if it were hurt or injured. It looked as if it were unable to fly. The cat gained confidence and rushed forward, but again the bird flew a short distance away and landed on the lawn.

Along about that time, Royce's lovely neighbor, Nelda appeared. She had been out looking for her cat. She saw what had transpired and explained to Royce that the bird was only pretending to be injured in order to lure the pesky cat away from her nest in the hackberry tree. She would risk her very life to save her offspring if necessary.

Then, Nelda asked Royce if he had noticed the large hawk circling above the treetops. "They have been known to swoop down without warning into the yard and carry away small, defenseless animals, such as cats and dogs," she said.

He remembered the time they had gone to one of the neighbor's garage sale. The neighbor had noticed Royce had been going over to Nelda's house late in the evening on several occasions. He politely told her, "Oh, I just like to go over there and watch 'HBO' while she gets her exercise." Nelda felt terribly annoyed that her neighbor, a devout, god-fearing woman and a longtime resident of the community would pry into her personal life so. Royce hoped that she hadn't felt insulted, embarrassed, or shocked in any way by the awkward revelation.

He remembered the time he lived in Florida as a young man. While eating a hamburger at Wendy's on the beach one day, after having gone swimming in the ocean, he noticed that two teenage girls seated nearby were trying to agree on their plans for the rest of the afternoon. One of them leered at passersby, cajoled, and grinned mischievously.

"I'll teach you to be a bitch," she proclaimed loudly and suddenly, to the amusement and delight of her companion, without any warning whatsoever or the slightest provocation, obviously acting out a scene from a soap opera drama, or repeating what she must have recently heard somebody say. You'd think that she would have been an embarrassment to her mother, squealing the way she did.

About that time, their friends showed up, with their surf boards. They were wet and dripping. The girls began to chatter enthusiastically with the surfers. They became animated, jumping up and down, and clowning around. Practicing their techniques. Her mother finished the morning shift at the hamburger stand. "Let's go, you little criminals," she said. They all piled into her station wagon. The surfers secured the boards on top with bungy cords.

Royce waited for his girlfriend. She was supposed to meet him there after work. A Marine Corps training officer, she reminded him of a character from a movie flick he'd once seen, *The Last Picture Show*. Only she was all grown up now. "Charlene Duggs" was in great physical condition! You might even say that she had "reinvented" herself. She was vivacious, charismatic, outgoing, and energetic. The complete package. The real deal. A total makeover. "All I ever needed was to meet a few good men," she once confided in him.

CHAPTER 59

Book review of the novel

HHhH

by Laurent Binet,
published in 2009, English translation in 2012.

When placed at the scene of the crime, the devil lies in the details.

The format of the novel, *HHhH*, by Laurent Binet, published in 2009, the English translation by Sam Taylor published in 2012, is not unlike that of a professional sporting event, televised on any given Sunday afternoon in the Fall. The author provides you with an interesting pregame report, the game itself with colorful commentary, and the post-game analysis with big-play highlights. Only the subject matter is of a much more serious nature. As serious as helmet-to-helmet contact and concussions. Such unsportsmanlike behavior on the playing field simply cannot be tolerated by the league any longer. Neither should it be tolerated in diplomacy. The similarity ends here. The subject of the book is war, not peace. The novel is about a wartime event that reportedly actually happened during World War II. The author relates the pertinent facts having bearing on the case. He tells you which side he favors in the conflict. He places you at the scene of the crime at the exact instant when it takes place. He discusses and describes the implications, repercussions, and reprisals which result. He gives you all the ammunition you need in order to decide for yourself the level of success or failure of the "mission." At this point, I merely want to interject and reiterate: "the devil is in the details."

On the subject of war-crimes, much has been written. I'm not certain that all of the judgments that have been passed are universally acknowledged and accepted, however. The terms "ratified" and "professional courtesy" come to mind for some obscure reason. Nevertheless, it has been said, "one man's resistance fighter is another man's terrorist." It has also been said that, "Might is right." In other words, whoever wins the war most likely goes unpunished. There are other considerations which follow, such as those involving collateral damage; namely, the innocent civilians, non-combatants, women, and children who become casualties of war. Perhaps the author does not adequately address these issues. Actually, he does not have to, because the book is a novel, not a treatise on government policy or a binding resolution in international law. He does not pretend to be a charter member of the Geneva Convention or a Supreme Court judge at the Hague either. Instead, he makes you think about these types of concerns. "How can the weak feudal state defend its humble fiefdom against the expansionist all-powerful, empire-building nation and become sovereign and independent itself?" one ponders. Remember, we are no longer competing at flag football on a level playing field with referees who are fair and impartial.

What actually transpired and was duly reported in great length in the book was no peaceful demonstration of protest. It was either an overt act of war, albeit, involving sabotage and espionage; or it was a prime example of a domestic dispute that spiraled totally out of control. Let us hope and pray that such an event does not ever repeat itself. Only the occurrence of another massive cataclysmic social upheaval could bring about such a dramatic change in the course of history.

R. Royce contemplated his life and deeds. He meditated. Breathing inward deeply and exhaling easily, he gradually began to relax and unwind. He remembered an early event from childhood. He was on a carnival ride, twirling around in circles on a simulated rocket-ship, clutched and suspended in mid-air by the whirling hydraulic metal lifting-arm mechanism. Lights of many colors scintillated and blurred all around him. Someone in the distance yelled, "Pull the handle." As he rotated around and around, someone called out again, "Pull back the handle." But Royce kept to himself, still and silent, as he took in the strange sights, musical sounds, the cotton-candy and caramel-coated popcorn smells. He was thrilled, excited, but not uplifted. Yet, he had somehow felt a keen sense of elation, similar to weightlessness. *Just as much fun as electric bumper cars*, he thought. Later in life, he considered going into the Air Force, but when someone told him, "Aim low, avoid disappointment," he enlisted in the Army instead. Much later in life, after he'd heard the immortal words, "No guts, no glory!" he began to realize that he was no hero. Definitely not a role-model either, but he had ideas and ambition. Had he pulled back on the handle, he would have risen high into the air and gone off like a Roman candle.

He reflected on the time when he was a little boy riding in the front seat of an automobile. Seatbelts weren't required to be worn back then, and most automobiles were not manufactured with headrests to prevent "whiplash" in the event of a collision. The driver sped around the curve to the service entrance in the alley of the Safeway store in Oklahoma City because he was in a hurry to pick up his paycheck. As he did so, the passenger-side door suddenly flew open. It had not been securely latched or locked. Perhaps Royce had pushed on the door handle by mistake at the wrong time. He flew out of the speeding vehicle, rolled on the concrete several times, and was momentarily stunned. The driver braked the car, reversed it, and pulled up alongside the boy, who appeared miraculously uninjured, and sat upright on the pavement. The driver, who must have been a neighbor or an acquaintance of the family, said, "Well, are you going to get in, or not?" As had been previously mentioned, he was obviously in a hurry. "You're lucky we didn't have an accident," he went on to say. As a result, and again, three or four cat-lives later, Royce had become much more security conscious. He actively tried to avoid risky, isolated incidents like being "thrown under the bus" and seeing "his life flash before his very eyes," which are generally preventable.

He saw a vision of loveliness. She was skiing cross-country, cascading over a snow-covered hill in her skin-tight, see-through spandex stretch ski pants and sky-blue down-filled zippered jacket with forest-green accents, topped off with cherry red lips and cheeks, bright, cheery eyes, an incandescent knit cap, and a smile. Royce picked up the phone. "What are you doing?" he asked.

"Oh, nothing really. Fifteen-minute workout on the Nordic track machine," Meghan replied.

"I'll be right over," he said.

CHAPTER 60

Review of the history book

The Storm Before the Storm:
The Beginning of the End of the Roman Republic

by Mike Duncan, published in 2017.

> *Virtue may be its own reward, but it does not take a military genius to figure out that the Consul of Rome did not ransack the city for its philosophy.*
>
> *It was not difficult to raise an army in Rome in the year 84 B.C.*

The book *The Storm Before the Storm*, by Mike Duncan, was published in 2017. The impressively well-researched, concise, and scholarly work relates to the stone-throwing, sword-wielding history of Rome during the time period roughly four to seven generations before the birth of Jesus Christ. A stark sense of foreboding begins to dawn on you when you read between the lines. You find the inference "raising an army in Rome was not difficult" has far-reaching implications. In addition, the author provides readers with an excellent English translation of an esoteric Latin quotation attributed to a wise and prominent philosopher at the beginning of each chapter. Insightful, the quotation drives home a major point, gives greater meaning to, and offers a unique perspective for the topic in question in each chapter.

If you are not already a well-versed lover of Latin linguistics, the author takes time to explain the meaning, usage, and function of certain obtuse, archaic, or technical terms, which have evolved or been incorporated into the daily lives of virtually every Roman citizen. You can't help but gain a deeper appreciation of the Forum, the Senate, and the Assembly, as well as many of their principal members and arch-enemies.

Who among us has ever heard of the dangerous exploits and grisly adventures of Gracchus, Marius, Jugurtha, Sulla, Mithridates, Drusus, or Cinna? I certainly haven't, until I began to delve into this particularly interesting book of antiquity. If you haven't heard of these several notable larger-than-life personalities either, and others, of whom the author mentions, you are in for a real treat. The author goes on to elaborate and elucidate, telling their individual stories, which are nothing short of incredible. The conflicted history of these terrible and terrific titans of Western Civilization turns out to be spectacular, overwhelming, and decimating. Yet, at the end of the day, the reader may pause and reflect that something good must have come out of all the strife and chaos they created after all. The possibility of peace, prosperity, and better government, for instance. Greater respect for humanity, human life in general, and personal dignity would only arrive a couple of thousand years later for some, the enlightened and fortunate ones. More drastic changes would be needed first.

R. Royce watched a professional bull-riding event on television. The commentator's advice for the average cowboy was, "You have to point your toes out and dig your heels in, if you want to stay on the bull." Royce had to think about that one for a minute. The object of riding a bull for the cowboy is to stay on top for at least 8 seconds with one hand raised in the air and one hand grasping the leather harness tightly wrapped around the bull's mightily muscular mid-section. Rodeo judges determine his score by how well he rides the bull. What the commentator neglected to mention is that a real cowboy wears silver spurs that jingle, jangle, and dangle on the heels of his boots. When he forcibly digs them into the haunches of the bull, the bull goes absolutely crazy, bonkers. The bull receives quite an unpleasant sensation, if not downright painful. He begins to jump high into the air repeatedly, writhing uncontrollably. He performs the most amazing contortions imaginable. He gyrates and spins around wildly, bucks, twists, and turns—anything to prevent the cowboy from digging the star-shaped metal spur points into the tender flesh of his flanks. So, technically speaking, digging his heels into the haunches of the bull, does not so much help the cowboy stay on the bull better, but it definitely helps him score more points with the judges, should he ride the bull for the required length of time.

Along about that time his friend and cohort Cornelius Korn telephoned. Royce picked up a nearby cellphone. He told Royce that the dental bridge in his mouth had come loose while he was biting into a casserole entre.

"The bridge is rock solid. It lasted about thirty years and the dentist offered to glue it back in on the spot," he said. But, Korn was more concerned about the strength of the teeth underneath. The dental assistant took some routine panoramic x-rays, and scheduled another appointment for the actual dental work to commence. "The initial shock of losing three teeth at the same time has worn off," Korn continued. But he was still uncertain whether to have the dentist fabricate and install a new bridge, or get an implant and three crowns."

"I'd definitely get a second opinion from the dentist who does implants," said Royce. "He should know if you are a suitable candidate for the delicate procedure."

CHAPTER 61

Book review for the novel

The Affair

by Lee Child, published in 2011.

Events leading up to his discharge from active duty military service.
  She offered her honor. He honored her offer.

Not everyone is cut out for military service. This is why the U.S. government in its infinite wisdom abandoned the military lottery system known as "the draft" long ago, and replaced it with the "all-volunteer army" concept in the later 1970s, sometime during President Nixon's administration. As America's fascination with war began to wane, it only made sense. You get soldiers who actually want to be in the military. Motivated to begin with, new recruits are more than willing to serve their country during times of strife, conflict, and outright war. They can be trained and managed to perform a variety of missions on a grand scale, using the most modern, sophisticated, and lethal weaponry mankind has ever seen. By means of thoroughly tough, rigorous training techniques and indoctrination methods, they become physically fit and mentally challenged. Those who endure, become stronger and more confident in their abilities than ever before in their lives. At least theoretically, they come out of basic training and their advanced specialty schools marching and singing to the tune of "The Ballad of the Green Berets."

Some common themes running through the "Lone Wolf," "Lone Ranger," "Billy Jack" "Bronson" Reacher series of novels, by Lee Child, including *The Affair*, which was published in 2011, include those pertaining to the aforementioned volunteer army, the rules of engagement, military downsizing during peacetime, uniformity and other strict military standards, upward mobility and promotion potential, opportunity to travel and see the world, exotic overseas tours of duty, military values in general, and my personal favorites, civil affairs and total control.

The local Sheriff in a small Mississippi town becomes completely perplexed, baffled and bamboozled by the main character, Major Reacher, and his undercover activities, when the mysterious stranger shows up unexpectedly in town. She cannot help but wonder, "How does he keep his composure in times of such crises?" and "How does he manage and react to the prolonged intervals of intense stress he endures time and time again?"

Whatever some individuals, many of them prior service members, may think about military values, they naturally begin to reflect on abstract, ideological terms like "honor, duty, country." Patriotism. The Stars and Stripes. Or, they simply remember the commercials on television. For instance, the one with the gallant soldier in the field who says with great candor and in all modesty, brimming with pride, "We do more before 9 A.M. than most people do all day long." It drives home a point.

Whenever I pause to reflect on "attention to detail," I remember the grass drills in particular, the extracurricular impromptu exercises performed by a targeted group of selected aspiring soldiers, who for whatever reason had neglected to pack a pair of leather gloves with their warm woolen liners into their field-packs for an upcoming road march. Or, in some cases, were too lazy or defiant to pull them out of their backpacks to show the drill sergeants in charge of the exercise as proof of their readiness. Or, because they were curious and just wanted to be able to participate in grass drills, for the sheer thrill of it all. Who knows what goes on in the minds of soldiers on the subconscious level?

Total control? That just meant your platoon was confined to post, for the duration of training or the latest mission. There would be no passes or leave or absenteeism anytime soon.

Civil affairs? That's the letter you received at boot camp or in the theater of operations from your girlfriend. Upon reading and reciting the letter word for word, you reflect on the contents and ponder. "End of story. That's all she wrote."

Rules of engagement in actual hand-to-hand combat between opposing forces in wartime? Kill or be killed. There are no two ways about it. For most other real-world scenarios, de-escalation of hostilities is probably the best policy. The threat of imminent danger being the predominant factor. Determent is always a practical expedient.

I saw an old classmate whom I hadn't seen or thought much about since high school. He dropped by my cousin's house the other day to pay his respects, since a member of the family had recently passed away. I was cheered by the sudden remembrance of my youth and vitality upon his arrival, and by the advice he had once given us way back then, when we wanted to run away and join the Marines. He had long ago proclaimed, "Eat the apple and forget the Corps!" On this particular day, however, he had to admit, "I made a pretty good living in the Marines." One thing about it, he obviously knew the importance of staying in shape as you grow older. He didn't appear too flabby or too shabby either. He had taken care of himself over the long haul. There was the issue of the neck-brace he wore, but then we all knew that he liked to spend time on the wild west and reckless side of town on occasion. Must have been due to an altercation, attitude adjustment, or accident.

R. Royce sat squarely on the cushioned seat of a BMW motorcycle in the recreational vehicle showroom. They have quick acceleration you know, and they have quiet, reliable, smooth-running engines. You can't beat the German engineering and metallurgy that goes into the manufacture of one of those things. They boast economical gasoline consumption. Plus, they represent freedom and pure escapism. What more could you want?

By way of comparison, Royce couldn't understand why anyone would want to buy a Harley Davidson motorcycle, without having a major muffler modification kit installed first. They're too loud, belligerent, and obnoxious sounding. Plus, the motorcycles need constant maintenance, care, and upkeep. It must be brand loyalty. Or the adrenaline rush you get while driving one. They are built in America. The company is coming out with an electric-powered version of the motorbike in the next few years. It might be worth a second look for someone wanting to purchase in the near future. Speedy, stealthy travel is now possible for the cyclist desiring a quieter, relaxing vacation getaway to paradise. They hardly make any sound at all as you drive along the highway. You are hurling silently through space in peaceful harmony with the universe. How exhilarating! You are riding smoothly, effortlessly along on a soft pillow-cushion cloud of warm air, enjoying the fine scenery as you go, gliding along without a care in the world. Up, up to the mountain peak you ride, high above the clouds until you finally make it over the hump. You've entered a blissful altered state of consciousness.

Meghan began tapping him on the shoulder, then. She said gently, "Earth to Major Royce! Your precious cargo ship on its way to Mars is about to smack into a big asteroid. You'd better change course."

At that point he stopped the show and removed the virtual reality goggles he had been wearing. He was almost sold on the idea.

"We were going to the mall and you were tagging along to help me pick out a new dress for the Spring Fling Formal garden party," she said. "Remember?"

"Your cheap skate prom date has arrived to escort you to the dance," Royce replied, grandiosely.

"I knew it," said Meghan. "An officer and a gentleman."

CHAPTER 62

Book review of the novel

Force of Nature

by Jane Harper, published in 2017.

"Hi Gene," she said to the motel manager in a small Rocky Mountain mining town, after twenty years.
Are you a happy camper?

Remember the fun stuff you did at summer camp? When you were a Boy Scout or a campfire girl? Bass fishing at the lake? Sightseeing in the national park? What can be more enjoyable than sitting around a bonfire toasting marshmallows, roasting hotdogs, and telling ghost stories on a warm, moonlit summer night? Singing "Home on the Range," "Good-bye Old Paint," and other traditional favorites. Hiking the trail, canoeing, spying wild animals in their natural habitats through your binoculars. How peaceful and serene it all seemed!

Or, perhaps, you went out to a scenic secluded spot in a remote recreational area just so you and your best buddies could drink beer and listen to the music on a newly installed AM-FM stereo radio-CD player played really loud, without disturbing anyone outside a radius of about two city blocks, while you listened to "Dark Side of the Moon." You thought about installing a C.B. radio underneath the dashboard as well, but you were twenty-one, on a limited budget, didn't really need one, and couldn't afford one anyway.

Now someone is thinking how the world has changed so very rapidly and dramatically, how nothing can ever really be the same as it once was. He probably thinks how he has more survival skills in his little pinky finger than all of the corporate executives combined gone fishing, hiking, birdwatching, or relaxing in their easy chairs, seated in friendly, comfortable surroundings, drinking aperitifs and telling jokes at the lodge for the duration of their long lost weekend in the national forest have in their whole bodies.

He wanted to relive the wonder years of his youth, so he volunteered as an active participant in the next corporate retreat to the great outdoors. The destination is none other than the incredible Outback of "Crocodile Dundee's" Australian wilderness. This is the gist of the novel *Force of Nature*, written by Jane Harper, published in 2017. The story becomes very interesting quite quickly. As suspense-filled and intriguing as the question I just made up is loaded: "Being strictly vegetarians, what were you able to survive on besides bush-meat?"

An avid book reader, one has a great tendency to look for the moral in the story—even if there doesn't appear to be one at first glance. For this particular book, although "laughter is not necessarily the best medicine," having slightly modified the title of the *Reader's Digest* periodical column, one might offer the aphorism, "He who laughs last, laughs best" as an alternative. But that's not right either. What transpires on their trip is no laughing matter.

All right. So I ask myself a simple rhetorical question, "What is the story about then?" The answer which immediately comes to mind is obviously too vague, and more of a riddle than an answer, but here goes anyway: "Close to, but not exactly the last desperate act of a dying man, going off the deep end in the secretarial pool, drowning in massive corporate debt." Indeed, such a blanket statement could be grossly misleading and quite plainly wrong.

Upon further reflection, perhaps wanting to revise my interpretation of the book altogether, I'm reminded of two basic bits of advice that any dedicated careerist may have heard repeated over the years: "Don't take your work home with you" and "Don't bring your personal problems to work."

Okay. That was another tangential point of departure for the rational thought process of an eccentric individual who obviously enjoys analyzing a promising work of fiction.

Trying again. The story is actually about a couple of federal investigators who endeavor to solve a stunningly serious, heinous, vexing and perplexing crime. This fact alone makes reading the book worthwhile. You can often tell from the first few pages that it's going to be a good novel from the rhythm and pace of the writing by an experienced investigative reporter and competent police detective.

R. Royce was deeply concerned that his ten-year-old niece might have become overly shy, withdrawn, and introverted spending so much of her time in front of a PC. He thought she needed a healthy and beneficial opportunity to break out of her shell, so to speak. Just before the upcoming Fourth of July weekend, he drove his brother Lehman and his daughter Lou Ellen to the lake one day to see if anyone was catching any fish. On the way, Lehman noticed that a fireworks stand was open for business and Royce stopped to let him buy some sparklers and firecrackers to liven up the outing a bit. All well and good. The two of them enjoyed the flashy, flaming noisemakers immensely, but Royce was not overly enthusiastic or satisfied by these less than impressive results. After they had their fun with the fireworks, the trio drove through the camp ground at the second spillway from the dam at the posted speed limit of 5 mph. Royce had an inspiration, then, wondering if the people they saw were sufficiently enjoying their vacations. He rolled down his window and got the attention of the first group of people they met, seated around a picnic table next to a smoking barbeque. He began chatting with them for a moment. He discovered that the family lived in Tulsa and were camping at the lake for the holiday weekend. When they drove on further, he asked Lehman and Lou Ellen if they could tell whether the other people they saw along the way, were also on vacation, or not. His brother played along and said, "I can't really tell at all. I think that you have to stop and ask them in person if you want to be absolutely certain whether they are on vacation or just out swimming for the afternoon."

"Let's see if we can find any happy campers," Royce said. He braked to a complete stop beside the very next campsite and suggested to Lou Ellen, "Why don't you roll down your window and ask?"

Bravely, fearlessly, his niece rapidly rolled down the car window. She leaned out of the window and inquired of the first person she met who was standing nearby, "Are you a happy camper?"

"I am definitely a happy camper," the dashing young fellow replied, cheerfully and enthusiastically; Eugene, a boy of her age and temperament, in his high-altitude jeans. "My family and friends are going to be here for the long weekend. We've already been fishing and swimming. Later on, we're going water skiing. Our boat and trailer is over there by the picnic table. Mom is grilling frankfurters for lunch. Want a soda?" The flood-gates had opened with his reply.

"No, thanks. Are you going to see the fireworks show tonight?" she asked, hopefully. She had come out of her shell in no time at all. They had no need of great concern. The two of them were after all, cousins. She would meet several more at the family reunion, planned well in advance, especially for this auspicious occasion. Distant relatives would be arriving soon from Wichita.

CHAPTER 63

Book review of the historical biography
Caesar: Life of a Colossus
by Adrian Goldsworthy, published in 2006.

Rome would grow weary wantonly waging world-wide war without end.

That Napoleon Bonaparte reportedly read the literary works of Julius Caesar extensively speaks volumes of the latter's influence on posterity centuries later. Author Adrian Goldsworthy, in his highly acclaimed historical and biographical work entitled *Caesar: Life of a Colossus*, advises us of this fact among others. Julius Caesar was born in the year 100 B.C. to a noble and aristocratic family which was well-connected in the Republic of Rome. He was intelligent and keenly perceptive about his social status. In addition, he had the additional benefit of pursuing a soundly tutored, logically focused, philosophical education, which would prepare him for the fast-track career of his choosing either as a civic-minded office holder or a uniformed military leader. Among his earlier achievements, he was appointed to the position of high priest. Go figure!

Later, he began to search for his true calling in life, practicing law as an advocate. He defended well-established, high-profile clients. But what most catapulted his career was serving in the capacity of a conquering military general. You might say that he had shown great potential for advancement in his chosen career path. He was given numerous military commands and led legions upon legions of Roman soldiers over the years. He was proven victorious, time and time again. Mostly on foreign soil, he won ever greater wealth, power, and accolades. You can easily see how possessing this type of information about a singular member of their own peer group might impress the likes of Napoleon, Churchill, Patton, and a great many other decorated officers of modern times. It certainly affected those of Julius Caesar's. Plus the fact that he went to great lengths in documenting practically every battle of every campaign he had ever fought with detailed precision, no doubt enhanced his fame and fortune. To say that Julius Caesar followed in the footsteps of Alexander the Great would be an understatement. This says a lot about the character of the man.

Besides documenting the life and exemplary deeds of Julius Caesar in his meteoric rise to become the most powerful man in Rome, if not in the entire civilized world in the last century B.C., the author delved deeply into what made the Roman leader "tick." Clearly, he was a product of his exclusive environment, the aristocratically led Roman Republic, for which he proudly stood.

In consequence, the author dug even deeper into the concepts involving the profound and far-reaching vastness of Roman government itself. He focused in on the opportunities which it afforded "certain qualified individuals," due to their birthright, their strong abilities, the competitive nature of their training, and just plain luck, being in the right place at the right time. He revealed how the complex system was organized, how its hierarchy functioned, how its laws were enacted and by whom, and how the system continued to change and evolve over the decades as a result of an ingrained "survival instinct" which kicks in during times of danger or great peril.

The reader soon realizes that once these "certain qualified individuals" have learned to climb the social ladder of success, they begin to rise like carbonated bubbles floating to the surface within the sweet, syrupy liquid that is government to even greater, more lucrative, powerful, and prominent positions. The process of advancement is analogous to working in the mailroom of a large corporation today, in order to get one's foot in the door, as they say, transferring to sales representative, becoming a marketing associate, then operations director, CEO, vice-president, and ultimately, president, "the big Kahuna." The bottom line is he had to keep those greedy stockholders satisfied with large profits and good returns on investment.

They quickly learned the competitive nature of the business in a vicious dog attack dog world. In the last century B.C., instead of simply firing the average individual applicant and giving him the opportunity to find a new job, the powers that be would exile him into oblivion, or simply execute him on the spot. Thus, there is a subtle difference between the Roman Republic as it was, and the much improved democratic laissez faire free-enterprise system of today.

The author went on to suggest that Julius Caesar's career may have been hampered by his unpredictable fits of epilepsy, but it might just as well have been his fits of rage. He had a terrible temper. The question of his virility was brought into play. Some inquired, "Was he a lover or a fighter?" Many experts believe that he was both. I think, he fought to protect his investment, and he made love for the same reason. I also believe that life in Rome might have been much improved had some of the Romans turned their swords into scissors.

As it was, a decent pair of center-pivot scissors would not be invented for another hundred and fifty years or so, from the time Julius Caesar was in the prime of his life. The modern version of the center-pivoting scissors was supposedly invented in Rome sometime at the end of the first century A.D. So, it was never easy to cut through all the bureaucratic red tape.

What could not be emphasized enough in the book, however, in my opinion, is the quintessential fact that there are greater forces at work on earth than Julius Caesar was able to conquer with his army, utilizing all of the military might of Rome. Such forces are peace, hope, and faith. He invaded the lands and scaled the walls of kings and queens. But, eventually he must have come to realize during some lucid moment in his life that the power of love is insurmountable. It is commonly believed that the authorities in Rome may have wanted to crown Julius Caesar as the king of kings, but such grandeur pales in comparison to the glory of God. Being largely self-centered, a mere mortal made man, he was never really able to break through to the other side spiritually in his lifetime, even if he did have royal blood flowing through his veins. He was never able to conquer the unconquerable, that which is divinely and devoutly religious. In the end, he must have had to learn a bitter lesson, "the grass is always greener on the other side of the fence."

R. Royce said, "As if property values around here weren't already low enough, we have drug dealers moving in and setting up shop."

"Isn't that why you bought the place?" asked Cornelius Korn, his longtime friend and business associate. "Buy low and sell high, on the assumption that property values would ultimately rise."

"Very funny. The big red brick building with its majestic marble columns was supposed to be a ground-floor opportunity for much needed improvement and community development," said Royce.

"Revitalization, is the term they often use," claimed Korn. "To bring back the beauty, grace, and charm of the old historical district downtown."

"We could convince the dealers to move their illicit business elsewhere," said Royce.

"Do you have a plan?" asked Korn.

"We could interdict their shipments," said Royce. "Disrupt their supply chain and open up their communications."

"We'll need active surveillance to track their personnel and run interference," added Korn.

"You'll have to involve detectives and lawyers to pull the plug on the key players," said Royce.

"You have to hit them where they live," said Korn. "Chicago, most likely."

"Can you make a few phone calls and get the ball rolling?" asked Royce.

"We can be fully operational within two weeks," said Korn. "Then, we'll wait and see what happens."

First they snared the lookouts. They got them off the streets and into "boot camp." One rolled over on the local dealer. One took out the bag man. The dealer gave up his supplier. The bag man snitched on his immediate supervisor.

The supplier revealed his source. The product dried up and went away. The boss took the fall and swallowed his losses. He had a crooked lawyer, but went to the penitentiary anyway. The lawyer cried to the heavyweight, his boss's boss.

R. Royce convinced the shark to take his business elsewhere. Then, to let the heavyweight know that there would be no hard feelings, he told him to "have a nice day, but go away."

The heavyweight was driving west on Murphy Boulevard the next morning about 10 o'clock when for some inexplicable reason his vehicle veered off course, careened across two lanes of opposing traffic, and collided with the solid concrete base of a large, shiny, stainless-steel traffic control box located in the grassy lawn area in close proximity to, but just south of the roadway, situated at the next intersection. Before the police, ambulance, and firetruck could arrive, Korn had extracted the dazed, bruised, and disheveled, but not seriously injured heavyweight from his vehicle and began transporting him to the airport. He put him on the next flight bound for O'Hare.

Two weeks later, Korn sold their investment property at a healthy profit to a real estate developer with vision. The buyer was relocating to the area and expanding his corporate headquarters. He said he wanted to broaden his tax base.

"That's what I'm talking about," exclaimed Royce, when Korn showed him the proceeds of a substantial wire transfer going into his personal bank account.

CHAPTER 64

Review of the nonfictional book

Bushwhacker Belles

by Larry Wood, published in 2016.

Good legal representation goes a long way toward preserving common decency, dignity, self-worth, and respect.

The most sure-fired effective method of weed control known to mankind is to pull them out one at a time by the stem base, roots and all, before they have a chance to really get started.

A shrewd businessman finds Nellie gainful employment working for the railroad. The local magistrate wants to have a word with her, before she assumes the position in another state. –Synopsis for an imaginative western.

*B*ushwhacker Belles, by Larry Wood, published in 2016, is a genuinely informative example of excellent journalistic reporting. The nonfictional book chronicles the actions taken, good, bad, or indifferent, by an interesting variety of women living in Missouri, during the Civil War years, based on available court and military records, newspaper articles, and other scholarly documentation. These women sprang from widely diverse social, economic, and political backgrounds. According to the information presented by the author, and my interpretation of the facts bearing on each individual case, they were generally young and charming, brash, outspoken, highly opinionated, self-assured, and independent-minded. They believed in America as the land of the free, the land of opportunity. They believed in life, liberty, and the pursuit of happiness. It just so happened that the Civil War created serious conflicts in their minds, which could not be readily addressed through otherwise peaceful or amicable means, or resolved through normal channels by town civic leaders, community church officials, or even the local sheriff.

Indeed, the issues confronting them were national in scope. They could simply not be dealt with on the Southern-state or local level. Carpet baggers from the Federal government, in their infinite wisdom, had already stepped in, probably about the time Kansas became a democratically elected Free-state, and John Brown's marauders commandeered rifle shipments from the Lincoln arsenal in Harper's Ferry, West Virginia, to exacerbate the situation.

What impressed me most by the book was how efficiently the military-judicial system worked during the Civil War years, concerning the processing of civilian non-combatants through the legal system. Good legal representation appears to have gone a long way toward preserving common decency, dignity, and self-worth. It ensures success, freedom, prosperity, independence, and security up to the present day. Not to mention, peace of mind, in my opinion.

Provost marshals and appointed judges alike appeared to have prosecuted the most serious of these cases with a measure of fairness and a certain amount of impartiality. I'd go so far as to suggest, and even go out on a limb, perhaps, to state unequivocally: "Justice was indeed served up on a silver platter!"

Beyond these considerations, I learned how and why the descendent families of so many acquaintances, school chums, friends, neighbors, and associates must have found themselves suddenly living in Oklahoma and Texas, who once upon a time would have been contentedly settled in the fine states of Kansas or Missouri. What tumultuous, cataclysmic events must have transpired to change all that? What a crazy, mixed-up world it is in which we live, yearn to be free, seek happiness, and desire prosperity!

Today, how I confront weed control on my lawn is not too different from the efforts initiated by the Provost Marshall during the Civil War years. Having discovered the most sure-fired method of getting rid of unwanted plants propagating on the lawn, I learned the hard way to simply pull them up one at a time, one by one, firmly grasping the base of the stem nearest the ground, pulling upward on the plant, forcibly if necessary, with single-minded determination, in one smooth, harmonic motion, and depositing it, roots and all, into the compost heap of posterity for recycling purposes. I call this process "better living through ecology." Hence forward, I began thinking more conservatively, if it's green, botanical in nature, and I can cut it back evenly and uniformly with my lawnmower, then I shall let it grow on my lawn. I call this "making progress." In stark contrast, some may consider it pro-grass.

On a different note altogether, I am reminded of the time a military associate and well-seasoned senior rater was explaining the purpose and function of the OER (or EER) document. It is an official military form which was expressly designed to report on the evaluation and progress which the soldier makes during the course of his active duty military career. Cited are such milestones as his individual awards, achievements, honors, and acts of bravery on the battlefield and in the face of adversity. What it is not supposed to report on is what his wife or girlfriend did or did not do in the meanwhile, he complained.

Meghan Thomas returned to the apartment carrying an original oil painting which was signed, sealed, sold, and delivered to her by Pierre Perrier. An indicator of its authenticity was stamped to the back side in indelible ink and included an unique eight-digit alpha-numeric identification code. It depicted a still life with fruit and wine on a wooden tabletop in a darkened room.

"What's it worth?" inquired R. Royce, at first glance.

"A cool million, give or take a few hundred thou," said Meghan, calmly.

"How did you come to acquire such a rare, beautiful, and valuable work of art?" he asked, skeptical.

"I purchased the painting from the original artist himself at an art exhibit," she said.

"It could be a forgery, an obvious fake reproduction," countered Royce. "The guy who sold you the painting might not have been the actual artist who painted it. Plus, you might have become an unwitting victim of fraud. How can you be sure the salesman was really Pierre, or the artist's exclusive, bonifide agent?"

"Simple. I had him extract his identification card and show it to me," said Meghan. "He had a recent California driver's license on him as well."

"Let me summarize what happened. You visited a flea market and happened to see his display of several fine-quality paintings. He represented himself as a starving artist who was trying to raise enough money to make it home to L.A. He was traveling from New York City, and Purcell, Oklahoma, was as far as he got before he ran out of gas. Broke, tired, and hungry he decided to sell the few paintings he had in his possession, so that he could continue on his long, lonely journey home," recanted Royce.

"Yes, he missed his family terribly, having been away for so many years, without being able to contact his loved ones, because of his dire circumstances," said Meghan, beginning to pout, and feeling lightheaded, giddy, and emotional all of a sudden.

"Okay, so how much did you pay for the painting?" asked Royce. The suspense was beginning to dawn on him.

"A hundred and fifty," she said.

"Where are you planning to put it?" he asked, obviously relieved. It was one of those priceless moments, generally experienced only in credit card commercials.

"Probably here in the den over the sofa," said Meghan.

"Did you ask him if he has any more of these?" inquired Royce, discretely, ever the consummate collector of rarely seen fine art, and art critic. "Did you mention to him that we may be in the market for another Picasso, possibly a Van Gogh?"

"Why don't you ask him yourself," she said. "He's standing on the other side of the wall in the living room."

"Lucky Pierre!" exclaimed Royce. "So nice to see you again. How have you been?" He reached for his elbow to usher him into the living room where he could feel more comfortable and offer him refreshments.

"What a pleasant surprise, Royce! I could be better, but the situation is improving by the minute. Have you been in the other room all this time?" asked Pierre.

"Why, yes. I live here. What a strange coincidence seeing you again. Meghan has been telling me all about you and your less than ideal circumstances. She hasn't been giving you the wrong impression, has she?"

"I do admit that I've been hoping for some ultra-extravagant accommodations in the immediate vicinity, until we can conclude our lucrative business dealings," Pierre went on to say.

"We have already made reservations for you in a lovely suite with an excellent view of the prairie in a five-star hotel comparable to the Hilton. It's located only a short scenic drive from here in beautiful downtown Paris, Texas. Here, let me help you with your luggage. They're expecting you on this very evening," said Royce. "Now, where's that Van Gogh?"

"He didn't really believe that he would be spending the night with a girl traveling under the alias of 'Paris Hilton,' did he?" asked Meghan, when Cornelius Korn called later. "When there are so many lovely Southern Belles promenading around the dance-floor, any one of whom would become his perfect, ideal date and mate. She is not at all his type or temperament."

"True, he might have somehow acquired that false impression from me, but I tried to discourage him every step of the way," admitted Cornelius, cleanly clearing the slate of any semblance of perceived ambiguity.

CHAPTER 65

Book review of the novel

The Late Show

by Michael Connelly, published in 2017.

It takes a special person to work graveyards.

The novel *The Late Show*, by Michael Connelly, published in 2017, proved to be an excellent primer on police protocol and procedure as followed by a rather unconventional, if not downright unorthodox detective working the nightshift in Los Angeles. She quickly demonstrates that she is not just another pretty face in the office. On the fly, she thinks fast on her feet. A good thing, too, since crime appears to be running rampant in the city. If unchecked, there's no telling where that would lead.

Anywhere else in the USA and perhaps the supervisor, chief, or head honcho calmly strolls into the meeting room at 9:30 A.M. sharp, looks around gawking, and hawkishly inquires, "What have you done for me lately?"

Or, hyperextending his arm out as if he's performing stretching exercises for the long arm of the law, he points his index finger in mock warning, menacingly and accusingly, like he's about to lower the boom on members of the audience, momentarily stunning the officers seated in the far corner, catching them completely off-guard, trying desperately to blend in with the woodwork while in their probationary periods, with the burning question, "Are you earning your keep?"

Crossing the path of two constables on patrol at the doughnut shop the very next day, he makes a snide, off-the-cuff comment, such as "Our tax dollars at work!" He gets a curt rebuttal in reply, "Skipping out on your anger management and sensitivity training classes again, Jefe?" Insulting, but what goes around comes around, as they say.

An agitator making instigating, highly offensive, smart-ass remarks, creating a hostile work environment in Charlotte, North Carolina, which is the quaint, modern, utopian setting of another graphic police-inspired novel currently housed on the shelf in the little neighborhood library, entitled *The Hornet's Nest*, by Patricia Cornwell, in front of the assistant director of the metropolitan police bureau, whom I pictured as being built like the proverbial brick outhouse, or a Kansas City Chief linebacker, take your pick—tall, athletic, muscular, strong as a rhinoceros, able to run forty yards in about four seconds—and she would probably knock his block off without a second's hesitation, not even blushing or breathing very hard afterwards; or at the very least, take him down a peg or two. Of course, I am exaggerating. Both novels provide interesting, informative reading material for a complete change of venue.

Which reminds me of a story. An ordinary fellow was waiting to catch a late-night bus at the Greyhound Terminal in downtown Tulsa, Oklahoma, many years ago on his way home to small-town America when two female police officers in full uniform unexpectedly walked around the corner, through the double-glass doors, and side-by-side through the crowded seating area as busses were being loaded and offloaded with passengers and luggage. Same scenario: built like Kansas City Chief linebackers.

One of them may have casually glanced over to the Creep slumped down on one of the long laminated seating benches in the room. His middle initial could very well have been a capital T, the mere mention of the name spelling Trouble. She might just as easily have stopped to have a brief conversation with him, leaning over in front of him, searching deeply into his scarred, scraggly, blank, expressionless face and opaque, glassy marble eyes, telling him in no uncertain terms, "Okay, give me one good reason," Clint Eastwood, "Dirty Hairy" style, but thinking all the while, *why I have to shoot paper targets full of holes using rubber bullets, inert and dummy rounds.* Women can be much more subtle. Instead, they stroll away without incident. He looked like he was the type who would sucker-punch an innocent traveler seated quietly next to him minding his own business, without any warning whatsoever, given the opportunity. He wouldn't particularly need rhyme, reason, or provocation. He appeared to be on the skids. Yet, he was rude and discourteous in his dealings with others. On probation, he wasn't supposed to leave the city. With a few bucks in his pocket, however, he'd have a ticket to ride. So, he acted as if he was in serious need of an attitude adjustment. But alas, the average person has not been fully trained as a criminal profiler. He does not possess the necessary skills, tools, and wherewithal, which qualifies him to make that call.

Later that night, the unsuspecting traveler was standing at one of the urinals when Trouble walked into the public restroom. He happened to glance around cautiously when the door opened and there he was. Fortunately for all concerned, an undercover detective walked into the facility about the same time and told him directly in no uncertain terms, "Don't even think about it."

The other's raised fist disappeared when he opened his hand. Surveillance footage would reveal an uneventful evening at the bus station. The detective had gained the subject's full cooperation and compliance after all. He knew how to deescalate a potential powder-keg situation.

R. Royce stared at the wall. He was thinking about a movie he'd just seen. An obscure aspiring actor, a complete unknown, really, has been thrown to the wolves. He's standing in the center ring of the WWF surrounded by three or four domineering and demanding Hollywood heavyweights, who would love nothing better than to choke the living daylights out of him, except that, metaphorically speaking, he is a pistol. He is the key. Completely oblivious to all which has transpired, his new girlfriend, the one true love of his life, calmly awaits his pending arrival at their chosen rendezvous point. Gainfully employed in the present tense, she has decided to throw it all away. She has prepared herself to embark with him on a long road trip, never to return to their old haunts ever again. She is an angel in disguise. They are blessed with great potential for living happily ever after.

Cornelius Korn reflected on the film he had recently viewed. He was lying prone on his back on the divan in the living room looking ponderously at the ceiling. No, it is not a mirrored ceiling. Two devious, demented, obviously deranged girls, undoubtedly outcasts, if not outright social pariahs, become dangerous and "damaged goods" in the film boasting a theme which is totally unrelated to anything that he has ever experienced himself and unrecognizable in the context of anything that he has ever heard or read about or witnessed in his entire lifetime.

"Can you elaborate on the plot?" asked Alexis Sue Shell, his confidant, business associate, and traveling companion. She was growing curious and a little concerned.

"They react in a cool, calculating, but coldblooded fashion as events unfold, as if they were originally intent on going to the mall one sunny afternoon for a new prom dress or maybe a musical compact disk, with a lively soundtrack they could enjoy in the car on the way back home, but suddenly decided to commit a serious crime of passion instead," said Cornelius. He was becoming uncharacteristically agitated, if not somewhat un-nerved at the prospect.

"There must have been some other way of resolving the inner turmoil of their deeply troubled and tortured souls," commented Meghan.

"It would be like trying to avert a natural disaster, such as the devastation caused by twin tornadoes, or in the present case, two twisted sisters," replied Cornelius.

"You didn't happen to watch that program on the Nature Channel, did you?" interjected Royce.

"How about you; kickboxing on the sports network?" retorted Cornelius.

"Now now, boys. Let's keep it friendly and rated G for General audiences, shall we," exclaimed Alexis Sue. "We get the picture. He is the ultimate fighter. The girls are psychologically dependent thrill seekers."

"We should all go back to our corners now and make preparations for the dinner engagement this evening," said Meghan. "We have to make ourselves presentable and time is of the essence."

"Very true. Henceforward, we should mind our Ps and Qs," said Korn, right on cue. "When the titles are signed and the transfers have been made, we take immediate possession of the vehicles."

"A half-dozen Ferraris, a half-dozen Lamborghinis, and a matched pair of stock Porsches, straight from the factory await clearance at the docks," said Royce, matter-of-factly.

"Transporters load six on each car-hauler. We ride shotgun in the Porsches to ensure safe delivery to our destination storage warehouses. We personally deliver them to buyers after they sell," said Cornelius. "Any questions?"

"Sounds like a plan to me," said Royce. "Sold a few paintings. Buy some cars. Sell out the Italians. Keep the Porsches. What can possibly go wrong?"

CHAPTER 66

Book review of the collection of short stories

Agents of Treachery

by Otto Penzler, published in 2010.

How to scandalize a nation in ten easy lessons.
The short hairs on the back of your neck stand up, shivers
run down your spine, and you get goose bumps all over.

There are two major differences between Otto Penzler's collection of short stories, entitled *Agents of Treachery*, published in 2010, and the selections which comprise Michael Rank's book, *Spies, Espionage, and Covert Operations*, published in 2014, besides the fact that one is completely fictionalized and the other is largely historical in nature, based on "declassified" or otherwise obtained secondhand information, even though both books involve a similar theme: international spies and spying in general. First of all, the operatives depicted in *Agents of Treachery* appear to be so much more vividly described and characterized. They appear "up close and personal" and "in your face," as some crude and callous rapscallion might perhaps declare. You get the distinct sense of being in the same room with the perpetrators; or, even worse, on the same battlefield in the heat of combat, with "bombs bursting in the air, ...bullets flying all around," and so forth.

The second major difference involves a matter of strict professionalism, intense training, philosophy, and politics. Specifically, Michael Rank's collection of spies demonstrated sound reasons, a solid rationale, or ingrained ideology for having acted as prescribed, or proscribed. The very survival of entire countries might well have depended on their surreptitious actions, and they delivered well within the parameters of expectations, fully cognizant of their nations' plight.

On the other hand, Otto Penzler's stories reveal the all-too-human side of the equation, in which awful mistakes were made, bad decisions were amplified, magnified, propagated, and perpetuated for posterity to sort out. Classic failures spiraled out of control, often with drastic or fatal consequences. As a result, the operation "went sideways," the mission suffered terribly, and critical agents in the field floundered miserably. They were "taken out." Nevertheless, the "Cold War" continued, societies kept up appearances, governments maintained the "status quo," and diplomatic efforts were re-energized. For, as we all know, life goes on regardless. The U.N. monitors national boundaries passively and voices dissent. The Hague rebukes, ostracizes, and condemns the worst offenders to a fate worse than death: infamy. Treaties are enacted, kept, and broken. Alliances are formed and reformed. Trade agreements are ratified, honored, and violated. The most civilized nations attempt to keep the peace and maintain law and order around the world and within their respective spheres of influence in the best way they know how.

In *Agents of Treachery*, you have all the elements for a first-rate spy thriller: the reality of third-world politics; the character of the spy himself, a candidly flippant, confident, resourceful professional—acting with a keen sense of purpose and urgency, in which the slightest mistake, one wrong move, or false misstep could wind up causing someone serious bodily injury, or worse; an assessment of the terrorist threat; a clever plot with great suspense, intrigue, shock, and surprise; classified secrets involving national security interests; and a conflicted agenda which is both complicated and convoluted by a combination of dedication, infiltration, betrayal, defection, and self-sacrifice. Put any ten of these sundry and miscellaneous ingredients into the mix with some ice cubes. Blend. Shake. Stir. Pour the chilled, frothy, effervescent liquid into a tall stemmed glass. Add an olive. You have the perfect frozen aphrodisiac that improves your love life on all levels. Then hang on tight. When take together all at once, drunk down like a double shot of whiskey, this rare brand of "intelligence" could present a potent storyline…

R. Royce was unable to suppress a smile at the mere mention of his nudist neighbors' antics. Someone must have told the Europeans that the nearby beach had gone "topless," and they took full advantage of their newfound freedom. They had recently moved into the remote, secluded community having an abundance of lush, tropical green vegetation, but their borders were open, without the high CBS walls or tall wooden privacy fences which typically surround the mansion estate grounds in the provincial neck-of-the-woods abode usually reserved for the well-established elite of New England suburbia. Actually, the road to their house would normally be accessible only from the curvy Banana Trail road by automobile, which traverses the isthmus running north and south; or, infrequently, by a vessel cruising in from the choppy waters of the Atlantic Ocean or through the intercoastal waterway to the west. Otherwise, someone would have to hack his way through impossibly dense undergrowth. "It's a jungle out there," say local dwellers in the area, who do not ever venture to travel that route without good reason, if at all.

"You can tell that they've gone completely native," said his good friend of many years and longtime business associate, Cornelius Korn. "See the Tiki hut bar and the hammocks strung up between coconut palms on the beach?"

"Frontal nudity doesn't offend me in the least," chimed in Alexis Sue, his other business associate, and unabashed travelling companion. Both were visiting Royce at the expansive vacation home retreat he calls "Paradise," the one with good "southern exposure."

"They like to squeeze lime wedges into their bottles of imported beer," observed Meghan, Royce's significant other, and another major player in the team's business dealings. "Naturally, we all love watching ocean waves cascading onto the beach and levelling the sandy playing field of obstacles in their path, depositing sea shell treasures as they go back to the sea."

After quickly selling their entire inventory of expensive Italian sports cars, making a hefty profit in the process, the two car-sales entrepreneurs, Royce and Korn, decided it was high time they entered into a different, much more lucrative and interesting line of work; namely, that involving the promising field of satellite communications.

Specifically, they wanted to broker a once-in-a-lifetime deal to sell a turnkey satellite communications system to the friendly startup "Telecommunications Linking Corporation," registered under the "TLC Inc." umbrella. The company headquarters had been centrally located within the principality of Luxembourg for several years now.

One of the last minute details for Royce's "sales team" was to obtain permission from the NASA administration to place their newly acquired technological wonder; that is, the latest and greatest version of the "Miracle" satellite, aboard the next scheduled launch of a U.S. Air Force Titan II test missile, which often has plenty of extra space available in the cargo hold for international space station equipment, etc.; "push it off" at an particular altitude; and "send it into orbit" in a uniquely predesignated outer-space trajectory, suspending it at a considerable distance above Earth's surface indefinitely. Royce still had connections within the military community and felt totally confident that he would be able to task them with the endeavor in the interest of national security.

Afterwards, the other three members of Royce's "Space-A team" could simply turn over the satellite-linking computers; all related hardware, software and applicable codes; and the keys to TLC, Inc.'s representatives—who happened to be none other than Royce's new, industrious and enterprising, open-minded neighbors, in exchange for a cool 550 million dollars, give or take a few hundred thousand.

"Do you happen to have the authorization documents with you in the cab?" the security guard asked Royce in a direct, but courteous manner. Royce flashed his white teeth in a manner of friendship and handed the uniformed officer the bulky packet of shipping documents he had previously set down on the seat beside him, which included a trip ticket, the manifest, packing list, and invoice. He was driving an oversized delivery van.

"The papers should all be in good order," said Royce, brimming with cordiality, yet he had a keen sense of purpose. He was a paragon of virtuosity. The guard verified his cartman's card and his driver's license, and noted the van's tag number. He logged in the shipment arrival date and time, then returned the shipping documents to the driver.

"Please proceed to Warehouse B for cargo transfer," said the guard, as he opened the front gate, which had been reinforced with tubular-steel cross-members as a precautionary measure.

After delivering the top-secret cargo to its intended destination, Royce exited the premises and contacted Korn immediately by cellphone to advise him that the cargo had been scheduled for liftoff within 48 hours. Two days later, the satellite was successfully launched into orbit.

"We've made the delivery of computers and hardware to our customer's local facility," reported Royce.

"We've delivered the keys to the office," said Alexis.

"We've verified that the specified funds have been transferred into our corporate account," confirmed Korn. Afterwards, he contacted Meghan via cellphone, advising her to deliver the encrypted equipment codes.

"We've passed along the manuals and codes the TLC technicians need to make the system work," Meghan reported to Royce, later on that eventful day.

"All systems go," Royce told Korn, using a common colloquialism utilized by astronauts on the job. "The customer is overjoyed. We beat all expectations."

"Did you manage to keep the Pfleugers in the loop the whole time?" inquired Royce, curious.

"Let's just say that the lovely couple will have to tune in when the rest of the world finds out that there is a powerful, new, easy-access, wireless, internet-based television service provider operating all over Europe and leave it at that," replied Korn. "Everyone concerned should be pleasantly surprised almost any minute now!"

"Then, we really can get this party started," exclaimed Alexis Sue. "Are we having fun yet?"

"Did you say dress casual?" asked Meghan. "I'm wearing 'Chic' capris over a modest pastel 'Speedy' bathing suit," she said, her discourse obviously shying away from the nothing-at-all concept, her soft, smooth skin glowing radiantly, her cheeks blushing cheerily. There were stars in her eyes.

"Have you been to the beach?" inquired their stunningly gorgeous and voluptuous new neighbor, Victoria Pfleuger, who was just then inhaling the warm, salty ambient air of a fresh ocean breeze deeply into her lungs, deliciously scented with vanilla beans, citrus, jasmine, a variety of exotic tropical flowers, cocoa butter and rich Hawaiian tanning oils. "The fragrance of tropical plants and the raw, salty smell of the ocean surf is an aphrodisiac for me," she admitted. "How exhilarating it is having you all here! Shall we go for a swim?" Alexis and Meghan did not hesitate, but plunged into the deep emerald green and turquoise blue water alongside Victoria for a cool, invigorating, and rejuvenating dip in the pool. They swam the length of the pool underwater for exercise. "Swimming laps helps you build up stamina," she confided in them. They tossed a beach ball back and forth for a while to unwind, and splashed about. Inevitably exhausted, they all retired to several comfortable beach recliners situated around the pool for lazy afternoon naps.

"Refreshments, anyone?" asked Cornelius, still dressed in a white suit and Panama hat, after they'd awoken and gone indoors. He opened an ice chest he'd stocked at a Treasure Coast convenience store for the occasion. As a token of their friendship, he handed Quincey, Victoria's gregarious husband, formerly outfitted in a sleek sharkskin business suit, presently wearing swim trunks and a tank top, a fifth of rare, specially blended and aged spiced rum from the Virgin Islands for his privately stocked liquor cabinet.

"Mission complete," Quincey acknowledged. He appeared elated to the point of becoming ecstatic. Their business had been concluded to the mutual satisfaction of both parties. He offered the guys high-fives and they bumped knuckles. He hugged the girls. The gigantic "mirrored disco ball" would revolve around the Earth for at least a hundred years. Twice as long, if TLC, Inc. could get a certified electronics technician up there to install a new solar-powered battery and make a few timely modifications.

"We're all going dancing later on tonight in celebration," suggested Royce. "A brass band will be playing in the hotel Ballroom at precisely 10 P.M." Everyone in the party expressed their unfettered approval and were sufficiently enthusiastic and motivated to participate in the adventure which was sure to change their lives forever.

"Come over here and give me some sugar," Alexis Sue said to Cornelius, amiably, inviting him to sit close beside her on the sofa for a pleasant diversion before they got up to dance. As a matter of fact, they all got up to dance at the same time, and they all had an enjoyable evening of refined musical entertainment. The quartet offered a toast to their new "best friends." The place was jumping. As a fitting end to a fine evening, the "Lawrence Welk," "Double Dee Disco" fans went home to retire in luxurious, extravagant surroundings.

"Isn't it wonderful to sleep in your own bed for a change," said Meghan, her personality incredibly charming, bubbly, and effervescent. R. Royce couldn't agree with her more. The couples slept in late the next day, and awoke fully refreshed. Their story has taken on new meaning and it had a life of its own. It was a new day indeed.

CHAPTER 67

Book review for Ursula K. LeGuin's
collection of short stories,

The Real and the Unreal

published in 2012, the individual stories published
separately from 1964 to 2014.

How are you doing my fine-feathered friend?
  Words of caution to live by: Watch out for falling rocks! Do not drive into smoke!

Ursula K. LeGuin's collection of short stories, *The Real and the Unreal*, was published in 2012. The individual stories were also published separately in the years from 1964 to 2014. The "Real" section contains 18 stories. The "Unreal" category includes 21 stories.

Initially, I thought that the Real stories would have been about the old American West taking place during the times of the last U.S. expansion, to the California frontier and the Great Northwest, something about which Louis L'Amour and his contemporaries might have written. Alas, it was not so. Yet, I wasn't at all disappointed. Pleasantly surprised, actually. Her stories turned out to be quite good. They depict times more modern, than riding the trail with a herd of cattle, settling your differences with the fast-draw of a fully loaded Colt .45 revolver, or going prospecting in the mountains with an intelligent and trusty burro pack-animal for company. Not at all. Not in the least.

She did write about the lush, fertile California valleys and the wild, rugged mountain region, but concentrated her attentions more on the inhabitants. Still, I got the distinct impression that the author was knowledgeable enough to avoid getting lost in the desert during the hottest part of the summer, but couldn't resist the lure of the Antarctic tundra and a visit to the South Pole from her stories. She places her focus on the human factor, on people who have been passively subdued by tacitly accepting the advent of suburbia, watching *Bonanza* and *Wild Kingdom* on television, dealing with the "Harper Valley PTA," and being treated by psychiatrists who administer anti-anxiety and antidepressant medication. Nobody has all the answers, to be sure, but those pill-pushing quacks couldn't have cured what ails you if they tried, in my opinion, whatever the prognosis. Basically, they didn't help at all. It must have been extremely frustrating for those "at the end of their rope"! So, they just lived out their lives as normally as possible and carried on in the best way they knew how. Or, they began to fantasize about a world of escapism, fairytales, and imaginary beings. "Mother Goose," the "Brothers "Grimm," the "Wizard of Oz," "Pooh Bear," and such.

Rather than experience this fate worse than death, you'd be inclined to think that these stories represent a reflection of their reaction to the status quo. Ordinary people struggling against incredible odds. Fighting against mediocrity with all of their might and power. History defines and conspires against them. Society molds them. The government controls them. But this assessment isn't altogether right either. Not at all. Not in the least. Not if you want to foster a better understanding of the human condition.

The author displays an uncanny knack and a keen ability for transporting you, the average, unsuspecting reader, from one place and time under certain given circumstances to a completely different milieu; yet, one just as interesting and captivating, or more so than the previous. We're not talking about "Greyhound therapy" here. She performs this singular sleight-of-hand achievement through the use of precise and descriptive narratives that put you at your desired destination amidst the turmoil, chaos, and confusion without ever having to leave home. You can clearly see for yourself exactly what has transpired and you are curious to know what happens next. She allows you to judge the outcome for yourself at the end. You wonder, was it all worth the effort? I believe so.

As you jump from one story to another, you perceive the strangest phenomenon: for a more meaningful life, all you have to do is simply follow in the footsteps of the author who merely tells a series of parables. Like following a roadmap and observing the signs along the way, you travel the scenic route of life. She guides you past the signs of the times. You can almost visualize those immortal words of caution signifying danger: "Do not drive into smoke!" and "Watch out for falling rocks!" Useful, important information, to be sure, for planning your next vacation.

She also points out in a round-about manner just how helpful it is to be aware that when you stop and visit strange places and are in totally unfamiliar surroundings—not necessarily your average tourist trap, that when you aggravate people who are already tired and stressed, they may snarl, growl, and snap at you—a tendency which is rooted in instinctual animal behavior. It is perfectly natural and must have something to do with self-preservation. After all, they don't want anybody to completely ruin their day, which has been going so smoothly up until then.

To continue the evaluation, the author appears to be socially aware of everything that is going on in her immediate neighborhood, much in the same way that everybody in a small town knows everybody else and their business. Thus, you have to be very careful about what you say and to whom you say it, because the fact of the matter is, they may be related to one another by blood or marriage. This much is obvious to most, but may be true insight to others. In all candidness, I'd have to admit that the author appears to know people much better than the average meteorologist working on a food truck serving up fine Mexican cuisine knows the weather. Just ask him if he expects cooler weather any time soon, and I wouldn't be at all surprised to hear him exclaim, "Chile tonight. Hot tamale."

How exactly do the "Unreal" stories differ from the "Real" ones? First of all, I believe the Unreal is a gut reaction to leading a plain, ordinary life, contrary to what many others may claim. It is what carries us beyond our everyday, humdrum existence that matters. More so than being noble or heroic; more than having dreams and imagination and fantasy. Certainly, you are ever mindful of these things. Of that, there is no doubt. As they say, "Action speaks volumes." Consequently, for all your aspirations, wishing and pretending didn't put a man on the moon.

The collaboration of advanced civilization, science and technology, hard work and persistence put the men on the moon, and someday soon in the near future will put people on Mars. This is no farfetched prediction, given the current rocketry skills and wireless communications expertise of NASA, SpaceX, and their numerous subsidiary corporations. Especially so, given the healthy competition and support generated by the prevailing ambitions of Earth's Super-powers, all of whom have lofty goals.

After mankind lands on Mars, I believe that humans will eventually advance to the moons of Jupiter, Europa and Io. It's only a matter of time. Beyond the farthest reaches of our own galaxy and we are back to square one, however. We are back to the realm of fantasy and imagination, especially considering that distances separating the universes are relative to the speed of light and measured in light-years. They only go that fast in *Star Trek*.

Who knows, though? There may be intelligent life out there somewhere after all, which may prove to be our ultimate salvation. If these Beings can somehow bridge the gap separating the universes. Or, if we and they have a simultaneous cataclysmic cosmos-sized "Big Bang" event. We may wake up one day to find that we have extra-terrestrial neighbors much closer than we ever thought possible.

"Uh-oh! Somebody must have reconfigured the Universe! Where did those extra planets come from?"

Hence, we have already discovered that imagining life on another planet is like having all the freedom and joy in the world, without any of the burden of responsibility for getting there.

R. Royce held up the gilded metal cage to the light so that he could look the bird directly in the eye. "How are you doing today, my fine-feathered friend?" he asked the bird, similar in size to a parakeet, only more plump.

The green, grey, and maroon plumaged creature began to whistle a melodious song of obvious contentment. Dumb bird doesn't have a single care in the world, thought Royce. We are in a dark, dank, clammy environment, but the bird is unfazed.

When his good friend and business associate, Cornelius Korn, and his constant travelling companion, Alexa Sue Shell, brought the pair home with them from a recent trip "South of the Border," he thought he overheard them say that they had named this one Bert, short for Pretty Birdie Bert, but that wasn't exactly right.

"Dirt is a contraction for dear heart and is obviously a term of endearment," explained Alexa Sue, most sincerely.

"Actually, Dirt likes to scratch around on the ground with his beak and claws like a chicken, poking around for chicken feed," elaborated Korn.

"The Crowned Princess Margaret loves him so," continued Alexa Sue, pointing to the other one of a matched set. "They are very affectionate towards one another, singing and chattering all day long."

"She's talking about their being lovebirds," said Korn, for clarification, now fully tuned in to the conversation.

"It only goes to show you," replied Royce, "that 'birds of a feather stick together.'"

On this particular day, Royce had transported Dirt into the mine Korn and he had recently discovered in some isolated region of the Rocky Mountains. He set the bird in its cage down on a wooden table top located in vicinity of the breezeway shaft, as a major safety precaution, while he labored with a pick and shovel in the cavernous depths. The place looked like a gigantic geodesic dome with magnificent, supernatural crystalline chandeliers that lit up when you shined a light on them. Like living inside a big hollowed-out geode, he thought. They had been hiking and climbing around for years, merely scratching the surface, as they say, but never found anything even remotely resembling this "Lost Dutchman's Mine," until recently. They'd dug and dug and dug some more in many places, but scarcely found an iota of minerals or metal ever worth becoming overly excited about. Enthused, perhaps. Eternally hopeful, definitely.

As any serious-minded professional miner knows, if the canary stops singing for any reason whatsoever, or keels over and passes out altogether from lack of oxygen or the presence of some strange, unknown gas, it is high time to high-tail it out of there. Quickly! You must get fresh air into your lungs immediately, Royce remembered.

It just so happened that only moments before, for some inexplicable reason, the roof fell in near the entrance to the mine. Perhaps it was a cave-in. Most likely, a rockslide. So, Royce was trapped inside the mine, with Dirt being his only companion. At least he could count his blessings that a grizzly bear hadn't wandered inside before the collapse. Or a wolf. Or a cougar.

"'Sylvester' is looking for you, 'Tweety,'" said Royce, as cynical as ever in a pinch, as he grew increasingly concerned about their prospects for survival. He knew it was crunch time. For one thing, his cellphone wouldn't function inside the cavern. Cornelius would come looking for him after a few days, but that might be too late.

On a whim, he decided to let Dirt out of his cage. The untroubled bird hopped about on the ground, probing his surroundings with the sharp claws of his feet, and pecking at a few pebbles with the point of his beak. Royce illuminated the area with his lantern. He aimed an LED flashlight into the dark, mysterious passageway which opened before them.

Quite unexpectedly, the bird flew away in the direction of the void that was a winding, meandering, and as yet unexplored passageway. Their path was punctuated and accentuated by stalactites and stalagmites, other unusual rock formations, tunnel detours, crevices, and a great abyss. Apprehensive and cautious, Royce followed the bird as he flew for short distances, or hopped merrily along the path.

Eventually, a few kilometers away, Royce spied a splinter of light at the end of the tunnel. There must be another entrance to the cave, after all, he thought. He breathed a deep sigh of relief. Dirt had saved him from a grave peril.

"The Crowned Princess has been waiting patiently in the 'Hatchery' for their joyous reunion," said Alexa Sue.

"Who knows! She may turn out to be 'the goose that laid the golden egg,'" said Korn.

"In light of recent events," said Royce, "I've been rethinking our exit strategy for the bird-sanctuary consignment of talking African Grays." He was as detail-oriented, conscientious, and rambunctious as ever. Back to being his old self again. Quite a card! Aren't they all?

Meghan Thomas had been away finalizing the sale of exotic birds. Upon her late arrival, Royce's significant other and business associate could not have helped but wonder, "Why do they call you Dirt?"

"It's because he narrowly escaped being buried alive in a landslide," explained Royce.

CHAPTER 68

Book review of

The Origin of Species

by Charles Darwin, published in 1859,
6th Edition printed in 2017.

Which came first the chicken or the egg?
Didn't he predict the existence of DNA, a full century before scientists broke the genetic code?

Charles Darwin referred to the effects of weather, climate, geography, and geology as "external conditions" in his nonfictional, scientific account of **The Origin of Species**, which is the title of his book, first published in 1859. A 6th edition was printed in 2017.

As an empirical scientist, astute intellectual, and highly knowledgeable naturalist, Darwin's main focus and emphasis was on the garden-variety organism, how it must have changed over long periods of time, perhaps over hundreds of millions of years and hundreds of thousands of generations. He concerned himself with the normal effects of altitude, terrain, wind, water, rain, heat, and cold on the organism. He did not particularly dwell on natural disasters caused by massive flooding, hurricanes, raging, out-of-control wildfires, and such. He was a practical pragmatist. So be it, if these kinds of events cause numerous species of creatures to become suddenly extinct. That he was acutely aware of what happened to the dinosaurs during the Ice Age, did not in the least detract him from his studies in the fields of biology and botany. Indeed, it spurned him on.

Darwin was more concerned with the living organism itself, "organic beings" and their—dare I say it, incredible, miraculous evolution, based on something the author referred to as "natural selection." He also called it "the survival of the fittest." Others might have described the phenomenon as "fate," "destiny," "God's will," or "just plain dumb luck." Some may have inferred at some point and time in their professional careers that the author used circular reasoning and convoluted logic in presenting his argument for how the species has come into being, exists and survives, but I think he has presented a solid case for his system of beliefs, which is nevertheless—despite what his detractors may have insinuated, based on sound logic and scientific proof. Having read the book, I have acquired a reasonable doubt that he ever lost an argument in the classroom, in the laboratory, on the lecture circuit, or in the barnyard, for that matter. He was the persevering type of researcher who would sail halfway around the world just to prove a point, namely, that his theory is irrefutable.

Totally consistent with his character, he was as stubborn, tenacious, and fast-thinking on his feet as the proverbial mule-deer buck, the elusive creature of the forest, which inevitably must have been descended from two or more modified varieties of distinct species—if I did my homework correctly.

Another of the more fascinating aspects of the book to me is Darwin's use of the term "plastic," perhaps a hundred years before the ubiquitous, organic material was invented, manufactured, and supplied to virtually everyone all over the world. Likewise, with his use of the term, "elasticity," long before the invention of "rubber," and similar manmade stretchable materials.

If he were alive today, I'm sure that Darwin would heartily approve of stretching your muscles as part of your cardio-vascular work-out routine and physical conditioning program. After all, he wouldn't want you to mutate into a flabby mass of beached whale blubber from the lack of exercise and a sedentary lifestyle. In order to drive home the point, besides being a modern-day fitness guru, the Darwin of today would have been a sole-survivor.

He would have been a survivor in the sense that he studied and delved as deeply into what it takes for creatures large and small to adapt to their environment as anyone, and come out victorious—or at least, to live another day, in the highly competitive world of competing interests. Having taken so much criticism for his theory over the years, he came out smelling like a rose. Obviously, he's learned from his vast experiences and experimentation. It's in his DNA. If he were alive today, I think he eventually would have cracked the genetic code, achieving a triumph in the process which ultimately would revolutionize and unify the sciences. He'd be able to tell us which came first, the chicken or the egg.

"Which should we take to Mars?" he could tell us.

R. Royce weighed the alternatives. A friend of a friend knew somebody who had heard something about the whereabouts and recent excavation of the complete skeletal remains of a most interesting subject. His longtime friend and business associate, Cornelius Korn had heard something similar. He wanted to investigate and compare notes.

A week ago, out of the clear blue sky, he had telephoned to say that he had acquired a large, heavy wooden crate of precious cargo and wanted Royce to sell the contents for him. "What's in the crate?" Royce inquired.

"Bones," said Korn. "They're very valuable bones." To make a long story short, Korn wanted Royce to meet with a prospective buyer in Cheyenne, Wyoming, and sell him the bill of goods for a museum of natural history exhibit.

"What does a sabretooth tiger have in common with 'Jimmy Hoffa'?" asked Meghan Thomas.

"Both are ancient history as far as I'm concerned," stated Royce, somewhat hesitant in making any reply at all. "The dirk-tooth cat lived during the Eocene and Pleistocene epochs, roughly during the period 34 million to 11,000 years ago. While there are approximately 45 genera of cats, each containing maybe one to 18 species, we have been looking at one of three species, including one of the largest ever found. They are descended from the Dinofelis, Paramachairodus, and Megantereon branches of the cat family tree. Specifically, we are most interested in the species S. Fatalis and S. Populator. These fascinating prehistoric creatures lived and roamed throughout North and South America. The first may have weighed anywhere from 300 to 700 pounds and was about 3 feet in height. The second species of 'Smilodon' weighed from 500 to 900 pounds and looked to be about 4 feet tall. It would have appeared similar to a large bear in stature, except—of course, for the long, curved incisors, which reached up to 12 inches in length. A large, complete skeleton in perfect, pristine condition could be worth a sizable chunk of a million dollars to us, if we could find the right buyer."

"And, in the other crate?" asked Alexis Sue Shell.

"Truthfully, we aren't exactly sure what the contents are," said Royce. "It was just another deal that fell into our lap. For all I know, it could involve the dispatch and disposition of a certain former American labor union president who reportedly had had a serious altercation with a few members of a known criminal organization which had been operating in Detroit, Michigan, in the 1970s. He'd gone to prison for jury tampering, fraud, and bribery prior to that time. He served a number of years of his sentence, then received a pardon from President Nixon. He was released on his own recognizance, and tried to resume his normal activities. Unfortunately, a few short years later—on July 30, 1975, it was, he disappeared off the face of the earth without a trace. He was officially declared deceased in 1982. No doubt, the world had changed a great deal in the interim."

"The crate could contain a weapon. IDs. Documentation. Evidence. Bones," said Cornelius. "Let's get rid of it, ASAP. Return to sender. No questions asked. Case closed."

"They were at the pinnacle of their respective food chains," said Alexis Sue. "Now, sadly enough, they're extinct forms of life, part of a bygone era. Powerful predators, who could bring down an elephant if they put their minds to it."

"They attacked in a group like a starving, salivating pack of fierce, ferocious timber-wolves. They were extremely vicious in their approach to taking care of business. Not unlike some of the Teamsters 'leadership.' The union was supposed to represent the average American worker, trying to earn an honest day's wage and make a decent living, but it had become totally corrupted, controlled, and taken over by shadowy organized crime figures, punctuated by their deadly predatorial practices and violent rampages, or so they say. The federal government had no choice but to step in and put a stop to the whole chaotic mess. Their rampant greed, their coldblooded tactics, and flagrant abuse of power was way over the top. There was no difference whatsoever between them and the pride of sabretooth tigers, who moved stealthily through tall grasses, then suddenly dashed out, leaping onto the backs of big mastodons, scratching, gouging, and digging deeply with their terrible sharp claws into the supple flesh of the gigantic beasts. One of the tigers would eventually clamp down hard with its huge powerful incisors onto the elephant's throat, ultimately piercing the jugular artery, sending down a flood of animal blood and a loud cry of brutalized anguish. The oversized, cumbersome, clumsy, awkward creature didn't have a snowball's chance in hell for survival at that point," said Royce. He was beside himself with empathy.

"Cars are just built better these days due to robotic automation. They drive better. They last longer. They are manufactured with computer brains, solid-state electronics, and space-age materials. You have a great selection of readily available repair parts and customizable components for upgrades and improvements. Best of all, when you see a salesman on television, you don't have to ask yourself, 'Would you buy a used car from this man?'" said Korn. "The quality goes in before the name goes on."

"I always sensed it had something to do with a smooth, comfort ride. Sleek styling and acceleration," said Royce.

"Don't forget good gas mileage," said Meghan.

"A terrific stereophonic sound system!" said Alexis Sue. "Having a full orchestra playing on satellite radio or from a Blu-ray music disk is the cat's pajamas, the living end."

"We may be missing the big picture here," said Korn.

"We may be missing a big payday, too, but I have to agree. Let the Feds handle it. They have more manpower. They can take the heat. We don't need the publicity," said Royce.

"As I've heard it said before, 'Friends will help you move. Good friends help you move bodies.' Now, where did you say that gold mine was?"

CHAPTER 69

Book review of the novel

Snowblind

by Ragnar Jonasson, published in 2010,
translated into English by Quentin Bates in 2015.

The Icelandic Saga continues.
The miniature tape-recorder implanted in his brain suddenly clicked on play-record.

In practically any Bronx or Brooklyn precinct PD you've ever seen on television, they always send the new guy out for coffee and doughnuts, half-expecting him to bring back bagels, lox, and cream cheese. Fortunately, for the most part, he blends in with the populace slightly better than Dennis Weaver playing "Marshall McCloud," who always seemed to have a couple of nefarious villains after him, shooters out, blasting and blazing. When you think about it, the situation is not too drastically different at the police HQ located on the big island northern Atlantic Ocean community which just so happens to be located directly on top of or in near proximity to a major fault line lying deep underneath the earth's surface, which also happens to be connected to a string of active volcanoes, any one of which could erupt violently on any given day with explosive devastation as the result.

He's typically introduced to everyone at the station, efficiently organizes his desk and cubicle, works the rest of the day, and goes home with half a dozen red herrings from the fish market. Fresh fish and a warm loaf of baked bread. Bagels and lox. What's the difference? It's all good sustenance for the body. He actually needs time to familiarize, acclimatize, socialize, and make himself at home. What he needs is no-nonsense QT. Quiet time. Quality time. Whatever you call it. A walk in the park. Someone who understands and cares. Perhaps he should establish a meaningful relationship and find somebody to reciprocate his feelings.

What he definitely does not need in his life at the present moment is to become friendly, intimate, or personally involved with violent, deceptive, pathological pariahs, "Pacman" piranhas, and deranged deviates, who engage in covert, risky, thrill-seeking behavior, some of whom may be prone to abuse painkilling medication. How that works out for him remains to be seen at this early stage in his career. One good thing for certain, he is neither a socialite nor a lone wolf. A happy medium, perhaps, somewhere in between. Mountain climber or social climber? It's too early to tell.

Priorities have been known to change, however. Longing for the simple life? He has found himself in a cozy, little scenic Christmas-card setting, well off the beaten path. A quaint, romantic fishing village up north out of "harm's way." A quiet, idyllic little getaway similar to what he's always dreamed about . Sandy beaches. Ocean waves. Plenty of sunshine. Romance. Or, so you'd love to believe.

The setting for Ragnar Jonasson's novel, **Snowblind**, published in 2010, appears to be bright, unpretentious, and promising. The English translation by Quentin Bates was published in 2015. What really should fascinate the average, impressionable, young reader, are the inhabitants who live there. You're curious about these "real people" and their enviable, untroubled lives. They could be the professionals who work in your own office or business. They could be your new neighbors. They are the people you meet every day who make a good first impression on you. After all, you do have a tendency to make friends quickly enough to form a good foundation for building a fruitful relationship.

Occurring just as suddenly as an inspiration or a flash of lightning, however, he quickly realizes that outward appearances can be deceiving. He's just an ordinary passenger on the *Orient Express*, in a manner of speaking. A non-suspect observer of the foibles of mankind. Initially, he might ask himself, "Who am I to judge humanity?" Then, he remembers quite clearly that he has a specific job with specific duties to perform: he has to discover what went wrong? Who committed the offense? Who should do the time?

"There's no glamour in the slammer!"

Once upon a time they sent him out for refreshments, a "constable on patrol," the new cop on the beat. The next thing he knows, he's returned and finds himself performing the duties of a seasoned criminal investigator. He's become the "Chief of Detectives," if only in function, and certainly not with any such official title. Or, is he a regular Dick? But he's good at what he does. He gets results.

Before very long he begins to learn the unsavory truth of the matter, the crux of the biscuit. The characters he's met begin telling tales. They reveal the complicated personal histories of their colorful, intriguing pasts, which would form the complete history of the town, were the puzzle pieces all joined together. He begins to learn what really motivates some of the suspects he has in mind. What makes them click and tick. The suspense mounts with each succeeding chapter of the book. The pressure builds like the powerful forces of unvented gases beneath a volcano about to erupt. He files a load of cases, solving some, adding some. Thus, the Icelandic detective saga continues, culminating in sudden, shocking, revolting, and unexpected revelations which may impact him personally someday and rock his world to the core.

You conclude that it's no small price you have to pay for the benefits of civilization, security, and stability in an otherwise uncertain world. You wonder if some of the perplexing people he encounters were descended from pagan or barbarian tribes. You consider the Vikings of the past, and their reputation for "raid, pillage, plunder" first and "ask questions" later. It must have penetrated through their thick skulls somehow and become deeply ingrained into their DNA processing machinery.

In today's world, be that as it may, the average modern-day professional in his office has been severely restricted as to his actions and the outlets for his inadequacies and frustrations. After a particularly stressful and tiring day at the office, he may determine that the only compelling option open to him which he could faithfully exercise on a daily basis is to go home, kick the dog, booze it up, punch the wife, and send the kids to bed without allowing them play video games. Indeed, life has become a vicious circle for him with no plan of escape. He should get counselling. After carefully studying and appraising the situation, he determines that some people are just too emotional, hot-blooded, and temperamental to settle down.

A former elementary teacher might have said, in his defense, "He was such a nice little boy. He must have picked up those bad habits after he grew up and moved away to Denmark in order to find work. It wasn't really his fault."

A high school science teacher might have expressed his circumstances best in an amusing anecdote about the sailors on a sleek, speedy Viking ship from yesteryear.

"Men, I have good news and bad news for you. The good news is we're rowing into the harbor of a fabulous city, with an abundance of wine, women, and food; a proliferation of music, dancing, frolicking, and feasting."

"The bad news is, the Captain wants to water ski."

Sitting on a park bench, R. Royce searched the moonless night sky above him and contemplated the universe all around him. It was too early for joggers. His future great-grandson should be able to retire comfortably someday on Mars, he thinks, after the dust settles and the way is paved. All a flourishing community really needs on the red-orange planet is a well-stocked lake, abundant vegetation, and a viable, oxygen-rich atmosphere. Plans and preparations should already have been made for the completion of thickly insulated suburban condominiums and townhouses, connected by a subway to the ultramodern underground city and industrial complex. City Planner. That's what he would call "job security."

Along about that time an unidentified man strolled up and sat down beside him on the weathered wooden bench, which had been painted a dark shade of green some months ago. He sat quietly in the shadows, away from the distant street lamp and appeared to reflect on the events of the coming day. He wore a long, warm, trendy, tan "London Fog" all-weather jacket, one with a plaid liner. It was all zipped up and buttoned. A warm woolen scarf was wrapped around his neck and draped over the shoulders. He wore black gloves that matched his distinctive leather boots. They had a dull-brushed finish to them. The stylish "Beaver" fedora hat that he wore, with its dashingly debonair, rakish, curved brim, shaped crown, and shiny band would have been all the rage in Wyoming had it been a taller and broader "Stetson." He gently placed a small tape-recording device on the seating space between the two of them. Next, he set down a dossier which had been bound into the certain format of an old rare-edition library book. It could just as well have contained someone's personal handwritten diary. He stood up abruptly, but nonchalantly remained standing, as if he were ready, but reluctant to leave. "As I was crossing a bridge one day, I met a man. He tipped his hat, and drew his cane," he said, according to the words of an obscure poem.

"And in this riddle, I told his name," said Royce, as if in reply. Afterwards, the man simply walked away. He vanished into the night. Royce flicked a switch on the recorder and the tape began to play.

"Good evening, Mr. Phillips! I trust that you've had a thoroughly relaxing and refreshing, if uneventful vacation in the tropics. It is so cordial and gracious of you to meet here on such short notice. A dreadfully catastrophic event is about to take place within the next several days. MI-7 needs you to find out the nature of the event, and put an immediate stop to it, before it occurs. The supplementary library material placed beside you contains a miniature thumb-drive with all of the pertinent background information you will require in order to become fully successful in your efforts, given the current level of your technical expertise, based on past experience. Should you choose to accept this assignment you must bear in mind that in the unfortunate event of your compromise, capture, or demise, our government will not acknowledge, recognize, condone, or approve of any of your actions, or any subsequent actions that you deem necessary. In other words, you are completely on your own on this mission. For your own safety and security, please step away from the bench at this time to avoid serious burns or otherwise severe injuries. As a further word of caution, you should be aware that the resulting smoke and fumes poses an inhalation hazard that may prove detrimental to your overall good health and general wellbeing. One final warning: the electronic device, the book, and all remaining contents will ignite, immediately catch fire, and completely melt down into ashes and oblivion within five seconds. Good luck and Godspeed."

Royce extracted the tiny thumb-drive from the book and left the scene without any hesitation on his part or comment. A few hours later, when he felt that he had attained a safe distance, far away from the rendezvous premises, having run through a series of maneuvers, a pattern of mazes, around and over numerous obstacles, he retrieved an anonymous cellular telephone and a stack of debit cards from their hiding place. He called his good friend and business associate, Cornelius Korn.

"I thought I was supposed to be 'Mr. Phelps,'" said Royce.

"How closely did you check the device?" asked Korn.

"There should have been a 'manufactured in Japan' data plate on it," said Royce.

"Good thing, Meghan decided to track the dapper gentleman with whom you met," said Korn.

"Has she developed any leads?" asked Royce.

"Not yet. The good news is, Alexis found the true messenger unconscious but alive, about a mile away among some shrubbery and bushes. He didn't pass all of the checkpoints. She revived him, and rerouted him to D.C. for debriefing. He had already destroyed the original, genuine tape-recorder before it could have been stolen," said Korn. "He has the burn marks to prove it. His attackers have been apprehended and appeared cooperative."

"Looks like we've had a serious breach of security. Any ideas?" asked Royce

"I guess we'd better open up a channel and contact HQ. The mission has changed for the worse," said Korn.

"It's definitely gone sideways. The information we have been given may be fraudulent, but not completely worthless. We'd better forward the thumbdrive to counter-intelligence, asap," said Royce.

"We also need to advise them of any Intel we acquire from 'Dapper Dan.' We're completely out of the loop now. Mission aborted," said Korn.

"Back to the old salt mines," said Royce, with an obvious sense of relief, but contented nonetheless. He'd followed protocol to the letter with amazing results.

"Have you ever noticed that you have a calming effect on some people?" asked Meghan. "They must trust you implicitly."

"The eyeglasses and disguise fooled them," said Royce.

"They'll trust you as far as they can throw you," retorted Alexis Sue. "Present company excepted."

"It bowls me over how we get into these SNAFUs," added Korn. "The good news is the check is in the mail."

"Are you suggesting that we planned it that way all along?" asked Alexis.

CHAPTER 70

Review of the nonfiction book

The Spy and the Traitor

by Ben Macintyre, published in 2018.

Hot-property prospect keeps business executive up late at night.

The Spy and the Traitor, by Ben Macintyre, published in 2018, is the definitive, highly informative, nonfictional account of the defection of a senior-level Soviet spy. He decided to go to the West in the summer of 1985 amidst a flurry of political instability and an uncertain future in the Kremlin. The book is jam-packed with significant historical events taking place on a massive global scale, many of which most of us have all but forgotten, if we knew about them at all. For example, Stalin's purge of 1936-'38, the Soviet invasion of Hungary in 1956, the construction of the Berlin Wall in 1961, the Soviet suppression of the Spring uprising in Czechoslovakia in 1968, and Britain's expulsion of 105 key Soviet intelligence officers in 1971.

Are we beginning to see a pattern here? Is history repeating itself? It's like looking at your reflection in a two-way mirror. You see life from "Both Sides, Now," as in the Joni Mitchell song from many moons ago.

Be that as it may, the book depicts interesting, biographical information about some of the most famous (or infamous) spies of the twentieth century from the U.K., the U.S., and the U.S.S.R. An excellent selection of photographs is included, which represents a virtual "Who's Who" gallery in high-resolution from the shadowy world of cloak and dagger. The book takes you on a virtual tour of the most conservative hotbeds of intrigue you can imagine from around the globe. Make no mistake about it. It's a no-holds-barred, kiss-and-tell book.

You can hardly miss, skimming the pages of this book, if you're on a fact-finding mission concerning the secretive intelligence community operating with impunity in the 1960s to the 1990s. What formerly had been considered classified, closely guarded secrets has suddenly "come alive" and become common knowledge. Shocking. I shiver at the mere thought of another "cold war." To think that all of these events actually transpired before the advent of super-fast, high-volume storage, internet-accessible personal computers, thumb-drives, and the foggy cloud of securely triple-encrypted data is mind-boggling.

"Where is Ed Snowden, when you need him to reset a password?"

Most of all, the book provides keen insight into what it takes to make it to the top of the bureaucratic hierarchy in the corporate boardrooms of spy craft. You are constantly reminded that longevity is never guaranteed in the spy trade. You find out the hard way that building a successful business career in "Her Majesty's" secret service is definitely no accident.

A good spy (and author) can fully describe, characterize, criticize, evaluate, and assess his subject within the space of two or three paragraphs, pointing out all of his flaws, failures, faults, weaknesses, shortcomings, and inadequacies in the process. He knows what he's up against. He reads his adversaries like a book. He knows their limits.

Good luck with that, James! There are ramifications for your actions. You're either on your way up or on your way out the door, when you mix and mingle with that sort of crowd.

R. Royce rode the beach cruiser in a northly direction to the park proceeding at a pleasant, leisurely pace. He stopped and leaned the bike against the trunk of an old walnut tree, to walk alongside a clear running creek. Oftentimes, he enjoyed reveling in and communing with nature. The weather was warm and sunny, for a winter day. The winds were calm. He noticed the brown paper grocery bag through the branches of a tremendously large, towering maple tree, all camouflaged and concealed by an abundance of leaves. One principal branch had fallen into a great depression in the muddy embankment, due to a lightning strike. It too was covered over with leaves, and partially hidden from the view of prying eyes behind some dense undergrowth and the trunk of a fallen oak. He quickly retrieved the item, then walked back to the bike. He placed the lunch-sack-size bag inside the waterproof, rip-stop fabric bike pack which had been Velcroed on top of the bronze anodized-aluminum rack, affixed to the back of the bike. The metal rack had been firmly attached to the titanium frame with small stainless-steel bolts, nuts, and washers, and fit stylishly over the rear wheel. The flat, broad surface of the rack thus placed in this manner had the added advantage of preventing water from spraying up his backside when he rode through water puddles on the sidewalks and in the roadway, much in the same way as a curved metal fender skirting would, but without the narrow space between the tire and the fender becoming clogged up with mud and debris, causing the bike to drag, and not roll as freely, almost effortlessly, as it should. He truly loved the technology, innovation, and ingenuity behind fine craftsmanship.

He climbed aboard the cruiser bike, thought about poor "Peewee Herman," and rolled away swiftly downhill. He was elated, and accelerated. It went faster than usual.

"Not bad for a day's work," said Royce, having returned to the apartment, well-exercised and exhilarated. He verified the contents of the bag, which might have contained sandwiches and cans of soda for an impromptu picnic. Except it didn't.

"Don't quit your day job," said Meghan, his constant traveling companion and business associate, seated on a flowery sofa in the living room.

"Some people would kill for a 'Pay-Day' like this," he said, taking a bite out of a warm portion of fruitcake, the shape of a candy bar. He began stacking bundles of $100 bills in two neat piles. The total added up precisely to a total of $65,000.

"One for me, one for you. One for you, two for me," she recited.

"Fair is fair," he said. "Who said money doesn't grow on trees?"

"As long as the assignment doesn't involve extortion, blackmail, or serious bodily injury, we can't lose," said Meghan.

"Simple arithmetic, security and surveillance are all important," said Royce. "Today's task reminds me of the country and western music we heard broadcasted over the public television station airwaves the other night. Two musicians were playing guitars, one acoustic, one electric."

"Their instrumentalist performance was flawless. They sounded absolutely fabulous. One of them sang a song, called 'The Walk of Life.' I don't think I'd exactly call it a recent hit. It sounded more like a popular Cajun tune of the 60s or 70s," said Meghan. "Sticks right in your brain."

Royce pulled out an old guitar case that was "stashed behind the couch," reminiscent of Glen Campbell, on his way to Arizona. He extracted an old wooden dulcimer and began to strum. She began to hum. She scraped a bottle cap over a corrugated, dull gray, galvanized metal washboard. Ecstatic, they played their roles to the hilt.

"You don't think, they'll miss the money, do you?" he asked.

"Not really. There's plenty more where that came from," she replied, confidently. "Cornelius said he would help the 'Small-Fry' out with a safer, more lucrative part-time job. It's honest work, with incentive pay. The job satisfaction he gains will make it even more rewarding in the long run."

"You're suggesting that 'the Rascal' keeps his job and isn't incarcerated?" asked Royce.

"What are friends for if they can't bail you out, when you make a drastic error in judgment that has the serious consequences and far-reaching implications of an international incident?" asked Meghan. "Selling public information for the greater common good may not seem to be that big of a deal, in all fairness, when your loyalist customer has an obvious need to know and the means to pay big bucks for it. Yet, as we have learned from past experience, there are more important issues at work in the marketplace than the latest fashion trends."

"However convoluted your logic is, I have to admit that making a fashion statement should be a matter of personal taste and preference," said Royce, reflecting for a moment on the gravity of the situation. "The affected individual must ultimately, rationally, and creatively decide for himself which role he is to play. Others will judge him accordingly, however wisely, collectively and humanely."

"Finders, keepers," said Alexis Sue, having been briefed about the operation on the following day. "Losers, weepers!"

"Right," said Cornelius Korn, the most farsighted and trustworthy member of the group of longtime business associates. "Except, we should have something to trade of equal value, for a win-win situation all the way around."

"They lost their investment capital in a volatile trading day on Wall Street. Our contact in Washington will square the deal. Shall we move on to new business?" asked Royce. He was growing impatient.

"Okay, done deal," said Korn. "By the way, do you know anything about the latest fighter jets?" he inquired, casually changing the subject.

"Not much," said Royce. "You'd need a squadron of military pilots to brief you."

"I can't help you in that department, either," said Meghan. "I've retired and lost my FAA certification."

"In that case, we should stick to strictly civilian pursuits," said Korn. "Keep a low profile and our feet firmly planted on solid ground."

"Agreed," said Royce. "I think we're running low on ammunition, anyway."

"We can always fall back and resume work on our mining interests," suggested Alexis Sue.

"Let's do it," said Meghan. "We're all out of hypersonic projectiles."

"We pull the plug on this operation, as of now," said Korn. "I'll notify Washington."

"See you back at the ranch," said Royce.

CHAPTER 71

Book review of the novel

Circe

by Madeline Miller, published in 2018.

Witch-Goddess I Chantel, bottled the heart-warming perfumed herbal remedy, with the Woman-Who-Means-Business Rising Star in mind, naming it Love Potion #925.

The wondrous re-telling of a timeless classic, mythical Greek tragedy.

Circe confronts her siblings, her demons, and other monsters of the deep in this first-person narrative novel entitled **Circe**, by Madeline Miller, published in 2018. The story is a wondrous retelling of a timeless classic, mythical Greek tragedy. The novel would make a superb Shakespearian play in five acts. The nymph witch-goddess would become the perfect drama queen, in my opinion; although, in doing so, she might not remain true to her character's role in accordance with the longstanding tradition of oral history. She most certainly was portrayed as a difficult, insecure child, but she also appeared as being compassionate, longsuffering, studious, and inquisitive. She listened carefully to her parents and elders. She observed and remembered everything that they said and did. She learned from them and sometimes imitated their actions. She could read minds and work magic. She displayed a super-abundance of women's intuition. She was quite crafty and could be a deceptive, "designing woman," when necessary. She proved to be an overprotective, doting mother at first, but gradually gave in and prepared her son for going out into the real world and fulfilling his destiny. Among the least powerful of the gods, Circe had to rely on many of her finer qualities in order to protect her loved ones from their enemies, including those who would cause them the most harm. Amusingly enough, I received the distinct impression that Circe would sometimes talk to herself; or, at least, think out loud, as she recollected her most reflective, revealing, and significant thoughts, given the extreme circumstances in which she was placed; thoughts which ultimately would affect her decision-making process the most, as she acted in a swift and appropriate manner. It almost seems as if she and the gods, in general, have an innate, divinely inspired, collective consciousness in which they can sense imminent danger and permeate the everyday pitfalls of life. In other words, they have premonitions of what will come to pass, and they react in unexpected ways.

While the novel has more than its fair share of suspense, surprises, and dramatic sequences, as compared with the average romance novel, I would also have to admit that it was among the best "self-improvement" books on interpersonal relationships that I've ever read, not that I've read that many. Case in point, how well Circe interacted with Prometheus. How well Circe interacted with Odysseus. Circe, with her siblings. She, with her son. She, interacting with one of the most powerful of all Titans, her own father. She and Hermes, the messenger. She and her archrival, Athena, daughter of the most powerful Olympian, the almighty Zeus. Thus, Circe proved time and time again that she was the most interactive goddess of all. There is no doubt at all in my mind, from having read the novel, that Circe represented "powerful medicine," as she faced grievous injury, battled overwhelming adversity, and had a definite problem with her own immortality. You could say that she didn't exactly play by the rules, either. In any event, in my humble opinion, her moving story was ten times better than any soap opera I've ever seen on television.

R. Royce stood in the crosswalk holding a large, red, octagonal-shaped sign, completely stopping traffic. Later that morning, having been recruited by his constant companion and the volunteer substitute teacher, Meghan Thomas, Royce found himself officiating some form of four-square, dodge basketball game activity during recess. He didn't quite know the rules. In the midst of a flurry of running and jumping around, a youthful sports enthusiast had suddenly dashed in and skirted around the unsuspecting dribbler at center court. In the blinking of an eye, she had deflected and stolen away the fully inflated, bright orange object of play from the other pintsize competitor.

"Now you know why they call me 'Quickie,'" she told him, smiling and beaming, obviously pleased with her prowess and agile athleticism. Afterwards, she returned to the far corner of the tarmac, confident, contented, calmly awaiting the next round of play.

At the end of recess, Royce casually mentioned the incident to Meghan. She said, "I should check the calendar for the next PTA meeting. The child is definitely bright, alert, and highly motivated enough. I'd like to meet her mother."

A few weeks later, Meghan told Royce about what had transpired at the PTA meeting. She said there was nothing at all to be concerned about. Both parents had been present and they seemed normal, pleasant, and well-adjusted. They were well-educated, steadily employed, and worked locally. She, part-time for an insurance agency. He, full-time in the shipping department for the large electronics manufacturing plant in the area. There was no cause for alarm—at least initially; until he gone missing for several days, and she received the ransom note in the mail.

"Have you ever worked for a detective agency?" Cornelius Korn asked his longtime friend and business associate, R. Royce.

"If you mean, like from the 'Yellow Pages' of the phone book," replied Royce. "Then, the answer is definitely and unequivocally, no."

"Maybe so, but we have been known to conduct private investigations on our own," said Korn, "when it affects our business interests. It's just that we don't advertise or solicit clients. "Essentially, we have been our own clients."

"That makes perfectly good sense to me," said Royce. "What are we planning to do? Investigate a detective agency?"

"Exactly!" said Korn. "That's our next assignment, in fact."

"You say we have a missing person?" inquired Alexis Sue Shell, Korn's significant other, his constant companion and close business associate.

"We don't exactly have him on our premises, per se, but we are keenly aware of someone who has presently gone missing," replied Korn. "Here's a copy of the ransom note."

"We have also obtained pertinent information from the recently hired detective agency, which doesn't seem to be getting anywhere near to solving the case," said Meghan.

"It's always good to get a second opinion on the matter," said Royce. "Especially since the client doesn't want the police involved."

"I am beginning to see the problem here," said Meghan.

"Particularly, when the wife doesn't seem overly anxious to get him back," said Alexis Sue.

"Searching for clues now," said Royce. "I've noticed that Mrs. Darla St. Johns has prudently taken out a sizable life-insurance policy on her dear husband a month or so after they were married. She must be a sensible woman, who's planned well in advance for the future stability and security of her family. Ten million dollars' worth of security and stability."

"That's enough to give anyone peace of mind and comfort the family in their time of grief, assuming the detectives can't find her husband, and the police don't either," said Alexis Sue.

"What's in it for us?" asked Meghan, playing the role of a practical sort of girl, and the average concerned citizen.

"Basically, we're slightly concerned about 'collusion' here," said Royce.

"I'm in full agreement there," said Korn. "Let's hope the detectives aren't in on it in some way, shape, or form." He, too, was a practical sort of fellow. He was not so much concerned about obtaining the sizable reward from a big corporate insurance conglomerate, as one might believe. True, he was an honest, standup kind of guy, who's had to look out for himself practically all of his entire life. But, be that as it may, he was more concerned about saving someone's life, namely that of Mr. Johnny St. Johns, who also happened to be a close friend of his.

Following a month of gumshoes pounding the pavement, it turned out that the detective agency had indeed hired a couple of unscrupulous P.I.s who were looking out for their own best interests, rather than that of their new client. They had held poor Johnny incarcerated against his will in a cabin surrounded by a national forest, since the time he'd gone missing. They would have continued to do so, had not Fate and Good Fortune intervened in the form of his concerned old Army buddy, Cornelius Korn, and R. Royce.

To make a long story short, the detectives were fired on the spot, and they lost their badges. They soon went into another less stressful line of work altogether.

Meanwhile, Mr. Johnny St. Johns was joyfully reunited with his loving family, which was comprised of his vivacious wife, Darla, and their charming daughter, Quickie. In consequence, Mrs. St. Johns continues to pay life insurance premiums. With a little help from Cornelius, now and then, she's never missed a payment, and most likely never will. As she grew older, her daughter's former nickname of dubious distinction has gradually evolved into "Cookie." She has since become a basketball star at the local high school and an instant hit "Celebrity Chef" on the internet. She says that her ambition is to attend the nearby community college after graduation. She wants to become a healthcare professional someday. And so, "as the world turns" 'round and 'round, "they grow up so fast," and live happily ever after.

"It just goes to show you," said Alexis Sue, philosophically. "Men aren't pigs. Pigs are loving and caring. They're kind and gentle creatures."

"Slam. Bam. Thank you, Ma'am," said Cornelius, ready to charge up San Juan Hill at a moment's notice. He should have kept his mouth shut. He must have been peeved, or irritable at some point, because he appeared somewhat miffed and isolated.

"You forgot the loyal and trustworthy part," said Meghan, not to be outdone.

"Actually, pigs aren't all that trustworthy or loyal. They'll escape from their pen at the first opportunity to run away. They love wandering through the briars and brambles and into the hollows and woods looking for roots, berries, and truffles. They'd run wild and go feral if you let them. They'd never come back," said Royce.

"Same thing for policemen," said Korn, to change the subject. "Once they change into plainclothes and go undercover, they never want to return to uniform duty."

"A truce," said Alexis. "Let's all go to the waterslide instead, and have some good, clean fun." There was no objection to her inspired suggestion. All was forgiven and forgotten. Life goes on.

"You said we're looking for a cannon ball from the Civil War era?" inquired Meghan.

"Very true, indeed," replied Royce. "There's a story behind the 'Cannon Ball Run.' According to the legend, two secretive chapters of Tau Kappa Epsilon Psi fraternity brothers from the University of Maryland and Virginia

Commonwealth University, respectively, decided in 1864 that they wanted the Civil War to end as soon as possible with a minimal loss of life and limb, mostly their own. One of the members discovered that Union soldiers were escorting a large shipment of gold bullion from the U.S. Mint to Fort Knox, Kentucky, concealed within a wagon-train of cannonballs destined for Gettysburg, Pennsylvania. The young men collaborated to abscond with the gold, but neither chapter wanted the Union or the Confederate side to have the gold. It would only prolong the war, they argued. So, they plotted to highjack and hide the gold in a safe place until after the war ended. But, again, neither chapter completely trusted the other one to follow through and do the right thing."

"That's right," continued Korn. "They were afraid the members of one chapter or the other would spend the gold on a lavish lifestyle. Or, they would get caught by Union or Confederate authorities. Either scenario would have defeated their purpose."

"So," said Royce. "They decided to swear the most trusted members of their sister sorority to secrecy and let their girlfriends hide the gold at an undisclosed location. 'Darla' and 'Jane' drove the heavily laden wagons concealing the gold and carrying six 'prisoners of war,' who were actually blindfolded fraternity members and provided the muscle-power for lifting crates, to the decided location. There, they quietly offloaded the gold bullion and sealed it inside an obscure cave. It had taken three days to arrive on the scene, they say, travelling only at night, under the cover of darkness, over meandering dirt roads, through pastures, along cow paths, and across deer trails."

"Flash forward to yesterday," said Korn. "We received a 'chain-letter' in the mail from one of Darla's sorority sisters in Virginia. She's cordially invited us to participate in the 'Diamond Jubilee Cannonball Run.' This year will mark the one hundredth year anniversary of the Cannonball Run, since they moved the gold to its new hidden location."

"You're saying, the sorority sisters went back and removed the gold from its original location, instead of returning it to the U.S. Mint after the Civil War?" said Meghan.

"They took the TKEY boys for a ride, didn't they?" commented Alexis Sue.

"Okay," said Royce. "According to the letter, the authentic commemorative and historical cannon ball in question has been hidden away near the

'Fountain of Youth' ride on the fairgrounds premises. Whoever finds the rare artifact, should promptly notify 'Jane' through the sorority's 'Gettysburg Memorial Fund." He is to place a ten-dollar bill inside each of two stamped and self-addressed envelopes, which have been generously provided, and mail them. He adds his own name to the bottom of the list and deletes the name at the top. Finally, he sends the newly compiled list to two trusted individuals of his own choosing, along with two more stamped self-addressed envelopes."

"I'm a little confused. I understand how we find the cannonball, but how do we get to the gold ingots?" asked Alexis Sue.

"Very simple," said Meghan. "Once the sorority sisters receive notification that you've found the cannonball, they send you another key clue to the gold as well as clues for finding the next serially numbered cannonball. There are ten of them in all. Whoever finds the tenth one, receives the treasure map leading to the gold; that is, assuming no one figures out beforehand where the gold is actually located from the clues they have already received."

"How many clues do we have?" asked Alexis Sue.

"I think we only need one more clue," said Cornelius.

CHAPTER 72

Book review of the novel

Hotel Sacher

by Rodica Doehnert. Translated by Alison Layland, published in German in 2016, the English translation published in 2018.

> *The apple doesn't fall far from the tree in this tawdry rhapsody of court intrigue.*
> *The Grim Reaper enters the castle through an open portal; glancing all around, spies Divine Love, unaware that she is immortal, making not a sound.*

Hotel Sacher is a fast-paced novel, intended for an audience familiar with Austrian, Hungarian, and Yugoslavian history around the turn of the 19th century; acquainted with the events leading up to the First World War; and having some basic knowledge of the royal monarchies and their business interests abroad. The reason is simple: These influential people and others from the vast military-industrial complex have dominated the headlines of major newspapers all over Europe. They have shaped society since time immemorial and would ultimately change the course of human history. On a negative note, it seems that not everyone in attendance at the European Conference held in Vienna along about that time was in favor of a peaceful resolution to the Napoleonic Wars. But, alas, all of that happened over a hundred years ago. Today, most of us; at least in this country, share but a few of the same values of the era, possibly excepting, those involving self-determination, freedom, and opportunity.

The author, Rodica Doehnert, has already made a successful television career for herself in recent years; and, so, her novel, published in 2016 and translated into English in 2018, could be easily converted into a BBC or Hollywood miniseries. It would make a great "Blockbuster" movie, as well. I believe, the author's success is partly due to her poignant style of writing and partly due to the sensational nature of her intriguing subject matter. People generally find members of the wealthy, powerful ruling class and the aristocracy, in particular, most interesting and compelling. They're like movie stars to many of us. While feudal society might not have actually appeared all that romantic to the average peasant worker-bee during the preceding medieval times, a good, wholesome "Cinderella" story always appeals to our better nature. We loved *The Sound of Music*, even if it wasn't entirely true, or quite as historically accurate as it might have been. We wouldn't be able get enough of the *The Phantom of the Opera*, had trustworthy detectives been sent in to solve the most diabolical and sinister of crimes.

Still at a loss, and just can't quite relate to the characters in the novel? Give yourself a break and watch Queen "Victoria" on *Masterpiece Theater* for illuminating background information. Or, you may want to flip through the cooking channels searching for fine dining cuisine and culinary delights. You just might discover that "Lars is upstairs showing the new English girl how to make a cream Danish."

On a side note, I wasn't exactly sure how to pronounce "Sacher," the name of the luxury hotel. Does it sound like "sacker" or does it rhyme with "slasher"? In either case, the cleverly written novel shines a spotlight on many of its own numerous redeeming qualities and ultimately makes for worthwhile reading.

Shouldn't we at least say a few words about the leading character? Love finds him in his castle, naked, unafraid, and unashamed; at Court, confronting oppression and conspiracy with diplomacy and dignity; on center stage of the Opera, her knight in shining armor.

A word of caution to those who may experience the gamut of intense emotions in reading the novel: overwhelming joy, undeniable sadness, and a profound sense of relief. The ending is enough to bring a sentimental, old fool to tears, adding a few more lines of sheer poetry to the story:

> The Grim Reaper enters the castle through an open portal,
> Glancing all around,

Spies Divine Love, unaware that she is immortal,
Making not a sound.

R. Royce looked calmly at his watch. Almost time for the changing of the guard, he thought. He listened to the FM band on the radio, "Eagles." They were singing "Hotel California." According to the hotel manager, however, "You can check in anytime in the evening, but the checkout time is 12 o'clock noon, unless you make prior arrangements."

Someone drove a large delivery truck out of the warehouse lot. A couple of blocks away, the driver turned left and went down Main Street. Moments later, Meghan Thomas had overtaken and intercepted him. She walked over to the driver's side of the vehicle as he pulled the truck over and parallel-parked near her sparkling clean, recently washed, waxed, and buffed cherry-red Mustang fast-back in showroom condition inside and out. Quincey exited the vehicle. Meghan stepped in and took his place behind the wheel.

"My God, Mr. Pfleuger! Aren't you cold?" she exclaimed. It was a chilly winter day and the wind blew in from the north. He wasn't wearing a jacket.

"I have a warm leather coat, fur-lined gloves, and earmuffs in the car," he replied, as he ran over to the Ford, got in, and sped away. He didn't look back. It wasn't really that cold, and he'd just wanted to show off his hot, vintage model-T illustration sweatshirt.

When Meghan passed Royce seated in the snazzy, sleek, charcoal gray Porsche along the way, he put it in gear, accelerated, and followed her at a safe distance. Cornelius Korn called Royce on his cellular phone to announce the rendezvous point. "Are you driving South on Main Street?" he asked.

"Yes, indeed, I just passed Lintemann's tuxedo rentals shop, across from Newtonia's five and dime. They have an impressive new lineup of dresses and gowns on display in their windows," said Royce. "Their selection of formal attire is the best in the business."

"Wasn't that fun?" broadcasted Alexis Sue Shell over the CB radio, having just advised Korn of two apparent accidents en route. She'd noticed the diversions on Wall Street right away. A stalled vehicle collision, blocking the intersection. A dumpster full of cardboard boxes on fire in the alley. She didn't know who had caused the accidents. Or, why. She wasn't a firebug and certainly didn't appreciate anyone who was. She merely went along for the ride to observe the foolishness and carelessness of others.

"That's always good to know," Korn told Royce, seconds later. "I'll keep that in mind. Incidentally, if you had gone the other route, there would have been an accident. We'll meet up later."

"Roger Wilco," said Royce. He sounded like an official in uniform, but wasn't. "We'll stick to the plan from here on out."

"What's in the back of the truck?" asked Victoria Pfleuger, when Meghan pulled into their circular drive and eased up to the residence.

"Six formal gowns and tuxedos; six designer dresses and leisure suits; complete with matching footwear, handbags, and accessories. As you must be aware by now, they have been exquisitely tailored to fit everyone perfectly," said Royce, beaming confidently, while extricating himself from the sports car.

"You haven't forgotten the crown jewels, have you?" asked Mrs. Pfleuger, partly in jest.

"I have all the glittery bling and trinkets we need for the party in the bag," volunteered Korn, holding up a plaid carry-on.

"The rest have been squirrelled away in a safety deposit box," said Royce, as he began removing boxes of garments from the cargo truck, using the hydraulic lift-gate attachment. Everyone present collected their items of wearing apparel and took them to their rooms for an impromptu dress rehearsal.

"The ball drops in five hours. Better get some rest," said Quincey Pfleuger. Once the cargo had been removed, he climbed into the cab. He drove off and returned the truck to the warehouse. Royce followed and gave him a lift back to the house.

"We can party like it's 1899 Vienna in these costumes," said Alexis, sashaying to and fro.

"Meanwhile, back at the Oasis," said Meghan. "We're ready to rock and roll." She enunciated each syllable in the decidedly exaggerated manner of a motivational speaker.

"Raawk and rowll!" repeated the others. "Drop another coin in the juke-box, darling." "We will, we will mock you," they sang, stomping their feet in unison, in the proper mood for any festive occasion. A New Year's celebration with friends and family!

Three days later, they put on their fashion-designer leisure suits and hopped aboard a charter flight to Florida for some fun in the sun and time on the beach. They had already made a substantial deposit into each of their bank accounts.

CHAPTER 73

Book review of

In Pieces

an autobiography by Sally Field, published in 2018.

The aspiring actress in situation comedy and slapstick takes on more meaningful, dramatic roles.

Sally Field's autobiography reminds me of an incident from my life which recently occurred, so there must be something universally appealing about her personal narrative, unless you're more interested in knowing the intimate details and finer points of pursuing an acting career in television and the motion picture industry. There's a considerable amount of information about that topic in her book, **In Pieces**, as well.

I saw my former sister-in-law in the Walmart parking lot around the Xmas holidays, loading groceries into the trunk of her sedan, and asked her how the young, skinny niece and her family is doing. She has four children, ages 3 to 13. Their family lives over by the lake, so I don't see them very often. Her husband frequently travels halfway across the state to Oklahoma City on poultry business. She works a full-time job herself, for some HHS entity. It beats heaving watermelons for a living.

Raquel told me, "I don't know how she does it."

They're deeply religious, god-fearing, and they pray, I thought, but didn't say so out loud. Their prayers are answered, because they persevere, I believe. But, saying so might be construed as being too intrusive into their personal lives on my part. Instead, I said, "She's a hard worker. Both parents are. They mean well, and only want to do what's best for their family." I wanted to leave it at that.

She continued, "Oh, Darlene and Kevinski will do just fine, now that they're both out of the military, and back home from Afghanistan."

I said, "They'll be okay as long as you're around to help babysit, and watch out for them. Incidentally, I drove by your mom's house to drop off some silk-screen T-shirts and dishes—tea cups and saucers, but no one was home."

She confided in me, "Mom's moved in with my sister. She caught the flu, so Abigail's been feeding her chicken soup until she can get her strength back. She's 93 years old, you know."

"Very well," I said. "I'd better get back to the house and check in on my own mother. She gets crazy as a loon when there's a full moon out. She's been that way all her life. Her fourth live-in companion had to go to a rest-home. He was falling down on the job all the time. And he wrecked his automobile. She said she can't take care of him anymore. When I asked her if she misses him, she gave me a blank stare and asked, 'Who?' I figured, she isn't getting any younger herself. Good thing Jeannie checks in on her practically every day. She has 'Meals on Wheels,' so at least she won't go hungry. I sold my house in North Texas recently and moved to Joplin to be closer to family—without being too close. Stuck in that big old apartment house, I would be afraid of going stark raving mad, like the strange character in that movie *Psycho*."

To tell you the truth, I didn't take Sally Field very seriously as a "starving artist." The author does prove her point that pursuing a career in television while raising three children can prove most challenging. Despite that, the photographs in the book, spanning six or seven decades, show what a wonderful family she has and depict what an incredible life she's lived so far. I fully expected that Sally would be charming, appealing, witty, funny, and wholesome in real life—like a cool glass of farm-fresh milk on a summer day. The book reveals the life and times of a modern television celebrity who expected more out of life and got it.

I imagine Ms. Field standing before "Britany Spears" and "Hannah Montana" as a film director one day, stating unequivocally, "You want a part that you can sink your teeth into," concluding their conversation with the fact that she has no intention whatsoever of "preaching to the choir."

Reflecting back in time, I think of other actresses who have "made it" in the business. Perhaps Sally Field may not have been as drop-dead gorgeous or nearly as glamorous as Marilyn Monroe, Elizabeth Taylor, Gina Lollabrigida, and Brigit Bardot in their day, but times have changed. People have changed considerably, too. Noticeably so. Then again, they still say "beauty is in the eye of the beholder." We've all experienced more of the world, and our perception of the universe has been rapidly expanding ever since. Yet, we can truly admit in all fairness that we have never seen Sally playing the role of a Tuesday Weld, Patty Duke, Ann Margaret, Heather Locklear, Jennifer Anniston, or Charlise Theron cloned lookalike, candy-striper, Elvis impersonator. The aspiring actress in situation comedy and slapstick had taken on more meaningful, dramatic roles. Totally unique in her approach, possessing a one-of-a-kind personality, Sally will always have her own special place in our hearts for the movie magic she has created before our very eyes, over the years.

Why did I read the book? Honestly, I was curious to know if Sally Field had been exploited as a movie actress like all the rest in the "me too movement." But mostly, I wondered if she had anything terribly derogatory to say about Burt Reynolds. While he had already built a large fan base previously in his career, Sally must have doubled it when she became his costar. No doubt, they became critically acclaimed superstars from the collaboration.

R. Royce sat on the sofa looking over a stack of passports. "Joaquin Garcia" and "Alejandro Nunez," he read. He knew they would be travelling to Juarez soon, across the border from El Paso, but he didn't think they'd be carrying false identification documents when they did so.

"What do you think?" asked Cornelius Korn, his longtime friend and business associate. "You look like one tough hombre, in your photo."

"Fine. You look as distinguished as ever in yours," said Royce. "As trustworthy as Benjamin Franklin on a crisp, newly printed bill."

"We'll be carrying more than a hundred dollars on this trip," said Korn, matter-of-factly. He held up a worn, weathered, tanned-leather satchel that looked like it might have been attached to some cowboy's saddle bags from before the Civil War. Probably Jesse James'.

"What's the plan?" asked Royce. His curiosity had obviously gotten the better of him. He knew that they were going to a bullfight as spectators, but wasn't quite aware of anything else on the agenda.

"First thing off the bat, we're going to make a sizable deposit into the Mercantile Bank in Juarez," said Korn. "Next, we'll meet our contact at a nice restaurant nearby. We'll enjoy a pleasant meal with lively conversation and a mariachi band for entertainment. We'll leave the waiter a big tip. I'll give Santa Ana Montoya a certified check as a deposit. Then we'll go to the bullfights for the rip-roaring, cultural experience of a lifetime all taking place on the single, solitary, warm, sunny afternoon that can only be described as Cinco de Mayo."

"I can deal with the culture shock of fireworks and Mexican Independence," said Royce, in confidence. "When do we get the goods?"

"When Santa Ana exchanges our saddle bags for his," said Korn. "What could be easier? The password of the day is 'simplification,' without complications."

"Joaquin. Alejandro. Andale, pronto!" shouted Meghan Thomas, emulating the immortal words from the large, silver screen of the magnificent Zorro. She was their chauffeur, already in the limousine driver's seat, projecting her voice, and insistently honking the horn. "Let's go to town."

"Hop in Gwendolyn. Time to move," she called out to Alexis Sue, smiling intently at the bonny bouncing bunny. They would follow the masked men across the Rio Grande; to the ends of the earth, if necessary; and Plano, Texas.

Having driven them to their destination, she would park nearby and blend in with the woodwork and scenery, while her two taxi occupants completed their financial transaction. She kept the meter running, as they say. Meghan is Royce's live-in companion and their longtime business associate. If necessary, she would help bring the deal to an agreeable conclusion, most beneficial to either one party or both parties, depending on favorable circumstances.

In a follow-on vehicle was the tightly knit group's fourth business associate, Alexis Sue Shell. She was also casually known as Korn's significant other. She slid a compact disk into the music player on the dash of the flashy Mustang as she drove. "What's that background sound?" asked Korn, who'd connected to her via his cellphone. She represented solid insurance..

"An old standby favorite of yours, 'Herb Albert and the Tiajuana Brass,'" said Alexis. "First selection, 'Lonely Bull,' followed by 'Never on Sunday,' then 'A Taste of Honey,' and finally 'South of the Border.'"

"How appropriate," commented Meghan. "Are you choreographing this Broadway play?"

The transaction went very smoothly, better than anyone had anticipated. The generous businessmen had tossed in a couple of kilo-size, porous, gray rock samples, which happened to be chock-full of gem-quality emeralds, and a velvet bag full of sparkling rubies. Freebies. A sign of good faith. Back in the living room at one of their hotel suites in El Paso, they divided the loot evenly. The next day, the vacationing couples drove their two vehicles on separate paths in different directions, like bank robbers avoiding a posse in hot pursuit across the burning sands, mesas, and sparsely populated badlands of New Mexico.

"It turns out," said R. Royce, "the 'Treasure of the Sierra Madre' was more valuable than gold."

"You've proved once again, that a good mechanic is worth his weight in platinum," replied Meghan, as he poured some liquid from a gallon jug into the radiator of their automobile, the motor still running to prevent the water pump from cooling down too rapidly and cracking the housing, or a rubber hose from leaking.

CHAPTER 74

Book review of the novel

The Gray Man

by Mark Greaney, published in 2009.

A weapons manufacturing consortium supplying N. Korea? Only one man in the world can breech security and poke a hole in that theory, if he's still alive.

Mark Greaney pulled out all the stops in his ambitious, fast-paced novel, *The Gray Man*, published in 2009. His main character has a long history of exercising his civic responsibility in a highly skilled, technical, and tactically proficient manner. At present, he is employed as an anonymous problem-solver, trouble-eliminator, and crisis management expert for a private firm worth trillions, after having been summarily dismissed from the CIA for inefficiency, insubordination, incompetence, or other such "politically incorrect" nonsense. He's had to prove himself ever since in order to polish and restore his tarnished sterling-silver reputation to its former glory. Now, he's the spitting image of the Tin-Star Man—I'm thinking of Marshall "Gary Cooper" here, fully re-tooled, steeled to the task at hand, sharpened, and re-assembled into the seven million dollar version of a "Robocop" prototype, or a reasonable fully human facsimile thereof, who must have recently escaped from Oz and the Emerald City. He is being sent on an entirely new mission altogether this time: save "Dorothy" from the terrible clutches of tyranny, in a manner of speaking, and possible torture. As I might have previously mentioned, having callously let the proverbial cat slip out of the bag, he is as tough as nails, in the peak of physical condition, mentally prepared, exceptionally skilled and very determined to follow through on the assignment he's been given, once he has deemed that the operation is necessary, sufficiently and significantly important, and ultimately worthwhile. In this particular case, "failure is not an option." There are two narrowly winding roads before him, "Do or die." He is tuned, wound, ramped up and ready to go, fully intent and totally focused on achieving the required successful outcome of his mission.

For example, you may ponder, what if a certain weapons manufacturing consortium, subject to a hostile takeover by unscrupulous rogue-raider businessmen has been surreptitiously supplying N. Korea, or other such sanctioned nation, with strategic raw materials, top-secret technology, classified support and guidance for advancing their WMD program?

There is only one man in the entire world who can breech their security and poke a hole in that theory, if he's still alive. The "Gray Man." What a stupendously powerful idea for a novel!

R. Royce decided that he's not going to be disturbed early on Sunday morning. He planned on watching television instead and relaxing around the house.

"What's on TV?" inquired his good friend and longtime business associate, Cornelius Korn, later in the day. He had a six-pack with him and sat down on the easy chair adjacent to the overstuffed sofa on which Royce was reclining, and thumbing through a glossy magazine.

"Same-o. Same-o," he said, lazily.

"Want to go out in the field and shoot some pheasants?" asked Korn. "'Tis the season."

"Not particularly," said Royce. "I'm more of a fisherman. I can tag along, though, if you want some company."

"Hiking through the woods will be good exercise for you," said Korn.

"I think so, too. Let's go."

"You can be the Caddy and carry the golf bag and equipment," said Korn, interjecting some humor into their adventure.

"Why not!" said Royce. "I should get out of the house and do something practical and constructive." He put on some boots, a sweater, a warm jacket, and a hat that folded down over his ears. He put some extra-warm woolen socks and fur-lined leather gloves in a nylon sports bag. Korn had all of the accouterments already stowed away in the trunk of his vehicle. They kept the firearms readily accessible. The rifles and shotguns were out of their hard-sided cases and had been placed in the back seat under some blankets.

"Looks like you're loaded for bear," said Royce. "I may want to do some target shooting myself."

At the end of the day, Cornelius returned the worn and exhausted Royce back home and watched over him as he dropped onto the living room sofa he'd left hours before.

"Would you like some warm tea?" asked Meghan Thomas, his live-in companion and their business associate. "Let me get you a blanket." When she returned with the tea and blanket, she stood next to him, put her arm around his shoulder and inquired discretely, "How was your hunting trip?"

"Well executed," said Korn. He could be strictly business, when the situation warranted attention to detail.

"Cornelius had casually neglected to mention that some people who were out and about looking for him had recently discovered his whereabouts," said Royce. "We led them into a trap at about the same time they were preparing to ambush us. The authorities were hidden behind a clump of trees onsite when the perpetrators made their presence known to us. We can thank our lucky stars that 'the desperados' had been stopped in the nick of time. The sheriff arrested them on the spot and his deputies transported them to the county calaboose without incident. We had a close call."

Recapping the events of the day, Alexis Sue Shell, the fourth member of their bridge club and garden party, said, "When Cornelius vanished from view, you dropped five in a row, sort of like the local community college basketball team on a hot shooting streak."

"I was wondering why you put me in the treetop blind with a tranquilizer gun," said Royce, "telling me not to come within a hundred feet of you." Korn had calmly walked over to each of the men where he lay prone on a soft bed of leaves. They were sleeping soundly and peacefully, Korn noticed as he covered each one up with a warm, woolen blanket.

Three others had been spooked and quickly fled the area when they heard a rapid succession of pump shotgun blasts in the air above their position. It momentarily froze them in their tracks. Alexis had noted the arrival of their vehicles earlier through the ruby-coated lenses of her binoculars.

Upon their safe return to town, they were all apprehended by local police officers. In a state of disbelief, the assailants were fingerprinted and automatically given a police record. They had been charged with the crime of littering. Their five aggressive friends were not so fortunate, however. Charged with illegal firearms possession and assault with a deadly weapon, they would go directly to jail.

The sheriff asked Cornelius about the incident after the fact. Korn said that he'd been out hunting and shot at a flock of birds that had suddenly sprung up in front of him. He asked if Korn had permission from the owner to hunt on the land.

"'The Thin-Man' owns the woods around here," said Korn, a serious look on his face. "A thousand acres of trees, rolling hills, natural grasses, and creeks, that are adjacent to the national forest game preserve. You've probably heard of him as 'Slender Man.' He's been in the news an awful lot lately. An apparition, ten-feet tall, some say, he has a very slender body with long, slender arms and looks as if he's walking around on stilts in the fog, if he's not actually floating in thin air. He wears a tuxedo, the formal dinner attire of a butler. Legend has it that he was once the harmful byproduct of children's imagination having run wild. People now say that he comes in through the LCD screens of their electronic devices, such as cellular telephones, televisions, and computer monitors, mostly at night. He appears like a magician, and slowly begins the methodical process of taking over their minds, making them do strange and bizarre things. They behave as if they were hypnotized and couldn't help themselves."

"Grownups just think of him as their worst nightmare," said Alexis Sue, sounding pleasant and convincing, yet having accepted the inevitable. "Don't you boys ever get tired of your camouflaged hide-and-seek paintball games?"

CHAPTER 75

Book review of the novel

The Gondola Maker

by Laura Morelli, published in 2014.

Hero on a sampan sitting at the stern, he don't think his boat will burn.
   The Reincarnation of Romeo and Juliet.
   He was caught up in a well-crafted, high-octane, whirlwind romance.

Laura Morelli's compelling novel, **The Gondola Maker**, published in 2014, commences in the year 1581 and takes place in the popular vacation destination of Venice, Italy. The narrator, "Luca Vianello," relates the incredible story of his life, family, and adventures during the waning years of the Renaissance period when Italian art, culture, and society were all the rage. His long-established and reputable family has been constructing and selling the sleek, swift, maneuverable wooden vessels that circumnavigate the Republic's canals, rapidly propelling the local population throughout the city, for generations upon generations. He proves his capabilities as a tried, trued, and tested master craftsman and "river-yacht" tradesman. His family touts their own particular brand and trademark of dealership vessels, as it were. It is not surprising that their boats are highly regarded as being among the finest manufactures anywhere in the then-known world.

One day, Luca decides to branch-out into the water-taxi business, and so begins the real adventure of a lifetime. He meets a certain "Guiliana Zanchi," and she zings him good, with one of Cupid's arrows. Their brief, fleeting, promiscuous, unexpected encounters dramatically change his perception of life, and his role in it, as he takes off in the "Daytona 500" fast lane. The adrenaline-rush coursing through his bloodstream is unlike anything he's ever experienced before. He feels as pumped and psyched as a man in flight. He becomes zestfully enamored and suitably enticed. Teased and pleased, true romance finally catches up to him. He acquires a sense of entitlement that should last him forever and a day.

Giovanni Boccaccio undoubtedly would have modified and retold the love story differently, had he heard it first, after a fashion, in his own ribald and risqué way, before including it in his "Decameron." William Shakespeare, arguably, would likewise have been impressed with the more modern, down-to-earth version of "Romeo and Juliet," quite possibly even preferring it to his own. This could be a slight exaggeration, however. In any event, the leading protagonist was caught up in a well-crafted, high-octane, whirlwind romance.

R. Royce was driving along a hilly, winding county road, having opted for the paved scenic route to their final destination. Seated beside him in the unrivaled Porsche was his good friend and longtime business associate, Cornelius Korn.

"Have you told Alexis Sue about the farm acreage you acquired out here, yet?" asked Royce. Alexis Sue is Korn's significant other and their business associate.

"She thinks we just hunt pheasants out in the County somewhere," said Korn. They continued on their way to their destination in muted silence. Korn provided timely directions, indicating the appropriate turnoffs and proper detours that they must make along the way, throughout the four-states region. He wanted to show Royce the property that he had recently purchased. He had already begun landscaping it.

"You wanted to surprise somebody?" asked Royce. "It looks like an ordinary mobile home to me, a rounded, silver-bullet 'Airstream' like you'd find in any recreational trailer park in America, only you have it isolated among a grove of shade trees on a hillside, near a clear-running creek, on about five acres of secluded land."

"Actually, it's more like thirty-nine acres of wilderness peace, joy, and serenity out here," said Korn. "Would you like the grand tour?"

"Certainly," said Royce. "By all means, let's hike around the woods and have a closer look. We can smell the roses and commune with nature in all her splendor."

"I can guarantee that you're going to be pleasantly surprised," said Korn. They walked along a meandering trail through the woods. Royce played follow the leader.

Before very long they had located an abandoned set of railroad tracks. The tracks had been converted into a paved bicycle path. They followed this path for a while. Then, they went on an off-road vehicle trail for a few hundred yards further. It led them to a large, obtrusive boulder. They went around its circumference to see what it might conceal from view. Sure enough, they found a smooth bedrock road leading up to the entrance of a cavern wide enough and tall enough for a full-sized automobile to drive into. They also discovered a spring-fed pool of sparkling pure, clean spring-water with a waterfall cascading into the creek far below.

They began exploring the cavern interior. Some of the limestone rock formation that was inside the cave must have washed out over thousands of years ago, leaving the solid rock interior hollowed out. Gigantic stalactites and stalagmites as big around as tremendous tree trunks merged like reinforced concrete columns in the center and throughout the cave, supporting the roof and tying into the metamorphic and igneous conglomeration that comprised the hard-packed rock floor. The enormously large room nature had created appeared to be architecturally and structurally sound. The temperature inside the cavern would be a dry, comfortable 60 degrees year-round, according to Korn. There was enough open space inside to park two dozen cars and couple of motor-homes. With its Southern exposure, the cavern appeared to be naturally illuminated. Royce noticed that Korn's beloved Mustang—his pride and joy, in pristine condition, had already been parked inside, where it was safely housed, secured, and hidden away, out of inclement weather.

"This is exactly where I want to be when the balloon goes up and the big one goes off," exclaimed Royce, somewhat excited about the rarified discovery.

"Jesse James must have said the same thing to his brother, Frank, when he revealed the location of the Gang's new hideout in 1862," said Korn.

"The old homestead definitely shows potential," said Royce. "The only possible downside I can see for the foreseeable future involves the proposed reservoir that the city plans to build some thirty miles downstream. The project will flood thousands of acres of fertile farm land in the valley south of here. I guess, your property value all depends on how high the water rises after they complete the hydroelectric dam. Excessive rainfall and global-warming may have an additional impact."

"There's no great concern here. We're at much higher elevation," said Korn, brimming with contentment and beaming with confidence. "I don't believe it will have any effect on us, whatsoever—unless we want to drive over to the lake and go fishing for bass and crappie."

"Then, I am suitably impressed," said Royce. "Can we store our cars in here out of the weather?"

"Whatever floats your boat," said Korn.

"What a fantastic cavern!" said Alexis Sue, a few days later, checking out the vista and panorama views. "Don't you just love a lush, tropical paradise? It's so romantic."

"This is what I'd call a real 'Man-Cave,'" said Meghan Thomas, having seen the hallowed halls for the first time. She stood by R. Royce 100 percent. They were all in.

"Now that we have a high-and-dry parking garage to store them in, we can broker another consignment of Ferraris," announced the always enterprising Cornelius Korn. "The last batch went too fast."

CHAPTER 76

Book review of the novel

Hunting Prince Dracula

by Kerri Maniscalco, published in 2107.

"But Father, why is there a fence around the cemetery?"
They go on a personally guided tour of the haunted, medieval castle late one night during a snow-storm by the light of a harvest moon.
It's all fun and games until somebody gets seriously injured or killed.

The novel **Hunting Prince Dracula**, by Kerri Maniscalco, published in 2017, is a cleverly written story about a couple of young lovers and forensic science students who travel to attend a medical seminar at Bran Castle near Bucharest, Romania, in the winter of 1888.

The gist of the plot reminds me of a well-written modern television series with excellent acting, called "Da Vinci's Inquest." The program has recently appeared on public television here and takes place in Vancouver, British Colombia. Da Vinci portrays the County Coroner, who is responsible for determining the cause of death in numerous instances of "wrongful death," or "foul play," usually involving suspicious circumstances. There is a similar theme at work in the novel. It's all fun and games until somebody becomes injured or gets killed, you think. In both the novel and the television series, the leading protagonists bring the right attitude to the job, in my opinion. They're a practical sort of professionals, keenly perceptive and positive-minded, with unswerving determination. They always follow through on obtaining desirable results, using radically and scientifically proven methods.

To continue on with the subject at hand, then; the novel is a superb gothic thriller, complete with a medieval castle and rural village, located in the remote Carpathian Mountain region of eastern Europe. The time period involved doesn't exactly correspond to or coincide with the Age of Enlightenment for many of the local inhabitants, be that as it may. Indeed, they are extremely superstitious and harbor deeply seated beliefs concerning the curious behavior of wolves, bats, spiders, strangers in their midst, and certain royal personages. You get an abysmally deep sense of foreboding and the macabre throughout the storyline. You quickly learn the meaning of what could most readily be defined as morbid, diabolical, and sinister. The author of this impressive novel attacks you with her wry sense of humor and assaults all of your senses with her avidly apropos descriptions. As a consequence, you may experience many of the overwhelming discomforts normally associated with the cold, the snow, darkness, shadows, isolation, vile creatures of the night snapping at your heels, and creepy premonitions of evil. It just goes to show you how a single, random, fear-fueled, imaginary thought can evolve into a terribly nightmarish concept too complicated for you to wrap your head around.

Had the novel been an interactive video game, you would have gone on quite an unforgettable, extensive, and pixelated tour of practically every chamber, meeting-room, passageway, nook and cranny in the medieval castle; onto the surrounding densely wooded grounds; and throughout the nearby picturesque village of Brasov, with its quaint little gingerbread houses. You'd probably hear Gregorian Chants, the spooky cacophony of Halloween, wild background noises, and suggested killer sound-tracks from such popular rock-and-roll bands as "Concrete Blonde," particularly, "Bloodletting (the Vampire Song)," and "Enigma," including the "Principles of Lust," "Knocking on Forbidden Doors," and "Back to the Rivers of Belief." Of course, you'd be haunted by the ghosts of kings, knights, princesses, damsels in distress, and other savory or not so savory characters; werewolves, other hairy hyaena beasts, and floating apparitions that go bump in the night and rattle their rusty old chains. There is no telling what kind of virtual-weapons you'd have at your disposal with which to defend yourself.

As a young child, I often went to the movies with friends from the neighborhood on Saturdays. Two of the absolutely scariest films I've ever seen; albeit, on separate occasions, involved a vampire and a huge, reincarnated monster. For that very reason, I've never read Bram Stoker's *Dracula* or Mary Shelley's *Frankenstein*. Perhaps someday, I shall summon up every ounce of courage I have in my body and read these two fine books, but I don't anticipate that happening anytime soon. Hence, I am totally in the dark, unable to compare and contrast the present novel with any such similar classics of literature. Regardless, I don't think you'll be too disappointed by this lack of information.

In summary, I think the book provides enjoyable light-reading for more mature audiences than *Harry Potter*. Fun-loving and romantic, it offers the genre a feisty, fresh perspective with a twist or two tossed into the mix.

Can you envision or imagine the heroine's daughter, "Audrey," as a child, strolling in the park with her wise, benevolent father one sunny Sunday spring afternoon in Bucharest?

She inquires, "But Father, why is there a tall, spiked iron fence around the cemetery?"

"Darling, that's so precocious little girls don't go picking their roses in the gardens," he replies.

"But Father, why are the brilliantly red roses so very colorful?" she asks.

"Most of the people around here think of them as burgundy, scarlet, cherry, plum, and apple roses. But, some of the local inhabitants think otherwise. They call them 'blood roses' instead. They claim that the roots of the reddest, red roses have soaked up all the blood from the dead bodies buried underneath, resting deeply in the ground. According to their rituals and beliefs, planting roses near grave sites is the only way that human spirits can escape and reach Heaven without their own blood relations weighing them down too much and holding them back," he explains.

R. Royce sat quietly and waited patiently for something to happen, a leaf to fall from a tree, a twig to snap, anything. He wasn't very good at communing with nature on this day. He thought about the time when he once had a good, steady job delivering mail and sundry items to cargo vessels in port from a certain steamship line operating in the Caribbean with its headquarters in Miami. Sure, the job had its occupational hazards, so you had to be watchful and cautious aboard ship. One of the first things he learned was not to hold onto the top rail, or gunwale, of the vessel to steady himself as he found his way to the Captain's or Purser's office. Whenever the ships stacked up, one on the outside of the other, there was a serious risk of smashing one's fingers between the two steel-hulled boats rocking and clanging against one another whenever the seas were choppy and swollen, or cresting waves crashed against the vessels. The effect would be worse than hitting your hand with a hammer; the repercussions, painfully disastrous.

Naturally, that reminded him of the time he met the "Rho-Rho," a large roll-on, roll-off vessel which transports vehicles across open seas, berthed along South Miami River Drive early one Saturday morning. It had been christened the "Silver Dawn." Usually, he'd meet the Captain in the mess hall and drop off the parcels of mail arriving weekly whenever the boat docked. They'd chat a while about current events, and he'd find out what supplies and cargo were being loaded onto the ship for export or offloaded stateside onto the docks. On that particular day, he'd met and conducted ship's business with the First Mate.

"The Captain on shore leave?" asked Royce, as he sipped a cup of coffee and, nonchalantly, took a bite from a freshly baked cinnamon roll.

"Not exactly," said the First Mate. "He fell into the hold from the top deck in Nassau yesterday. He was killed the instant he hit the floor." Which is the second thing Royce has learned about working on a ship. You never lean over too far while looking into the cavernous hold of a cargo ship, especially when you have only limited means of supporting yourself in case you slip, trip, or tip over the edge.

Which reminded him of the third thing he'd learned while working on a ship. When the crew has been busy sprucing up and swabbing the decks with soap and water, and you step aboard from the gangplank onto the top deck, you will inevitably accelerate and slide all the way across from port left to starboard right; that is, from one side of the vessel to the other, without meeting any resistance whatsoever. You'd better be wary, and be able to handle the situation like a surfer riding an ocean wave, if necessary.

When he mentioned the fact of his reminiscing to his good friend, Cornelius Korn had replied, "Do you think the good, courageous Captain fell, or was he pushed?"

"Good question," said Royce. "We both know very well how bossy and pushy drug smugglers and gambling racketeers can be in their everyday business dealings."

"Best to avoid them whenever possible is my policy," said Korn. "Did you know that detectives eventually caught up with the culprits involved in the murder? The apprehended drug dealers lost a boatload of narcotics and their freedom to the U.S. Marshalls. They went away to prison for a long, long time. Their conveyances were seized and sold at public auction, including the vessel itself. Interestingly enough, two suitcases with several million dollars cash inside went missing. They were never recovered by the original owners or the authorities. Must have something to do with poetic justice."

This thought led Royce to reflect on the good times he'd had with a former girlfriend from up the coast. She had provided understanding and much-needed companionship whenever he'd felt lost and alone, over the years. She'd meant much more to him than a pleasant diversion, really. He could always depend on her when the way proved too arduous, and he's had to become stronger, both mentally and physically, in his dealings with others. He thinks he is tough enough now.

"I had a baby," said Mariska, when she'd walked up to Royce out of the blue on the beach one day, to say hello and see how he was doing.

"How did that happen?" inquired Royce, discretely. He hadn't seen her in months.

"Close friends invited me to take in the penthouse view from one of the tall harbor buildings around the corner and down the street from U.S. 1 and New Haven late one Friday night. We went onto the roof-top to see the stars, and one thing led to another," she said.

"Stranger things have happened," said Royce. "We know about those hot summer nights."

Along about that time, Cornelius Korn pulled up alongside Royce's Porsche in his slick Mustang and rolled down the window. He handed over a rectangular bundle wrapped up in plain white butcher paper. "Your share of the sales proceeds," said Korn.

"Muchas Gracias, Amigo," said Royce.

"Can you give Meghan Thomas her share as well?" asked Korn.

"Sure enough, I'm dropping by her Condo for a luncheon date now," said Royce. Korn handed him a second bundle, and Royce placed it on the floorboard in front of the passenger's seat alongside the other one.

"Nice doing business with you," said Korn. "Hasta la Vista, Caballero!" he called out, as he sped away. He always preferred dividing up the earnings as promptly as possible, once the transaction had been completed. There was less confusion that way and fewer complications down the road. Plus, receiving 113K each was nothing to sneeze about. All in a day's work in the luxury sports car market, as they say. They'd received, transported, and sold four fast Ferraris in the past four days and two Lamborghini's last week. Cash and carry, right off the boat. They liked doing business in Florida and Texas.

CHAPTER 77

Book review of the autobiography

Line Rider

by Joe Pearce, published in 2015.

Seahorses and the Pony Express.

Line Rider, by Joe Pearce, is an informative historical autobiography about a rancher and Arizona Ranger who lived from 1873 to 1958. I read the book for useful background information about the cowboy and state law enforcement officer.

R. Royce sat on a poured concrete dock in downtown Miami, Florida, waiting for his ship to come in. Sure enough, there she was, the "Silver Dawn," moving up the river. She was a "Rho-Rho," a metal-hulled ship that hauls automobiles and such, with a large metal ramp that drops onto the pier, like the drawbridge of a fortified castle over a moat. You can drive cars on or off the end of the vessel. The oceangoing ship was expressly designed to transport cars for quick import and export.

Royce had been parked alongside Miami River Drive that fateful Sunday afternoon. He'd been watching for ships coming up the river. It was a cloudy and humid day. He was hungry, so he started up the old, beat-up Chevy Impala, drove around the bend, and up the avenue to find an open bodega for a carryout lunch of rice and beans, and a soda. There had been a cloudburst and downpouring rain, before the skies cleared up enough, so that he could safely return to the marina and boat ramp parking lot. When he did finally return, he noticed that a tow-truck had backed up to the boat ramp and was in the process of pulling a completely submerged car out of the river by the rear axle. Royce got out of his vehicle, walked over and asked the tow driver what happened.

"Four people were riding in a vehicle along Miami River Drive, when the driver missed the curve and drove down the boat ramp into the river," he explained. "Apparently, they couldn't see where they were going in the pouring rain. The divers pulled the bodies out of the car. The ambulance took them away."

"Did any of them survive?" asked Royce.

"Afraid not," said the tow-truck driver.

Cornelius Korn walked up to Royce shortly afterwards. "Do you recognize the vehicle?"

"It's the tan sedan you put a tail on," said Royce.

"The four accident victims were drug dealers," said Korn. "We're in the clear."

"They're no longer after us," said Royce, stating the obvious, and sighing with a deep sense of relief.

CHAPTER 78

Book review of the novel

The Texas Ranger

by James Patterson and Andrew Bourelle, published in 2018.

"What do you know, Geronimo? Where did they go, the Alamo?"

How anyone can write about honkey tonks and country music in Texas without once mentioning Bob Wills, Hank Williams, Jerry Lee Lewis, LeAnn Rimes, Miranda Lambert, and a great many others is beyond me, but they do. Must have something to do with changing musical tastes and attitudes. Do we go to Billy Bob's, Gilly's, the "Midnight Rodeo," or Abby's on Saturday night? Decisions. Decisions.

I slid the "Dixie Chicks" music disc into the CD player on the dashboard of my vehicle, skipped forward to "Lullaby" and drove to the lake. Fully satisfied, listening contentedly, I inserted another disc from the stack of them on the front seat and it began to play. Tanya Tucker was singing about "Lizzie and the Rain Man." I was in the zone, in seventh heaven, moving on, into the wild blue yonder.

We're talking about basic human necessities here, such as food, clothing, shelter. How can I forget to include fuel for the ole jalopy pickup truck? Sure, it's a changing world out there, with more choices than Standard Oil and Texaco, but let's not overdo it by running out of steam. Gas can in hand, I hiked to the nearest convenience store.

Texas has always been synonymous with Big Oil, but now we're in a complete state of culture shock. It's affected the way we live. Oil is imported. It comes out of a platform floating in the middle of the ocean. They fracture it out of rocks underground in South Dakota. They make it out of corn and soybeans in Nebraska and called it ethanol. When they talk about the hottest prospects for an burgeoning energy company, they're actually referring to a windfarm extending for miles and miles along the ridge outside of town. What's the world coming to? It's all a mystery, I think, like the inner circle dealings of oil and gas industry giants.

To prove my point about how little many people know about Texas tradition, some of the most skeptical people once believed that if an oil well out west ever goes dry, a tycoon like "J. R. Ewing," as portrayed in the television series *Dallas*, can make a few phone calls and a crew of engineers and roughnecks automatically brings in dozens of big rigs and tanker cars. Then, they simply fill the oil wells back up again with new product. They call him a renewable energy source.

Be that as it may, *The Texas Ranger*, a novel written by James Patterson and Andrew Bourelle, which was published in 2018, quickly grabs your attention and won't let go anytime soon. The plot is as fast-paced as the cars on the track at the "Texas Motor Speedway." The story hits you harder than a runaway freight train locomotive rolling through town at breakneck speeds. Luckily, you can catch your breath for a few moments of calm before the storm, since the authors provide a considerable amount of polite conversation on the part of the principal characters, which no doubt adds local flavor to the story, like basting barbecue sauce on a rack of ribs in an outdoor smoker grill at a tailgate party. Most people around here eat that good stuff up like there's no tomorrow. Plus, they can't get enough of community gossip and the associated gospel revelations. Wash it all down with a few bottles of beer and you have some mighty interesting reading material.

Because I wanted to dig deeper and delve into the mind-set and mentality that makes up the Texas Ranger persona and mystique, I did further research and read a couple of pertinent autobiographies. I wanted to gain a better understanding of the archetype character involved. The first book I read was *Jim Bridger, The Grand Old Man of the Rockies*. He was a trapper, tracker, guide, and scout who lived from 1801 to 1881. He displayed great courage, tenacity, and prowess in his abilities. He was a true pioneer of the prairie, mountains, forest, and stream. His qualities were not unlike those of the modern-day Texas Ranger.

The second book I read is called *Line Rider*, by and about Joseph H. Pearce, who lived more recently from 1873 to 1958. He was a rancher, tracker, forest ranger, and an Arizona Ranger. He displayed similar traits as Jim Bridger did throughout his long, illustrious career, which included possessing unique problem solving skills, particularly those involving conflict resolution.

In addition, I began skimming a third nonfictional book for even more background information, called *Rangers and Pioneers of Texas*, by A. J. Sowell, published in 1884. It provides critical insight, gives a concise history, and offers a sense of the social climate operating in the Texas Territory during the 1800s. Ostensibly, a great many forces were at work on the psyche of the American settler during that turbulent century when Texans were trying to achieve statehood and gain their independence from Mexico.

Hence, I now have a basic idea in mind of what to say when a Texas Ranger approaches your home or business, politely knocks on the front door, and starts asking a considerable amount of questions about recent events that may have made the evening news on television and generated front page headlines in the newspaper.

If he asks, for example, "What do you know, Geronimo?" or, "Where did they go after the Alamo?" you'd better think twice before giving him a bum steer.

I reflect on the first words I ever heard sung by a new musician performing at a roadhouse in Denton, Texas, years ago. It was simply beautiful the way she carried on with her little red electric violin. The manager wouldn't let her go on stage until very late in the evening. Apparently, she had to wait her turn, after two rock bands got their opportunity to perform before a live, exhilarated audience, some dancing, some gyrating, slightly inebriated. I saw her seated quietly in the shadows of a booth along the sidewall, practicing and pantomiming in generally unobserved silence, non-deterred, and definitely not dissuaded. I was eager to hear her play. A few days after the event, I thought of some lyrics to go along with the song she sang like an angel. The verse went something like this:

"She met a man in Reno at the Dillard's Department Store.
He could have been a major disappointment, but he knew the big time score.
She was a honey, and he had the money.
Darlene was enchanting and Zoot-suit was kind of funny.
They high-tailed it out of town on the noon train, lightning fast.
Just in Texas for a high school reunion, they really had a blast.
The mere thought of it now makes him wince,
but they've been going together ever since
he'd run away with the girl of his dreams.
Somedays, when she screams, he screams
and they all scream for sundae ice creams."

R. Royce sat on a secluded, unassuming, poured concrete dock in out-of-the-way Port Arthur, Texas, waiting for his ship to come in. Sure enough, there she was, the "Silver Cloud." The vessel appeared on the horizon remarkably similar to another "Rho-Rho," from Miami, Florida, he thought. A Rho-Rho is a metal hulled ship that hauls automobiles and such. A large metal ramp drops onto the pier, like the drawbridge of a fortified castle over a moat. You can drive cars on or off the end of the vessel. The oceangoing ship was originally designed to transport cars for import and export. Some dozen and a half vehicles on the ship for this particular voyage belonged to Royce and his long-time business associate, Cornelius Korn, who was having a bite from a spicy empanada and sipping a V-8 vegetable juice in the shipping company warehouse. Three car-hauling trucks were parked at the ready for the long-haul north over the road to Missouri.

When the vessel docked and Royce saw the courageous Captain, he was momentarily stunned. "I thought you were dead!" he exclaimed.

"Let's just say Cornelius Korn and company saved my life and put me in the 'witness protection program,'" said the grateful, good Captain, modestly.

"How did you get back into the U.S. from the Bahamas?" asked Royce.

"That was the easy part," said the Captain. "We commandeered a high-speed cigarette boat on a special delivery consignment, and went for an island-hopping excursion en route. We eventually made on our way back to the Miami Yacht Club, and returned the speedboat to its rightful owner. From there it was a hop, skip, and a jump home." Most people were unaware that he would have been equally proficient navigating the mangrove-choked coastal inlets, the lazy rivers of Lake Okeechobee, or the backwaters of the Everglade swamps had the situation been warranted, as he was in sailing the deep blue seas of the vast ocean.

"The Silver Cloud looks awfully similar to the vessel you once piloted in Miami," commented Royce.

"As you must know, the U.S. Marshalls seized the 'Silver Dawn,' in an early morning raid on the Miami River, and the government sold it at auction a few weeks later," said the Captain. "This is the very same ship. Cornelius bought the vessel, lock, stock, and barrel, with a cashier's check on the day of the sale. He was the best and highest bidder."

"In the meantime, he must have had the vessel renamed and reflagged," said Royce.

"The truth be told, we weren't sure whether to name it the 'Silver Ghost' or the 'Silver Geist,' but decided on the 'Silver Cloud,' instead. It's much less ominous sounding," said the Captain, smiling.

"So, Cornelius kept you on as the Master of the Vessel," said Royce. "What do you do when you're not transporting sports cars?"

"The Silver Cloud is easily modified and can be completely overhauled. For instance, we usually have it outfitted as a commercial Gulf coast fishing trawler, which, incidentally, is my day job," said the Captain.

"Sounds like a dream come true," said Royce, as men from the warehouse began driving vehicles down the ramp, off of the ship, and into the parking lot. They walked quickly toward the warehouse.

"Greetings and salutations! Come on into the office," said Korn. "Have you had breakfast yet? You can help yourself to the food and beverages on the table. We'll sign the pertinent cargo documents afterwards. While we're at it, we might as well transfer ownership of the Silver Cloud into your name, if you are agreeable."

"Like Royce said before, a dream come true," reiterated the good, courageous Captain. He was beginning a new life, starting over with a clean slate. Royce witnessed the proceedings instigated on behalf of the Captain. His had been a life full of promise. He'd finally found the pot of gold at the end of the rainbow. He was more than ready to live the good life. There was no stopping him now. Once known throughout the free world and Caribbean as the flamboyant Captain Eldorado Kidd, he had completely reinvented himself as the low-key Gulf fishing boat operator otherwise recognized as Captain Francis Drake Goode.

"May I call you Sir Francis?" asked Korn, suddenly inspired, as they continued to sign the shipping documents.

"Hello, darling!" interrupted Mariska, having sauntering into the office, unexpectedly, quite unannounced. To say that the Captain had been surprised and taken aback, would have been a profound understatement. He ran to her side of the room without any hesitation whatsoever. It was as if a flame had been ignited, their former intimate relationship, suddenly rekindled. The effect was that of the Biblical burning bush, of all-consuming love. Not to downplay the intensity of their personal and emotional involvement at the moment, but the words of Bill Shakespeare were most applicable to the predicament in which the present party had now found themselves: "All's well that ends well." And they lived happily ever after.

CHAPTER 79

Book review of the novel

The Huntress

by Kate Quinn, published in 2019.

He doesn't really know the woman he married.
Marrying axe-wielding Brunhilde has distinct advantages.

Reading *The Huntress*, by Kate Quinn, published in 2019, proved to be an interesting, but gut-wrenching experience. The book challenged many expectations. Sometimes, it defied logic. At times, it broadened horizons. Events unfolded from vastly different perspectives. Once in a while, flashes of brilliance were discovered in the prose. People, dates, and places were beginning to converge upon one another. Then, it became personal.

In this subtlest of novels, an Austrian woman is accused of killing a British soldier at her residence in Poland during the waning months of World War II. After the war ends, three concerned citizens from a foreign nonprofit organization attempt to locate her, shake her down, and bring her to justice. All she needs is topnotch security and a good lawyer to defend her rights and honor, I think. Of course, I could be way off base in my assessment.

Maybe I've been watching too many reruns of *Boston Legal* on television lately, but I think a good lawyer can get her off with a minimum sentence and light probation. After all, it can be readily shown beyond a reasonable doubt that the suspect—or, in this case, the real victim here, had been inundated and surrounded by enemies practically her entire life. She never knew whom she could trust. Fleeing from a pack of ferocious wolves, as it were, she jumps into shark-infested waters and has to fight for her very life. Suffice it to say that war makes for strange bed-fellows. Believing herself rescued aboard a luxury ocean liner, she is once again surrounded by false friends, who have the sole purpose and intention of obtaining incriminating evidence against her and gaining vital information about her, such as her banking and credit card transactions, all without her knowledge or consent, of course. Essentially, in doing so, they betrayed her faith in humanity fully and completely, without having any legal authority for doing so. Neither did they follow the due process of the law. The highly organized team of bounty-hunting vigilantes had the unmitigated gall to continue dogging her, grilling her, and raking her over the coals, without any form of search warrant, and without having given her the required police "Miranda warnings" upon arrest. They pushed her over the precipice of sanity and decency, speaking figuratively. Hence, she should have gone directly to a psychiatrist and gotten her head examined for trusting such an aggressive mob of vicious, self-serving, fame-seeking, jail-baiting misfits, who continuously confronted, interrogated, abused, shamed, and accosted her throughout the whole, ugly ordeal. She must have thought at some point and time in the harassment process, no more "funny games."

Any qualified, respectable lawyer with a good conscience would easily understand the primary motive for her past actions. She must have concluded that she had no other alternative, at that very instant of her momentous decision, but to shoot the midnight intruder, the home invader, the enemy spy, or whatever he was, who suddenly appeared in the midst of her loving family environment without any warning whatsoever to do them harm. He'd violated curfew. Evidently, he had to be a robber, a thief, and a violent murderer. For obvious reasons, she pounced on him in self-defense when he least expected it. She would have bombed him into oblivion, had she had the opportunity and means, I think, epitomizing the political climate of the times.

There is one additional point bearing on the case worth considering, I believe. DNA testing would have helped immeasurably in solving a particular detail the case in question left unresolved; namely, the determination of who really kidnapped "her inner child," held her for ransom, and made her lash out so violently, furiously, suddenly, and passionately. Without a doubt, in my opinion, she just couldn't help herself or act in any other civilized manner. Instead, she was forced to rely upon her basic instincts. Make no mistake about it. Anyone would have defended her home and family under similar circumstances, although maybe not in the same exact way. Most Europeans living in the soon-to-be-defeated Axis countries at the time had been extremely brainwashed by the very persuasive propaganda machine of the Third Reich. Presumably, there had been several reports of enemy activity in the localized area during that time period of heightened fear, uncertainty, and danger.

Upon her release from the judicial system, I believe, she would find another husband easily enough in the capitalistic west, during such a promising time of peace and prosperity. No doubt about it. They would quickly rebuild their lives together and move on. It's in their nature. It's in their DNA. Optimistically, you want to look into the future to see how they evolve.

After twenty years or so, her husband looks out from the towering castle walls, overlooking the Danube River and, not so loudly so as to be overheard by anyone specifically, proudly proclaims, "marrying axe-wielding Brunhilde definitely has its advantages."

Listening carefully, he could hear the quaint, mysterious chords of a violin playing faintly, but harmoniously in the distance, accompanying the orchestra of sweet songbird melodies, emanating from the evergreen forest, on such a particularly warm, sunny, glorious spring day.

R. Royce searched the skies and wondered, what if. He suddenly went into a dream. Maybe it was a trance. His good friend and business associate, Colonel Cornelius Korn had volunteered for a routine NATO training exercise in Poland. Was it somewhere in Romania or the Czech Republic? He wasn't sure. Doesn't matter, the event was a massive tactical military assault with certain goals to achieve and objectives to be met. He was leading a regiment of M-1 tanks, the M-1 being the main battle tank of the U.S.A.. They were edging ever closer toward the hypothetical Bello-Ruskan front. Regiments of French Mitterands, Belgian Waffles, Italian Alfa-Omega Romeos, British Centurions, and German Panzers, rolled forward alongside his in a seemingly endless, long sweeping assault line. Onward they proceeded en mass toward the border. None of the units encountered any resistance whatsoever in their march to the sea, since their combined forces had assembled close air support by squadrons and squadrons of fighter jets from among the numerous NATO allies, Mirages, Harriers, F-16s, Messerschmidts, you name it. Of course, it was only a routine military exercise. The Bello-Ruskan opposition forces, called the OpFor Army, was nowhere to be seen. Really, they were all "paper targets" anyway. It didn't matter. The tanks had been loaded with the typical shells they normally fired on the range and actual "live-fire" bullets, however. So, the exercise was realistic in that sense. The reason behind this is the fact that some uniformed "big-wig" with stars on his hat and collar, a general officer, made the point that NATO soldiers should "train the way they fight." So, the soldiers were using real ammunition and live rounds.

It just so happened that the M-1 tanks being utilized in the exercise were the only battle worthy tanks available in the entire U.S. arsenal, so the regiment wanted to put on a good showing in the exercise. That is, they wanted to meet their objectives, achieve their goals, and come out victorious, smelling like roses. This meant that they needed to attack all of their paper targets and score direct hits on them.

As the NATO armor units pushed forward over hill and dale, they lined up in attack formation for an all-out assault on the OpFor. The signal was given to breech the so-called "Bello-Ruskan border," but, for some inexplicable reason, the only tanks which drove across the border to engage with the enemy were those of the American regiments. The other NATO units stopped abruptly at the border line and would not proceed one inch further. It was a precariously freaky predicament in which the American regiments found themselves.

All at once, out of nowhere, the Ruskan OpForces revealed themselves en mass. They came in from 270 degrees of the compass in the two dimensional plain. In consequence and short order, the army of M-80 enemy battle tanks had completely surrounded the American regiments. Their armored units quickly, efficiently, and methodically overtook and overwhelmed the American regiments. Their tanks ambushed them, smashed their resolve, and then blew them to smithereens. The American tanks erupted in terrible plumes of smoke and exploded into "great balls of fire." The Americans had been caught completely off-guard and taken unaware. As a result, the regiments had to be written off as a complete loss.

Apparently, some very real and larger-than-life Russian military leaders still believe that "unless soldiers are killed in their training exercises, then the training isn't realistic, or tough enough." NATO was forced to call off the exercise soon afterwards, without any explanation given.

That's when R. Royce woke up and smelled the coffee. Cornelius Korn was on the telephone. "This is no joking matter," he said.

"I just replayed the same video game scenario in my head," said Royce. "It's come to my attention that we can't afford to perform our mission isolated and alone anymore, in this violent world of rapidly changing circumstances. We have to have fully operational backup units onsite and a viable backup plan in place if we are to come out at all successful. As you know, we really shouldn't go to certain regions in the world today, even if we are mobilized and mechanized, without a full battalion of conditioned and motivated uniformed soldiers to support our efforts, and get us up and running again after our objective is met."

"A lesson well learned," Korn said over the cellphone, when he called in a progress report on the new video game he was playing on the large-screen, high-resolution television in his living room, a harmless form of entertainment he could enjoy in the privacy of his own home without unnecessary interference or interruption. "The Ruskan Air Force just decimated all of our NATO fighter jets. Some of them never left the ground."

"Better press the reset button and start over," said Royce. "Somebody just whitewashed our highly maneuverable armored vehicles and their associated weaponry with the unvarnished truth."

"I notice that we can change the console settings on our newest virtual reality game," said Korn. "For example, I changed the tactical situation parameters from 'win-lose' or 'lose-win,' to 'win-win.' That's a first for any game I've ever played. It features totally unheard-of scenarios. Next, I disabled the 'divide and conquer' feature and maximized some of the 'force multiplier' features; eliminating others. What do you think that will do for us?" It was a rhetorical question. "I guess we'll find out soon enough."

"Definitely a changing world out there," commented Royce. "You must adapt to the situation and react decisively at the moment of truth, if you want to survive and come out alive."

"Remember, it's only a game, Royce," said Korn, the compassionate, magnanimous one. He wasn't about to start another dog-fight scenario. Bombs can produce more mass casualties and inflict greater devastation, he reflected; but hand-to-hand combat is just as bloody and ruthless.

CHAPTER 80

Book review of the historical biography

Isabella of Castile

by Giles Tremlett, published in 2017.

Too many burdens and too much tragedy for one woman to bear in one lifetime.
  Never caught napping or eating bonbons in a "Lay-z-Boy" recliner during a turkey-shoot.

Isabella of Castile, by Giles Tremlett, published in 2017, is an excellent example of scholarly research. It's an historical account, which you might otherwise think—had you not read the book carefully, depicts the meteoric rise to incredible wealth, power, and glory of a modest, soft-spoken, 15th-century woman, coming from a poor, humble background and a rural origin. At least, you may wish to believe this kind of Cinderella story. But, actually, you discover upon closer reading that she had been the keenly observant and highly educated daughter of a proud, but ineffective King Juan II, who relied on "Grandees," noblemen or select private individuals to perform the difficult work of governing his province, while reaping the benefits. When his son, Enrique, inherited the throne, he continued to rule likewise, lazily delegating his duties and doling out his responsibilities to others. So, the kingdom's royal power remained in a perpetually weakened, impotent state of limbo, which had become the status quo for the nation.

Questions arise, with the Queen's authority. For instance, what does the devoutly religious, yet profoundly ambitious Princess, facing an uncertain, shifting political climate do—particularly, when she suddenly and unexpectedly grasps the enormous opportunity of becoming the sole Sovereign of a sunny, prosperous nation of loosely connected, largely autonomous city-states, gently guided along the path toward civilization by the faiths of three principal religions? What happens next, when her once mousy little kingdom of shepherds, weavers, and fruit growers is quickly expanded and radically transformed into the wealthiest, most powerful empire the world has ever seen, all with the Pope's blessing? The answers may be found in the subject matter of this fascinating and intriguing book.

More questions. How well did Queen Isabella handle crises and complex affairs of state as startling new situations developed and spiraled out of control? With grace, eloquence, and dignity? Tolerance, and understanding? Looking back over the years, would she be considered a kind and benevolent ruler? How did she maintain hegemony and harmony, and keep the peace in troubled times? I think the answers to these questions are an emphatic "no, definitely not," "no, not really," "not very well," or "unsuccessfully, according to today's standards." But then, these are all loaded questions. So, if you really think deeply about it, none of these things appeared to have mattered very much to her. They didn't give her life purposeful meaning.

At some critical juncture in her life, Isabella had come to recognize that her true calling in life involved the herculean task of instilling the fear of God into the minds of lowly, struggling Christians, thus motivating them to lead righteous lives. Paradoxically, by the end of her illustrious career, I wonder if Isabella herself was very fearful of God. Arguably, ironically—

perhaps it is blasphemous to say so, were it possible with love so pure and divine, would God grant her an exemption and recreate Himself in order to correspond to the ideal image she had of Him in her mind? I don't know.

Regardless of the answers to the above probing questions, the vast empire Queen Isabella left in her wake continued to grow and prosper for over three centuries. Decidedly and in dramatic fashion, she changed forever the European's perception about the world around them, when she sent Columbus on his famous, fateful voyage, and he discovered the brave New World.

You have to admire a woman who sticks to her guns. Resolute, she held firm convictions. She did not gladly suffer fools. She achieved most of the goals she had set for herself in life. Any woman today like her would not be caught napping or eating bonbons in a "Lay-z-Boy" recliner during a turkey-shoot.

She had fought too many battles, carried too many heavy burdens, overseen too many bullfights, and experienced too much tragedy in her own lifetime to suddenly stop short. Some may argue against too many burdens and too much tragedy for one woman to bear in one lifetime. They say bad things happen when you mix church and state issues. You get court intrigue. You get incredible insight into the dark ages. You get an eye for an eye with your apple pie. You fear for your ears. You do what you must to placate the plague. Then, for some reason, life simply evolves and moves on. Today, some medical researchers want to test for "super-bugs," but they shouldn't count out other "super-beings," especially the saintly Homo sapiens variety.

R. Royce punched in the number he'd obtained from the classified advertising section of the newspaper early that morning, along with the extension, 2-2-1-1. The telephone at the other end of the line began to ring. Raquel, picked up on the line and said in a calm, soothing tone, "Hello, Royce. So nice of you to call."

"Great to hear your voice again, Meghan," he said. "I just arrived back in town. Are you very busy?"

"Not at all. I'll just drop everything and come get you," she said. "Where are you?"

"Fourth and Main," he replied, delighted with the news.

"I'll be there, soon. Five Mikes," she said, calculating, and hung up the phone.

"I like your choice for our new office location," said Royce, upon their arrival. "We have an exceptionally scenic view of the Arkansas River."

"You said you wanted a modern, out-of-the-way place without too many prying eyes," she said. She showed him her new driver's license.

"Your new identity?" he asked.

"Yes," she said. "Raquel Remington, originally from Aurora, Colorado."

"A practical American. A solid citizen. An unassuming settler of the plains," he said. "I heartily approve. Plus, we have the same initials now."

"Did you bring the funds?" she asked, pointedly.

"They're in a locker at the bus station," said Royce. "We should collect them right away."

"Inside the sports bag?" she asked.

"Yes, let's grab a cup of coffee, and go get it," suggested Royce.

"Where's the sleek, metallic gray Porsche? Still at the airport?" inquired Raquel, as they drove along, slower than the speed limit.

"Where I parked it on the lower level, hopefully. We can retrieve the car later. That's low priority," he said.

"Do you have the key to the locker?" she asked, when they'd arrived at the bus station. She was in strictly business mode.

"Here it is," said Royce, handing her the uniquely-numbered specialty key, made of hardened, distinctly orange plastic and bronze. "If you retrieve the bag, I'll shadow you from a safe distance." She recovered the item containing the funds, without a hitch. They brought it with them to the Mustang and promptly left the area. Transportation back to the office had been uneventful. They deposited the funds into the hidden wall safe, having taken appropriate precautions first.

"Shall we go and collect the Porsche from the airport now?" asked Raquel.

"That's not a bad idea," he said. "Are you driving?"

"Of course! Let's go!" she said. Raquel dropped him off at the circular drive-way departures gate, then went to park her vehicle in the short-term lot at street-level. Royce went to the underground covered parking lot where he'd left the Porsche. When he located the car, he noticed three bodies lying in prone positions on the pavement nearby or at least in the vicinity. Unperturbed, he got into his vehicle and drove away without further incident. Raquel had acknowledged the situation from a safe distance away. Unconcerned, she also left the scene as it was, largely undisturbed. Afterwards, driving down the highway, the Porsche and the Mustang were observed traveling in a southwesterly direction. The tandem turned off at the proper exit, and eventually arrived at an upscale complex of newly constructed townhouses.

"How'd it go?" asked Cornelius Korn, their business associate, and Royce's longtime friend of many years. He had been sipping a soda and watching television. He turned off the TV. Silence permeated the room like the vacuum in outer space.

"Very well, thanks," said Royce, after a brief pause and a lull in the conversation. He'd performed a rapid perimeter check of the living room area.

"Except for the bodies you left lying on the concrete in the airport parking lot. Alexis Sue's aim must have improved considerably with practice." She was Cornelius Korn's constant companion, his significant other, and their fourth business associate. She had covered their backs.

"We thought you might be tailed, so we exercised extra precautions. The assailants never knew what hit them. When they finally wake up, they'll be wondering what happened," said Korn. "Alexis is having them followed as we speak."

"You've put those tranquilizer guns we've acquired to good use, lately," said Royce. "Thanks for saving my car from hoodlums and thieves."

"I strongly suspect that they were more interested in the sports bag you left on the passenger seat," said Korn.

"Two million USD transferred into your bank account early this morning," said Royce. "All the bag had in it was a quick change of clothing."

"Another fully successful mission is in the bag," said Korn. He was more trustworthy and confident than anyone Royce had ever met in his entire life. They began to relax and unwind. They had bubbly liquid refreshments and snacked on slider sandwiches.

"Know anything about the paintings up for auction at Sotheby's?" Korn later inquired.

"I've heard that the three we were interested in sold at much higher prices than anticipated," said Royce, obviously contented with the outcome.

"What do you expect from a masterpiece?" said Raquel. It was a rhetorical question.

"Clues. Less profit than finding sunken treasure from the wreckage of a Spanish galleon on the sandy shelf beneath the ocean reef off the Caribbean island coast," replied Korn, speaking out of turn, but ready to provide an honest appraisal, in case anybody was interested.

"Hmm. I thought they were just old paintings of wooden sailing ships in the harbor," said Raquel.

"Which island?" asked Royce, seeking more specific information.

"Good question," said Korn. "Nobody knows for sure. Sailors enjoy drinking rum in port and telling tales more than venturing out and going island hopping."

"You'd have better luck talking with deep-sea divers and trophy fishermen," continued Royce. That ended the discussion for now. They lacked facts, compass bearings, and GPS data. Speculation on vacation is for the birds. They didn't intend to cruise, booze, snooze, or lose.

CHAPTER 81

Book review of the novel

McNally's Risk

by Lawrence Sanders, published in 1993.

Having curbed their appetites and urges, they instinctively return to some semblance of routine normalcy, or homeostasis.

Lawrence Sanders, the author of numerous novels, including ***McNally's Risk***, published in 1993, hints that there might be some measure of truth to his fiction. If you ever read the newspapers at all in South Florida, or watch the ten o'clock news, you can see for yourself what the hubbub is all about. It's not your usual television series *Bachelorette* party. Years ago, having barely eked out a living, working long hours in Hialeah and the surrounding community for a good number of years, I paid my dues, paid the bills, and put food on the table. I was, for all intents and purposes, like the lowly horse handler at the track, who feeds them hay and oats, gives them cool, refreshing water, exercises them, combs the cockleburs out of their manes, and cleans out their stalls. He never complains, but works determinedly day in and day out, season after season, listening, observing, learning, biding his time. He labors for years and years, scrimping and saving every penny, putting it all in the bank, until one day, out of the clear blue sky, he bet his entire life savings all on a thousand-to-one longshot "trifecta" and wins big, a veritable fortune. He collects his bundles of large-denomination bills at the teller window, puts it all in a big cotton duffle bag, and nonchalantly strolls away. He walks around the corner and disappears, like a ghost into thin air on a foggy night. He doesn't return to work the next day. In fact, he never returns to his job ever again. They don't know where he came from. No one knows where he went. He left no forwarding address. They don't even know who he was, for that matter. He didn't leave a calling card. He didn't have a verifiable identification, such as a driver's license. You might say that he had a sketchy employment history. One thing was for certain, he knew his horses. After he'd left the premises for good, the other horse handlers remembered him in awe as "Juan in a million." That's how an ordinary groom became a legend and an unsung hero in the pungently aromatic, behind-the-scenes world of horseracing, or so I've heard repeated, according to the story told by at least one decent-minded journalist with imagination.

Instead of following his lead, I simply decided to go with the flow and invest my dismally mediocre funds in the stock market over the years. You go in thinking, "I might not actually win the jackpot sweepstakes, but maybe someday I can eventually walk away with enough modest earnings over the long-haul to retire in relative security and comfort for the rest of my life." It doesn't always happen that way. But, sometimes it does.

I remember meeting the extraordinarily beautiful girl at the airport. The boss told me to pick her up. She'd been carrying saddle bags, boots, rope, and other such accoutrements with her. I'd been living in a typical concrete block stucco apartment off the beaten path, renting from a couple of jockeys—two brothers from New Jersey, in Hialeah, near Flamingo Park, the once-famous horseracing venue, which is probably still registered on the list of national historical places, even though the Track is now long defunct. So, I was naturally, intensely curious about her itinerary and made a discrete inquiry about her ultimate destination. She said, "To the stables in West Palm Beach." She went on to confide in me that she'd recently sold a horse and was traveling with the animal in order to keep it calm and safe from injury in flight. You can't have a big, muscular, wild animal kicking down doors in a jet aircraft at 30,000 feet because it was spooked by turbulence, or an unexpected thunderous bolt of lightning. She broke down in tears, suddenly. Evidently, she'd raised the darling foal from the time of its birth. She'd spent years training it and riding it, becoming a prize-winning, competitive, jumping horse equestrian on the European circuit in the process. The by now, fully grown and fully developed horse had become her best friend and constant companion. Their parting ways was too tough to speculate upon. A private consortium in WBP had recently purchased the magnificent beast from her father. They were going to transform it into a stellar-performance polo pony. Dominating league play, it might even have wound up on the pampas in Argentina, but I didn't tell her that. She loved the horse and was destined never to see her close friend ever again. It was a heartbreaking scenario. On a positive note, she did receive a small fortune in exchange for the horse. I could always relate to a big payday. She could always find another horse to raise, I concluded.

One of my colleagues in S. Florida offered me a revelation worth pondering, along about that time of my life, when I'd been excessively preoccupied with seriously avoiding the dire, debilitating effects of traffic, crime, and poverty. At the time, when I couldn't see much farther than beyond the end of my nose.

He said, speaking plainly, "While you're here sweating your gonads off in Miami, there are 13,000 millionaires living the good life in West Palm Beach." I believed Boca Raton would have been the more accurate locale, but who's complaining about random comparisons?

It's enough to make you think about the prospects of prosperity in your own endeavors. Picking and grooming championship polo ponies could turn out to be a great job after all! There must be other professions just as lucrative in the field, I reflected, of interest to me, personally. The same kind of windfall profit could happen to practically anybody in any one of dozens of communities across the U.S. of A. if he would simply reach out, grab, and latch onto the opportunity. For example, when I eventually transferred jobs myself, years later, and moved to a small, rural cow-town in N. Texas, I asked a coworker upon my arrival why so many people move to Dallas. He quoted statistics. "For every millionaire in Fort Worth," he said, "there are sixty in Dallas." There you have it. That's what they'd like you to believe. Wherever you go, money matters most and motivates people to action. And to think all along I'd been more concerned about my health, fresh air, exercise, and BFI, up to that point. That's "body fat index," in case you're wondering, not yet having won my first major horse race as an owner, trainer, or jockey, or become famous in any way, shape, or form.

Archibald McNally is the main character in the novel. His verbosity and pomposity proves highly entertaining. He is chock full of amusing anecdotes.

Youthful in appearance, he may seem callous, snobbish, self-centered. He represents the embodiment of an egotistical prude, but he is respectful of his parents. He is mindful of where he came from. "He knows on which side his bread is buttered." Ivy-league educated and very perceptive, to his credit, he has a good working knowledge about how S. Florida high-society functions, and uses it well to his advantage. Archy reminds me of a character in one of Sander's other novels I'd read maybe twenty-five years ago, about a corporate insurance fraud investigator. I don't remember the name. Archy displays similar redeeming qualities as a private investigator in his own right. He appears unnecessarily reckless and daring in his approach, however. His motto could very well have been, as the saying goes, "live fast, die young, and leave a beautiful memory." He behaves like "a walking contradiction," sometimes, perhaps, but leaves the favorable impression that he can stand on his own two feet. He has a solid sense of self-preservation, nonetheless. Although, he displays a peculiar habit of committing social blunders or multiple faux pas, he also projects the keen ability to "talk a pig into a ham sandwich," especially when cornered.

Hence, through his characters' clever expressions, commentary, and exclamations, the author quickly demonstrates time and time again his wide-range and excellent use of specialized vocabulary and profound word choice at the right moment in the narrative. In other words, he knows exactly what to say, and precisely when to say it. He could have gone into high-pressure sales or run a successful boiler-room operation, just as easily as writing. When the world around them appears to be going up in flames and utter chaos reigns, the main characters in his novel instinctively return to some semblance of routine normalcy, or homeostasis, fully satiated, having curbed their appetites and urges. Sure, the book might have been dedicated to more prurient and salacious interests, or youthful indiscretions, or sublime philosophical discourse. Who knows? Be that as it may, the gem of a story features a multifaceted plot, clearly written by a fiery, brilliantly talented author.

R. Royce considered the consequences of his actions, for once in his life. He would look this time before he leaped into the foray by initiating an unexpected counterattack. Three adversaries had cornered Cornelius Korn with the intention of beating him to a pulp, if not actually killing him. What could he do to put a stop to this nonsense at once?

Luckily, he had a Taser on his person in a pancake holster attached to his belt and carried a tranquilizer rifle. He decided to shoot the closest, most menacing perpetrator first with the rifle, without warning. Next, he would confront the other two with the Taser and try to resolve the situation as quickly as possible with a minimum of injury to the friendly parties, namely, himself and Korn.

It worked according to plan, like a charm. Two men were down. The third appeared about to give up without a struggle. Royce was relieved.

"I was wondering what you were going to do next," said Raquel, having sneaked up behind the leery and cautious Royce. Then, she shot the third individual, almost point-blank catching him completely unaware, before he had a chance to react to the changing situation as it developed. She also carried a tranquilizer rifle. She took no prisoners. Her policy was to shoot first and ask questions later.

"These things some in quite handy," said Korn, pointing to one of the rifles. He was recovering from the assault, much more quickly than the others had anticipated.

Royce began to collect the identifications of the fallen perpetrators. He inspected their driver's licenses and checked their credit cards. He jotted down the names and numbers on a notepad. "Shall we go?" he asked.

"Definitely," said Korn. "It wasn't a very good ambush."

"We'll be in touch," said Raquel, as she departed the scene.

"Alexis Sue will have them followed, after they wake up," said Royce. "Then, we can pay them a visit sometime in the near future, when they least suspect it, and remind them of the error of their ways."

"Do I see a common theme running through this plot?" inquired Korn. "Am I getting a sense of deja vu?"

"This scenario has played out before. We've just experienced a rerun from an old television crime series," said Royce. "It's nothing we can't handle."

"Let's put a stop to it right away," Korn said. "We can't have these guys meddling in our affairs."

"They're either random troublemaking hoodlums or organized-crime thugs," said Royce. "Either way, it's not good for business; particularly, theirs." He could be a standup type of good guy, with a strict moral code of right and wrong. He would bring in the local PD, detectives, National Guard, or FBI, if necessary, as the situation warranted, at the drop of a hat.

"Let's pass the buck," said Korn. "Have Raquel drop off the IDs with the Sheriff."

"That should do the trick," said Royce. "We should get out of Macon County, asap. We don't have any business to keep us here any longer."

"True enough, the car-haulers have come and gone," said Korn. "Next time you can be the guinea pig."

"They don't know with whom they were dealing," said Royce. "Or what. The vehicles on the car-hauler aren't ordinary sports cars. They may look like expensive sports cars, but they're actually space-age prototypes. They're land-speed-record holding machines. They are as adaptable to Baja 500 competition as they are for Martian planetary exploration. They represent the google-plex, nano-technology of the future. They're made of lightweight, durable carbon-fiber and titanium-strength materials. They have satellite transponders hidden in the frames, in case they become lost in vast, unknown terrain."

"Plus, they're fun to drive," said Korn. "I thoroughly enjoy winning these kinds of top-secret, lucrative, government research contracts that put men on the moon. Don't you?"

CHAPTER 82

Book review of the novel

The Kite Runner

by Khaled Hosseini, published in 2003.

No clear winner in the bearded man contest for the asylum-seeking refugee.

What is the novel about? Government authority, religious tolerance, family tradition, individual freedom, social values, economic conditions, the justice system, and environmental concerns. Variables and constants of life for practically any group of people, anywhere in the world.

Where does the novel take place? In a modern, war-torn, impoverished nation of simple, independent-minded, family oriented, devoutly religious tradesmen, craftsmen, shopkeepers, and farmers. Specifically, Afghanistan.

What's the big deal? Communists took over the country in 1978. The Russian military invaded. The leaders of the constitutional monarchy fled. Life went on much as before. The military left, about a decade later. Religious extremist factions rose to prominence and proceeded to divide the country. Some religious fanatics gained strength and began to consolidate their influence. The strictly intolerant, fundamentalist Taliban took over the country, having fought and defeated the others. After the attack on the NYC World Trade Center by Muslim terrorists in 2001, the U.S. military arrived in Afghanistan to combat terrorism. They've stayed over 18 years, and counting. They've been fighting the Taliban ever since.

Current status? Not much has changed in the country. The poor people continue to suffer. The quality of life has not improved in the least. There is a total lack of and disregard for civil rights, legal representation, economic development, opportunity for advancement, and fair, impartial justice for all. Ordinary people look on apprehensively as bullets, rockets, and self-destructive bombers dispense justice.

Complications? Poppy cultivation and narcotics production may be a contributing factor to social unrest in the country and in destabilizing the surrounding region, since Afghanistan is reputed to be a major supplier of heroin to the most civilized nations of the world. Hitherto unknown individuals, even anonymous groups of rugged-looking, bearded mountain men, may have become exceedingly wealthy and powerful distributing this type of commodity, obtaining weaponry to protect the trade and sowing discord in the process.

Recommendations? Somebody ought to do something about raising the collective consciousness of the people, even if he only flies kites for healthcare awareness, or runs marathons for Red Cross disaster relief. There's a lot to be said for a good education, as well, in a nation of illiterates, who can't think for themselves. Other than that, in my opinion, only a continued military presence has any chance of stabilizing the region.

Odd to think so, but this book review on **The Kite Runner**, by Khaled Hosseini, published in 2003, could have made a great beginning for a classified CIA report on any number of militant third-world countries they'd better keep a close eye on, in the interest of national security and improving diplomatic relations.

On a personal note, the average reader can tell at first glance that the narrator of the story loves his family dearly and has developed lifelong, respectful friendships from the time of his early childhood. He's made mistakes, certainly, but he has learned from them. He's grown. He knows right from wrong. He has found his rightful place in the community. He has finally acquired a sense of spirituality. What more should you expect? Forgiveness? A trip to Mecca?

R. Royce thought about attending a high school football game north of Fort Worth at one of the large magnet schools situated there. A big event, locally speaking. In late August or early September it can be very hot outside, dry or steamy-humid, depending on changing weather conditions, even during the evening of the game. But, he would endure these extremes without complaint, patiently waiting for a cool breeze. It was part of life. One of the things that most impressed him was the energy and enthusiasm displayed by all of the youthful, active participants and spectators in attendance. He'd casually walk over to get a soda at the concession stand and there would be throngs of kids and parents milling about in long lines and in the foyer, chattering happily, cheerfully, excited to be part of the pageantry that has become a proud, Texas tradition.

He carried the container of icy-cold drink beverage over to the stands in the stadium—

one which rivals stadiums at the college level in many communities in the states to the north, and took a long look all around him at the players on the field, the marching band, the cheerleaders, the fans in the stands. It was an impressive sight to behold, a glorious event that brought all kinds of people together, from all walks of life. It was a carefree time for relaxation, fun, and frolicking. Music was in the air. Laughter mingled with the sounds of brass instruments and drums. Students and friends and neighbors who hadn't seen one another for the entire summer, since school had been let out, met one another as for the very first time in their lives. It all felt new and different, somehow. Fresh and alive. Splendid and joyful. A carnival of sights and sounds. Popcorn. Syrupy soft drinks. Cotton candy.

The best part of all: none of them yet knew his permanent place in society. No one told them this is where you are supposed to sit. This is what you are supposed to do. Nobody told them they had to sit down and be quiet. They were completely free to enjoy themselves, the festivities, and the sporting activities which presented themselves as they presented themselves. It was a good feeling to enjoy complete freedom, even if they didn't realize that's what it was, and a sense of security. They felt confident, bold, gleeful, and beautifully inspired. They would have a bright future before them with incredible challenges and vastly diverse opportunities. This, indeed, was something worth celebrating.

Of course, by later on in the season, most of them would have found their seats, gone to them, and learned more about the type of acceptable behavior which was expected of them. For now, they all had infinite dignity and infinite possibilities. It was another matter entirely for season-ticket holders.

They were the pillars of the community. The founding fathers of the city. The matriarchs of the establishment. People looked up to them, for the most part, and respected them. They mirrored society. If the students represented the future, they represented the present and the past. They were historically significant.

His good friend, Cornelius Korn was on the telephone. "Care to fly to Iceland for the weekend?" he inquired. "I found a pilot and guide who's located a rocky outcrop, at the leading edge of a melting glacier, where we can find all the rubies we can possibly carry."

"All we have to do is go and dig them out," said Royce, jubilantly. He'd instantly deduced the truth of the matter.

"I think, I'd rather stay at home instead, and skip this trip," said Raquel.

"What ever shall we do without you boys?" inquired Alexis Sue.

"Pull weeds in the flower garden?" suggested Korn.

"Re-paint the living room?" Royce offered up. Life goes on.

CHAPTER 83

Book review of the novel

Enquiry

by Dick Francis, first published in 1968.

Oddsmakers play the percentages.
"Personally, I like to pick a horse with personality, Mr. Ed."

When I recently read the novel **Enquiry**, by Dick Francis, first published in 1968, I immediately thought of the classic movie starring Robert Mitchem and Deborah Kerr, called *The Sundowners*. In both stories, an interesting family captivates your heart, as they gallantly try to make a go of it, under harsh, adverse living conditions. They approach life as if it were some great adventure and they were world-renowned explorers. They do so with delightful gusto and rambunctious humor, fully appreciating the majesty and grandeur which surrounds them. Both storylines involve the fine sport of horseracing. The have the opportunity to strike it rich, or at least, to win the big race with the big purse, hoping to obtain the grandest reward of all for their efforts. The novel depicts the more modern of the two adventures and takes place in Great Britain, while the film is set in Australia, before the advent and proliferation of the automobile. It is quite a contrast, to be sure, between the high society of Lords and Ladies, and their rustic, rural, working-class counterparts, the rosy-cheeked neighbors from down under. The common thread of racing for the championship and striving for the crowning achievement which victory ultimately brings runs throughout both, hopefully, you think, without anyone having to taste the "agony of defeat," according to "Wide World of Sports" spectacular extravaganza tradition, as portrayed during the 1970s on television, or as "another one bites the dust," according to the prolific "Queen" song, decades later. They'd much prefer tasting champagne, to be sure. All thrills, no spills.

"Kelly Hughes," a professional horseracing jockey, narrates the novel, telling about the general difficulties he's faced in his compelling life story. In particular, how he loses his livelihood and license to race horses on a highly lucrative, competitive basis, at the apex of his career. He reveals what changes he has been forced to make in his life as a result of his loss. He focusses on jumping through fiery hoops, in making the valiant attempt to win it all back. It is a cleverly written detective story, in which he becomes the self-appointed chief investigator. He represents himself and the stable's horse trainer, who has also become an outcast, a shunned social pariah. He goes to great lengths attempting to find out what really went wrong, how, and why. It's a masterfully well-written whodunit tale of drama, mystery, and intrigue. Hughes proves to readers time and time again that he really understands people inside and out, and what makes them tick. In the course of pursuing his probing investigation, he becomes an excellent judge of character. The story evolves into a fast-paced thriller. As might well be expected, given his level of sophistication and the area of his expertise, not many will argue the point that he knows his horseflesh just about as well as the fact that horse-sweat forms on their animal hides during the heat of the race. It's something he rather anticipates. In other words, he demonstrates incredible insight, persistence, and horse-sense in his endeavor. He makes the necessary Sherlock Holmes-type, brilliant deductions in order to solve the case. No horse feathers.

On a side note, this amazing novel does not suffer in the least from the one fundamentally fatal flaw, for which a lesser known author of some, perhaps, not quite as popular fiction may not be forgiven, in my opinion; namely, that he does not simply kill off a potential rival character, an archetype antagonist, without first revealing something significant about him in the plot of the story, through flashbacks, or in historical footnotes. Apt and accurate descriptions are preferable for this purpose, rather than long, drawn-out explanations, flimsy excuses, and a name generated on an obscure list.

Such an author would be completely out of his depth, considering the complicated nature of his subject matter. The reader gets that sinking feeling.

He walks away, shaking his head, wondering what the individual character did that was so very wrong as to deserve being targeted and murdered so ruthlessly and calculatingly in cold blood, while seated in the lap of luxury in the privacy of his own hotel room, hypothetically speaking, of course. Really, I must be thinking of another book entirely, here.

Was it because he ran with the wrong crowd? Did he grievously injure or deeply offend someone important? Wouldn't play cricket? Worked for a competing corporate interest in a cut-throat, dog-eat-dog environment? Gained notoriety somehow? Politically incorrect? Or, was he merely in the wrong place at the wrong time? Where is the truth and poetic justice in the world, when all you get is a bunch of Hollywood hype, without the concrete proof to accompany it and any form of epistemology or intelligence to back it up? On the other hand, I guess there's no point in beating a dead horse.

R. Royce rose to the occasion. Raquel Remington, his vested business associate and constant companion, had already downloaded the contents of the perpetrators' cellphones and all of their vital contact information into his computer. He was about to trace their phones, track their recent whereabouts, and look into their daily business transactions. That way he could get a fairly good idea about with whom he was dealing. Big picture stuff, and so forth. What the team could potentially be up against. Hardly a glimmer of mob activity. No foreign connections. These guys acted independently. They were completely on their own. Three inexperienced, two-bit hoodlums, essentially. They hadn't quite made adequate preparations or thought the job through to completion. You could tell, they weren't chess players, or well-versed in scientific method. Cornelius Korn, his esteemed colleague and inveterate business consultant, had arranged to meet each of them at the Macon County Jail.

"Snazzy-looking orange jump suit you're wearing," said Korn, smiling. He was going to discuss the situation with John, first, who was the youngest at age 19. He planned to offer each of them a deal. One they couldn't very easily refuse, mostly because of his winning personality.

"Who the hell do you think you are?" spouted John. "My newly appointed courtroom lawyer?"

"On the contrary, John. I represent the business interests with whom you tried to interfere, when you failed in your miserable attempt to ambush our convoy of specialty vehicles," said Korn. There was a deafening silence in the interrogation room. He continued, unabated. The defendant appeared willing to listen. All ears.

"Judge Savage sends his regards, by the way. He's a close, personal friend of mine. He says you're lucky that you haven't been assigned to Judge Padloch. He wanted to put you away for twenty years for committing such a potentially heinous federal crime. They might just as well lock you up and throw away the key, as far as he's concerned. You and your chums are lower than pond scum in the food chain, according to his humble opinion, because of your recent hostile actions and pernicious threats. Plus, you made the major mistake of adding insult to injury, after you were duly apprehended and incarcerated. Such foolishness and pathetic behavior won't be tolerated in the prison system." He spilled a glass of water on the table

"Look at what you've done. You're disgusting! He pounded on the table. Unless you make amends immediately, you'll be sorry for the rest of your worthless life. What do you have to say for yourself now, tough guy?" Korn figured that he might as well cut to the chase and get to the point.

"I've already met Father Cross, the Chaplain," chirped John. He was not exactly thrilled by how the meeting was progressing. Smart alecks don't get very far in this world, he'd discovered. He would soon begin to sing like an uncaged canary perched on the windowsill to freedom.

"I'm here to make you a deal that will change your life forever," said Korn. "The way I see it, you have only two choices. Army or Marines?"

"I want my lawyer," said John, resisting the inevitable.

"He won't help you. He doesn't want to talk to you. In fact, he doesn't even want to see you ever again. I've discussed your available options with him. He has agreed to the plea-bargain. You're very lucky, generally speaking, that you are young, appear to be in fair physical condition, and enjoy reasonably good health."

The realization began to dawn on John. First stop, basic combat infantry training. Next stop, Afghanistan.

"Marines," said John, finally. He'd been totally convinced. He was ready to sign on the dotted line.

Later that day, Royce dropped by for a cordial visit at Colonel Cornelius Korn's elegantly decorated, picturesque, hillside abode, obviously designed by an architect with Frank Lloyd Wright style and flair. Alexis Sue Shell, Korn's significant other, constant companion, and the fourth business associate brought him a tall, refreshing glass of cool mint tea on ice.

"You are an excellent Army recruiter after all!" confided Royce. He admired Korn and was proud of all that he stood for.

"Today's score, two potential Army infantry soldiers; one tough, future Marine," Korn stated, for the record. He felt a distinct sense of accomplishment.

"A little sensitivity training goes a long way. It makes you a better person, all the way around," said Raquel, as she strolled into the living room from the art gallery, having thoroughly enjoyed studying the dozen Norman Rockwell paintings hanging on the walls in the adjacent room. She stood quietly near the sofa, sipping her tea, contemplating the implications of an even brighter future.

"They'll go a long way, all right," said Royce.

"The best part of the charade operation was when the Sheriff's Department planted bloody-mannequin bodies at the crime scene, and a few of the deputies dressed up like walking wounded on Halloween," said Alexis Sue. "The County's Rescue Training squad hauled them away in ambulances, along about the time our three perpetrators finally woke up from their tranquilizer-gun naps, and were arrested for various high crimes and misdemeanors."

CHAPTER 84

Book review of the biography
Marie Antoinette: the Journey
by Antonia Fraser, published in 2001.

Anarchy reins. Justice prevails. The people form a new government.

I fell fast asleep after having read the incredible biography of Marie Antoinette. Later on, in the middle of the night, I'd been startled wide awake, having sensed a spiritual presence in the room. It became larger and was gradually coming closer. Looking toward the open doorway of my bedroom, I saw a brightly illuminated light, as if from a candle. There before me stood a pale, flaxen-haired lady in a plain white dress. She seemed to hover in the air and watch over me. She appeared as a vision of loveliness, an angel of mercy. Her voluminous, shiny, wavy, amber hair cascaded down over her shoulders and onto the front of the finely woven garment she wore. She positively glowed and beamed. She seemed to radiate pure energy. I couldn't help smiling and thinking, how so unlike the style and grace of any woman I'd ever met or seen in person. Then, she abruptly vanished in an instant, thus breaking the spell. The room went completely dark again. It had been like viewing a real person in the midst of a hologram. I rolled over, went back to sleep, and slept soundly for the remainder of the night.

Antonia Fraser picked quite an interesting subject, when she wrote the historical biography **Marie Antoinette: The Journey**, which was published in 2001. Marie Antoinette is probably the most famous and memorable Lady in French history, bar none. She began life as the daughter of an Austrian Queen. Her father was the Emperor of the Holy Roman Empire. Pretty powerful stuff, no doubt. Born in the middle 1700s, when the world was ruled by wealthy, omnipotent rulers called monarchs, whose authority supposedly came directly from God, or was at least divinely inspired and unquestioned, Marie Antoinette married the King of France, in an arranged marriage. The idea was to preserve the peace among the various nations, which wanted to maintain their mutually beneficial interests in trade, enterprise, prosperity, and for purposes of expansion throughout the known world.

Selfishness and greed is what usually throws a wrench into the works of the best laid plans, and so it was that many of the nations and principalities were often at war, or preparing for war. At the time of Marie Antoinette's rise to prominence, France's Seven Years' War was just ending and times of peace and prosperity were looming. It just so happens that certain ambitious individuals, often highly organized, over vast geographical regions see this as an opportunity for making themselves as rich and powerful as the monarchs. They do so, by many diversified methods and means. Some publish pulp fiction. Some bake bread and make fried potatoes. Some manufacture durable goods. Some manufacture arms. Some go into the gambling business. Some sell alcohol. Some sell precious metals and jewelry. They build ships. They venture to the New World. They go into Theater, Opera, and Ballet. We call it making progress, today.

To make a long story short, large groups of well-educated individuals, lawyers, professional soldiers, statesmen, and prominent businessmen collaborate, organize, and decide to take over the function of government entirely. They put themselves in power with the intention of ending the rule of the unsuspecting monarchs, associated noblemen, and aristocrats. They plan to cut them out of the picture all together. They call their noble efforts a revolution, and put themselves in power in their place. They become the new ruling class, in effect.

Unfortunately, in the new scheme of things, justice is not often dispensed with fairness and impartiality. The punishment does not always fit the crime. The new system is crude. Inhumane. Cruel and unusual punishment is the order of the day. Government becomes an ugly and unpleasant business. They rob Peter to pay Paul. They don't always pay the piper for his services.

Caught up in the ensuing chaos and madness is King Louis XVI of France, his Queen Marie Antoinette, their family, their associates, and their closest friends. They become libeled, scandalized, and suffer the dire consequences. You can't help but feel sorry for certain adversely affected persons, who are forced to experience life-altering events beyond their control. Many are forced to undergo difficult transitions in their lives, which not all can endure without hardship and suffering. I must admit, after reading Chapter 19, the situation was starting to look bleak. It wasn't looking very promising for the home team, so I impatiently skipped to the Epilogue, looking for redemption, before resuming my reading of the closing chapters.

One curious observation I made, after all was said and done, was that, while modern laboratory technicians, having analyzed surreptitiously obtained DNA tissue samples from the body of Marie Antoinette's youngest son, they did not explicitly reveal who had been Louis Charles' actual father. Or, maybe I missed something in the rapid reading of this fascinating book. On the other hand, I was pleasantly surprised to discover that someone significant, Marie Antoinette's daughter, Marie Theresa, had somehow survived captivity.

R. Royce somehow obtained a sample of the latest element of the periodic table to be recently discovered, number 131, in the row of super-nova elements. Miners call it stardust, golden sunshine, or radicon. He wanted to have it independently analyzed, for his own peace of mind, and appraised right away. He wondered, if it is completely stable. Is it safe? And, what is it worth? He did not attempt to open the lead-lined box into which it had been placed, as it sat there ominously on the coffee table in his living room.

"What a novel conversation piece!" said Cornelius Korn, walking in unannounced and spying the object of their curiosity. He was a longtime friend and business associate. "I bet you can't find a Pandora's Box like this one anywhere in China." He knew what was going on. He'd been briefed.

"Are you going to let us in on the big secret?" inquired Raquel, Royce's significant other, and their business associate. "Or are you going to keep us guessing?"

"They don't have an approved name for it, yet. It's so new, that scientists have only assigned it a letter so far, element K. I call it special-K," said Korn. "You aren't going to believe this, but there are already a number of proposed uses for this revolutionary new product. Melting a small quantity of the substance at high temperatures, pouring it into a mold, and allowing it to cool, transforms it into an impervious metal, more durable than gold, and just as pleasing to the eye. Combining the substance with quartz, sand, or other crystalline minerals, under intense heat and pressure, and it can be transformed into gemstones, harder, clearer, more fiery and precious than diamonds."

"So, special-K is quite valuable, then," said Raquel.

"That's not the half of it," continued Korn. "In the form of a fine powdery compound, the chemical substance can be made to dissolve in saltwater or ordinary tap-water."

"That doesn't sound so impressive," interrupted Royce.

"Not to the seasoned mall shopper or average guy in the street," said Korn. "But when you consider some of its other extraordinary chemical properties, you begin to see its really strategic usefulness. If properly trained Hazmat teams are able to inject the powdery special-K compound into containers of nuclear material, the compound instantly reacts with the material to form a completely harmless byproduct, commonly known as garden-variety fertilizer. In other words, it becomes a manageable, granulated mixture of nitrogen, phosphorous, and potassium—NPK. Alternatively, the end-product could just as easily be Portland cement, or even masonry bricks. As you know, chemists and chemical engineers are only limited by their imaginations. Essentially, adding Special-K can render nuclear material of all types, into something non-radioactive, non-lethal, and non-threatening, such as ordinary building construction materials."

"In theory, or practice?" asked Royce.

"You'd have to ask Dupont or Dow Chemical about that," said Korn.

"I'm all in favor of better living through chemistry," said Alexis Sue Shell, the fourth member of the bridge club and garden party, having just arrived. "But, I was under the impression that special-K originates from black holes at the edge of the universe."

"That's the next row of elements in the periodic table, the black-hole elements," said Raquel. She could be a highly informative subject matter expert.

"Most people believe that once matter goes into a black-hole, due to the immense pressure of gravitational forces, it never comes out again. The exception is when the black-hole is a hole in the shape of a doughnut. I think of it as a glazed chocolate funnel cake doughnut. Matter goes in, becomes forever transformed, and exits out the opposite side of the funnel. The miners call these black-hole element substances moondust," explained Royce. "They also call them crystal moonbeams, because they contain particles of light, like a fire opal."

"They remind me of a lava lamp I once bought at a gift shop on the beach," said Alexis Sue.

CHAPTER 85

Book review of the novel

As the Crow Flies

by Jeffrey Archer, published in 1991.

> *"The Lord is thy shepherd. He maketh thee to lie down in green pastures. Thou shalt not want."*
> Charlie picks himself up by the bootstraps.

As the Crow Flies, by Jeffrey Archer, published in 1991, depicts the lives of several principal characters, spanning the course of the turbulent decades between 1900 and 1970 in Great Britain. Written in first person narrative form, the author somehow manages to put the often momentous, sometimes cataclysmic events, which helped shape the lives and livelihoods of two prominent London families into perspective. "Charlie," "Becky," "Daphne," "Colonel Hamilton," "Mrs. Trentham," and "Cathy" all provide their uniquely distinct points of view for the evolving storyline, giving the novel spice, flavor, and plenty of pizzazz. They live their lives as if they were on an endless rollercoaster of frills, thrills, and spills. The reader watches scenes unfold, becomes enthralled in earth-shattering revelations, and sometimes enters into an altered state of utter disbelief, as if he were looking through an unusual pair of high-powered, long-range binoculars with colorful, scintillating, kaleidoscopic lenses, while riding aboard a rocket-propelled time-machine. At times, he feels exasperated and overwhelmed by what he is permitted to see. At times, he feels completely baffled and decidedly perplexed. Joyously elated. Perhaps deeply saddened. It all depends on the circumstances which transpire inevitably, reminding me of the Scriptures. "The Lord is thy shepherd. He maketh thee to lie down in green pastures. Thou shalt not want." I begin to wonder about Charlie sometimes, about whom much more might have been written. Beginning with, "He picked himself up by the bootstraps." Certainly not ending with, "He turned the reins of the Kentucky derby winning corporate horse over to his chosen successor."

R. Royce travelled around the U.S. looking at specific, privately owned, classic European driving machines, principally Porsche 911s from the 1970s, 80s, and 90s, personally inspecting each one himself, test-driving the sports cars in much better than average running condition. He believes in putting them through their paces, over a grueling racecourse of hills, valleys, and curves. He likes driving them fast, swerving around the turns, especially the stealthy, deceptively lightning-fast Lamborghinis.

"How many have you purchased so far?" inquired Cornelius Korn, his good friend and longtime business associate, calling long-distance on a cellular telephone.

"Two more to go," said Royce. "The others are securely located at our rendezvous point, ready for immediate pickup and transport."

"One of the car-haulers is en route as we speak. He should arrive at the storage units in Springfield by tomorrow afternoon at the latest. He can load and transport half a dozen of the sports cars onto his rig," replied Korn.

"Sounds like a sure-bet winner," said Royce. "You have the green light to go ahead with the plan. Raquel and Alexis Sue should make arrangements to move the vehicles pronto."

"How soon on the remaining two cars?" asked Korn.

"They'll both be in storage units there by Wednesday afternoon," said Royce. "Barring unforeseen circumstances."

"Be careful on the road! The last two cars are extra special," said Korn. "Brand-spanking-new, high-performance racing engines were installed in them only a few of months ago. The vehicles purr like kittens in town, but they roar like lions when you go speeding down the highway."

"I have first dibs on the British racing green crown jewel," said Royce, adamantly.

Meanwhile at the storage facility in Springfield, Raquel Remington was in the process of inspecting the merchandise, when the first car-hauler pulled up. "Hello, Mr. Pfleuger," said Raquel. "Are you ready to take possession of your vehicles?" He was another business associate and a close, personal friend of the team.

"Of course. Most certainly. That's exactly why I'm here," he said excitedly, but professionally all the same. Alexis Sue Shell had already lined up three of the vehicles in the parking lot for loading onto the car-hauler.

"Here are the keys to the peachy yellow Porsche," said Raquel.

"It goes on the top front," said Quincey Pfleuger. "I'll load them in the order that you have them parked." In no time at all, he had the three vehicles loaded onto the transporter. By the time he was finished, Alexis Sue had parked three more in close proximity.

"That's all for now folks," said Alexis Sue. Mr. Pfleuger proceeded to load the final three to complete the load.

"Here are the transportation documents," said Raquel, handing him a bundle of folders containing copies of the pertinent six car titles, with their corresponding bills of sale and plates.

"We'll see you soon in Denver," said Alexis Sue.

On Wednesday, Royce dropped off the final Porsche sports car at the Springfield storage facility. After a quick bite to eat at a nearby Denny's Restaurant, he strolled back to the storage facility. "Been waiting long?" he asked the lingering transporters.

"Arrived ten minutes ago," said Korn. "Are you about ready to get this show on the road?"

"Naturally," said Royce, wagging an index finger and pointing off to the distance. "As you may have noticed, I have three cars already queued up for loading."

"This is Mr. Henry Dobbs," said Korn. "He will be loading the vehicles onto the car-hauler and moving them onward to their final destination." He is new.

"Pleased to meet you," said Royce. They shook hands enthusiastically. He handed Cornelius a set of car keys. "I'll go and remove the final three cars from their storage units now and have them ready for loading aboard the car-hauler, pronto." The loading operation went as smooth as silk. He handed the long-haul driver six document packages. He drove away contentedly, seemingly without a care in the world.

"This is the easy part," said Korn. He was referring to moving a dozen classic sports cars in pristine condition to Colorado for detailing and resale.

"The hard part was moving the horde of treasure we'd recently discovered and discreetly recovered from the sunken Spanish galleon we found in the Caribbean onto dry land in Georgia, concealing the treasure from prying eyes, and then transporting it to our out-of-the-way little mine, hidden in a nondescript location, somewhere in the Rocky Mountains," said Royce.

"Our own private Fort Knox," exclaimed Korn. "The best part of all was when we transported the vast wealth of treasure concealed under the backseats and inside the trunks of ordinary clunkers and junkers, which we acquired through classified ads and later sold at a discount to interested afficionados, enthusiasts, and other classic car restorers, after having first judiciously removed all of the gold bullion and doubloons, the silver ingots and coins, and carefully placed them into a secure storage-locker facility."

"Because you made such a tidy profit in our last venture, we want you to have really nice sports cars of your own as a personal reward and a token of our appreciation and esteem," said Raquel, most eloquently.

"We know how much you enjoy traveling in style," said Alexis Sue.

"It's true that we can flash the cash whenever it becomes necessary," said Korn. "And you know very well that we'll do whatever it takes to keep up appearances."

"But most of all, we're lovable and cuddly, eager to please," said Royce, amicably.

"Teddy bears," said Raquel, affectionately.

"All ribbons and curls," said Alexis Sue. They were the best girlfriends anyone could ever hope for. They enjoyed life to the fullest with relish. They loved their treasure-hunting, sports-car-driving, paint-balling boyfriends. They believed in them completely and trusted them inherently. Predictably, it would all work out according to plan.

"Incidentally, have you located any more sunken Spanish galleons?" inquired Royce.

"Lately, I've been thinking about buying thoroughbred horses," said Korn, dismissively. Up until this point, he'd been preparing himself for a long, well-deserved period of rest and recreation, rather than tackling a new enterprise. The Kentucky Derby was a done deal, as far as he was concerned. Royce was getting psyched for adventure.

CHAPTER 86

Book review of the novel

The Hitchhiker's Guide to the Galaxy

by Douglas Adams, published in 1979.
Afterword, published in 2004.

A light-hearted, adventure story about an imaginative fellow who goes on a long trip with friends.

Getting where you're going, enjoying the company you keep, making the trip of a lifetime.

When you know for certain that identifiable flying objects piloted by aliens are in close proximity and you have the coded electronic boarding pass granting you unlimited access to go anywhere in the universe.

The Hitchhiker's Guide to the Galaxy, by Douglas Adams, published in 1979, is a thrilling work of science-fiction and highly entertaining to read. It is a well-written book, with a surplus of thought-provoking ideas. The prose conceals flashes of brilliance and unearths pearls of wisdom. The characters are themselves illuminating, with respect to their sharp perceptions, astute assessments of the situation, quick reactions, and outright candor. You get the impression that the story could very easily have been about a likable group of college students who plan to go on a road trip for spring break, so that they can experience all that life has to offer, let off a little steam, and reduce some stress before final exams.

But, alas, the book is more complicated than that. It is more like, what if you know for certain that identifiable flying objects piloted by alien beings are in close proximity, and you have the coded electronic transporter boarding pass, granting you unlimited access to go anywhere in the universe, right there in your hot little hand.

You find that this quite interesting group of individuals demonstrates great camaraderie and superlative rapport in their timely interactions. They provide keen insight, regarding their interpretations of recent events and take on a variety of germane subjects. Such as: "what should we do next in order to survive imminent disaster?"

Basically, they learn to get along exceedingly well together as they travel through the galaxy in a space ship they've somehow managed to commandeer and fly out to distant points as yet unknown. The space ship, incidentally, as it turns out, incorporates the latest and greatest technology ever seen anywhere.

Again, the book is cleverly written, of a deeply philosophical nature, and incredibly fun to read. I'd recommend it to anyone. *The Restaurant at the End of the Universe* is the next title in the book series.

R. Royce saw the note attached to the refrigerator with a small magnetic ornament in the shape of a wildflower. It read, "We decided to let you sleep in. Be back in a jiffy with your truck of chinchillas."

"Good morning, Royce," said Cornelius Korn. "Are you ready to travel?"

"Where is everyone?" asked Royce.

"They went to gas up the vehicles for the trip to Minnesota. As you know we need to deliver four truckloads of the cute, cuddly critters to the new chinchilla ranch up near the Canadian border," explained Korn.

"I thought we were still in the early planning stages for that assignment," said Royce. "How'd you get the ball rolling so fast?"

"In case you weren't aware, the democratic process can work miracles in times of great need. The majority voted we go now," said Korn. "Plus, we have just received a sizable cash advance on our proceeds, the amount we get upon final delivery."

"Apparently, you didn't need my vote," said Royce. "Doesn't matter. I'm all for the plan."

"The Montana rancher sold us all of his chinchillas, but he's holding on to the minks and sables," said Korn.

"Makes perfect sense to me," said Royce. "You can make very expensive, complete fur coats out of mink or sable. They manufacture the chinchilla fur hides into fashionable leather coat collars, hats, gloves, and accessories. It involves different manufacturing processes entirely."

"Some people keep them as pets, as well," added Korn. "They're docile, playful, and curious. Intelligent creatures."

"You say that we're delivering paired couples of chinchillas to the rancher in Minnesota?" asked Royce. "And we get a share of the profits for the first litters?"

"That's right," said Korn. "$20 bonus, for each baby chinchilla born upon or after arrival at the destination. $80 each, for the redhaired, striped, or spotted blondes. That's because they're rarer breeds and much in demand."

"I can see how this venture might prove profitable," said Royce. "What do the girls have to say about our travel prospects?"

"Mostly, they want to experience fine dining along the way, stay in scenic hotels, and go to the International Mall in Minneapolis," said Korn. "Who can argue with their logic?"

"Not me," said Royce. "Here they are now. Let's get this show on the road. Shall we?"

"We're all fueled up and ready to roll," said Raquel Remington. "I've been thinking about those chinchillas. Maybe we should do some additional research."

"I agree," said Alexis Sue Shell. "There may be a big demand for chinchilla oil in the field of medicine."

"Or, for the wild, musky chinchilla scent, in the perfumery industry," continued Raquel.

"We'll definitely have to look into the matter and make discrete inquiries accordingly," said Korn, nonchalantly. Which probably meant that he had other sticks in the fire, as well. For all they knew, he might already have sold some of the cute, furry creatures to NASA for their Mission to Mars program. His next detour: The Biology Unit, Life Support Section, Advanced Obscure Scientific Research Corporation, a subsidiary of NASA. It was inevitable, and so conveniently nearby the chinchilla ranch.

CHAPTER 87

Book review of

Oil and Marble
A Novel of Leonardo and Michelangelo

by Stephanie Storey, published in 2016.

The rich, powerful, and influential beat a path to the famous artist's doorstep.
Il Gigante. The Duccio Stone. Someone should make a statue out of the big block of marble.

O*il and Marble*, written by Stephanie Storey, published in 2016, is a novel taking place during the years 1499 to 1504, presumably when the artists, Leonardo de Vinci and Michelangelo Buonarroti, most likely crossed paths, which was generally during the time period when they both lived and plied their trades in Florence, Italy. Along with being able to follow two amazing, interwoven storyline threads, about the personal lives of the two artists, the reader is treated to a the gradual unfolding of a fascinating fabric blend, a tapestry of culture, art, and art history. He learns firsthand that what's involved in creating a masterpiece is a vastly different from what goes into making a great classic Bologna sandwich, for example. Back in the 1500s in Italy, the local craftsmen weren't cranking out paintings or statues on anything remotely resembling a Ford mass-production assembly line. Instead, they made them individually, one at a time, and the results were generally considered original works of art.

There is a certain amount of genius that went into writing this novel. The author compares and contrasts the personal lives of the two great artists,

Leonardo and Michelangelo, as well as the significant features of their two principal art mediums, the oil painting and marble statuary. For me, the riddle of the ages lies in resolving the impetuousness, raw muscular strength, and unbridled passion of youth with the patience, cleverness, and wisdom of old age. You might just as easily compare photography and taxidermy.

An unusual comment to make? Suffice it to say that most mid-western people around here would be more inclined to go to a "Bass Pro" shop or "Cabellas" to see the nature exhibits than to travel the great distances involved in a trip to the "Metropolitan Art Museum," or other such venues, in order to view abstract art they don't understand. By in large, many relate more directly to wild animals in their natural settings, even if the larger, more dangerous animals are stuffed, in my opinion. Plus, they really appreciate seeing live fish in clear-running streams as part of the exhibits, and the aquariums. And the harmless little creatures, such as chipmunks, scurrying around.

Similarly, they would have a greater tendency to turn to the local newspaper to see photographs of local athletes in the sports pages and young ladies and gentlemen dressed up in gowns and tuxedoes in the society pages, rather than viewing paintings or pottery at an art gallery. Plus, they can always go to a formal or family photograph studio for portraits of their loved ones.

As for the artists, themselves, in the novel, I didn't think Leonardo would do anything too incredibly foolish or take unnecessary risks, being the older, wiser, and more established of the two. I half expected Michelangelo would be the one who might get his "ass kicked" for making smart remarks to the "football team" after school.

It is worthy of mention that gossip, rumor, innuendo, speculation, and conjecture often works just as well in a novel, as the truth. Be that as it may, I definitely learned more than a few details about the artists and their subjects that I never knew previously or realized before reading this book.

I've finally concluded that a certain fundamental process must be involved in completing the work of any great artist. The famous artist creates a masterpiece. The rich, powerful, and influential beat a path to his doorstep, trying to capitalize on it. The process is plain and simple. Even better, when there's an interesting story to tell, behind the painting or statue.

For instance, I see Leonardo searching his entire life trying to discover the perfect photographic mental image for the supreme subject of his art. Perhaps he is deeply in love for the first time in his life, yet harbors serious, lingering doubts and misgivings. At their last portrait meeting, he stares at her for the longest time.

Ramona Lisa notices and says softly, "Why don't you just take the picture. It will last much longer." The statement is a form of reality check.

"How true! Your husband would only lock it away in his private library, or put it in a walk-in closet for safekeeping," replies Leonardo. He becomes reflective and has gone on the defensive.

"What he enjoys most is how little the painting resembles me, his wife. He already knows that he can easily resell the woman of mystery to the highest bidder for a tremendous fortune." She is merely being practical, not at all vain, about the investment opportunity.

In stark contrast, I see Michelangelo at the unveiling of his wondrous marble statue. He's been thinking, *I have finally become a highly successful and respectable member of society. Never again shall I be beaten down, bullied, harassed, cajoled, and intimidated. Never again will my character be dragged through the mud, and besmirched.* His illustrious career has been catapulted into stardom by a mere mortal man carrying a crude slingshot. When we were kids, we called it a bean-flip.

R. Royce observed the lone buffalo standing tall on the ridge. In a moment the statuesque creature would be gone. His instinct was to migrate. Instead, a large-caliber rifle slug hit him broadside. Then another. The rifle report had cracked and echoed. The first bullet caused him to hesitate for an instant. The second bullet stopped him in his tracks. He knew immediately from the impacts that he had been seriously injured. He was no doubt grievously wounded. He toppled suddenly and fell heavily sideways onto the tall prairie grass. Dead. He'd been shot once through the heart. Once in the massive shoulder muscle. His eyes clouded over and grew increasingly dull, as he lay where he fell.

Soon, a large, dually flatbed pickup truck with two occupants drove toward the buffalo. They didn't see Royce. They came to claim their kill. He wasn't particularly angry or annoyed. He only wanted to see if the two young cowboys had the required hunting permit. They did.

"Good shot," said Travis.

"Expert," said Cody. They began to winch the animal carcass onto the heavy-duty flatbed truck, when Royce walked up out of the trees.

"Greetings, fellows," said Royce, friendly like. "Looks like you bagged yourself quite a trophy."

"We definitely won the lottery with this one," said Travis. "Are you the game ranger?"

"No, just an interested bystander. Some friends and I are moving part of the buffalo herd from here to a state preserve in Nebraska. They want to increase the numbers to the herd already existing there," said Royce.

"Well, you won't be moving this one," said Cody. "We've got the official permit. We're taking the hide to the taxidermist and the meat to Valentine's meat market in Manhattan, near Fort Riley. The rest is going into the freezer for the top-sirloin restaurant in town."

"May I see the hunting permit?" asked Korn, politely. He'd just walked up. "We have to protect our own business interests. We wouldn't want anyone to accuse us of rustling, or shooting buffalo without a valid permit."

"This is my good friend and business associate, Cornelius Korn," introduced Royce.

"Perfectly understandable," said Travis. "He handed him a copy of the serially numbered document."

"Thanks," said Korn. "See any other buffalo in the vicinity? We're looking to round up six or eight more."

"There's a creek in the valley over the next hill to the west of here. Some of the herd likes to graze near there," said Cody. "None are as big as this one, though."

"That's just fine with us," said Royce. "It makes them easier to transport to their new habitat."

"Are you driving them, or loading them into semi-trucks for the trip?" asked Travis.

"No. That's way too slow. We'll put them on military aircraft, either fixed-wing C-130 or C-141; or heavy-lift helicopters."

"You're with the military, then?" asked Cody.

"Independent private contractors," said Royce. "They've given us permission to use their assets and resources."

"If you need a job, sometime," said Korn. "you can look us up." He handed them each a business card.

"Midwestern Buffalo Wings?" asked Travis.

"Not to be confused with the restaurant chain often seen advertised on television during football season," said Royce.

CHAPTER 88

Book review of

Doris Lessing Stories

published in 1978 as a collection of stories,
individual stories originally published from 1953-1975.

Farmer's Market, Fun in the Sun City, 1985, he gingerly uncrates plantains from the plantation. Carefully placing them on the table, he looks around optimistically for the first customer of the day.

She was licensed and certified to practice what she preached.

You know what's supposed to happen at the top of the food chain, and at the bottom of the food chain, but what actually occurs somewhere in the middle of nowhere is anybody's guess.

Doris Lessing lived from 1919 to 2013. She was a prolific English writer of poems, plays, novels, and short stories. From the age of five, she lived approximately 25 years in Rhodesia, which has since been renamed and divided into two countries, Zambia and Zimbabwe, on the subcontinent of Africa. The experience may have had a profound effect on her deepest heartfelt thoughts in her formative years as well as on the subject matter of her prose later in life. Such is a prime example of understatement—taken exponentially to a higher power, speaking in terms of abstract mathematics. Hence, her collection of *African Stories* was published in 1951. She also wrote many short stories which appeared in numerous magazines over the years. Some of these were included in her collection of stories entitled *The Real Thing*, published in 1987. A third collection of short stories, which I have also recently read, is entitled *Doris Lessing Stories*, and was published in 1978. These stories were originally included in anthologies. They were published from 1953 to 1975. At least one of these was selected for an anthology of stories which college freshmen typically read for their 1970s English Literature 101 course, namely "To Room 19." Practically any student alive could tell you the author must have been an exceptionally good writer, but most of them probably didn't understand the story. They couldn't relate to it, possibly due to their prissy attitudes, sheltered upbringing, inflated egos, or the testosterone levels in their blood. I may be exaggerating slightly here, and grasping at straws.

So, decades later now, I begin to wonder what has made her "a good writer" after all is said and done. To my knowledge, she didn't win any "Pulitzer Prizes" for her journalistic efforts. That was probably because she wrote more fiction and poetry than sticking to the facts. Stuff that you couldn't put a finger on or print on the front page of the newspaper, because it wasn't exactly or technically true. Believable, certainly. Plausible, no doubt. Fundamentally grounded in reality, indeed. But embellished and enhanced by a wild, vivid, fertile imagination. I went on to rate the stories of hers I have recently read. The ratings were based on my humble opinion of them, however biased, and shouldn't impact on what others may think or believe.

Doris Lessing Stories, 33 of 35 were good and interesting; 8 excellent, sensational, incredible, or just plain great.

African Stories, 29/32 good and interesting; 9 excellent, sensational, incredible, or just plain great.

The Real Thing, 17/18 good and interesting; 8 excellent, sensational, incredible, or just plain great.

Next I decided to categorize the stories of all three collections. These stories fall into the following seven categories:

Wilderness Survival and the State of Nature; The Occupations of Hunting, Farming, and Mining; The Strife of Big City Life; Social and Political Unrest; Dreamers, Visionaries, and Those with Mental Health Issues; Serious Concerns about Marriage and Other Interpersonal Relationships; and, finally, The Residual Effects of War on Everyday Life.

Essentially and cumulatively, this is what these stories are all about. If you want to read about hunting, farming, and mining, *African Stories* is your ticket. If you want to read about city life within the last century, *Doris Lessing Stories* or *The Real Thing* is a sure bet. If you want to read about the war or man versus nature, forget *The Real Thing*.

Which stories did I like best? From *Doris Lessing Stories*: "The Woman," "Wine," "How I Finally Lost My Heart," "A Room," "Our Friend Judith," "Homage for Isaac Bable," "Report on the Threatened City," and "An Unposted Love Letter."

From *African Stories*, "The Black Madonna," "The Trinket Box," "Traitors," "Old Chief Mshlanga," "A Sunshine on the Veld," "The Nuisance," "Eldorado," "A Mild Attack of Locusts," "Flight."

From *The Real Thing*, "Debbie and Julie," "Sparrows," "The Mother of the Child in Question," "Pleasures of the Park," "Casualty," "In Defense of the Underground," "The New Cafe," and "Her."

After having read these stories, one can begin to understand why the steering committee selected her to win the 2007 Nobel Prize in Literature. Her lifetime achievement in the field of fiction writing is quite simply overwhelming. The Rhodesian scholar opened up a whole new world to the average reader.

R. Royce thinks about his good friend and business associate, generally known as Cornelius Korn. He's late for work as usual. He gingerly uncrates the plantains brought over from their Caribbean island plantation. Carefully and gently placing them on the crude, unvarnished, roughly hewn wooden table in front of him, he looks around the Farmer's Market cautiously for the first customer of the day. He is very optimistic about their sales potential.

Standing by him is Meghan Thomas, his significant other, personal assistant, and constant travelling companion. She has been telling him about a couple of movies she's seen, *Somersby* and *Martin Gere*, that share a similar theme, while biding their time.

"A husband goes away to war for several years and his wife is left behind to run the family's farm. She struggles but somehow manages to care for the barnyard animals, harvest the vegetables from the garden, and put enough food on the table to feed the family through hard times," says Meghan. "When he finally does return home, she discovers much to her chagrin that fighting in the war has changed him so drastically and dramatically that his own dog doesn't recognize him. He tries his best to resume a routine life on the farm and the normal relationships with his wife, family, friends and neighbors, but finds it exceedingly difficult. Over time, he gradually learns to readapt to his former circumstances and surroundings, then begins to fit in more quickly and completely. His present life becomes a vast improvement over the way it once was, before the war."

"In fact, on the very same night of having slept with his beautiful and voluptuous wife for the first time in several long, lonely years, she rolls over onto her side of the bed, looks deeply into his face and eyes and suddenly exclaims, 'Hey, wait a minute, you're not Young Jack, you're better than Young Jack!'"

"None of us were ever really the same after the Civil War," he says, calmly. Completely satisfied with his reply, she falls fast asleep and sleeps soundly throughout the entire night, more contented than she's been in years. Clearly, from that moment forward, she has become happily married once again and for the rest of their idyllic life together."

"I certainly do enjoy a story with a happy ending," said Royce, sheepishly.

"I love golden fried plantains with rice and beans myself," said Korn, having arrived just in the nick of time for lunch. Shall we indulge in the fine cuisine from Javier's food-truck? They have picnic tables set up for us. And he's bought all of our produce."

CHAPTER 89

Book review of

Dorothy Parker Complete Stories

by Dorothy Parker, published in 1995 by Penguin Books,
stories written 1924 – 1958.

Cornered, she gets the upper hand, without biting, kicking, scratching, throwing punches and daggers.

Dorothy Parker was born on August 22, 1893, and went to meet her maker in 1967. In her lifetime, she published numerous short stories for popular magazines of the day, including *Vogue*, *Vanity Fair*, the *Saturday Evening Post*, the *Ladies Home Journal*, *Everybody's*, and *Life*. She wrote poetry for the *New Yorker magazine*. Accordingly, there are 48 short stories and 9 sketches included in the compilation, *Dorothy Parker Complete Stories*, published in 1995 by Penguin Books. They are among the best stories I've read in recent months—if not, years.

Dorothy Parker's writing is just as incredibly perceptive, insightful, intelligent; clever, and witty; refreshing and alive, whether she is describing an ordinary domestic arrangement or a quaint social gathering. In the process, she gets the same rise and gut reaction out of me that I would achieve if I were attempting to scale Mount Kilimanjaro, from the storyline of some dramatic adventure novel. Her uncanny ability to drive home her point impresses me just as much, as if I were about to ascend to the peak. She does so without actually coming out and specifying what she means, by way of long drawn-out explanations or tawdry apologies. Not by any stretch of the imagination. She gives me the impression of having been an adamant, difficult, and unyielding woman. An unflappable character from the Roaring 20s. Cornered by adversity, I think she would have gotten the upper hand, without having to resort to biting, kicking, scratching, throwing punches and daggers. As they say these days, "It is what it is."

Then, just when you begin to think the author must have been "tough as nails" in her day-to-day business dealings throughout life, she reveals her vulnerable, insecure, all-too-human side. "Bless her heart." You get the distinct feeling that you should emulate her; be more compassionate and considerate of others. You want to hug somebody, protect them, cover a loved one with a warm blanket, and bring her some hot cocoa.

On the flip side, she could be a real fashion plate. You can see it through her characterization. Meticulous. No detail too small. Glamorous. Stunning in her debut. Decked out in her finest jewelry. She knew her place in society and possessed all of the social graces and proper etiquette. It was sufficient enough to turn the wheels of commerce.

R. Royce opened the statement from the bank and glanced at the most recent deposit amount. He thought about their job assignment in Atlantic City several years back at a modern hotel, owned by the eccentric entrepreneur, "Mugsy" Malone. The assignment was still paying regular dividends, so to speak. Until Cornelius Korn, his friend and business associate, got involved, running the hotel had been a simple, straightforward collaboration, run by Malone, himself, the hotel accommodations manager, the food and beverage manager, and the entertainment director. The establishment was not too extravagant, but profitable, without having any gaming devices or gambling machines on the premises. The guests were attracted mainly by the hotel's fine cuisine, the rotation of talented musicians, a relaxing, carefree atmosphere, and the affordability of the rooms. Essentially, it was a nice place to stay for a few days, hassle-free and thoroughly enjoyable.

One day, during the winter offseason, there was a severe snowstorm and some of the employees asked Malone if they could bring up cots and spend the night in a couple of vacant suites. He readily agreed, not wanting anyone to become stranded on the way home; or call in the next day, due to lack of transportation services. He soon became aware that several employees had organized a dollar poker game in one of the suites. He didn't particularly mind, but at the same time, he did not want anyone losing their grocery- or rent-money to any unscrupulous card sharks among the group. So, he limited their activity. He provided a nominal Christmas bonus to each of the card players and declared that the game would have to end at or sometime before midnight, so they could be fresh and alert at work the following day.

All of the participants thoroughly enjoyed the small-stakes poker game. It was an icebreaking event and a pleasant diversion from their daily activities. So, Malone allowed the practice to continue, on an infrequent, seasonal basis, so long as things did not get completely out of hand.

One cold, snowy day, the following winter, he went up to one of the vacant suites to see how the employees spending the night were doing. There was plenty of laughter and holiday cheer, as might be expected. He was surprised to find that the employees now had three poker tables set up, a dollar, a ten-dollar, and a hundred-dollar table, with players all around. Naturally, Malone grew concerned that things were really beginning to get out of hand. Before long, his hotel would be hosting poker games for their guests, without his knowledge or consent, which would invite all kinds of problems and legal concerns he didn't need. He decided then and there to put an end to the poker games at the hotel altogether.

About that time, Malone contacted Cornelius Korn's *Executive Security Agency* for assistance and professional advice. Korn readily agreed that Malone should put a stop to the poker games in his hotel.

"They invite nothing but heartache and trouble," Korn told him. Always thinking outside the box, however, Korn added that if Malone were serious about getting involved with the spectator sport of poker, maybe he should consider sponsoring an annual poker tournament somewhere in the Caribbean Islands, where it would be completely legal and taxes are low or nonexistent. He came up with the idea of live-streaming, internet-based, pay-for-view, *fantasy poker*.

"You've heard of 'fantasy football,' right," said Korn. "It would be very similar. Customers, using their credit cards, access a live poker game in progress on some obscure island nation in paradise. They pick a particular player of their choice and follow the poker game for as long as they like for a fee. The added benefit of picking the player is, the customer is allowed to view the cards that the player is dealt, see the bets he makes, and monitor his stacks of chips. Plus, he gets to view practically every winning hand, the exception being, of course, when a winning opponent is not required to show his hand, because all of the other players decided to fold. Admittedly, you have to agree, these are powerful features. Most importantly, the customer gets the thrill of watching a complete poker game, without incurring any risk of gambling losses whatsoever."

"You may have latched onto a brilliant idea," said Mugsy Malone, "that could prove to be worth a sizable fortune. I'm going to do further research into the matter. There's a creative I.T. consultant I know personally, who can follow through on the project."

Cornelius Korn telephoned R. Royce. "Did your deposit from Switzerland post to the bank yet?" he inquired.

"A sure bet," said Royce. "The premium-quality $59,000 annuity came in like clockwork."

"Ditto here," said Korn. "Do you remember how we avoided the potential problems we encountered at Malone's Hotel?"

"Very clearly," said Royce. "Like it was yesterday. Alexis Sue walked up and asked you a simple question about a couple of smart-aleck hoodlums trying to set up a new poker game in the hotel. She opened her purse and was about to extract a subcompact semiautomatic."

"That's right," said Alexis Sue. "I asked Cornelius if he wanted me to do them both then and there. They were belligerent and disrespectful by their very nature. Rude, crude, and terribly insulting."

"We had just returned from following them in separate vehicles. We found out where they lived and worked," said Raquel Remington, the fourth member of their security team. "You immediately silenced her, by putting your index finger up to your lips, saying that we might want to check into their backgrounds first."

"You can never be too careful who's listening," said Korn. "Suffice it to say we resolved the issue by running the necessary background interference."

"If I remember correctly, you contacted the wise-guys' Big-boss, who happened to be their Grandfather, and convinced him to take their business elsewhere. He reluctantly agreed," said Royce.

"The competition is killing me," *the Grandfather* had said at the time.

"Yes, he certainly had to consider the longevity and profitability of his own gaming interests," retorted Korn. "He backed away quickly, when the subject of the New Jersey *State Gaming Commission* was mentioned. They simply shut down their tables and removed themselves to another location. Therefore, the matter was resolved peaceably without too many more complications."

"We had Mugsy Malone to thank for that," said Royce. He never gave in to outside pressures. He ran a clean, debt-free, highly successful hotel business. And he always dealt fairly and squarely with his partners. God rest his soul."

"The newspaper reported that 27 bullets were fired into his vehicle late one evening. No witnesses stepped forward." said Raquel. "Any of three that hit him in the upper torso, may have been the ones that killed him."

"We know better than that, don't we?" exclaimed Korn. "Who do you think signs our security checks?"

CHAPTER 90

Book review of the science-fiction novel

Dune

by Frank Herbert, published in 1965.

Zealous mother and enterprising son go on a camping trip. He should earn a Boy Scout merit badge in survival skills.

The science-fiction novel **Dune**, written by Frank Herbert and published in 1965, might just as easily have provided the pre-curser literary materials for a "Hallmark Home for the Holidays" screenplay as it would have for any of several *Star Wars* episodes. It is a meaningful, versatile, very adaptable novel. The book is good and offers deeply religious connotations. It provides historical significance, dating back from ancient times, and suggests serious implications for the future, involving social and political stability.

Ostensibly, the story follows a doting, overly protective, single mother who wants only what is best for her son. She takes him on a camping trip, in order for him to win the equivalent of a "Boy Scout" merit badge in survival skills. Basically, his task is to provide food for the family in the wilderness. If he can find the right bait and put it on a hook to catch a fish for dinner, he all but assures himself of attaining the merit badge he seeks. The problem is, they soon discover that the lake has all but dried up. The waters have receded, or they have been diverted, somehow. Hence, he has to hunt for alternative sources of food. Simple enough, you think. Except, you remember that the novel is pure science-fiction. Things get hairy in a hurry and out of hand very rapidly, and the various outcome scenarios become numerous and unpredictable. The storyline becomes even more interesting later on, when the son decides to attend his first rodeo.

Perhaps, the single mother has mistakenly slipped a bottle of "Mescal" Mexican tequila into her backpack, instead of the "cooking Sherry," which she had intended to bring along on the trip "for medicinal purposes." While cooking over the proverbial open campfire, she must have been sipping some form of potent alcoholic beverage, causing her to dream, and possibly, hallucinate. The manufacturers even put a little grub-worm into the bottles of this particular tequila, out of an abundance of caution as a warning; or for aesthetic reasons, I imagine. Not too unlike, the "green dragon" or the "genie in the bottle," appearing on the label of a libation otherwise known as absinthe. In her dreams, or perhaps because of her vivid imagination, then, the harmless, one-inch, standard-size grubworm is transformed, becomes magnified, or otherwise enlarged by the mysterious processes of her mind, into a gargantuan monster 5,000 times its normal, original size. This is where the science-fiction part enters the story. Thus, a potential whirlwind romance is transmogrified into something completely out of this world. It evolves into a tantalizingly amazing and profoundly appealing tale of adventure. Again, I'm reminded of the classic *Star Wars* saga, which first appeared in movie theaters twelve years after the novel *Dune* was first published.

In the course of natural events, the mother of the impressionable, young lad fondly reminisces about living in their former home far, far away by incredibly great distances of measurement, somewhere over the curved spectrum of colorfully diffracted light-beams known as a rainbow, beyond eons and eons of cosmic clouds in the time-space continuum, having a normal climate, an abundance of rainfall, mild weather, with clear lakes and cool-running streams, something quite radically different from the dire circumstances in which they presently find themselves. She smiles graciously and is pleasantly reminded of swimming in the ocean like an Olympic athlete; the outdoor public showers on the beach; washing the salty water out of her tousled and tangled hair, rinsing her skin clean and vibrant again; noticing the sand in her bikini panties.

But now, however it came to pass, she is much more immediately concerned about gang violence and her youth blasted into oblivion by laser-light guns. Even worse, their exposure to harmfully volatile cartridges of electronic cigarettes; risking addiction; and, ultimately, being "vaporized" by an atomizer. Vanishing into thin air.

R. Royce rests on a long, weathered wooden pier, the wharf overlooking the intercoastal waterway from a hidden cove. Here, he goes by the nickname "Johnny Questar." He's looking into the deep, clear, greenish tinted water for a big spearfish. He recollects parts of a song from way back when and modified them on a whim, including a variety of vaguely enigmatic lyrics, as follows:

"In the year 2625, there'll be no husbands; you'll have no wife, since she'll be married to her career for life...."

"From the year 3735, propaganda will rule for thousands of years. Tremendously egotistical, there's nothing too terrible their great leader fears...."

"In the year 4845, robotic androids are running wild... They'll achieve great feats of magic, but can't seem to bear a child...."

"In the year of Reckoning, 8310, the Supreme being should have made a cameo appearance by then. He'll certainly have something important to say, for it's the time of evolution and Revelations Day..."

"By the year of our Lord, 9495, if mankind hasn't given in to his predestined plight, there'll be no more wars; we'll experience no further strife. We'll begin to see an everlasting light..."

"Then, after ten million years have come and gone, assuming mankid has not met its demise by then, surely we'll have completed the ultimate trophy race and won. We'll live comfortably on a new planet; feeling generally euphoric and majestically contented..."

Hence, R. Royce recited the poetry he made up as he went along, a distinct mutation and deviation from the original version, written by Rick Evans in 1964 that became a number-one hit by the duo "Zager and Evans" in the summer of 1969 and topped the music charts in both the U.S. and the U.K.

"We'll start all over again in another galaxy, my friend, in the promising age of Re-enlightenment," sang the high-spirited Cornelius Korn, chiming right in. People in the area know him by the popular namesake, George Jetsam."

"We'll transport oceans of water for the next ten thousand years," predicted Royce in conclusion.

"How is it, that people like us always wind up going to strangely exotic destinations such as the Florida East Coast and on remote desert islands?" asked Alexis Sue Shell, now answering to the name "Wilma Flint."

"Probably because we've adapted so well to hot air, palm trees, sandy and salty water. The natives are friendly and they generally mind their own business. We love the carefree lifestyle here. Plus, whenever we're ready, we can sail away," said Raquel Remington, presently known as "Betty Revelle."

"Anything on the agenda for today?" asked Royce, suddenly businesslike, ever the practical one, and exuding confidence.

"I've located the two grandsons from New Jersey," said Korn. "We're meeting them in a nice, quiet setting on the beach this very afternoon, at Hooligans."

"I have good news and bad news for you," confided Royce, later, at the restaurant. "The good news is you are no longer obligated to pay Mugsy Malone what you owe him, since he's met with an unexpected and untimely demise. You probably read about it in the newspapers."

"Oh, how did that happen?" asked Kashmir, one of the wise guys he'd met in New Jersey at Mugsy Malone's Atlantic City hotel months ago, feigning innocence. "What's the bad news?'

"Some weeks before his sudden departure, Mr. Malone authorized my security firm to make good on the debts his more prolific business associates owe him. In other words, we're here to collect on what you and your cousin, Nehru, haven't yet paid him. With expenses and interest, the amount due today comes to half a million. Can you cover it with cash, certified cashier's check, or a bank-to-bank transfer?"

"We're on vacation in South Florida," said Nehru. "We don't normally carry that kind of cash around with us."

"Your grandfather was very cooperative. He advised us that you're doing quite a lucrative business in the vicinity. He said that you're involved in the tourism and travel industry. You've been making money hand over fist here," said Royce. He'd certainly done his homework on the pair's financial dealings.

"All we have available at the moment are 100 Super Bowl tickets, 100 reservations to Disney World, 100 tickets to Universal Studios, and four repossessed luxury tour busses, formerly owned by country and western musicians," said Kashmir. He obviously wanted to settle their differences amicably and put an end to the matter at once. Smart. He actually wanted to avoid risky, protracted conflicts with formidable adversaries.

"That should cover your overdue account debt. We humbly accept your generous offer," said Royce, indicating Kashmir's metallic briefcase containing legal documentation, tickets, and bus keys. "Thanks for putting us in the tourist business. Trusted associates from the firm will contact you shortly to iron out any details and finalize the transaction." He calmly strolled away, taking the briefcase with him. Kashmir and Nehru felt a sense of relief that there were no complications to derail their plans.

"Chump change," George Jetsam said later that evening, as they all began to relax and unwind in their hotel suite. "But it pays the bills and keeps peace in the family."

"I think you handled the situation admirably, Royce—I mean, Johnny," said Betty Revelle.

"Looks like we're back in business again," said Wilma Flint.

"Yes, indeed! Travel agencies to contact, tickets to sell, and buses to lease," said Johnny Questar.

CHAPTER 91

Book review of the novel

Boundary Waters

by William Kent Krueger, published in 1999.

The raging river growled like a grizzly bear, the swift current dragging her into the gurgling chaos.

The cascading river roared like a lion, the rapids boasting more thrills, spills, and general excitement than a demolition derby.

Theirs was not to be a gentle, scenic float trip down a cool, lazy river on a hot summer's day.

When I was looking for a new novel to read, I had never even heard of the author William Kent Krueger. Nor did I realize that he had written so many novels about the farthest reaches and isolated wilderness of North America encompassing both sides of the U.S. and Canadian border. He really is a prolific writer on the topic. You can tell right away that he's the real deal. His knowledge about the indigenous peoples living on the razor-sharp edge of civilization and their stone-wedge culture goes unrivalled and unparalleled in modern times. He clearly demonstrates an intimate knowledge of the folklore, myth and legend. He understands the terrain and the lay of the land, like the back of his hand. He relates to the lakes, vegetation, and forests as if they had personality and feelings. As I live and breathe, the reader can easily identify with the main characters in the story. They're likeable. They have good intentions. They are the salt of the earth.

I wasn't sure which book to read first, so I just picked the second one of the series at random, *Boundary Waters*, published in 1999. It turned out to be a fairly interesting novel, a quixotic page-turner that kept me inspired, interested throughout, and curious enough to wonder periodically what could possibly happen next, "to make their day." The suspense was surely killing me by degrees.

The river roared like a lion. The rapids boasted more thrills, spills, and general excitement than a muddy, bloody demolition derby. Egads, theirs was not to be a gentle, scenic float trip down a cool, lazy river on a hot summer's day.

Does the book promote the greatest achievements ever undertaken by mankind? Probably not. Does it include the most famous and memorable characters from throughout the scope of history and literature ever assembled together in one place and time, the toast of the city, upper-crust dignitaries, or controversial, civicminded and great military leaders? Probably not. But, it does convey an interesting plot. Plus, the author has done more than his fair share in conducting the necessary background research on the residents living in the immediate area—

something, which is enticingly fascinating in and of itself, and their illustrious neighbors, who try their darndest to fit in peacefully and harmoniously—particularly, the former sheriff, now retired, his close-knit family, and their diverse assortment of odd-fellow acquaintances and nearest, dearest friends. For, somehow, a great, terrible danger has been imported and incorporated into the scheme of natural events from outside the normal boundaries of the reservation.

The potential interlopers, agitators, and trouble-makers which prove to be the cause of all of the commotion have obviously been attracted by the lure of the glamorous nightlife of flashy casinos, excellent fishing, and the pristine scenery of a pure, unspoiled wilderness, a pastoral natural setting, the sanctuary of forests, and 10,000 lakes. Oh, what a tangled web of deceit and duplicity that they must weave! How can our heroes get to the bottom of this, find the truth and solve the crime, in such a sometimes frosted-cold, sometimes slippery, wet cold-case environment?

R. Royce had no idea how to get out of his present predicament. He'd been set up. They wanted their tour buses back. They had only been leased for the season—not sold outright to him and his cohorts, as he had initially believed.

"Give them back their buses," suggested Cornelius Korn, his longtime friend and business partner. "We have nothing to lose."

"Why should we?" asked Raquel Remington, Royce's better half. "What do they plan on offering in exchange?"

"I have to admit," replied Royce. "Now that I've seen them up close, the completely remodeled and fully accessorized busses have to be worth quite a bit more than the half million and change that Kashmere and Nehru owed us." The two executives from New Jersey had recently expanded their operation to include the Atlantic coast of Florida.

"Nehru says they can let us have four, brand-new, twenty-footer cargo trucks instead, if we choose to go that route, with cash-in-hand to make up for the difference," said Korn, in reconciliation.

"Personally, I'd prefer going into the business of moving furniture and sundry items of freight, rather than transporting irate and noisy passengers, mostly senior citizens and large families going on vacation to Disneyland, to other well-known attractions and amusement parks, and major sporting events," said Alexis Sue Shell, Cornelius Korn's main squeeze. Her assessment of the situation was spot on.

"People are horrible to deal with," agreed Raquel. "I'd prefer moving priceless paintings, sleek automobiles, and gold bullion, any day of the week. Such inanimate objects don't argue or talk back."

"Cargo trucks and cash have always worked for me," said Korn. He could be incurably optimistic.

Nehru was now on the telephone with Royce. "There's been a terrible accident!" he exclaimed, sadly. "The busses have all been completely destroyed in an unexpected warehouse fire, where they were being stored out of the weather. Burned to a crisp. Fortunately, as we have recently learned, they have been fully insured for the cost of replacement."

"Like I told you the last time we spoke, cash works for me," said Royce. He was not an overly sentimental fool. He was not particularly in the mood for romance, or excessively concerned about any love lost between the two parties.

"Fireworks?" inquired Raquel, coquettishly.

"Try explaining the situation to the poor people of Paradise, California," said Alexis Sue. "And see how much sympathy you get in return."

"Looks like we are going to make a substantial profit on our return after all," expostulated Korn, disregarding Alexis Sue's extraneous viewpoint. "A 50-50 split of the proceeds is now entirely possible. It's a win-win situation all the way around," he quickly extrapolated, without exaggeration.

Nehru called back shortly, however. He had no misgivings whatsoever. He retorted, "The buses that burned weren't yours after all. It was just a big misunderstanding. We've located your cargo vehicles at a different warehouse facility. You can collect them anytime at your convenience." He was beside himself with joy. He was especially anxious to bring their business dealings to a satisfactory conclusion.

"Looks like we're all going on an exploratory assignment of in-depth investigative journalism," said Korn. "Because you can't always believe everything two wise guys from New Jersey tell you, even if they do make a good first impression. They are dangerous political animals in that respect."

"If the deal sounds too good to be true, it probably is," recited Raquel.

"Lead, follow, or get the hell out of the way," repeated Alexis Sue, which had the effect of jogging Royce's memory. Something he'd overheard.

Stacey reflected on his brief stint in the Army. The Drill Sergeant had been tasked with providing each of the members of his platoon with individualized career counselling. He'd been allotted 10 to 15 minutes one Sunday evening, per soldier.

"How do you like the Army so far?" inquired the drill sergeant.

"Honestly, I don't really care to get up so early in the morning and have to make my bed," said Stacey, plainly and simply.

"Yo mama," said the DS.

"Army chow doesn't appeal to me very much, either," Stacey continued. "Too bland. Needs more spices."

"Yo mama," said the DS.

"We haven't had a day off, since we arrived. The Sergeants yell at us no matter what we do," said Stacey.

"Yo mama," repeated the DS.

"Drill Sergeant, why do you keep interrupting and saying 'yo mama' every time I try to explain anything to you?" asked Stacey, obviously perplexed and exasperated by the whole process of counselling at this juncture of his career.

"Because I ain't Yo Mama," stated the DS, loudly and unequivocally. "My job is to keep you alive on the battlefield."

CHAPTER 92

Book review of the novel

Six Months to Kill

by Enzo Bartoli, published in French in 2017; English translation, published in 2019 and translated by Alexandra Maldwyn-Davies.

He tells a convincing story without revealing too much all at once, and spoiling the surprise ending.
Another Freudian slip-up, or some sort of "Death Wish."
Quasi susceptible to the subliminal power of suggestion.

Enzo Bartoli has written a superb novel, entitled **Six Months to Kill**. He published the book in French in 2017, and Alexandra Maldwyn-Davies translated it into English in 2019. I'm not sure how I can write about the book without revealing too much of the plot and spoiling it for the reader, but I'm going to try. It's going to be a challenge, since I perceive that the novel appears to have an ultrathin storyline, and has been written using a minimalist style of writing. In other words, the author does not appear to sway or deviate much from his intended purpose, nor does he go overboard with excessive or obsessive descriptions of people, places, or superfluous scenery. He does what he has to do to get to the climax point of the story, without mincing his words or wasting them. He doesn't beat around the bush, either, once he achieves his objective, but gets right down to business.

Just suppose the leading character of the novel finds himself in the unenviable position of being judge, jury, and hangman, whose perceived job is to bring criminals to justice, exact a sentence, and mete out punishment for their violent acts of wrongdoing. Assume that the main character has self-esteem issues, together with a tremendous ego, which causes him to overreact to the everyday problems he encounters. Do you begin to see the challenge with which I'm faced?

Okay, so let's take a different tact. How would you like to get even with anybody and everybody who's ever done you wrong? First, you generate a bucket list. You add names to the list. People whom you perceive to have caused you harm at some point and time in your past and in your lifetime, in general. In column two, jot down specifically what they did to cause you the injury, be it an actual physical injury, emotional duress, or some other slight or infraction. In the third column, you will want to get really creative. Describe an exacting, suitable or otherwise appropriate punishment for the perceived crime or crimes they allegedly committed. You are meticulous in following directions. Being quasi-susceptible to the subliminal power of suggestion can be helpful in achieving your goals. As they say, "The strength of the effort is often a measure of the results." True, you want to "do the right thing," but you know you can't always. You have to accept this inevitability.

The trick, then, is to "get even" with the perpetrators, without being caught like a fish in a net yourself. Obviously, you want to avoid being apprehended and punished by lawful authorities at all costs. These dedicated members of local police departments, sheriffs, detectives, and other investigators have been professionally trained to put you in jail for a long stretch of time. They would sting and tie you down faster and more permanently than the Lilliputians did when they incapacitated "Big, Bad John," the "Giant of a Man" from Jonathan Swift's novel *Gulliver's Travels*.

You may conclude from the above information, however factual and accurate it may initially appear, that the story is merely a flaky, "fractured fairytale" with somewhat flaky, quirky characters in it. Or not. Perhaps, they are just as normal as you and I; but you will have to agree that we all do live in a pernicious, potentially dangerous world. There are people out there who want to get you. Cause you harm. Their intentions may well be spiteful and malicious. Nevertheless, you want to continue feeling safe, secure, and protected. You want to experience that warm and fuzzy feeling. Live a long, normal life and prosper. Be that as it may, some are more determined than others in their supremely motivated efforts to dissuade you. They seem to have some sort of a "death wish." They have a seriously psychological or deviate, psychotic condition which must be overcome; exorcised, in my humble opinion, in order for any of them to realize their maximum individual potential, something which can be exacerbated by the occasional Freudian slip-up.

I sincerely hope that I haven't divulged too many sordid details; given away the plot; or revealed any sudden surprises in store for the avid reader. That would be like reading a few chapters, growing increasingly frustrated, then skipping to the end of the book to see how it turns out. Naturally, doing so would tend to spoil the surprise. I do not recommend taking this approach here.

R. Royce delivered the fourth cargo truck to its intended destination. He parked it beside the other three in their warehouse. Inside each of the four vehicles was a late-model corvette, in immaculate showroom condition. The low-mileage sports cars were prepared and ready for special-delivery to eager shoppers in the eastern Colorado high-plains.

"You have to stick with what you know," said Cornelius Korn, upon his arrival at the designated facility in Joplin, Missouri. "Tomorrow, we travel to Pueblo."

"Our customers are depending on us," said Raquel Remington, "to get their shipments through." She was there to pick up Royce and take him back to their hotel for a well-deserved good night's rest.

"We meet here tomorrow morning at 9 o'clock sharp to begin the convoy north and west to Colorado," said Korn.

The next day, however, the group arrived only to discover that their cargo trucks and the valuable commodities they contained had vanished into thin air.

"Any idea what happened?" asked Royce, having arrived in the hotel shuttle van.

"Someone must have absconded with the trucks and cargo," said Korn. "I suspect Nehru and his cousin, Kashmere are involved." Fortunately, he had placed a transponder in each cargo van, and secreted similar electronic devices, known as "Mantrackers," in the Corvettes.

"You just can't be too careful these days," said Royce. "Our laptop security program shows a detailed satellite map, pin-pointing the location of each vehicle. They're heading north, toward Kansas City." They were actually about to make a detour on their way to Fort Leavenworth.

"If we hurry, we can intercept them," said Alexis Sue Shell.

"There's really no need," said Korn. "I've already contacted the Pfleugers in Florida. They have retrieved the four missing Country and Western musician tour buses, which Nehru and Kashmere had so conveniently misappropriated and misplaced a few weeks ago. They provide additional insurance that the deal goes right."

"I've contacted their grandfather to update him about the progress of our present transaction. He's arranged to have 'the boys' return the cargo trucks immediately," said Royce. "We can always trust him to do the sensible thing, especially when it's in his best interest to do so."

"I just got off the phone with John Q. Pfleuger," said Raquel. "He says that he spoke with the drivers who stole our cargo trucks, via cellular telephone. He offered them all jobs as tour bus drivers on the spot, and they gladly accepted. It was the only decent option left on the table."

The very next day all four of the cargo trucks had been returned to the warehouse in Joplin with full tanks of gasoline. They were washed, waxed, and detailed. The oil had been changed, fluids were topped off, air-filters replaced. The high-jacking had only put them a day behind schedule. The "A-team" of initial drivers would drop off the four corvettes in Canon City and pick up four shiny new Lamborghinis for the comparatively uneventful return trip east. Net profit could have been $800,000 for the sale of the latest modern marvels of cutting-edge technology, not including the additional income generated from the buses. Nehru and Kashmere were lucky they hadn't been ridden out of town on the rail. They would stay in business. It was indeed a kinder, more gentle world in which they lived.

Later in the day, Royce became curious about something he'd noticed during the trip. He made a point to ask Korn about it at the first opportunity.

"I was wondering about something, Cornelius," said Royce.

"Fire away," said Korn. "Something troubling you, Royce? Get it off your chest!" He could bolster you with the courage and confidence you needed at times. He was a tower of strength. He demonstrated the most magnanimous of qualities. He was respectful of others.

"Were there any last-minute details concerning our previous consignment about which you've neglected to mention?" inquired Royce. "Something was very odd about it."

"The raised platforms gave it away?" inquired Korn.

"Yes. You didn't by any chance squirrel away a little something extra in the crawlspace between the platform and the cargo bed, did you?" asked Royce.

"Could be. Have you checked your financial statement recently? A deposit in the amount of five million dollars has been wire-transferred to your personal bank account as of yesterday," declared Korn. "Two dozen 'Sidewinder' missiles requisitioned by the U.S. Air Force have been duly delivered into their hot little hands through official channels, per our original, invoiced agreement."

Royce had nothing further to add to the conversation. He was surprised, certainly, but not flabbergasted. He'd known his good friend Korn for years. He knew him well for the capable, resourceful businessman that he was.

CHAPTER 93

Book review of the novel

Malevolent

by E. H. Reinhard, published in 2014,
the first book in the Lt. Kane crime series of six books.

Simplified brain-washing techniques for the predisposed and so inclined.

E. H. Reinhard has come up with an eye-popping tale of criminal mischief, when he wrote the novel **Malevolent**, published in 2014. The book is the first in a series of six crime-fiction novels. They follow the day-in-the-life and day-to-day routines of the magnanimous "Lieutenant Carl Kane," a competent, dedicated, and hard-working police officer who reports to precinct headquarters in the Tampa, Florida area. Here, he finds himself in a race against time trying to locate and put a stop to someone who commits "particularly heinous" crimes, right under the very noses of the police department. He becomes increasingly frustrated when the news media gets involved, as well as the FBI, an ever-expanding network of detectives, and police officers from the other jurisdictions nearby and surrounding municipalities.

He and his police department take the heat for not being able to solve the crime quickly enough, when the unit comes under intense public scrutiny due to leaks to the press. He and his team of detectives do everything they can to follow police procedure and protocol, but to no avail. They come up empty-handed at every turn. They hit one snafu after another. They run into nothing but roadblocks and dead-ends, while the perpetrator continues his crime spree unimpeded.

The offender obviously has an hidden agenda, but the persevering Lt. Kane, and company, can't for the life of him figure out what it is. Calling in an FBI profiler seems to put things into proper perspective and helps the police focus on an archetype of possible suspects, but it really doesn't generate many solid leads. It is like saying they are looking for an older suspect who might have once played with matches; tortured small, defenseless animals; and didn't play nice with the other kids in the sandbox. Insecure and emotionally troubled, he must have developed deep-seated, prolonged feelings of inadequacy. Either he had become an aggressive bully by his very nature, or he might have at some critical juncture in his hideous life been beaten up and bullied himself, never to forget the debilitating or excruciating experience. It is difficult to tell, really, when, how, or why he needs constant supervision.

When the bodies began piling up, one thing was for certain. He had become downright despicable, a dirty, mean, and totally nasty character in the minds of law enforcement. An irresistible force to be reckoned with, he revealed himself as having diabolical, sinister, evil, and cruel tendencies. In short, he had become a terrible, terrifying monster. It was Lt. Kane's job to give the department the straight dope on how the criminal investigation was proceeding and how much actual progress they were making toward solving the crime. At the time, the police were completely buffaloed, stymied, and baffled. They didn't have a single, significant clue to go on. Because of the preponderance of media attention, members of the public at large had become horrified, shocked, and fearful for their own safety and wellbeing. It was chaotic. They have to get him off the street.

Meanwhile, the elusive criminal, although he may not exactly yet be defined as being a smooth operator, continues to prove that he is the cold-blooded animal, devoid of feelings, that everyone thinks he is, in every way, shape, and form. He does not empathize with the plight of others, particularly that of his victims. He is a thoroughly bad, bad guy, with absolutely no redeeming qualities of which to speak. He is decidedly intelligent, a devious, sneaky, problem-solver. Therefore, he has skillfully and repeatedly avoided capture. He has been extremely difficult to catch, despite life being full of little coincidences, on which the police fail to pick up. He must have gone from one abusive relationship to another. In this scenario, he is clearly the abuser. There is no doubt about the observable facts. When he goes from attempted brainwashing to conducting brain-salad surgery, his crimes become particularly evil-natured. If not dispassionately predisposed, they are so inclined. The police are still in need of articulable facts, bearing on the case. What fiery hoops must they jump through in order to put an end to the madness?

R. Royce decided to take a break from the job, go out, enjoy life a little, and take time to smell the roses. He had enough money in his bank account to shop around and buy an island. He thought about the possibility of designing a submarine base which would provide safe haven for the underwater vessels from many nations around the world. His deep-harbor base would offer all the amenities required by submarine commanders on the go, and give their pent-up crewmembers the opportunities to get out a little for fresh air, sunshine, and exercise. Conceivably, they would be able to socialize in a completely natural, healthy, carefree, tropical environment. Adequate repair facilities, supplies, and necessary accommodations could be made available to all requiring them.

"You can't have foreign navy trawlers wandering around aimlessly in our waters, looking for a submarine sandwiched between a rock and a hard place," said Cornelius Korn, his good friend of many years and creative business partner. He has a great tendency to create opportunity for himself and his associates as he continually seeks to diversify his holdings.

"Perhaps, we should think about rapidly expanding, and having submarine bases operating in each of the world's major oceans," suggested Royce.

"We just need to get out our tourist-travel brochures, pick and choose from among our favorite islands in paradise and the hot-spots around the globe," said Korn. "You can take it from there."

"Did you discover any safe, deep harbors, yet, leading to modernized facilities nearby, having adequate, hardened overhead protection, such as from fjords, mountains, and steep cliffs?" inquired Raquel, rather boldly and indiscreetly.

"Well, no, but I did meet a very handsome and loquacious foreign yachtsman on a shore excursion," said Alexis Sue. "He was looking for something similar in the way of accommodations."

"He looks rich and resourceful enough to engineer secret underwater entrance passageway construction," said Royce.

"I'm having dinner with him this evening," Alexis continued. "I just bought the perfect shimmering, iridescent, long, formal gown in the most luscious shade of evergreen you've ever seen, to wear to the Moonlight Ball."

"We're all going be there with bells on," said Korn. "The festive occasion of which you speak will prove to be quite memorable, as you soon shall see."

"You aren't planning on kidnapping and interrogating him, are you?" asked Royce.

"Lest you forget, we represent the *Executive Protective Service*," said Korn. "We are ever mindful of our patriotic duties and civic responsibilities."

"You didn't answer the question!" exclaimed Royce.

"Global warming, the environment, narcotics, terrorism, border disputes, and dubious circumstances beyond our immediate control will always be emotionally charged, hot-button issues," expounded Korn, evasively. "I don't know what to tell you, Royce."

"Your attempt at being completely transparent, open and honest is greatly appreciated," said Royce. "At least, we know you are a trustworthy undercover detective and on our side."

"If he turns out to be a rogue intelligence officer, we can always hand him over to the CIA," suggested Raquel.

Later that evening, Alexis Sue was having the time of her life at the Ball. "You can park your denizen of the deep at my house any day of the week," she whispered breathlessly to Cornelius.

CHAPTER 94

Book review of the novel

The Godmother

by Hannelore Cayre, published in 2017 in France,
translated by Stephanie Smee in 2019, from French into English.

> *What's legal isn't always right; what's right isn't always fair; what's fair and reasonable isn't necessarily good for her. In other words, she needs a good lawyer.*
> *The straight dope on how the deal went south.*

Hannelore Cayre wrote an illuminating novel about the more practical aspects of dealing street-level drugs in modern France, entitled ***The Godmother***. It was originally published in French in 2017. Stephanie Smee translated the book into English. The translated version was first published in 2019. The book is definitely a winner. It is rock solid and has substance. It provides the straight dope on how the deal went south from numerous angles and knowledgeable sources. Readers should find the book thoroughly thought provoking, if not mildly stimulating. The mind-numbing plot intoxicates and simply overwhelms the senses. The storyline defies everyday logic and common sense. It plays on the emotions of the leading character, "Patience." You quickly discover that she is not your typical "Fairy Godmother" from the Brothers' Grimm fairytales. She takes advantage of every situation which presents itself. Then, she goes to great lengths and shows in great detail, with the aid of masterfully revealing, excruciatingly complex minutiae just how far she would go in seeking to attain her ultimate goals in life; how devious, sneaky, and underhanded she could really be when she sets her mind to it, gets down, and applies herself.

Some readers may agree with the convoluted, half-baked statement that any intellectual of average intelligence might have made, that what's legal isn't always right; what's fair and reasonable isn't necessarily good for you—but this merely involves a question of semantics. It begs the question. As I may have casually mentioned before, she has already thrown caution to the wind and logic completely out the window. She has no need for recognition. She has no need for attention. Or anybody's seal of approval, for that matter. In fact, she would prefer complete anonymity and the utmost secrecy in making absolutely certain that her "French Connection" inspired business transactions become a fully functional reality, and a model for posterity.

In the Arab world, the woman's place is in the home. It is her principal domicile. Apparently, because of this narrow view, women have been severely limited, hampered, and restricted in their actions, activities, and achievements since time immemorial. One may even say that they have become totally oppressed, repressed, and submissive as a result of the bargain they have made with society as a whole. In sharp, dramatic contrast, as in the highly exceptional case of the leading character, Patience, specifically, we soon learn "who wears the pants in the family." Nevertheless, we are also surreptitiously led to believe that she still has only two options open to her: she can either learn the easy way, or she has to learn the hard way. You object! You are probably thinking, but she has sailed a massively difficult ship to navigate across treacherous waters, and rowed an unwieldy, awkwardly unstable dinghy to shore, figuratively speaking. Once on dry land, she has discovered that the prized cargo she carries is actually "a tough row to hoe," but lucrative. You think that all of her hard work should pay off. Alas, but we can only pause and reflect, surmise the outcome, and sympathize with her, because of her plight. How can she possibly behave in a truly heroic fashion under such obvious duress in the long run? How can she survive her fate? You gasp in horror, with fear and trepidation.

We know that Patience has stubborn tendencies and is a very determined woman, so we have to persevere for the duration of her trials and tribulations in order to learn the true result of the endgame. We follow along placidly, merrily, dreamily, sweeping in and gliding gently, virtually hovering about in order to get a closer aerial bird's eye view of the culmination of her caterwauling career, as the authorities rapidly close in on her, in the ensuing, climactic chase scene. We begin to read each paragraph much faster. We turn the pages more quickly now; finally, with utter abandonment, and in eager anticipation.

R. Royce was enjoying life to the fullest. He had acquired a mixed lot of jewelry recently, including those formerly owned by some royal family, it seems, made of the finest gold and platinum, and having the most precious diamond, sapphire, ruby, emerald, tourmaline, and topaz inlaid gemstones. The multitude of large, faceted stones flashed with dazzling brilliance, fire, and clarity. The items should fetch a tidy sum in the range of twenty to twenty-two million USD, he thought. A bundle, in short, yielding a tidy profit. He made only one tiny, little mistake along the way, when he decided to wear one of the distinctive diamond rings in public, which happened to fit his finger perfectly, like a kit leather glove. A man with whom he was intent on dealing recognized the item immediately and took it upon himself to inform the original owner of its whereabouts.

His Royal Highness King Richard III "The Lion Hearted" Ishtabuhla, formerly known as the "Wandering Prince of Budapest" introduced himself to Royce while he was seated on a rickety folding chair on the old wooden wharf not far from Satellite Beach in Florida, a fishing pole in hand, and another leaning up against the railing. He appeared mysteriously out of the wild blue yonder one day. Debonair and unassuming, he was casually dressed in light, loose-fitting clothing and comfortable sneakers. He looked about the area nonchalantly and was apparently pleased with the natural beauty of the surrounding scenery and the tranquility of the secluded location.

"Catch anything?" inquired the King, twice removed, impoverished by the sudden, unexpected disappearance and untimely sale of the crown jewels in the past.

"They stopped biting," said Royce. It was getting warmer outdoors with the rising sun. "Caught several sea bass earlier this morning, though. They're in the cooler over there." He pointed to the nearby ice chest.

"And the big one that got away?" asked the King. He'd heard plenty of fisherman's tales in his time.

"I was using a heavyweight line, with a long, stout metal leader and swivels, a lead sinker, and a large, sturdy hook on the end. It must have been a snook or a barracuda that hit the line and took off. I fought and fought for at least half an hour, trying my level-best to reel him in. Eventually, though, the line went slack. I thought the big fish had snapped the line in two, causing me to lose the hook, line, and sinker. But when I reeled in the line, to my chagrin, I discovered that the hook, line, and sinker was still attached to the line as before. What was most unusual about it was, the once gracefully curved and sharply barbed hook had been bent completely straight, the barb sheared off, broken. That must have been why the fish slid off the hook and got away."

"I was watching through binoculars when you were busy reeling in the big snook," said Richard the Lion-Hearted. "A big grouper bit into the snook. Then, an even larger fish swallowed them both. You were lucky the bloody shark did not pull you into the water with them."

Royce invited his new friend, Richard, to take up the other fishing pole and try his luck, to which the King readily agreed. Eventually, they returned to his condominium, where he introduced him to his friends and acquaintances, namely Cornelius Korn, Alexis Sue Shell, Raquel Remington, and Heather Meriwether, who looked an awful lot like the beautiful television celebrity and blonde bombshell, Heather Locklear. They'd recently met her at the beach, looking for sea shells. Richard took to her like a duck takes to water. They quickly became friends.

Eventually, King Richard III, the Lion Hearted, had to come clean and get something off his chest, which must have been troubling him for a long time. He did not reveal his true identity to the group, however.

"Might I be so bold as to inquire about the gold ring that you are wearing, Royce?" he asked. "Where did you get it?" They'd been sipping on spiced island rum and Cokes on ice.

Royce was taken aback and became reticent and introspective. He reflected, before he gave an answer. "Raquel gave me the ring over the holidays as a token of our love and friendship," he said, finally.

"This particular item had been included in an estate auction. We'd purchased numerous items jewelry recently through an auction service in Miami Beach. We purchased the majority of a large quantity of fine jewelry pieces, thinking they would soon make a sound business investment," Raquel elaborated. "We had originally planned to sell all of the items we bought to a collector in New York, but I thought we should keep the ring for ourselves. It appears to be quite stylish and most unique. As they say in the credit card commercials, 'Simply priceless.'"

"I don't personally believe that the diamond is actually real," confided Cornelius Korn. "It must be one of those Russian-manufactured diamonds, since it appears so completely flawless. They make artificial diamonds, using complex machinery which operates under extremely high pressure and at very high temperatures. These diamonds may be expensive to produce and expensive to buy, yes, but, in my opinion, they are not the genuine article, driven by the forces of nature; exploding volcanos, colliding continents, and shifting tectonic plates, as Mother Nature had intended."

"I can assure you that you have the genuine article," said Richard III, calmly and evenly. "The ring has been engraved with my initials and it once belonged to me." The other members of the group were genuinely surprised, that they were in the presence of one so intimately knowledgeable about the apparently and relatively insignificant trinket in their possession. The apparent predicament in which they now found themselves aroused their curiosity, and they became greatly concerned. How is it that fate has brought these people together in this manner, uniting them with the expert in the matter? They sensed that their latest deal was beginning to come unraveled at the seams.

"So, tell us truly, Richard, dear friend. Do you want your magnificent, shining ring back now, after all has been said and done, for sentimental reasons?" asked Korn, in sincerity. It must have been a terribly delicate subject to broach.

"Actually, I would be more interested in exploring partnership possibilities for newly constructed submarine bases," said the wandering King-maker, and spokesman for a proud, traditional, and as-of-yet undisclosed European nation. "Perhaps, we can include the islands to go with the bases in the deal." He had long since located and bought back the missing crown jewels from the business associates that they had in common in New York, at reasonable prices and fees. This was no longer a concern.

"Of course, you may keep the ring as a token of our friendship," added Richard, with considerable authority and finality. "I just thought you'd like to know a little about its considerable history."

He did not specify exactly, but there were actually 13 of the rare rings originally created by the finest craftsmen deep inside the frozen mountains of the Scandinavian North. They had been perfectly designed, refined, and tooled. They are easily identifiable to this very day. The first King Richard, the Lion Hearted, had once called them rings of friendship, before his untimely imprisonment, centuries ago, dating back to medieval times and knights in shining armor. The party suddenly felt subdued by the somber mood of silence and secrecy which fell upon them. They were given a purpose, direction, and a new lease on life.

CHAPTER 95

Book review of the short story collection

Ridden Hard — Put Up Wet

by Fredrick W. Boling, published 2000 to 2001, 12 stories.

A big, glass Mason jar of pickled pig's feet to go with the yarn.
"That dog won't hunt."
Moonshine, ribs, pickled pigs' feet. All the meat, potatoes and gravy you can eat.

There are twelve stories in Fredrick W. Boling's collection of short stories, ***Ridden Hard — Put Up Wet***. They were meant to captivate, interest, beguile, intrigue, and enlighten you. All in all, they have been well-crafted and neatly packaged for this express purpose. You discover to your delight and chagrin that they are genuinely inspired, authentic tales of the wild west. They are the type of stories often heard around the camp-fire and repeated during the holidays, spanning approximately 80 years from the 1890s to the 1970s. Without a doubt, it rapidly becomes self-evident that the author's encyclopedic knowledge of cattle, horses, mountainous terrain, leather saddlery, harnesses, boots, bits, spurs, cowboy hats, the wide assortment of firearms, jail-houses, saloons, and "home on the range" is considerable. The colorful, descriptive language he uses in his narrative, often cites and expounds upon a great many local euphemisms and long, all but forgotten pioneer thoughts and prayers. Included as well are numerous instances of traditionally Native American wisdom.

What else makes the book so exceptionally endearing? It depicts the great progress made by Western Civilization, in general, and tells of golden opportunities that followed in its wake, from the perspective of the enduring people who were there and lived through those turbulent times. People with vision, foresight, determination, pride, and ambition. Their stories remind me of articles you used to see in the "Old West" magazines from the 1960s and 1970s that my father and all of his friends from work, his army buddies, and the neighbors read regularly, if not exactly religiously.

The magazines portrayed frontier towns, ghost towns, and historical mining towns. They described the rugged and risky way of life in the old west with all of its wildflower glory, charm, natural beauty, and heartache. Most of all, they told and retold the bold, adventurous tales of prospectors, gold hunters, and all manner of treasure seekers. Thus, they provided prime examples of heroic men and women who best demonstrated the true pioneering spirit. Pioneers who approached life with a keen sense of humor, no matter how difficult the challenge; how rough, tough, and tumble the situation and dire the circumstances had become. Essentially, as it turns out, what really mattered most then is almost exactly the same today as it was yesterday, in those yesteryears.

What really mattered in the 1960s and 1970s? Family and, basically, the same things that mattered in the 1890s. Namely, you had to put food on the table. Rabbits and squirrels, if you couldn't get venison or find a prairie-chicken. You had to chop enough firewood to keep warm in the winter. You had to have walls to surround you with a good measure of security and a roof above you that kept out the wind and the rain; wolves, cougars, bears, rattlesnakes, and other predators. You had to pay rent on your house if you lived in town. You had to find and keep a steady job in order to maintain an income. Nothing too complicated, other than what affected their basic survival; that is to say, their very lives and livelihoods. I'd even go so far as to say that the entrepreneurial skills, which they developed in the process along the way and the indomitably defiant sense of humor which they innately possessed might actually have contributed to keeping many of them alive under unbelievably harsh conditions, and in accordance with no great stretch of the imagination.

Nevertheless, it didn't always work out that easily or predictably for everyone. If harsh environmental conditions, desperados, other mean, despicable hombres, or just plain bad luck didn't catch up with the vast majority of them, then the Law certainly would and did, in the form of a heavy-handed, nickel-plated revolver wielding Sheriff, or a sawed-off, double-barrel shotgun toting

Marshall. Life could be a three-ring circus during those times. There was no getting around it. Practically every one of the transplanted, migratory individuals living in the era, walked the precarious balance-beam tight-rope, or else they swung from the "trapeze," however adaptable, rugged, "young and invincible" they thought themselves to be in the moment of truth or consequences. It just didn't pay enough to stray very far away from the straight gate and narrow way.

Which of the stories did I enjoy most or liked best? Well, I can't rightly say. I thought they all provided excellent, first-rate, top-drawer reading material, obviously intended for the publisher's first perusal, who then presented them to the perhaps ignoble, unsuspecting public-at-large, in the form of pages and pages of vastly useful, definitive, and interesting information, bound together beneath the classic cover of graphic cowboy artwork. These crisp, pristinely printed pages would eventually and inevitably reach voracious readers like myself throughout the land; readers seeking pearls of wisdom, trying to expand their horizons, and becoming more educated to the ways of the world, both in this sometimes wicked world, as well as in the hereafter. Expecting anything less, losing sight of the ultimate goal, forgetting the big picture, lowering your lofty standards? "That dog won't hunt."

R. Royce was about to scream bloody murder, but he was not a particularly flighty or emotional man. Hence, he ceased and desisted with the theatrical antics. He sat down quietly and pondered his plight. The man he counted on most recently had run off with all of his money. He had to do something. Seek advice. He was struck by what the armorer once told him years ago. "The safest place to keep your gun is in its holster."

"He took your $3.5 million?" asked Cornelius Korn, Royce's longtime friend and trusted business partner.

"He certainly did," said Royce. "There are no two ways about it."

"It isn't like he had a gun pointed to your head. Why did you let him have all of the funds at once?" inquired Korn.

"I thought the merchandise was good," said Royce. "The Bill of Sale was genuine and the papers were all in order." He handed Korn a stack of documents.

"You bought a thoroughbred Arabian racehorse?" asked Korn, upon reviewing the papers, shaking his head in bewilderment.

"Not just any thoroughbred," said Royce. " 'King Tut's Heavenly Reward,' appropriately named after the famous Egyptian Pharaoh."

"The top contender for the next triple crown. Reportedly known as the fastest horse in the world?" said Korn. The animal's reputation had preceded him.

"He's never lost a race," bragged Royce. "I was hoping we could to run him at the Santa Anita Park in California, and see how he does." Unfortunately, the horse had never won a race in these United States. He had only been raced in Europe.

"Where is the horse, now?" inquired Korn.

"Missing, presumed stolen," exclaimed Royce, like a little whipped pup. "The former owner has returned to New York and can't be reached by telephone."

"Let's call Nehru and Kashmire's Grandfather. They have contacts there," said Korn. "Maybe they can help locate Abduhl and our horse." They had been business associates in New Jersey and Florida.

A couple of days later, Prince Abduhl had personally arranged for a meeting with Royce. He was truly sorry for any inconvenience he might have caused. He went on to apologize about the missing thoroughbred.

"I wanted to run King Tut's in one more race, before I turn him over to you. I sincerely hope you don't mind," said the prince. The rich and powerful think differently than the rest of us.

"Okay. Where are you racing him?" asked Korn. "I want to place a bet."

"Gulfstream Park, in South Florida tomorrow afternoon, the third race," said Prince Abduhl, cordially. He didn't believe that he did anything exceptionally wrong or particularly out of the ordinary. It was business as usual for him, another day at the office.

"May we pick up the horse at the track afterwards?" inquired Royce, humbly. He was a modest, but unassuming man. You have to know how to talk to royalty.

"Most certainly," said Prince Abduhl. "We had a deal, didn't we? I plan to honor it."

"We'll see you at the finish line, then," said Royce. His confidence was returning, slowly, but surely.

To make a long story short, Royce and Korn were indeed physically present at the racing event of the season the very next day. They had placed their wagers in person, and they had won their bets. A good time was had by all. After the race, Royce and his newly recruited partner, Cornelius Korn, collected their winnings and their horse. They drove away together in a late-model F100 pickup truck with the horse in an attached covered trailer. Contented and now jovial, they were somewhat wealthier and wiser as a result of the edifying experience. They behaved a lot like the rambunctious Henry Fonda and Glenn Ford in the 1965 Hollywood movie *The Rounders*, washing down their pickled pig's feet from a big, glass Mason jar, with moonshine whiskey from a gallon crock jug.

Two weeks later, they entered King Tut's Heavenly Reward in the fifth race of the day at the Santa Anita track. "Their horse easily won," to paraphrase the Helen Reddy song about vanity. A solid investment after all was said and done, they sold the horse for a sizable profit immediately after the race to a highly successful breeder and the proud owner of a winning string of fine steeds himself. His ranch was well-known in the community, and was steeped in tradition. The new owner had long ago established his name and fame, from the stables centrally located in the blue-grass state of Kentucky. Royce and Korn obviously felt elated after King Tut's victory, but they didn't want to push their luck too much by racing him repeatedly at the tracks all over the country for an entire season. They could have much more easily put him out to stud and made a fortune that way. But, instead, they decided to sell the animal outright. It was a done deal.

Yes, indeed, they wanted to maintain the status quo. Tentatively, they were still in the market for an entirely new "base of operations," and didn't want to jeopardize or become too distracted from this construction project by gambling on horses. Raquel and Alexis Sue, their enterprising significant others, had already lured several potential investors to their secluded island in the Caribbean Sea. Royce and Korn were on the way to meet them there, pronto. Conceivably, the newly designed submarine base would someday rival the Panama Canal, Hoover Dam, and other similar, largescale marvels built using the latest modern engineering methods; widely known around the globe as one of the eighteen wonders of the world.

CHAPTER 96

Review of the nonfictional book

Genghis Khan and the Making of the Modern World

by Jack Weatherford, published in 2004.

Henchmen intercepted, humiliated, tortured, and put to death the humble emissary of peace, not yet knowing the full wrath of Khan and the mighty Mongol army behind him.

Upon reading Jack Weatherford's historical account of ***Genghis Khan and the Making of the Modern World***, published in 2004, you begin to see the Chinese calendar in a whole new light. The author has given it literary and historical significance. You can finally relate the year of the horse to 1212, when Genghis Khan rode out on his trusty stallion and restored the Khitan monarchy to all its power and magnificence; the year of the pig to 1215, when Genghis Khan and his Mongol horde first brought fine meaty delicacies, such as ham and pork chops, back to his starving people from conquered civilizations to the east; the year of the rabbit to 1219, when he and the Mongols proceeded westward—dashing, zig-zagging and, hopping around like a programmable "Eveready" Easter bunny on steroids with a computer chip for a brain toward the citadel of Khwarazm, liberating untold wealth and achieving the pinnacle of success; the year of the dragon to 1220, when he and his behemoth Mongol army captured Bukhara to the south, known as the jewel of Islam; and so forth, until the fierce, fire-breathing Mongol army conquered every major city in Turkey, Arabia, and Persia in the greatest show of strength, prowess, agility, and military might which the inhabitants of this vast, wide world have ever experienced up to that point and time in history. Thus, the author continues to provide anxious readers with useful gems of information throughout the entire book, constantly mining for facts, refining the details, expounding and elaborating upon the major historical events as he narrates the story. Ultimately, he sets it all on the table and puts everything to the test. In a nutshell, he gives the incredible story of Genghis Khan the breath of life, cinematic-quality, and panoramic perspective. The Khan becomes a dominant, larger-than-life, archetype character, the main driving force, in his leading role as a great military leader and guru. Specifically, perhaps speaking facetiously, you can glean more common sense wisdom out of absorbing the facts, figures, details, and events, which the author cavalierly presents in this esoteric book, than you might otherwise digest in the course of a lifetime of oblivious, sedentary, gravitationally challenged occupations in an exercise in futility, like watching TV soap operas all afternoon, before suddenly waking up, smelling the coffee, and attaining enlightenment at some point in time, as follows:

It was once said, but rarely repeated, that in the not too distant past, perhaps hundreds or even thousands of miles away, a group of rough and tumble henchmen intercepted, humiliated, tortured, then cruelly and unceremoniously put to death a poor, humble emissary of peace, not knowing the Great Mongol Khan and his mighty army horde was right behind the envoy, just over the next hilltop, and would not be denied.

Utilizing the military tactics learned over the years from the mighty Genghis Khan, after his death in battle in 1227, his sons and grandsons picked up where he left off, having grasped the tactical importance of a variety of attack modes, including the "dogfight," "silent attack," "lightning strike," and "divine wind."

In the "dragnet," for example, you never know what kind of hoofed animals and wild hogs might be scooped up for a Royal Mongolian Barbeque.

Therefore, in long, protracted wars, and laboring under all conditions, the Mongols perpetuated their reputation as having a viable, unified, highly organized, and very effective fighting force. Reading between the lines, you learn what happens when an irresistible force meets an immovable object.

In 1236, the year of the monkey, Batu's leading general attacked the Volga River region of Bulgar. A few short years later, in 1240, the year of the rat, the

Mongols attacked Kiev. Afterwards, Khan Batu came to be known as Czar Batu. He has left an impressive legacy.

After the death of Genghis Khan's sons, Ogodei and Batu, their sons continued the aggressive actions of their fathers before them. Ogodei's sons attacked China and Batu's sons attacked Europe, automatically assuming command in their places.

In 1241, the three Princes of Mongolia, Batu, Buri, and Guyuk began squabbling among themselves for a time, halting progress in their invasion of Europe. It is not clear whether or not their differences were satisfactorily resolved, but this did not prevent the Mongol army from attacking the German knights and defenders at Walhstatt. The Mongols had easily lured the knights into a trap and defeated them handily. Duke Henry II was killed in the battle. But, according to the author, the battle had been fought merely as a diversion for the Mongols. The real objective for the Mongol army was Budapest, Hungary. Within three days march away, the invaders killed an estimated 100,000 Hungarian and Polish soldiers who came out to greet them. King Bela IV was forced to flee, and miraculously escaped the carnage.

Near the end of 1241, Khan Ogodei died, and the full-scale invasion of Europe suddenly ceased. The Mongols left without a word, without further ado, perplexing all concerned. In 1242, the year of the tiger, the Mongols simply withdrew from W. Europe altogether, back to their expanding Russian stronghold base. By 1255, all four of Genghis Khan's sons had died. So, it came to pass that the men fought the wars, but their women ruled the empire, as suggested by the author. So it was the Mongols who must have coined or invented the term, "the power behind the throne."

In July, 1251, Mongke Grand Khan was proclaimed the supreme ruler of the Mongolian empire. He was the son of Genghis Khan's youngest son, Tolui. His mother, Sorkhokhtani, ruled N. China and E. Mongolia. Definitely worthy of mention is the fact that all four of her sons would become Khans: Arik Bok, Hulegu, Kubilai, and Mongke. The family certainly had a complicated genealogy.

In 1253, the year of the ox, Mongke Khan set forth a magnificent celebration, feast, and a religious debate among the prominent religions of Buddhism, Muslim, and Christianity. There were years of peace and prosperity and they must not have had anything better to do at the time. In August, 1259, as the author faithfully relates, Mongke Khan died.

In 1260, Arik Bok became the Great Kahn. But he was ousted by his brother Kubilai Khan in a coup soon afterwards. He died in 1266, under mysterious circumstances. Definitely suspicious. You wonder what really happened.

Kubilai Khan's greatest achievement was in conquering and unifying all of China by mostly peaceful means. Essentially, he unified China through the use of a strong army, influential propaganda, a benevolent administration and instituting fair policies. The author makes several such perceptive inferences in that chapter of history. You may draw your own conclusions. Brilliant deduction, Sherlock. We know why they built the "Great Wall of China."

The stories themselves and the timeline presented by the author certainly provides a firm framework for analytical readers who want to dig, delve, and dive deeply into material of the book in order to discover juicy pearls of sensational facts and fascinating multifaceted, ruby-red details about the numerous countries involved; the so-affected and impacted regions of the then-known world; and their powerful, enigmatic, illustrious leaders, hitherto largely unknown entities. History may ordinarily be considered a dry, tedious subject in general, but, I am positively certain, that reading about the great Mongol horde will quickly become a worthwhile endeavor for anyone with an inquiring mind, particularly those who want to know exactly what "the enemy" has been thinking all those years.

Particularly, when they are skeptical that a large, motley, scattered band of poor, illiterate, back-woods marauders could possibly have traveled over such great distances for so many years to fight battle after battle together against trained soldiers protectively ensconced on solid foundations and secured behind the dense, thick rock walls of fortified castles. It boggles the mind to think that they could shoot up Main Street in town on Saturday night like drunken cowboy outlaw revelers; or attack the Fort, like a renegade tribe of wild North American Indian warriors, massacring everyone inside, then moving on to the next fortified city. Perhaps, it is speculative science fiction to think so, but I begin to wonder if there hasn't been a massive cover-up about a thousand years ago, or even farther back in time; if there wasn't an undisclosed "Area 51, Roswell, New Mexico" from some technologically advanced civilization hidden within the dense forests and inside rugged mountain caverns, somewhere in the more remote, desolate, and isolated regions of Mongolia. Where exactly did the space ship land? Where did all the flying saucers go? Farfetched as it may seem, Europe, China, and the Middle East might actually have been invaded in the medieval ages by alien beings, originating from another planet in a far distant galaxy, who suddenly appeared on Earth in human form, and infiltrated the Mongol army horde, solely in order to have them turn the tide of history in their favor. On the other hand, maybe they were just looking for the "Lost Ark of the Covenant," and the raiders had to fight everyone along the path to get there. Only the physical evidence and concrete proof is missing.

R. Royce was snorkeling at an as of yet undisclosed location when he noticed a school of sharks pass beneath him in the oceanic depths. He thought, *I should have stuck to noodling for catfish in the tributaries of the Missouri River.*

That made him think about something he told his sister some months ago, "Don't let your mother and your daughter drive you crazy and let them ruin your life." All of them have such willful minds. They are stubbornly determined, persistent, and totally committed to their actions. "Can't they just let it slide for a change?" Elders don't want change. They can't deal with it. Youth wants to try a fresh, novel approach. She's stuck in the middle and can't escape her destiny.

Later on the beach, Royce called Cornelius Korn, his business associate and longtime friend on his cellular telephone. "The sharks have arrived to have the barnacles scraped from their bellies, ingest their vitamins, and get their shot records updated," he said. "How are things going on base?"

"Couldn't be better," replied Korn. "Three subs will arrive within the month for routine maintenance and resupply. Technicians will modify and upgrade their electronics equipment. The excavation and construction project is moving along like clockwork."

"The O-club has been bustling with activity, as have the USO office and Recreation Center. The troops couldn't be happier," said Royce. "Island Adventures is a trip out of this world."

"There's no shortage of pirate booty in Bluebeard's Duty Free Store, either," said Alexis Sue Shell, Cornelius's girlfriend, grinning.

"Let's go, Buck-O," said Raquel Remington. "But, I don't want to pressure you in any way." They had been happily sipping Margaritas in the shade and cool tropical breeze of a nearby Tiki hut. "Talk about an ocean view!"

"Hickory liquory daquiri dock. See the surfers on the boardwalk," sang Alexis, enthusiastically. She was poetry in motion.

"Why, they're none other than the famous Hollywood movie moguls and Italian film directors, Royce and Korn," said Raquel, as they walked toward them and bellied up to the bar.

"We eat spaghetti westerns for breakfast," said the jovial Korn.

"Trinity is still my name," said Royce, referring to an Italian movie of the same name.

"My red, swollen feet hurt terribly," exclaimed Korn, suddenly mildly irritated, pointing down to his bare appendages. The sandals he was wearing exposed his tender feet.

"You probably thought you'd stepped on a jelly fish, and he turned out to be a Portuguese man of war," said Royce, now smiling congenially.

"Definitely not a Squid or a Navy Seal," retorted Korn.

"Yes, he might have kicked your derriere, otherwise," said Royce.

Along about that time another couple strolled up, Richard Ishtabuhla and Heather Meriwether. He was the former King Richard III in exile and she was his Lady. They were travelling incognito, and mum was the word. The last to arrive was Sailor Dan Sandhurst, another undercover operative, and business associate of the present party. He came to pass along a message. The Phluegers would be arriving in a few days to make final preparations for the sale and transfer of the newly constructed corporate headquarters building on the island. It was a big deal about to bear fruit. Official now, the navies from a dozen or more allied nations had signed a 99-year lease for the use of the land and facilities at the proposed top-secret subterranean submarine base.

"We plan on catering to all of their military needs," said Sandhurst. He was actually a highly competent contract, procurement, and logistical officer. Someone misquoted him as having said, "If the Navy wanted you to have a wife, they would have issued you one." Before too long, he was happily engaged and living in paradise.

"You come highly recommended by my young Aunt," confessed Daisy Mae Jones, his sweetheart, when they first met at the Academy.

CHAPTER 97

Book review of the novel

The Visionist

by Rachel Urquhart, published in 2014.

Back biting, foot stomping, teeth chattering, shivering cold, chain rattling, wintry wind chill.
   Blame the Puritans, admonish the Amish, chastise the Philistines, but make her a Shaker?

The darkly somber, strangely foreboding, yet mysteriously uplifting novel depicts the life of "Polly," a young girl who is dropped off at a Shaker settlement in rural Massachusetts in 1842 by her fleeing mother in the middle of the night. Hence, author Rachel Urquhart has written a refreshingly different kind of book, which was published in 2014. The title of **The Visionist**, *suggests* supernatural "paranormal activity," that may include spirit possession, telekinesis, and clairvoyance. I shall leave it to readers to decide for themselves the nature of this awkward business of "mind over matter." A word of caution, as you are no doubt aware, "the spirit is willing, but the flesh is weak."

A few extraneous thoughts immediately come to mind: "You work your fingers to the bone, and what do you get? Boney fingers." "Cleanliness is next to godliness." "You are next in line for a miracle." Her mother must have been looking for the "Ronald McDonald House," and found the Shakers', instead. You read a few chapters of the novel to develop a sense of direction for where the story is intent on leading you. Clue you in to the gist of the twisted tale? A potential cornucopia of earthly utopian delights awaits, but doesn't cover the half of it. You are in for a powerfully shocking, gut-wrenching reaction.

You think, they can blame the Puritans, admonish the Amish, chastise the Philistines, but can't seem to make 'er a proper Shaker, in a manner of speaking. The sudden, irrepressible feeling of a back-biting, foot-stomping, teeth-chattering, shivering-cold, chain-rattling, wintry wind-chill, Arctic air blast appears like a phantom. A maddening apparition, a cloud in human form, if not actually in the flesh. Only then, the narrator begins to reveal the wisdom of her years.

Plainly and simply, you anticipate having to solve a most difficult mystery as the story continues to unfold. Add a go-getter gazetteer, an investigator, who once worked for a prominent, but unscrupulous county attorney. He is "Simon." He's looking for answers for himself personally, and on behalf of his latest client. Along the way, he encounters civic-minded townspeople who guide him on his quest for the truth. He meets a lawyer who has a staked interest in the matter. He greets a Shaker with an attitude. He makes the acquaintance of a true believer. Carefully analyzing the culpable alternatives for a possible crime, he has to sift through the evidence and sort it all out. He is on the rebound from having decided once long ago to break off all ties with family and friends. He wants to start over again with a clean slate, like Henry David Thoreau, but he becomes puzzled and has second thoughts. He has a change of heart.

Add another talented, saintly close companion, and you have all the necessary character ingredients for an explosive thriller. She is Polly's dear friend, "Charity." She is a real pistol, rather a smoking gun.

There is no doubt in R. Royce's military mind. He has come this far, and plans to see the mission through to completion. The man in his sights has been juggling hand-grenades for his own perverse amusement. Dressed in Kevlar, loose-fitting denim slacks, a cool Hawaiian cotton shirt, and hiking boots, he is prepared for a day of fun and rugged adventure in the big outdoors. His church is as big as the great outdoors. In fact, it is the great outdoors. You can't confine a guy like that. You can't restrict or constrain him, either. He has unlimited potential. He has the means. He used to be ambitious, but has grown overly complacent in recent years. Too much success has made him lazy. He lacks the necessary motivation to be a key player on the big stage. He does have more than adequate resources.

Royce took careful aim and shot him squarely in the shoulder with his tranquilizer stun gun. The stately, studly personage fell to the floor with a loud, screeching thud. He was a big, muscular dude, who must have once pumped iron on a regular basis. At the moment, he was totally incapacitated, unable to lift a finger in his own defense. The shot had been an effective one. Hand-grenades rolled about the gleaming varnished hardwood floor in every direction all around him.

Cornelius Korn was the first to reach him. He lifted the man up and sat him back in a comfortable chair. He zip-tied his hands and feet, so he wouldn't get very far if he decided to make a break for it. Alexis Sue Shell collected up the grenades, carefully placing them in a wicker basket as if they were Easter eggs, gingerly putting the basket on a high shelf in the closet in the adjacent room, out of harm's way.

Royce strolled up accompanied by his able-bodied assistant, Raquel Remington. She had a similar rifle with her, at the ready, in case he missed his target.

"How long before he wakes up?" inquired Raquel. She has decided to fix sandwiches for the group. It would be like a picnic, she figured. The forested view overlooking a remote trout stream and clear blue sky was magnificent. They could all sit on the verandah, relax, and unwind, before they got down to business. The sublime scent of evergreen trees was everywhere. Cedar, spruce, birch, wildflowers in bloom.

"Twenty or thirty minutes, tops," said Royce. He was serious.

Raquel found a thick slab of Canadian bacon and began frying slices of it in an iron skillet. She toasted bread. Alexis diced some Idaho potatoes and prepared to fry them as well, using the same skillet. Korn cut a large beefsteak tomato into thin portions, put them on a platter, with some shredded lettuce, pickles, and olives.

"Nothing better than BLTs on a cold, crisp day in the mountains," said Korn.

"I may follow the path through the woods to the stream and catch us some rainbow trout for dinner, a little later on in the day," said Royce.

"I found the wine cellar," said Alexis, bringing up a few bottles of the good stuff, French, Italian, and California's finest bubbly. She also put on a pot of coffee and made some fresh-squeezed orange juice. She opened a glass jug of ruby red grapefruit juice. Royce made omelets. The expansive A-frame cabin was well-lit with large picture windows, near the rough-hewn mahogany dining room table, long enough to seat a dozen guests, next to the well-provisioned kitchen.

"Nothing like a good, hearty breakfast to jumpstart your day," he said.

"Hungry?" Korn asked the overly sedated adventurer, slowly regaining consciousness. He gradually awoke, became more cognizant of his changing surroundings.

"Who the hell are you? What do you want from me?" asked Richard Ishtabuhla, visibly stirred, but not shaken.

"We were going to rob and kill you, but suddenly decided not to," said Royce, jovially, "when someone casually mentioned that you're worth more to us alive, Richard, the Lion-Heart."

"How do you know my true identity? And how did you find me?" asked Richard III. He was still feeling drowsy, apprehensive, and more uncomfortable by the minute. He felt exposed like a turtle turned on its back in the middle of the road, arms and legs flailing away. Or, rather, he would have been flailing away, had the flex-cuffs on his arms and legs been removed.

Along about that time Heather Meriwether was awoken by all the commotion emanating from the living room area downstairs. She put a warm terrycloth robe on over her pajamas and put on some fuzzy pink house slippers. She looked radiant, as if she had enjoyed a good night's sleep and had had the sweetest of dreams.

"Good morning everyone; Darling," she said, floating and lilting down the spiral staircase, as if she were walking onto a million-dollar yacht, or about to receive an Academy Awards presentation for Best Actress and Best Picture. "A toasted muffin and cream cheese for me, if you please, with OJ."

Richard relented. They untied his hands. They gave him a western omelet on fine china, a silver fork, and a cup of coffee. Everyone sat around the mahogany table to enjoy their breakfast. It improved Richard's mood and disposition immensely, to know that they would become good, close friends over the next several days, and the present company was infinitely more agreeable. He eventually forgave Heather for initially leading him to believe that they might have become the gruesome victims of a grisly home invasion. After a time, the now convivial party moved over to the seating area surrounding the fireplace.

"The first order of business is liberating our money-laundered funds from the principal branch of the 'Exchequer,' sometimes commonly referred to as the 'Cambio.' These businesses are never actually insured or even recognized by the FDIC, or any legitimate government for that matter. We have accrued over 30 million dollars in our account there and plan on withdrawing it all at once. Some might suggest that this amounts to wholesale robbery, but they're entitled to their opinion. We know better. The funds just move considerably faster through the Cambio system, than it does through normal banking channels, making it much more convenient for us to track, follow, and use," explained Korn.

"It's just that we need a legitimate, well-known, and well-respected businessman, such as yourself, to front the operation. Specifically, we need you to walk into the Cambio bright and early on Monday morning, complete the necessary withdrawal form, and exit with a certified check for the entire amount of funds that are in the account at present," said Royce. "What could be easier?"

"You want me to hand you a certified check worth 30 plus million dollars on Monday morning at the exact moment when I walk out of the Cambio with it in my hand. Sounds easy enough to me," said Richard III.

"Then we are going to buy an island," said Korn. "Unless you happen to already own one we can buy from you."

"As a matter of fact I own several islands. Since we have become formal business partners, you may pick and choose from among the ones you like best. I shall have my solicitor draw up the deed document details right away," stated Richard III. He was not in the least dissuaded from following through on a deal of which he wholeheartedly approved. As he well knows, you achieve a certain amount of independence owning your own island nation.

The two couples were subsequently invited to spend the night at the cabin to watch an "Ultra 4K" movie on digital DVD disk, instead of returning so late and disheveled to the Skiing Lodge. "I've never seen *Rosemary's Baby*," said Alexis Sue. "What is it about?"

After the planned Monday morning visit to the financial institution, Cornelius Korn cordially accepted the check from Richard Ishtabuhla, and deposited it across town into their trustworthy, large federally insured bank without further incident.

"You didn't have to come in with guns blazing, making demands, and tossing canisters of smoke into the lobby after all," exclaimed Richard III, obviously delighted by the recent turn of events. He had completely given up juggling grenades and chainsaws. He and Heather cheerfully returned to the secluded cabin, normalcy, and their fine new collection of wind-up tin soldiers and sophisticated yoyos, a gift. They were once young juvenile delinquents, wet behind the ears. Now, they have been made experienced, wise beyond their years. They are confident, expert, trustworthy. Knights of the round table. Teammates and dream dates.

CHAPTER 98

Book review of the novel

March Violets

by Philip Kerr, published in 1989.

The authorities can sugar-coat the truth, but they can't pull the wool over everyone's eyes.

Herr Gunther is the leading character in Philip Kerr's historically relevant detective novel, **March Violets**, published in 1989. He is a hard-hitting heavyweight, who would probably have prospered in the ring as a professional boxer. He can deliver a formidable knockout punch as well as the appropriate punchline to any spiced-up hamhock of a juicy, news story, depending on the right sort of circumstances. The setting of the novel is the risqué Berlin of the 1930s, after World War I ended and before the start of the second World War, just as Herr Hitler and the National Socialists were rising to power. We learn what happens when people believe everything a politician tells them. We learn what happens when the local yokels blindly trust in a totalitarian dictator, however charismatic he seems and appealing are his promises. Yet, there is no way to completely mask and disguise evil. They can sugarcoat the truth, but they can't pull the wool over everyone's eyes.

With a bustling metropolis of some 4 million people living in Berlin, Germany, at the time of chaotic social unrest due to terrible inflation, horrible poverty, high unemployment, and lack of opportunity, it is no wonder that there is a political upheaval going on in the country, marked by frustration, violence, and crime. Did I mention scarcity and hunger? Deplorable working conditions? That some malcontents have been beaten into submission and jailed in order to gain their full cooperation? Paradoxically, it is the perfect climate for law enforcement officers desiring job security. In fact, preserving state security is how Herr Gunther got his start, before going off on his own years later as a crackerjack independent private investigator. He had finally found the perfect job for an experienced police detective, who wants to be his own boss, have his own business, and work his own hours, without the massive confusion caused by an overstepping bureaucracy wearing uniforms and flaunting tremendous egos.

Herr Gunther is a little rough around the edges. He is neither very romantic, nor excessively sentimental. He may appear rude and crude, at times, but he is believable and trustworthy. It has been said on his behalf that he doesn't normally screw over his friends and informants. As an able-bodied, conscientious investigator, he follows police protocol down to the letter. The procedures he follows for solving crimes are as sound and solid as a silver dollar. He's competent and proficient at what he does, despite the fact that detective work can be dangerous at times. Some consider being shot at occasionally as an ordinary occupational hazard. In my opinion, it could be a real showstopper. Thus, he has developed a healthy skepticism when dealing with certain members of the public, particularly those who have something to hide or something up their sleeves. He most certainly needs a sixth sense, for the sake of his own safety, and a reliable back-up. As a hobby of sorts, he's become quite proficient at sniffing out corruption, something he's learned on the job with Berlin's criminal police, "Kripo." In the process of fine-tuning the skills of his profession, he has familiarized himself with the operations of several localized precincts of prolific, high-profile policing agencies, such as the state intelligence service, "Sipo," SS stormtroopers, and the infamous Gestapo. It is fascinating to see how the more dominant of their leaders with type-A personalities manage to interact with each other and still get things done. Take Goering and Himmler, for example.

Herr Gunther hasn't even scratched the surface, when it comes to wheeling and dealing with these megalomaniac military bureaucrat types, when he gets involved with and is forced to confront the most powerful, wealthy, and eccentric industrialist business executives that mankind has ever seen assembled together in one place on the whole continent of Europe. They are the types of bosses who absolutely must "have their cake and eat it too," in a manner of speaking, up to a point, until their house of cards comes tumbling down, when the war-mongering National Socialists ultimately wrestle power away from them and overwhelm most of their political rivals; the more moderate, watered-down version of Social Democrats, supporting social security and common sense; and the working-party Communists, supporting a curious mixture of egalitarianism and utilitarianism. It is insane the lengths to which the Nazis go, when the world finally realizes that there's no stopping the war machine, once it gains momentum. After reading such inciteful passages in the book, I felt the urge to get away from it all, drive into town to do some grocery shopping, and try to calm down a little. That stuff all happened in the distant past. It is all history now, dead and gone. It can't ever happen again. On the way, I rented a DVD home movie, *The Good Liar*. Later that evening, viewing the film footage gave me a splendid opportunity to put major events of the last century into proper perspective.

R. Royce merely tested the waters. He was not the type to debunk a myth. Expound upon a legend. Characterize great fiction. Tell tales of knights in shining armor. Or discuss heroism in depth. He wasn't trained or qualified to do any of that. What he could do was relate in simple, honest terms what happened on the night of October 2, 2001, a palindrome of a date. Not that very long ago, in a pleasant, out of the way place off the beaten path. He was on a long journey, far away from home. Camping out by the lake. He'd finished working on a construction project taking several months, saved his money, and decided to take a well-earned vacation for a couple of weeks, before embarking on a new venture. Maybe, see the sights and scenery. Relax and unwind from the pressures imposed on him by the job, and, in general, by the obligations of everyday existence.

He thought about the aviation unit in the Middle East, with whom he'd served. It was a detachment of Huey helicopters, used for transporting supplies to the Ranger or Delta units in the vicinity, and for purposes of medical evacuation. The unit was highly mobile and maneuverable, but ostensibly stationed at an undisclosed location somewhere in the middle of the desert. Nothing was there but wind and sand; blazing sunshine during the day; chilly, cloudless, starry nights. It was isolated and remote. They didn't anticipate visitors. The area was not identified on any map, but they had GPS and could pinpoint exactly where they were with grid coordinates from a satellite. The mission was top secret and none of them were allowed to tell outsiders which country boundaries they had breached. Mum was the word on that sensitive subject.

Royce had been lately assigned the task of latrine duty. It's a dirty job, but somebody has to do it, as they say. He cordoned off a small area about 75 feet downhill and downwind from their exercise and sleeping quarters areas, and began digging two holes the size and depth of foxholes. Next, he constructed two wooden frames which he situated over the holes. Essentially, what he'd built was two outhouses, only the surrounding walls were made of tent canvas, instead of wooden boards, for quick and easy set-up and even faster tear-down removal. He'd inherited the job from his predecessor, and predecessors before him, who'd completed their tours of duty, and returned stateside.

One interesting feature of desert latrine duty was the unit traditionally planted two or three trees beside each outhouse for posterity. Once the trees began to grow and prosper, the unit would find a new location and move the unit there. They were a nomadic, mobile outfit. They would continue to reconnoiter, reconnaissance, rendezvous; and do what they normally did elsewhere.

Whenever the unit had an important VIP, or other high-ranking guest arrive, they would routinely break camp and move to a past location, where the unit had once been previously located perhaps years ago, and set up the camp there. Then, they would bring out a wide, comfortable hammock made of sturdy knotted rope, attach the connecting end-loops to two of the large tree trunks growing there and invite the VIP over for a siesta. He could have a nice relaxing nap beneath the welcoming shade of the trees. Swaying ever so gently to sleep, cooled by a fresh, invigorating breeze, he was able to forget all of his problems, cares, and concerns for a while. When he awoke, he would be all rested and refreshed. By and by, nighttime operations would commence. Most everyone else tried their best to sleep on the shifting sands in camouflaged sleeping bags, in the area and along the perimeter of the bivouac area. Everyone except for the security detail. They were on high alert.

On that particular October night in 2001, Royce strolled along a path beside the lake, eventually climbing to the summit of the hill and steep bluff overlooking the lake. It was a moonlit night and all was peaceful and quiet, except for an occasional fish leaping up out of the water, causing the sound of a splash.

Up ahead, he'd noticed a tan four-door sedan. Someone had parked the automobile on the hilltop, overlooking Lovers' Leap, a popular summer destination for the younger set on Saturday night. But summer was over. The kids are all back home with parents, at school-sponsored sporting events, or away in their dorms at college.

What do have we here? thought Royce. Someone was dragging a body out of the front seat of the vehicle toward the cliff. He'd lifted and heaved it over the edge, and the body dropped into the deep end of the lake directly below, right before Royce's very eyes. The stranger hastily returned to the car, hopped in, and sped away. Royce immediately reacted to the situation that played out before him.

He ran up the path and leaped into the depths of the lake after the body, falling feet-first near the center of the big splash it created, but not too close. Reaching and searching about, he found the body quickly, grabbed hold of it tightly, and propelled them both to the surface of the water. He swam for the shoreline with the body in tow, gasping for breath.

The girl he'd found was alive and breathing after all she'd been through that night. Her hands and feet had been bound, but she was going to be okay. He untied her, and sat with her on the beach until she began to recover. His camp was only a short distance away, so he covered her with dry leaves in order to keep her warm, and told her to wait. He ran to his vehicle and returned with warm blankets, pants, a shirt, and a towel. He had a warm thermos with coffee. She drank from the thermos cup.

"What's going on?" asked Royce, obviously concerned. "Jealous boyfriend?"

"It was a bad deal all the way around," said Raquel. "They picked an incompetent two-bit hoodlum to conduct a Mafia-style hit."

"We'd better get you home immediately," said Royce. "Do you want me to call the police for you?"

"No, it's high time I left town anyway," said Raquel. She was adamant. "You aren't from around these parts, are you?"

"Just passing through," said Royce. It is beginning to look like he'd found himself a new girlfriend. Fate must have interceded on behalf of both of them.

"Won't take me long to pack up, and then we can skip town," said Raquel, a matter of fact. "You don't mind the company, do you?" She was beautiful and vivacious. He did not object to her game plan.

"You can tag along, if you want," said Royce. "I was planning on leaving town in the morning, anyway."

"Do you think we're compatible?" she asked, searchingly. She didn't have a lot of viable options open to her at present.

"Must be love at first sight," said Royce. "We're can't continue meeting like this, though, when we actually start dating." He didn't have anything better to do than get involved with a perfect stranger.

"I travel light," said Raquel. "One medium suitcase of personal effects."

Of course, she had one more stop to make before leaving town. Apparently, unbeknownst to her, the store manager for whom Raquel had worked part-time for only about two weeks' time, filling in for a friend, who'd gone on vacation, had gotten himself involved in a big business deal with gemstone distributors from Mexico, who'd sold him a hundred thousand dollars' worth of cut diamonds, rubies, emeralds, citrines, topazes, and fire opals. The items were supposed to be discretely placed inside a cardboard box normally containing glass jars of picante sauce. Mild, spicy, and hot. Raquel slid the tow dolly underneath the pallet, stacked with cartons of picante sauce, from a delivery truck backed up to the warehouse dock, and began to pull it inside the storeroom, where the salesman and the store manager had been anxiously waiting to receive the products, when she noticed that there was a couple of extra cartons in the nose area of the box-van. From the advertising, she saw that the items were described as "guacamole salsa," not the picante sauce they'd ordered, and naturally thought that they were free complimentary samples given to the store manager for generating new sales orders. She set the two cartons aside and forgot all about them. Then, she pulled the pallets of picante sauce forward into the storeroom on the tow dolly. The store manager and salesman began to count the cartons of picante sauce and opened a few boxes for quality assurance, which is when they eventually discovered that the cut stones they were expecting to find had not been placed inside any of the cartons of picante sauce. The cut stones had gone missing to the chagrin of both parties. Meanwhile Raquel went back to place the two boxes of guacamole product in the sample cage for temporary storage. It was a variety of imported guacamole salsa in 16-ounce glass jars. She would later discover that this particular brand of salsa tastes absolutely delicious when topping the large, warm, well-seasoned, fried potato wedges prepared daily by the deli and offered for public consumption.

Along about that time, Raquel overheard an argument ensue between the store manager and the salesman about some missing rocks. The argument almost led to violence. The manager was tempted to shoot and kill the robber salesman on the spot. Fortunately, the two men came to a mutual agreement. They decided to settle the matter the next day, when the salesman would have more of an opportunity calm down a little and look into the matter further. Maybe his sales team had neglected to transport the gemstones with this particular shipment of picante sauce. Maybe they wanted to be sure their client had the cash first.

Before closing that night, Raquel went into the caged storage to examine the new product samples and decided to taste-test the guacamole sauce herself. When she did so, she noticed that someone had placed several sealed plastic baggies of loose, cut gemstones that looked all too real, inside one of the cartons. Curious and enterprising girl that she was, she would soon return and replace the baggies of genuine gemstones with baggies containing colorful plastic beads, the type of which may be readily and cheaply obtained from a hobby shop or the fabric section of any department store, until she could find out exactly what was going on here. They were supposed to be selling groceries, not precious gemstones, potentially worth millions.

The store manager flew off the handle with rage when he discovered the plastic beads placed in the cartons of guacamole sauce early the next day. Late that evening, he had an emotionally charged confrontation with his temporary, part-time shop-clerk, Raquel, became terribly enraged all over again, and decided to throw her off the cliff at Lovers' Leap to put an end to the matter once and for all. It wasn't the most rational decision he'd ever made, or thing he could have done.

"Want to make a sound investment?" inquired Raquel, cautiously. Royce looked like the type who could be trusted.

"Sure," said Royce. "Is there any risk involved?"

"Not much. I had to contact a wholesaler in Mexico about the parcel of jewels he recently sold us, so that he wouldn't worry about receiving his payment in full," said Raquel. She showed him the gemstones.

"A good friend of mine is always in the market for quality merchandise," said Royce, reassuring her. He called Cornelius Korn on his cellular telephone, and pressed on the speaker-phone button. A few days later they drove to his condominium in the Rocky Mountains.

"Delighted to finally meet you, Raquel," said Korn. "You will be pleased to know that your business associate from Mexico has already been paid in full." She handed him the gemstones, for which she received a generous finders' fee and an invoiced receipt.

"Looks like we're in business together," said Royce.

CHAPTER 99

Book review of the collection of short stories

Blow-Up and Other Stories

by Julio Cortazar, published in 1967,
translated by Paul Blackburn.

Basic component stereo set: pre-amp, power amplifier, turntable, speakers.
   Basic camera outfit: 35mm single lens reflex, 50mm lens with polarizing filter, extra 50-160mm telephoto lens, tripod. Quiet on the set. Sound, action, camera. Roll 'em.

The gist of each story in Julio Cortazar's collection of 15 superb short stories, ***Blow-Up and Other Stories***, published in 1967, may be succinctly expressed in a single sentence or a simple phrase, as follows:

1. "Axolotl" — The most dangerous creature from the ocean isn't a lionfish, an octopus, or a non-aggressive, striped sea krait.

2. "House Taken Over" — More scary, supernatural, paranormal activity, the government or some pesky neighbors moving in.

3. "The Distances" — They go on a honeymoon in Hungary, but she has a secret agenda.

4. "The Idol of the Cyclades" — They dig up a cursed archeological artifact.

5. "Letter to a Lady in Paris" — Raising rabbits is simple and easy.

6. "A Yellow Flower" — Contemporary thoughts on reincarnation.

7. "Continuity of Parks" — Perhaps the most baffling story in the collection holds the key to solving the mystery in another one.

8. "The Night Face Up" — Commuting to work on a motorcycle, he winds up in the hospital, chased by Aztec warriors.

9. "Bestiary" — A little girl spends her summer vacation in Argentina with a family of zoologist caretakers.

10. "The Gates of Heaven" — Best friends reminisce about ballroom dancing and catch "Saturday Night Fever."

11. "Blow-Up" — An amateur photographer captures a scene in the park with his trusty 35mm SLR that might have made the cover of "Time" magazine.

12. "End of the Game" — A game of Charades for youths with big dreams.

13. "At Your Service" — Unusual temporary employment opportunities.

14. "The Pursuer" — A biographer-critic and a famous musician come to terms.

15. "Secret Weapons" — A love story with a twist of lemon and a bitter remorse.

These stories remind me of a simpler time in my life and my youth, when music and photography captured the best moments of my college years. A song, an image. They bring back loads of memories. I remember having lived in a three story, red brick fraternity house one summer and spent every nickel I had on a new component stereo. The components included a loud, four-channel, 60 watts per channel, Pioneer integrated amplifier with a built-in frequency equalizer; a good-quality 33 rpm-LP album turntable, with a steady, solid aluminum platter, an anti-skate device, and a Shure diamond-tipped cartridge; and four large, walnut-enclosed, three-way Altec Lansing speakers, each one having a bass, mid-range, and tweeter. The other students in the building used to drop by bringing records to test out on the sound machine. Some even brought their musical instruments to accompany the recorded music. Those were fun times. The best of times.

Wanted to borrow a camera, go out and take some pictures. Basic camera outfit: 35mm single lens reflex, 50mm lens with polarizing filter, extra 50-160mm telephoto lens, tripod. "Quiet on the set. Sound, camera, action. Roll 'em." We shall see what develops.

During those years, the 1970s, I often enjoyed going out and watching foreign movies. I happened to catch one with the title *Blow-Up*. Recreation Services would play films in the Student Union cafeteria on weekends, and several of us would go see them once in a while. Interesting stuff, but life goes on. We move on and grow up so fast. Go our separate ways.

"Well, I laid around and played around in this home town of mine. Summer's come and gone. I must be truckin' on. Truckin' on, truckin' on."

"Aberdeen. Aberdeen. Prettiest town that I've ever seen was Aberdeen, Aberdeen. My Aberdeen. Prettiest girl that I've ever known was Abby Marlene, my Abby Marlene. Abigail Marlene." I digress.

Eventually, the movies went from VHS tapes and players to DVD disks and digital devices, for home viewing. Years ago, I purchased *Blow-Up* on DVD, but never got around to watching the movie. Now, what seems like 40 years later, and I just pulled the disk out of a drawer in the garage, unviewed, the cellophane package never even opened, this morning and put it by the television set. Having finished reading the *Blow-Up* stories in e-book reader format, I planned on watching the movie version later today. A plethora of ideas already spring to mind about how the book must have made an impact and had a profound influence on the film producers, director, and actors. Possibly, on the audience, as well.

What if you can create a fictional archetype character in your film from combining the traits, personalities, tendencies, and predilections exhibited and shared by the narrator and leading characters in the story book of one of your favorite authors; Julio Cortazar, for example, and incorporate them into the film of the same exact title, or at least a similar one? You begin to sense how the stories interrelate among themselves and can then influence the film in so many subtle ways. You think it would be a wonderful exercise to cultivate your imagination. What kind of larger than life character would you have created?

Perhaps he is a complicated, or conflicted character, who appears disjunct, disconnected, on the outside looking in, or on the inside looking outward, but never totally, intimately involved with his subject; always chasing pipe dreams, forever seeking escape, but never achieving full release from his bonds. He is not a contented individual, someone seated naturally beside the fireplace, where the home fires are warmly burning, delivering in the joyous holidays with family and close friends bearing gifts, decorations, and sweets. No, this is not the hallmark of his success story. He is the type who would annihilate his very own existence, if he thought he could get at the kernel of truth. But when he finally arrives at the truth, he discovers a deeper meaning. All he sees is lies and deception up to that point. He does not live in a happy place, at least not in the book of short stories envisioning his own private purgatory. You might not want him for a friend either, once you've seen how he behaves in the film.

He doesn't have many friends. He doesn't need them. He doesn't want to get close to anyone. He doesn't want anyone to get close to him. He's a loner. He immerses himself in his work. He can't "see the forest for the trees." He is more of a nihilist, than one approaching from a narcissistic point of view. He should have put things into proper perspective. He makes people angry. He must have been a difficult child, but neither particularly artistically, nor autistically inclined. He never really wanted to grow into maturity. He always did things his way. Went off on a tangent. That's the cold, hard, calculated assessment of the situation as I see it unfolding. Plus, he has destructive tendencies. And yet, he wants to stay aloof and remain unaffected by the changing circumstances surrounding him and an increasingly constricting environment in which he suddenly finds himself. To summarize, he is as solid as the Rock of Gibraltar, reminiscent of a "Simon and Garfunkel" song about naturally dense, earthy material which has risen up out of the ocean. He's a prince among the populace.

Preparation is the key, I think. I've read the *Blow-Up* stories and found that the author's writing is fluid and dynamic enough to make it harrowingly interesting. It captures the imagination. It flows spontaneously, like a rapidly flowing river cascading down the mountainside over large, rounded smooth, granite rocks. I'd like to think that I can relate to a little of what he was trying to write about, but I am not too sure about that. The plot is too vague and leaves me in the dark. Watching the DVD version is next on the antique bucket list, to see how they compare and contrast, and how much of the re-run I can remember.

I saw the movie yesterday afternoon and recollected some of the scenes quite well, and many of the details that were fuzzy in my mind, are now much clearer. I see how the book might have once inspired the film, but they are really two entirely different stories, with different principal characters and locations. One is an obviously highly educated professional in foreign service, and an amateur photographer on the side, but competent and talented, a good Samaritan. The other is an experienced professional fashion photographer, who would rather go on an undercover assignment as a hard-hitting photojournalist, exposing social injustice. The "birds" don't do that much for him anymore. He is focused. The other is somewhat disillusioned. Both get more than they bargain for, when a shady deal takes on a more sinister tone.

R. Royce strikes up the band. He had been eavesdropping on the neighbors for the past three days, alternating between a pair of high-powered, low-light hunting binoculars and a celestial telescope. He could tell they were up to no good. They were about to make their move, judging by the fact that they put their guns on the table by the sofa, and loaded them. They were not to be trifled with in their present state of mind. Not a good time to stroll over, introduce himself, and borrow a cup of sugar. He sensed danger. They put on their hats, jackets and overcoats, and appeared ready to depart.

His telephone began to ring, and Royce answered it right away. His longtime friend and business associate was calling for a progress report. He was awaiting further instructions.

"They're getting ready to move," said Royce. Two vehicles, both four doors. One is a tan Mercury Marquis. The other is a gray Chevy Impala. I texted you the plate numbers.

"We're on the way," replied Cornelius Korn, his cohort. Alexis Sue Shell was in the cherry-red Mustang with him. They began tailing the Mercury.

"We'll follow the Impala," said Royce. Raquel Remington was with him in their car, a green Dodge Charger. She was ready to pounce. Royce was not so sure of himself.

They proceeded south on Harry Hines Boulevard and ended up at the railyard, keeping back at a safe distance. What were the perpetrators up to? They wondered. It would be illegal, whatever it was, they surmised.

Turns out, they were after a brand spanking new, gleaming, shiny red firetruck. Apparently one of the rural area Volunteer Fire Departments had been in serious need of a new hose and ladder truck for quite some time and didn't have the resources necessary to just go out and purchase one, not even a used one. They can be quite expensive, at around $850,000 a pop. So, Billy Bob, Bubba, Ted, and Fred stepped up to the plate and decided to find them a firetruck on their own and sell it to the volunteers really cheap. Seemed to make sense at the time.

They collected the keys and documents from the rail foreman, and drove the firetruck away, without much fanfare or any complications. Dallas Firemen were expected to collect the vehicle that very afternoon. The thieves just needed to present a certified check for the shipping charges and collect their new truck. It was a piece of cake.

Royce followed the firetruck and the Impala shotgun vehicle. Korn continued to shadow the Mercury. Bob returned the Mercury to their house in the city without incident. Bubba and Fred drove the firetruck, and Ted drove the Mercury in a westerly direction across town and out into Denton County at a leisurely pace, which didn't necessitate a hot pursuit on the part of Royce and Raquel. It didn't take a whiz kid to figure out where the Possum Kingdom boys were going with this. Bubba and Ted collected a nylon duffle bag containing bundles of cash from the Volunteers who shall forever remain anonymous, and they immediately left the area in the Impala, the deal completed to the satisfaction of both parties.

The reward wasn't much for recovering the stolen firetruck, but it was significant enough for a sizable down-payment on a good pre-owned one. The volunteer fire department in rural Montague County appreciated the kind gesture on the part of Cornelius Korn.

"How come we made so much money on a deal that went sour so fast?" inquired Royce, when Korn handed over a couple of bundles of cash to each of them.

"Bowie managed to repossess Alvord's firetruck, when their gas-wells came in unexpectedly," Korn explained. "With the newly generated tax revenues they represent, both communities were able to purchase new firetrucks. We happened to be in a position to offer them the second firetruck at a discount."

"It pays to be in the right place at the right time," said Alexis Sue.

"I know where we can get a good deal on a new road-grader," said Raquel. "Some of the streets around here have pot-holes and need repaving."

CHAPTER 100

Book review of

Conquistador

An historical account of the life and times of Hernan Cortes, written by Buddy Levy and published in 2008.

> *Cortes lays deep in a coma. The loss of Montezuma's treasured friendship weighs heavily on his mind.*
>
> *Driving the party wild, dancing around a huge bonfire, beating war drums, chanting banana banana beer; banana banana beer; beer beer banana; beer beer banana; banana banana banana, they eventually ran out of beer and bananas.*

Buddy Levy has written quite an ambitious historical piece in ***Conquistador***, which was published in 2008. The book chronicles the life and times of Hernan Cortes, who lived in the early 1500s, and was in the prime of his life. As some readers may already be aware, he was an early Spanish explorer who sailed to the New World in search of adventure, fame, and fortune. Although he was initially sponsored by the Governor of Cuba, Diego Velasquez, other powerful businessmen, such as his own wealthy father, and a good number of investors, Cortes generally acted independently on behalf of the greater common good; namely, that of the sovereign of their nation, King Charles V of Spain. In doing so, he had a marked tendency to behave as an ambitious upstart and an adept social climber, who well understood his place in society and in the larger scheme of European politics at the same time; yet, by the same token, he acted on his own recognizance in the capacity of a completely dedicated legal professional and freelance diplomat. In short, he became a self-appointed self-made man in the capacity of a high-ranking politician, if not a demigod, having proven himself on numerous occasions as a highly charged emissary, judge advocate, and competent military commander, over the years. His most immediate, lofty goal was to claim "Mesoamerica" for Spain, and convert its people into up-standing, law-abiding citizens, devout Christians, and good taxpayers. But, as Cortes discovered the hard way, "this was easier said, than done."

Fortunately for him, Cortes met a great many proactive and influential people along the way who would contribute to helping him realize his goals and ambitions. A long list of these people would have to include the following, and many others besides:

Antonio de Alaminos, the ship's navigator; Diego Velasquez, Cortes's benefactor; Pedro de Alvarado, ship's captain; Melchior, Mayan interpreter; Bernal Diaz, expedition journalist; Jeronimo de Aguilar, priest and translator; Malinche, interpreter; Cuitlalpitoc, Aztec chief; Ambassador Tendile, Aztec representative; Tlacochcalcatl, Totonac chief; Olintetl, Xocotlan chief; Xicotenga, Tlaxcalan chief; Father Olmeda, counselor; Cacama, King of Texcoco and Montezuma's nephew; Montezuma, Aztec emperor; Juan Velasquez de Leon, Spanish military leader; Gonzalo Sandoval, Spanish military leader; Diego de Ordaz, Spanish military leader; Martin Lopez, carpenter and shipbuilder; Panfilo Narvaez, Spanish military leader; Cuitlahuac, Aztec chief, ruler; Matlatzincatzin, Aztec chief; Maxixcatzin, Hueyotlipan chief; Andres de Duero, Spanish investor and friend; Franciso de Eguia, African ship's porter; Catalina Suarez Mercaida Cortes, Hernan Cortes's wife; Cuauhtemoc, the 8th Aztec emperor; Coanacochzin, King of Texcoco; Ixtlilxochitl, Aztec chief, Montezuma's nephew, ruler; Julian de Alderete, Royal Fifth treasurer; Antonio de Villafana, Spanish soldier; Cristobal de Olea, Spanish soldier; Cristobal de Olid, Spanish military commander; Charles V, King of Spain, Holy Roman Emperor; Juan de Fonseca, the Bishop of Burgos; Alonso Garcia Bravo, architect; Don Pedro Montezuma, Mexico City administrator, surviving son of Montezuma; Jean Florin, French pirate; and Martin Cortes, son of Hernan Cortes and Dona Maria Malinche.

I know, the list doesn't exactly read like the cast of characters in your typical Shakespearean play, but the contributions they make to the book is why it is so particularly interesting. You want to go on vacation and visit some of the places for yourself, see their museums, take a closer look at their statues, meet these people in person.

Mitigating and aggravating circumstances, which might have assisted or impeded the progress Cortes was making toward achieving his goals include the following, and many others besides:

Smoking and actively erupting volcanoes in the region; the Aztec and other Indian practices of making human sacrifices for religious purposes; conflicts caused by warring tribes and unwavering factionalism; the harsh, diverse weather patterns, whereby the Spaniards were freezing cold in the mountains one day, and in stifling hot and humid conditions in the low-lying plains on the next; a preponderance of mosquitos and malaria; the sudden exposure of the local inhabitants to smallpox by infected crewmembers disembarking from the vessels of the Spanish armada; the shocking introduction of Christianity to the unsuspecting Mesoamerican population at large; the wide variety of wildlife, dangerous, exotic animals, birds, flora, and fauna; the resounding clash of Spanish and Aztec cultures; the bizarre presence of Aztec gods; and shortages of fresh drinking water.

Pronunciation is the least of our concerns over the many names of persons, places, and gods encountered upon reading the book, which is enough to slow down the average reader, who wants to persevere nonetheless in making a gallant attempt at conquering the mystery that surrounds the history being lavishly portrayed; its heritage so rich and meaningful. The reader wants nothing better than to gain a precise understanding of what actually happened in Mesoamerica, and who exactly were the aggressors, responsible for causing such terrible transgressions and calamities. The "few, proud, and brave" claiming knowledge of the truth may purposefully state, perhaps with a vengeance, that it was a complicated, unchecked chain of events that ultimately led to an inevitable conclusion.

I wonder what Cortes and Montezuma might have done differently in order to alter the course of human history any further. If that were even possible. What could they have done to avoid so much of the brutality and hostility, chaos and devastation, the murder and intrigue?

First of all, Montezuma made the drastic mistake of trusting the Spaniards and cordially inviting them into his happy home; men, who were hell-bent on conquering his nation and taking all of the vast treasure for themselves, given the opportunity.

Secondly, Montezuma made the drastic mistake of blindly trusting the highly suspect and superstitious Aztec Priesthood for divine guidance and advice, most notably those of whom may have had absolutely no idea whatsoever as to what the intelligent life is and what it involves that rules the universe. Obviously, they never would in their bleak, dismal short-lived future, whereby there is only the power struggle between mere mortal men on earth that seems to matter. Some may suggest, that these spiritual guides must have been total frauds and pretenders, "fruits and nuts," worshipping and idolizing ferocious predatory animal spirits, such as the imaginary jaguar, eagle, and poisonous snake creatures. I wouldn't know for sure, myself, but being invited to dinner, and then finding myself battered, breaded, and boiling in oil in a large, round, iron cauldron over a hot-burning fire would have convinced me otherwise of the soundness of their religious beliefs.

I, for one, would have liked to have read that Leonardo de Vinci was among the crew of new arrivals in Hernan Cortes's party to Tenochtitlan. A practical, scientific man, he would have seen right away that if the loyal Aztecs were bound and determined to throw people off of their temple rooftops as a mere matter of routine, he might at least give them a fighting chance by fitting them out with hang-gliders beforehand, so they could make a fortuitous attempt at flying to safety; thus, testing out a few of his theories about full-fledged flight on the "Aztec Air Force."

Naturally, I continue to ponder on Hernan Cortes's role in the grand scheme of things as well. He could have done things radically different himself. An acting scene from a possible future Broadway play, based on the book, comes to mind:

"Cortes lays deep in a coma. The loss of Montezuma's treasured friendship weighs heavily on his mind."

Next, I begin to consider the thousands upon thousands of misguided, restless natives wandering around in the wilderness. They are homeless, frightened refugees. What would they have done differently if they truly had had a choice, free will, and a mind of their own? Conduct poetry in motion? Face the music like the good community college brass band they emulate, when their very lives depended on it?

"Driving the party wild, dancing around a huge bonfire, beating war drums, chanting banana banana beer; banana banana beer; beer beer banana; beer beer banana; banana banana banana, they eventually run out of beer and bananas. They roam around in the darkness, and yet, miraculously, are no longer afraid."

From where in the world did they originate? Speculating, I would tend to hazard an educated guess that some eons ago, perhaps millions and millions of years ago, when South America and Africa were part of the same continent, many of the people there had lived in the African part, and some lived in the far western part, which just so happened to have quaked, crumbled, and broken off in a great cataclysmic, geological rift from the main continent. It slowly began to float and drift across the vast Atlantic Ocean, and gradually formed its very own, isolated continent, having grinded to a complete stop due to massive amounts of heat and friction; reconnected and fused with the solid rock shelf lying just above the earth's molten lava core at its present location.

Much later on, probably at some time during the ice age, a great many of the peoples living in this new continent of South America began to migrate northward toward tropical Central America, where the climate was much warmer and food was plentiful. There they settled and there they lived out their lives, for generations upon generations. Primitive, half-naked and unashamed, these lost and abandoned, extended families could have been escapees from Moorish, African, Indian, Egyptian, and other desert tribes. Or, then again, I could be completely mistaken. Maybe they did drop out of the sky. The results of those DNA tests have not come in.

R. Royce is looking for answers. He wants to buy a bass boat for backwater and lake fishing, but he is uncertain as to which manufacturer's brand he prefers, "Bass-tracker" or "Ranger." He considers the optimal shape of the hull, the boat lengths, horse-power, "Mercury" and "Evinrude" motors, canopy style. He likes the idea of a canvas Bimini top above the steering wheel console.

He would settle for twin-engine outboards, swivel chairs on pedestals, a flat-top deck, with the look and stability of an aircraft carrier, and stainless steel railings all around the bow, so he wouldn't suddenly take the plunge into the lake if the water becomes too choppy due to inclement weather, or go overboard in the event a cresting wave comes sweeping over the deck, while he was trying to reel in a fish.

"Let's go to Florida and go fishing in the ocean," said Cornelius Korn, his friend of many years and longtime business associate.

"I haven't ever thought about buying an oceangoing yacht," replied Royce. "Aren't they expensive?"

"They can be. Buy a big enough boat, and you can sink your entire life savings into it," said Korn. "Or, we could just go to one of the marinas and charter a tall cabin cruiser, one that's completely stocked with food, beverages, fishing poles, and bait."

"We can always go out for a day trip and see how well we like it," said Royce. He suddenly became animated and enthusiastic about the prospect."

"There are plenty of good resort hotels nearby where we can stay in the meantime," said Korn. "If we find out that the life of ocean fishermen appeals to us, we might want to sail down to Belize or Mexico for marlin and tuna."

"We'll fly the girls down to Vera Cruz or Belize City for a vacation, upon our arrival," said Royce. He was all aboard now with the plan.

What Korn had judiciously failed to mention was the fact that sailing the vessel to Central America was actually going to be their latest job assignment. Their task was to deliver a newly purchased yacht, imported directly from the manufacturer in South Korea, which had recently arrived at the Port of Dodge Island in Miami, Florida, promptly to its ultimate destination and new owner in Vera Cruz, Mexico.

"We'll just hug the coastline in a southerly direction, when we cross the Gulf," said the Skipper, Captain Francis Drake. "After we get in a few days of good fishing for marlin, grouper, and red snapper."

"Of course, we have to make sure the 'Donna Maria' is seaworthy," said Royce. He was eager to reel in his very first large ocean fish.

Unfortunately, the vessel was taken over by three armed pirates intercepting them with a cigarette speedboat on the high seas just off the southeastern coast of Florida before they could catch a single fish. They meant to rob Royce, Korn, and the good Captain of their valuables, throw them overboard, and steal away with their vessel. It was not a pretty picture that was developing.

"Why don't you let me fix you a nice lunch before you depart?" offered Korn, cordially. "I make a sensational margarita and an equally superb daquiri."

"What do you say? Take the cash, watches, and jewelry. Leave us the life-raft," suggested Royce. He sounded convincing. "We won't tell anybody what happened. The yacht is fully insured. Everybody wins."

"Take the ship. It's brand new. Worth a fortune," said the Captain, pleading for his life. "Put on a coat of new paint, fiberglass, redesign the hull and interior. Reregister the vessel in Panama. Nobody will recognize the old girl."

Along about that time something really strange and bizarre happened. A large marlin leaped up over the back starboard side of the ship and would have landed on the deck, had not one of the pirates been standing directly in the path of its trajectory. Tragically he was run-through by the swordfish's long, sharp-pointed sword and pinned solidly to the nicely lacquered mahogany deck, while the big fish flopped around trying to free itself from its predicament. The men stood by aghast, not knowing exactly what to do to save the man's life. The sword and teeth had gored a large gaping hole in the middle of the man's chest. He was bleeding profusely. The other pirates could not react quickly enough as Royce and Korn each brandished matching .357 caliber, stainless-steel, magnum revolvers and knocked the men unconscious. They bound and gagged the two men. They could do nothing for the third pirate. He had expired quite suddenly from shock and blood-loss. The quick-reacting Captain grabbed a gaff hook off the wall and subdued the large marlin, having repeatedly punctured its brain with the hook and holding on for dear life, until it too expired.

"Our fish only weighed 600 pounds, said the Captain, modestly. "The largest of the marlins around here usually weigh in at a hefty 800 to 900 pounds." The three fishermen gained the full cooperation of the two remaining pirates and had them clean the fish, cut it into fillets, package the pieces in large zip-lock freezer bags, and transfer them into the cold-storage unit for another, much more pleasant, auspicious occasion.

"Have you ever considered going into another line of work?" Korn asked the two would-be pirates. He proceeded to actively engage the men in a meaningful conversation which lasted more than an hour and a half, during which time they returned all of the items and cash that was stolen. They provided the fishermen with all of the requested information as to their identities, where they lived, and where they worked. Then, they washed away "the blood of the lamb." They removed the dead body from the yacht and put it on their cigarette boat.

"I think they've learned their lesson," said the Captain. He felt sorry for the two fellows, having heard the pathetically sad, terrible story of their lives. They had obviously gone wrong as teenagers, had never been caught before today, but wanted an opportunity to change for the better, perhaps the only chance they would ever get in order to redeem themselves. They were definitely up for rehabilitation. So, Royce and Korn decided to let them go.

"Accidents happen," said Raquel Remington, somberly, when the party met up a few short weeks later to celebrate the successful delivery of the Donna Maria to its rightful, proud new owner in Belize. She was Royce's significant other and their full-fledged business associate.

"I've never caught so may fish in my life," exclaimed Royce.

"Me neither," admitted Korn. He had not only insured delivery of the vessel, but he also functioned as the yacht broker who sold the vessel, and quite a few others besides over the years.

"The funds have been electronically transferred to our bank accounts early this morning," reported Alexis Sue Shell, the fourth member of the party, Cornelius Korn's significant other and formal business partner.

CHAPTER 101

Review of the nonfictional book about
an investment capitalist,

Red Notice

by Bill Browder, published in 2015.

A perfectly legal & legitimate way of raising capital.
  Born with a silver spoon in his mouth, holding on for dear life to his parents' coat tails and apron strings, until he manages to inherit a great deal of money and put it to work for him? I don't think so.

Red Notice is a nonfictional, autobiographical account of an American investment capitalist who acquires a British passport and freely conducts business in Russia, by Bill Browder himself, written in 2015. He manages a lucrative investment fund and tells about the ups and downs involved in the world of high finance.

Meet Bill. Bill is in emerging markets. He is an affable people person. He evaluates their abilities for achieving lofty goals. He avidly encourages and enables qualified individuals with the vision to do their jobs better. Likewise, he studies prospective businesses from developing nations. He generates a short list of them for further consideration, based on certain economic criteria. Finally, he invests in the few remaining companies from the ones selected, those which he deems most worthy. As it must have been suggested on more than one occasion, he produces the best results when he matches the most talented personnel with companies demonstrating the most unlimited potential for success and having vast resources. The truth of the matter is, he manages to raise a tremendous amount of capital for the businesses he turns around and makes them incredibly profitable. Plus, it's all perfectly legal and legitimate.

Bill is very perceptive. Although, he notices an irregularity here and there, identifies an inconsistency once in a while, introduces a sticking point into the mix, and generates a controversy, he, almost miraculously, achieves guaranteed results. Thus, he makes a ton of money for his clients. As naive as he is perceived to be at this particular point in time, Bill has come to learn that if you throw enough money at a problem, no matter however large, complicated, and insurmountable it may appear, the problem eventually goes away. Then, the fascinating theory of large numbers comes into play. The good life reveals itself with infinite possibilities and his mega-fund proves immeasurably profitable.

"Who says, 'Money doesn't grow on trees'?" some investors inquire.

Due to the unpredictable nature of economic forces beyond his control, however, he becomes a billionaire one day, and seems practically broke the next. "Looks can be deceiving. The figures don't lie. It just doesn't compute," they rationalize, and try to explain what happened. He keeps chipping away at the old rock.

"Can't we just make it all go away?" he must have wondered at some point, when the pressure becomes too great and unbearable. "No strings attached."

Unfortunately, to make matters even worse, Bill also learns after a number of years of solid experience in the field, and because of his finely tuned sense of expertise in "the school of hard knocks," that being rich is no substitute for being endowed with both wealth and power. Particularly, when the powerful can take all of the money away from the rich at any time it serves their purpose. Thus, Bill suddenly becomes motivated by the politics of the situation in which he found himself dramatically immersed, but with drastic consequences, and to which he was forever more inextricably connected. In other words, he can't ever get out of that contract.

The framers of our Constitution wouldn't believe where they were going with this piece of legislation, I thought to myself, having read through three-quarters of the book. *Apply enough heat and pressure to an ordinary lump of coal, and you think you'd eventually get a diamond.*

"Who's proselytizing now?" I wonder.

R. Royce remembers what his father told him many years ago, in the early springtime of the year, the last time he saw him: "You have a good heart." They had been seated on two of the orange vinyl rocking chairs located in the sheltered concrete pad enclosure that doubled as a back porch area and a secure bunker, which he and his friends had built in 1976 during tornado season, or thereabouts, while drinking cans of "Milwaukee" beer.

He remembered what his neighbor had once told him about his soft-spoken grandfather: "The lifeless, rigid bodies of the soldiers had been stacked from the worn, splintered wooded floor to the faded painted-metal ceiling; flat, prostrate, one on top of the other in the freight cars of the now halted train in the chaotic, but strategic Stalingrad railyard. He found an empty, isolated, vacant space in one of the cars, when no one was looking. The fighting was over. He did not hesitate in the least, but climbed right on in and immediately fell fast asleep, half-starved, severely wounded, presumed dead. When he finally awoke, he found that he had been dutifully returned to his Homeland. Over time, he had recovered in the warm feather bed of a makeshift hospital ward, but the doctors had had to remove part of his intestines. It made digesting his food difficult."

"Aren't you glad to be alive?" asked Cornelius Korn, his good friend and business partner of many years.

"Every morning when I wake up and look around," said Royce, smiling gleefully. "See the sunshine, and smell the coffee."

"Sophie told us an entirely different version," said Raquel Remington, Royce's significant other, and their business associate.

"Who's Sophie?" asked Alexis Sue Shell, the fourth member of their bridge club garden party, business associate, and Korn's constant companion.

"She was his grandmother's dearest neighbor, and a close friend of the family. They owned two of the guest-houses in town," continued Raquel. "She said your grandfather returned home one fine day, wearing a leather jacket, leather pants, thick-lens goggles, and driving a shiny, screaming motorcycle with a side-car. Rolf was beside him, riding contentedly in the sleek, polished cubicle formed around the attached seat. They drove in circles around the town square to announce their impending arrival. He had had the magnificent machine stored in the unassuming garage belonging to a family of farmers from the surrounding community housing farm implements. They'd even kept Rolf for him while he was away."

"Who's Rolf?" inquired Alexis Sue.

"His best friend and faithful companion, a good Shepherd. They're highly intelligent, you know. They understand what you say when you talk to them," said Raquel.

"He's never attended obedience school. The grandfather wouldn't let him go," said Korn. He too had heard some amazing stories about Rolf from Royce. "Whenever Godfrey would whistle—sounding an awful lot like a bomb dropping out of the sky from a B-24 aircraft before it struck paydirt, most other dogs would simply lie down and cover their heads with their paws. But no, not Rolf. He might run for the trees, but he would never cower."

"Can you tell us about the time your grandfather played a trick on you?" said Alexis. "I like that story."

"Godfrey had the policeman son of a friend drive us to the city where she lived to visit my grandmother in a nice, late-model green Opel. No one had ever told me that she was in the hospital, during the several weeks' time I had spent visiting that summer, until that very moment," said Royce. "We arrived at the hospital and were patiently waiting for her in the waiting area, when two orderlies noisily rolled in a large bed on squeaky wheels, with a matronly looking lady in it, wearing a nightgown. She might have once been a queen, judging from all outward appearances. But, clearly, at the present time, she did not look at all well. The sight was too shocking for words for this young lad. I had no idea that she had even been ill. Not so much as a cold. I became visibly upset and was almost ready to cry, when the members of another family stepped forward to see their mother. They began talking quietly among themselves. I wasn't sure exactly what was going on at that point. About that time, my real grandmother walked into the room as calmly as you please. She glided over to Godfrey, looked him directly in the eyes, and asked, 'Can we keep him?' He put his arm around her. You see, I hadn't seen my grandparents in thirteen long years, since I was five, and could barely remember them at all, having moved away to America long ago with my parents and new baby brother. My sister hadn't yet been born."

"She was the hospital administrator," explained Alexis.

"You haven't yet told us the rest of Godfrey's story," said Raquel. "What else did he bring back from the war?"

"There's nothing much left to tell," said Royce. "He brought back Rolf. He brought back a muddy motorcycle, cleaned it up, and restored the vehicle to BMW showroom condition, having first rebuilt the motor. I guess, I must have neglected to tell you about the Luger and 'crown of thorns.'"

"You see, during the time of the Russian invasion, someone stole the 'crown of thorns' from the preserved dead body exhibited inside a glass enclosure which had been temporarily and generously placed on display by an Eastern European museum in one of our local churches. It had completely vanished without a trace during the war," continued Royce. "Godfrey had somehow found the missing 'crown of thorns' and returned it to its rightful owners. Plain and simple."

"And the Luger?" persisted Raquel.

"I believe, he acquired the semiautomatic pistol from an old art and antiquities dealer in Berlin, through an anonymous mutual acquaintance," said Royce. "He alluded to the possibility that it might have been the actual murder weapon which contributed to the demise of the esteemed Fuhrer, but didn't elaborate further. He gave the gun to me for safekeeping as a family heirloom, but I planned on selling the item in pristine condition some years later, including the original bullets, as soon as I determined what it was worth."

"What a coincidence! I was able to purchase a similar pistol only recently; the one with the next consecutive serial number in the sequence," said Korn. "The matched set had been given to two of the rarely irascible dictator's most trusted and loyal bodyguards in 1937 at a most solemn awards ceremony."

"Same dealer?" inquired Royce. He mentioned the name of a man and a street.

"A distant relative of the very same distinguished gentleman," said Korn, in affirmation. "He was a legend in his own mind."

Royce flipped through the channels. Ray Price singing a Roger Miller tune, how interesting. Royce suddenly felt jovial, rowdy and boisterous. He began singing a medley he made up on the spur of the moment.

"Open freight car, late night train, destination Berlin soccer game. Rented tuxedo and canvas shoes. I don't carry the business-class blues…a man with options and a dozen tall tales, 'King of the Rails'…You can't roller blade in an antelope herd…They're gonna put me on Broadway. They're gonna make a rock star out of me. All I have to do is behave congenially. A guiding light and a beacon of hope, that's what I am." Clickety clack. Clickety clack. Clickety clack."

"I bet you think twice next time, before assuming the identity of a long-lost Hungarian war hero," said Raquel, "and the crowned Prince Galahad living in a fairytale castle with its towering stone walls and rugged ramparts, overlooking the glittering, green, and deceptively swift current of the gently flowing Danube River, with the beautiful Lady Gwendolyn of the medieval manor by his side, his eternal flame and secret admirer. May the people come to love him and not despise him."